Henry Wood

Under the Rose

Henry Wood

Under the Rose

ISBN/EAN: 9783337078836

Printed in Europe, USA, Canada, Australia, Japan

Cover: Foto ©Andreas Hilbeck / pixelio.de

More available books at **www.hansebooks.com**

UNDER THE ROSE.

BY THE AUTHOR OF

"EAST LYNNE."

"She's beautiful; and therefore to be wooed;
She is a woman; therefore to be won."

Shakspeare, Henry VI.

NEW YORK:

Copyright, 1873, by

G. W. Carleton & Co., Publishers.

LONDON: S. LOW & CO.

MDCCCLXXIX.

CONTENTS.

I.

LOSING LENA.

WE lived chiefly at Dyke Manor. A fine old place, so close upon the borders of Warwickshire and Worcestershire, that many people did not know which of the two counties it was really in. The house was in Warwickshire, but some of the land was in Worcestershire. The Squire had, however, another estate, Crabb Cot, all in Worcestershire, and very many miles nearer to Worcester.

Squire Todhetley was rich. But he lived in the plain, good old-fashioned way that his forefathers had lived; almost a homely way, it might be called, in contrast with the show and parade springing up of late years. He was respected by everybody, and though hot-headed and impetuous, he was simple-minded, open-handed, and had as good a heart as anybody ever had in this world. An elderly gentleman now, was he, of middle height, with a portly form and a red face; and his hair, what was left of it, consisted of a few scanty lightish locks, standing up straight on the top of his head.

The Squire had married, but not very early in life. His wife died in a few years, leaving one child only; a son, named after his father, Joseph. Young Joe was just the pride of the Manor and of his father's heart.

I, writing this, am Johnny Ludlow. And you will naturally want to hear what I did at Dyke Manor, and why 1 lived there.

About three miles' distance from the Manor was a place

called the Court. Not a property of so much importance as the Manor, but a nice place, for all that. It belonged to my father, William Ludlow. He and Squire Todhetley were good friends. I was the only child, just as Tod was; and, like him, I had lost my mother. They had christened me John, but always called me Johnny. I can remember many incidents of my early life now, but I cannot recall to my mind my mother. She must have died—at least I fancy so— when I was two years old.

One morning, two years after that, when I was about four, the servants told me I had a new mamma. I can see her now as she looked when she came home: tall and thin and upright, with a long face, pinched nose, a meek expression, and gentle voice. She was a Miss Marks, who used to play the organ at church, and had hardly any income at all. Hannah said she was sure she was thirty-five if she was a day—she was talk ing to Eliza while she dressed me—and they both agreed that she would probably turn out to be a Tartar, and that the master might have chosen better. I understood quite well that they meant papa, and asked why he might have chosen better; upon which they shook me and said they had not been speaking of my papa at all, but of the old blacksmith round the corner. Hannah brushed my hair the wrong way, and Eliza went off to see to her bedrooms. Children are easily prejudiced: and they prejudiced me against my new mother. Looking at her by the improved eyes of maturer years, I know that though she might be poor in pocket, she was good and kindly, and every inch a lady.

Papa died that same year. At the end of another year, Mrs. Ludlow, my step-mother, married Squire Todhetley, and we went to live at Dyke Manor; she, I, and my nurse Hannah. The Court was let for a term of years to the Sterlings.

Young Joe did not like the new arrangements. He was older than I, could take up prejudices more strongly, and he took a mighty strong one against the new Mrs. Todhetley. He had been regularly indulged by his father and spoilt by

all the servants; so it was only to be expected that he would
not like the invasion. Mrs. Todhetley introduced order into
the profuse household, hitherto governed by the servants.
They and young Joe equally resented it; they refused to see
that things were really more comfortable than they used to
be, and at half the cost.

Two babies came to the Manor; Hugh first, Lena next.
Joe and I were sent to school. He was as big as a house,
compared with me, tall and strong and dark, with an imperi-
ous way and will of his own. I was fair, gentle, timid, yielding to him in all things. His was the master spirit, swaying
mine at will. At school the boys at once, the very first day
we entered, shortened his name from Todhetley to Tod. I
caught the habit, and from that time I never called him anything else.

And so the years went on. Tod and I at school being
drilled into learning; Hugh and Lena growing into nice
little children. During the holidays hot war waged between
Tod and his step-mother. At least *silent* war. Mrs. Todhetley was always kind to him, and she never quarrelled; but
Tod opposed her in many things, and would be generally sarcastically cool to her in manner.

We did lead the children into mischief, and she complained of that. Tod did, that is, and of course I followed
where he led. "But we can't let Hugh grow up a milksop,
you know, Johnny," he would say to me; "and he would if
left to his mother." So Hugh's clothes in Tod's hands came
to grief, and Hugh himself sometimes. Hannah, who was
the children's nurse now, stormed and scolded over it: she
and Tod had ever been at daggers drawn with each other; and
Mrs. Todhetley would implore Tod with tears in her eyes to
oe careful with the child. Tod appeared to turn a deaf ear,
and marched off with Hugh before their very eyes. He
really loved the children, and would have saved them from
injury with his life. The Squire drove and rode his fine
horses. Mrs. Todhetley had set up a low basket-chaise drawn

1*

by a mild she-donkey: it was safer for the children, she said. Tod went into fits whenever he met the turn-out.

But Tod was not always to escape scot-free, or incite the children to rebellion with impunity. There came a day when he brought himself, through it, to a state of repentance and self-torture.

It occurred when we were at home for the summer holidays, just after the crop of hay was got in, and the bare fields looked as white in the blazing sun as if they had been scorched. Tod and I were in the three-cornered meadow next the fold-yard. He was making a bat-net with gauze and two sticks. Young Jacobson had shown us his the previous day, and a bat he caught with it; and Tod thought he would catch bats too. But he did not seem to be making much hand at the net, and somehow managed to send the pointed end of the stick through a corner of it.

"I don't think that gauze is strong enough, Tod."

"I am afraid it is not, Johnny. Here, catch hold of it. I'll go indoors, and see if they can't find me some better. Hannah must have some."

He flew off past the ricks, and leaped the little gate into the fold-yard—a tall, strong fellow, who might leap the Avon. In a few minutes I heard his voice again, and went to meet him. Tod was coming away from the house with Lena.

"Have you the gauze, Tod?"

"Not a bit of it; that old cat won't look for any; says she hasn't time. I'll hinder her time a little. Come along, Lena."

The "old cat" was Hannah. I told you she and he were often at daggers drawn. Hannah had a chronic complaint, ill-temper, and Tod called her names to her face. Upon going in to ask her for the gauze, he found her dressing Hugh and Lena to go out, and she just turned him out of the nursery, and told him not to bother her then with his gauze and his wants. Lena ran after Tod; she liked him better than all of us put together. She had on a blue silk frock, and a white straw hat with daisies round it; open-worked stockings were on her pretty little legs. By which we saw she was about to be taken out for show.

"What are you going to do with her, Tod?"

"I'm going to hide her," answered Tod, in his decisive voice. "Keep where you are, Johnny."

Lena enjoyed the rebellion. In a minute or two Tod came back alone. He had left her between the ricks in the three-cornered field, and told her not to come out. Then he went off to the front of the house, and I stood inside the barn, talking to Mack, who was hammering away at the iron of the cart-wheel. Out came Hannah by-and-by. She had been dressing herself as well as Hugh.

"Miss Lena!"

No answer. Hannah called again, and then came up the fold-yard, looking about.

"Master Johnny, have you seen the child?"

"What child?" I was not going to spoil Tod's sport by telling her.

"Miss Lena. She has got off somewhere, and my mistress is waiting for her in the basket-chaise."

"I see her just now along of Master Joseph," spoke up Mack, arresting his noisy hammer.

"See her where?" asked Hannah.

"Close here, a going that way."

He pointed with the hammer to the palings and gate that divided the yard from the three-cornered field. Hannah ran there and stood looking over. The ricks were within a short stone's throw, but Lena kept close. Hannah called out again, and threw her eyes over the empty field.

"The child's not there. Where can she have got to, tire-some little thing?"

In the house, and about the house, and out of the house, as the old riddle says, went Hannah. It was jolly to see her. Mrs. Todhetley and Hugh were seated patiently in the basket-chaise before the hall-door, wondering what made Hannah so long. Tod, playing with the mild she-donkey's ears, and laughing to himself, stood talking graciously to his stepmother. I went round. The Squire had gone riding to Evesham; Dwarf Giles, who made the nattiest little groom in the county, for all his five-and-thirty years, behind him.

"I can't find Miss Lena," cried Hannah, coming out.

"Not find Miss Lena!" echoed Mrs. Todhetley. "What do you mean, Hannah? Have you not dressed her?"

"I dressed her first, ma'am, before Master Hugh, and she went out of the nursery. I can't think where she can have got to. I've searched everywhere."

"But, Hannah, we must have her directly; I am late as it is."

They were going over to the Court to a children's early party at the Sterlings. Mrs. Todhetley stepped out of the basket-chaise, to help in the search.

"I had better fetch her, Tod," I whispered.

He nodded yes. Tod never bore malice, and I suppose he thought Hannah had had enough of a hunt for that day. I ran through the fold-yard to the ricks, and called to Lena.

"You can come out now, little stupid."

But no Lena answered. There were seven ricks in a group, and I went into all the openings between them. Lena was not there. It was rather odd, and I looked across the field and towards the lane and the coppice, shouting out sturdily.

"Mack, have you seen Miss Lena pass in-doors?" I stayed to ask him, in going back.

No: Mack had not noticed her; and I went round to the front again, and whispered to Tod.

"What a muff you are, Johnny! She's between the ricks fast enough. No danger that she'd come out when I told her to stay!"

"But she's not there indeed, Tod. You go and look."

Tod vaulted off, his long legs seeming to take flying leaps, like a deer's, on his way to the ricks.

To make short of the story, Lena was gone. Lost. The house, the out-door buildings, the gardens were searched for her, and she was not to be found. Mrs. Todhetley's fears flew to the ponds at first; but it was impossible she could have come to grief in either of the two, as they were both in view of the barn-door where I and Mack had been. Tod avowed that he had put her amid the ricks to hide; and it was not to be imagined she had gone. The most feasible conjecture was, that she had run from between the ricks when Hannah called to her, and was hiding in the lane.

Tod was in a fever, loudly threatening Lena with unheard of whippings, to cover his real concern. Hannah looked red Mrs. Todhetley white. I was standing by him when the cook came up; a sharp woman, with red-brown eyes. We called her Molly.

"Mr. Joseph," said she, "I have heard of gipsies stealing children."

"Well?" returned Tod.

"There was one at the door a while agone—an insolent one, too. Perhaps Miss Lena——"

"Which way did she go?—which door was she at?" burst forth Tod.

"'Twas a man, sir. He come up to the kitchen-door, and steps inside as bold as brass, asking me to buy some wooden skewers he'd cut, and saying something about a sick child. When I told him to march, that we never encouraged tramps here, he wanted to answer me, and I just shut the door in his face. A regular gipsy, if ever I see one," continued Molly; "his skin tawny and his wild hair jet-black. Maybe, in revenge, he have stole off the little miss."

Tod took up the notion, and his face turned white. "Don't say anything of this to Mrs. Todhetley," he said to Molly. "We must just scour the country."

But in departing from the kitchen-door, the gipsy man could not by any possibility have made his way to the rick-field direct without going through the fold-yard. And he had not done that. It was true that Lena might have run round and got in the gipsy's way. Unfortunately, none of the men were about, except Mack and old Thomas. Tod sent these off in different directions; Mrs. Todhetley drove away in her pony chaise to the lanes around, saying the child might have strayed there; Molly and the maids started elsewhere; and I and Tod went flying along a bye-road that branched off in a line, as it were, from the kitchen-door. Nobody could keep up with Tod, he went so fast; and I was not tall and strong as he was. But I saw what Tod in his haste did not see—a dark man with some bundles of skewers and a stout stick, walking on the other side of the hedge. I whistled Tod back again.

"What is it, Johnny?" he said, panting. "Have you seen her?"

"Not her. But look there. That must be the man Molly spoke of."

Tod crashed through the hedge as if it had been so many cobwebs, and accosted the gipsy. I followed more carefully, but got my face scratched.

"Were you up at the great house, begging, a short while ago?" demanded Tod, in an awful passion.

The man turned round on Tod with a face of brass. I say brass, because he did it so independently; but it was not an insolent face in itself; rather a sad one, and very sickly.

"What's that you ask me, master?"

"I ask whether it was you who were at the Manor-house just now, begging?" fiercely repeated Tod.

"I was at a big house offering wares for sale, if you mean that, sir. I wasn't begging."

"Call it what you please," said Tod, growing white again. "What have you done with the little girl?"

For, you see, Tod had fully caught up the impression that the gipsy *had* stolen Lena, and he spoke in accordance with it.

"I've seen no little girl, master."

"You have," and Tod gave his foot a stamp. "What have you done with her?"

The man's only answer was to turn round and walk off, muttering to himself. Tod pursued him, calling him a thief and other names; but nothing more satisfactory could he get.

“He can’t have taken her, Tod. If he had, she’d be with him now. He couldn’t eat her, you know.”

“He may have given her to a confederate.”

“What to do? What do gipsies steal children for?”

Tod stopped in a passion, lifting his hand. “If you torment me with these frivolous questions, Johnny, I’ll strike you. How do I know what’s done with stolen children? Sold, perhaps. I’d give a hundred pounds out of my pocket at this minute if I knew where those gipsies were encamped.”

We suddenly lost the fellow. Tod had been keeping him in sight in the distance. Whether he disappeared up a gum-tree, or into a rabbit-hole, Tod couldn’t tell; but gone he was.

Up this lane, down that; over that moor, across this common; so raced Tod and I. And the afternoon wore away, and we had changed our direction a dozen times: which possibly was not wise.

The sun was getting low as we passed Ragley gates, for we had finally got into the Alcester road. Tod was going to do what we ought to have done at first: report the loss at Alcester. Somebody came riding along on a stumpy pony. It proved to be Gruff Blossom, groom to the Jacobsons. They called him “Gruff” because of his temper. He did touch his hat to us, which was as much as you could say, and spurred the stumpy animal on. But Tod made a sign to him, and he was obliged to stop and listen.

“The gipsies stole off little Miss Lena!” cried old Blossom, coming out of his gruffness. “That’s a rum go? Ten to one if you find her for a year to come.”

“But, Blossom, what do they do with the children they steal?” I asked, in a sort of agony.

“They cuts their hair off and dyes their skins brown, and then takes ’em out to fairs a ballad-singing,” answered Blossom.

“But why need they do it, when they have children of their own?”

“Ah, well, that’s a question I couldn’t answer,” said old

Blossom. "Maybe their'n aren't pretty children—Miss Lena, she is pretty."

"Have you heard of any gipsies being encamped about here?" Tod demanded of him.

"Not lately, Mr. Joseph. Five or six months ago, there was a lot 'camped on the Markis's ground. They warn't there long."

"Can't you ride about, Blossom, and see after the child?" asked Tod, putting something into his hand.

Old Blossom pocketed it, and went of with a nod. He was riding about, as we knew afterwards, for hours. Tod made straight for the police-station at Alcester, and told his tale. Not a soul was there but Jenkins, one of the men.

"I haven't seen no suspicious characters about," said Jenkins, who seemed to be eating something. He was a big man, with short black hair combed on his forehead, and he had a habit of turning his face upwards, as if looking after his nose —a square ornament, that stood up straight.

"She is between four and five years old ; a very pretty child, with blue eyes and a good deal of curling auburn hair," said Tod, who was getting feverish.

Jenkins wrote it down—"Name, Todhetley. What Christian name?"

"Adalena, called 'Lena.'"

"Recollect the dress, sir?"

"Pale blue silk ; straw hat with wreath of daisies round it ; open-worked white stockings, and thin black shoes ; white drawers, finished off with tatting stuff," recounted Tod, as if he had prepared the list by heart coming along.

"That's bad, that dress is," said Jenkins, putting down the pen.

"Why is it bad?"

"'Cause the things is tempting. Quite half the children that get stole is stole for what they've got upon their backs. Tramps and that sort will run a risk for a blue silk, specially if it's clean and glistening, that they'd not run for a brown holland pinafore. Auburn curls too," added Jenkins, shaking his head; "that's a temptation also. I've knowed children sent back home with bare heads afore now. Any ornaments, sir?"

"She was safe to have on her little gold neck-chain and cross. They are very small, Jenkins—not worth much."

Jenkins lifted his nose—not in disdain, it was a habit he had. Not worth much to you, sir, who could buy such any day, but an uncommon bait to professional child-stealers. Were the cross a coral, or any stone of that sort?"

"It was a small gold cross, and the chain was thin. They could only be seen when her cloak was off. Oh, I forgot the cloak; it was white: llama, I think they call it. She was going to a child's party.

Some more questions and answers, most of which Jenkins took down. Handbills were to be printed and posted, and a reward offered on the morrow, if she was not found previously. Then we came away; there was nothing more to do at the station.

"Wouldn't it have been better, Tod, had Jenkins gone out seeking her and telling of the loss abroad, instead of waiting to write all that down?"

"Johnny, if we don't find her to-night, I shall go mad," was all he answered.

He went back down Alcester Street at a rushing walk—not a run.

"Where are you going now?" I asked.

"I'm going up hill and down dale till I find that gipsies' encampment. You can go on home, Johnny, if you are tired."

I had not felt tired till we were in the police-station. Excitement keeps fatigue off. But I was not going to give in, and said I should keep with him.

"All right, Johnny."

Before we were clear of Alcester, Budd the land-agent came up. He was turning out of the public-house at the corner. It was dusk then. Tod laid hold of him.

"Budd, you are about always, in all kinds of by-nooks and

lanes : can you tell me of any encampment of gipsies between here and the Manor-house ?"

The agent's business took him abroad a great deal, you know, into the rural districts around.

"Gipsies' encampment?" repeated Budd, giving both of us a stare. "There's none that I know of. In the spring, a lot of them had the impudence to squat down on the Marquis's——"

"Oh, I know all that," interrupted Tod. "Is there nothing of the sort about now?"

"I saw a miserable little tent to-day up Cookhill way," said Budd. "It might have been a gipsy's or a travelling tinker's. 'Twasn't of much account, whichever it was."

Tod gave a sort of spring. "Whereabouts?" was all he asked. And Budd explained where. Tod went off like a shot, and I after him.

If you are familiar with Alcester, or have visited at Ragley or anything of that, you must know the long green lane leading to Cookhill ; it is dark with overhanging trees, and up-hill all the way. We took that road—Tod first, and I last ; and we came to the top, and turned in the direction Budd had described the tent to be.

It was not to be called dark ; the nights never are at midsummer ; and rays from the bright light in the west glimmered through the trees. On the outskirts of the coppice, in a bit of low ground, we saw the tent, a little mite of a thing, looking no better than a funnel turned upside down. Sounds were heard within it, and Tod put his finger on his lip while he listened. But we were too far off, and he took his boots off, and crept up close.

Sounds of wailing—of somebody in pain. But that Tod had been three parts out of his senses all the afternoon, he might have known at once that they did not come from Lena, or any one so young. Words were mingled with them in a woman's voice ; uncouth in its accents, nearly non-understandable in its language, an awful sadness in its tone.

"A bit longer ! a bit longer, Corry, and he'd ha' been back

You needn't ha' grudged it to us. Oh——h! if ye had but waited a bit longer!"

I don't write exactly as she spoke; I shouldn't know how to spell it: we made a guess at half the words. Tod, who had grown white again, put on his boots, and lifted up the opening of the tent.

I had never seen any scene like that; I don't suppose I shall see another. About a foot from the ground was a raised surface of some sort, thickly covered with dark-green rushes, just the size and shape of a gravestone. A little child, about as old as Lena, lay on it, a white cloth thrown across her, just touching the white, still face. A torch, blazing and smoking away, was thrust into the ground and lighted up the scene. Whiter the face looked now, because it had been tawny in life. I'd rather see one of our faces dead than a gipsy's. The contrast between the white face and dress of the child, and the green bed of rushes it lay on was something remarkable. A young woman, dark too, and handsome enough to create a commotion at the fair, knelt down, her brown hands uplifted; a gaudy ring on one of the fingers, worth sixpence perhaps when new, sparkling in the torchlight. Tod strode up to the dead face and looked at it for full ten minutes. I do believe he thought at first that it was Lena.

"What is this?" he asked.

"It is my dead child!" the woman answered. "She did not wait that her father might see her die?"

But Tod had got his head full of Lena, and looked around "Is there no other child here?"

As if to answer him, a bundle of rags came out of a corner and set up a howl. It was a boy about seven, and our going in had woke him up. The woman sat down on the ground and looked at us.

"We have lost a child—a little girl," explained Tod. "I thought she might have been brought here—or have strayed here."

"I've lost *my* girl," said the woman. "Death has come for

her!" And, in speaking to us, she spoke a more intelligible language than when alone.

"Yes; but this child has been lost—lost out of doors! Have you seen or heard anything of one?"

"I've not been in the way o' seeing or hearing, master; I've been in the tent alone. If folks had come to my aid, Corry might not have died. I've had nothing but water to put in her lips all day."

"What was the matter with her?" Tod asked, convinced at length that Lena was not there.

"She had been ailing long—worse since the moon come in. The sickness took her with the summer, and the strength began to go out. Jake have been down, too. He couldn't get out to bring us help, and we have had none."

Jake was the husband, we supposed. The help meant food, or funds to get it with.

"He sat all yesterday cutting skewers, his hands a'most too weak to fashion 'em. Maybe he'd sell 'em for a few ha'pence, he said; and he went out this morning to try, and bring home a morsel of food."

"Tod," I whispered, "I wish that hard-hearted Molly had——"

"Hold your tongue, Johnny," he interrupted sharply. "Is Jake your husband?" he asked of the woman.

"He's my husband, and the children's father."

"Jake would not be likely to steal a child, would he?" asked Tod, in a hesitating manner, for him.

She looked up, as if not understanding. "Steal a child, master! What for?"

"I don't know," said Tod. "I thought perhaps he had done it, and had brought the child here."

Another comical stare from the woman. "We couldn't feed these of ours; what should we do with another?"

"Well: Jake called at our house to sell his skewers; and, directly afterwards, we missed my little sister. I have been hunting for her ever since."

"Was the house far from here?"

"A few miles."

"Then he have sunk down of weakness on his way, and can't get back."

Putting her head on her knees, she began to sob and moan. The child—the living one—began to bawl; one couldn't call it anything else; and pulled at the green rushes.

"He knew Corry was sick and faint when he went out. He'd have got back afore now if his strength hadn't failed him; though, maybe, he didn't think of death. Whist, then, Dor," she added, to the boy.

"Don't cry," said Tod to the little chap, who had got the largest, brightest eyes I ever saw; "that will do no good, you know."

"I want Corry," said he. "Where's Corry gone?"

"She's gone up to God," answered Tod, speaking very gently "She's gone to be a bright angel with Him in heaven."

"Will she fly down to me?" asked Dor, his great eyes shining through their tears on Tod.

"Yes," affirmed Tod, who had a theory of his own on the point, and used to think, when a little boy, that his mother was always near him, one of God's angels keeping him from harm. "And after a while, you know, if you are good, you'll go to Corry, and be an angel, too."

"God bless you, master!" interposed the woman. "He'll think of that always."

"Tod," I said, as we went out of the tent, "I don't think they are people to steal children."

"Who's to know what the man would do?" retorted Tod.

"A man with a dying child at home wouldn't be likely to harm another."

Tod did not answer. He stood still a moment, deliberating which way to go. Back to Alcester?—where a conveyance might be found to take us home, for the fatigue was telling on both of us, now that disappointment was prolonged, and I, at least, could hardly put one foot before another. Or down to the high road, and run the chance of some vehicle overtaking us? Or keep on amidst these fields and hedgerows, which would lead us home by a rather nearer way, but without chance of a lift? Tod made up his mind, and struck down the lane the way we had come. He was on first, and I saw him come to a sudden halt, and turn his head to me.

"Look here, Johnny!"

I looked as well as I could for the night and the trees, and saw something on the ground. A man had sunk down there, seemingly from exhaustion. His face was a tawny white, just like the dead child's; a stout stick and the bundles of skewers lay beside him.

"Do you see the fellow, Johnny? It is the gipsy."

"Has he fainted?"

"Fainted, or shamming it. I wonder if there's any water about?"

But the man opened his eyes; perhaps the sound of voices revived him. After looking at us a minute or two, he raised himself slowly on his elbow. Tod—the one thought upper-most in his mind—said something about Lena.

"The child's found, master?"

Tod seemed to give a leap. I know his heart did. "Found!"

"Been safe at home this long while."

"Who found her?"

"'Twas me, master."

"Where was she?" asked Tod, his tone softening. "Let us hear about it."

"I was making back for the town" (we supposed he meant Alcester), "and missed the way; land about here's strange to me. Agoing through a bit of a grove, which didn't seem as if it was leading to nowhere, I heard a child crying. There was the little thing tied to a tree, stripped, and——"

"Stripped!" roared Tod.

"Stripped to the skin, sir, save for a dirty old skirt that was tied round her. A woman carried her off to that spot, she told me, robbed her of her clothes, and left her there. Know-

ing where she must ha' been stole from—through you're accusing *me* of it, master—I untied her to lead her home, but her
feet warn't used to the rough ground, and I made shift to carry her. A matter of two miles it were, and I be not good for
much. I left her at home safe, and set off back. That's all,
master."

"What were you doing here?" asked Tod, as considerately
as if he had been speaking to a lord. "Resting?"

"I suppose I fell, master. I don't remember nothing, since
I was tramping up the lane, till your voices came. I've had
naught inside my lips to-day but a drink o' water."

"Did they give you nothing to eat at the house when you
took the child home?"

He shook his head. "I saw the woman again, nobody else.
She heard what I had to say about the child, and she never
said 'Thank ye.'"

The man had been getting on his feet, and caught up the
skewers, that were all tied together with string, and the stick.
But he reeled as he stood, and would have fallen again but
for Tod. Tod gave him his arm.

"We are in for it, Johnny," said he aside to me. "Pity
but I could be put in a picture—the Samaritan helping the
destitute!"

"I'd not accept of ye, sir, but that I have a child sick at
home, and want to get to her. There's a piece of bread in my
pocket that was give me at a cottage to-day."

"Is your child sure to get well?" asked Tod, after a pause;
wondering whether he could say anything of what had occurred, so as to break the news.

The man gazed right away into the distance, as if searching
for an answer in the far-off star shining there.

"There's been a death-look in her face this day and night
past, master. But the Lord's good to us all."

"And sometimes, when He takes children, it is done in
mercy," said Tod. "Heaven is a better place than this."

"Ay," rejoined the man, who was leaning heavily on Tod,

and could never have got home without him, unless he had crawled on hands and knees. "I've been sickly on and off for this year past; worse lately; and I've thought at times that if my own turn was coming, I'd beglad to see my children gone afore me."

"Oh, Tod!" I whispered, in a burst of repentance, "how could we have been so hard with this poor fellow, and roughly accused him of stealing Lena?" But Tod only gave me a knock with his elbow.

"I fancy it must be pleasant to think of a little child being an angel in heaven—a child that we have loved," said Tod.

"Ay, ay," said the man.

Tod had no courage to say more. He was not a parson. Presently he asked the man what tribe he belonged to—being a gipsy.

"I'm not a gipsy, master. Never was one yet. I and my wife are dark-complexioned by nature; living in the open air has made us darker; But I'm English born; Christian, too. My wife's Irish; but they do say she comes of a gipsy tribe. We used to have a cart, and went about the country with crockery; but a year ago, when I got ill and lay in a lodging, the things were seized for rent and debt. Since then it's been hard lines with us. Yonder's my bit of a tent, master, and now I can get on alone. Thanking ye kindly."

"I am sorry I spoke harshly to you to-day," said Tod. "Take this: it is all I have with me."

"I'll take it, sir, for my child's sake; it may help to put the strength into her. Otherwise I'd not. We're honest; we've never begged. Thank ye both, masters, once again."

It was only a shilling or two. Tod spent, and never had much in his pockets. "I wish it had been sovereigns," said he to me: "but we will do something better for them to-morrow, Johnny. I am sure the Pater will."

"Tod," said I, as we ran on, "had we seen the man close

before, and spoken with him, I should never have suspected him. He has a face to be trusted."

Tod burst into a laugh. "There you are Johnny, at your faces again!"

I was always reading people's faces, and taking likes and dislikes accordingly. They called me a muff for it at home (and for many other things), Tod especially; but it seemed to me that I could read people as easily as a book. Duffham, our surgeon at Church Dykely, bade me *trust to it* as a good gift from God. One day, pushing my straw hat up to draw his fingers across the top of my brow, he quaintly told the Squire that when he wanted people's morals read, to come to me to read them. The Squire only laughed in answer.

As luck had it, a gentleman we knew was passing in his dog-cart when we got to the foot of the hill. It was old Pitchley. He drove us home: and I could hardly get down, I was so stiff.

Lena was in bed, safe and sound. No damage, except the fright and the loss of her clothes. From what we could learn, the woman who took her off must have been concealed amidst the ricks when Tod put her there. Lena said the woman laid hold of her very soon, caught her up, and put her hand over her mouth, to prevent her crying out ; she could only give one scream. I ought to have heard it, only Mack was making such an awful row, hammering that iron. How far along fields and byeways the woman carried her, Lena could not be supposed to tell : " Miles ! " she said. Then the thief plunged amidst a few trees, took the child's things off, put on an old rag of a petticoat, and tied her loosely to a tree. Lena thought she could have got loose herself, but was too frightened to try ; and just then the man, Jake, came up.

" I liked *him*," said Lena. " He carried me all the way home, tnat my feet should not hurt ; but he had to sit down sometimes. He said he had a poor little girl who was nearly as badly off for clothes as that, but she did not want them now, she was too sick. He said he hoped my papa would find the woman, and put her in prison."

It is what the Squire intended to do, good chance helping him. But he did not reach home till after us, when all was quiet again : which was fortunate.

"I suppose you blame me for this ?" cried Tod, to his step-mother.

"No, I don't, Joseph," said Mrs. Todhetley. She called him Joseph nearly always, not liking to abbreviate his name, as some of us did. "It is so very common a thing for the children to be playing in the three-cornered field amidst the ricks ; and no suspicion that danger could arise from it having ever been glanced at, I do not think any blame attaches to you."

"I am very sorry now for having done it," said Tod. "I shall never forget the fright to the last hour of my life."

He went straight to Molly, from Mrs. Todhetley, a look on his face that, when seen there, which was rare, the servants did not like. Deference was rendered to Tod in the house-hold. When anything should take off the good old Pater, Tod would be master. What he said to Molly nobody heard ; but the woman was banging at the brass things in a tantrum for three days afterwards.

And when we went to see after poor Jake and his people, it was too late. The man, the tent, the living people, and the dead child—all were gone.

II.

FINDING BOTH OF THEM.

ORCESTER Assizes were being held, and Squire
Todhetley was on the grand jury. You see, although
Dyke Manor was just within the borders of Warwickshire, the greater portion of the Squire's property lay
in Worcestershire. This caused him to be summoned to serve.
We were often at his house there, Crabb Cot. I forget who
was foreman of the jury that time: either Sir John Pakington,
or the Honourable Mr. Coventry.

The week was jolly. We put up at the "Star and Garter"
when we went to Worcester, which was two or three times
a-year; generally at the assizes, or the races, or the quarter
sessions; one or other of the busy times.

The Pater would grumble at the bills—and say we boys had
no business to be there; but he would take us, if we were at
home, for all that. The assizes came on this time the week
before our summer holidays were up; the Squire wished they
had not come on until the week after. Anyway, there we
were in clover; the Squire about to be stewed up in the county
courts all day; I and Tod flying about the town, and doing
what we liked.

The judges came in from Oxford on the usual day, Saturday.
And, to make plain what I am going to tell about, we must
go back to that morning and to Dyke Manor. It was broiling
hot weather, and Mrs. Todhetley, Hugh, and Lena, with old
Thomas and Hannah, all came on the lawn after breakfast to see
us start. The open carriage was at the door, with the fine dark

horses. When the Squire did come out, he liked to do things well; and Dwarf Giles, the groom, had gone on to Worcester the preceding day with the two saddle-horses, the Pater's and Tod's. They might have ridden them in this morning, but the Squire chose to have his horses sleek and fresh when attending the high sheriff.

"Shall I drive, sir?" asked Tod.

"No," said the Pater. "These two have queer tempers, and must be handled carefully." He meant the horses, Bob and Blister. Tod looked at me; he thought he could have managed them quite as well as the Pater.

"Papa," cried Lena, as we were driving off, running up in her white pinafore, with her pretty hair flying, "if you can catch that naughty kidnapper at Worcester, you put her in prison."

The Squire nodded emphatically, as much as to say, "Trust me for that." Lena alluded to the woman who had taken her off and stolen her clothes two or three weeks before. Tod said, afterwards, there must have been some prevision on the child's mind when she said this.

We reached Worcester at twelve. It is a long drive, you know. Lots of country-people had arrived, and the Squire went off with some of them. Tod and I thought we'd order luncheon at the Star—a jolly good one; stewed lampreys, kidneys, and cherry tart; and let it go into the Squire's bill.

I'm afraid I envied Tod. The old days of travelling post were past, when the sheriff's procession would go out to Whittington to meet the judges' carriage. They came now by rail from Oxford, and the sheriff and his attendants received them at the railway station. It was the first time Tod had been allowed to make one of the gentlemen-attendants. The Squire said now he was too young; but he looked big, and tall, and strong. To see him mount his horse and go cantering off with the rest sent me into a state of envy. Tod saw it.

"Don't drop your mouth, Johnny," said he. "You'll make one of us in another year or two."

I stood about for half an hour, and the procession came back, passing the Star on its way to the county courts. The bells were ringing, the advanced heralds blew their trumpets, and the javelin guard rode at a foot pace, their lances in rest, preceding the high sheriff's grand carriage, with its four prancing horses and their silvered harness. Both the judges had come in, so we knew that business was over at Oxford; they sat opposite to the sheriff and his chaplain. I used to wonder whether they travelled all the way in their wigs and gowns, or robed outside Worcester. Squire Todhetley rode in the line next the carriage, with some more old ones of consequence; Tod on his fine bay was nearly at the tail, and he gave me a nod in passing. The judges were going to open the commission, and Foregate Street was crowded.

The high sheriff that year was a friend of ours, and the Pater had an invitation to the banquet he gave that evening. Tod thought he ought to have been invited too.

"It's sinfully stingy of him, Johnny. When I am pricked for sheriff—and I suppose my turn will come some time, either for Warwickshire or Worcestershire —I'll have more young fellows to my dinner than old ones."

The Squire, knowing nothing of our mid-day luncheon, was surprised that we chose supper at eight instead of dinner at six; but he told the waiter to give us a good one. We went out while it was getting ready, and walked arm-in-arm through the crowded streets. Worcester is always full on a Saturday evening; it is market-day there, as everybody knows; but on Assize Saturday the streets are nearly impassable. Tod, tall and strong, held on his way, and asked leave of none.

"Now, then, you two gents, can't you go on proper, and not elbow respectable folks like that?"

"Halloa!" cried Tod, turning at the voice. "Is it you, old Jones?"

Old Jones, the constable of our parish, touched his hat when he saw it was us, and begged pardon. We asked what he was doing at Worcester; but he had only come on his own account. "On the spree," Tod suggested to him.

"Young Mr. Todhetley," cried he—the way he mostly addressed Tod—"I'd not be sure but that woman's took—her that served out little Miss Lena."

"That woman!" said Tod. "Why do you think it?

Old Jones explained. A woman had been apprehended near Worcester the previous day, on a charge of stripping two little boys of their clothes in Perry Wood. The description given of her answered exactly, old Jones thought, to that given by Lena.

"She stripped 'em to the skin," groaned Jones, drawing a long face as he recited the mishap: "two poor little chaps of three years, they was, living in them cottages under the Wood—not as much as their boots did she leave on 'em. When they got home their folks didn't know 'em; quite naked they was, and bleating with terror, like a brace of shorn sheep."

Tod put on his determined look. "And she is taken, you say, Jones?"

"She was took yesterday, sir. They had her before the justices this morning, and the little fellows knowed her at once. As the 'sizes was on, leastways as good as on, their worships committed her for trial there and then. Policeman Cripp told me all about it; it was him that took her. She's in the county gaol."

We carried the tale to the Pater that night, and he despatched a messenger to Mrs. Todhetley, to say that Lena must be at Worcester on the Monday morning. But there's something to tell about the Sunday yet.

If you have been in Worcester on Assize Sunday, you know how the cathedral is on that morning crowded. Enough strangers are in the town to fill it: the inhabitants who go to the churches at other times attend it then; and King Mob flocks in to see the show.

Squire Todhetley was put in the stalls; Tod and I scram-

bled for places on a bench. The alterations in the cathe
dral (going on for years before that, and going on for years
since, and going on still) caused space to be limited, and it
was no end of a cram. While people fought for standing
places, the procession was played in to the crush of the organ
The judges came, glorious in their wigs and gowns; the
mayor and aldermen were grand as scarlet and gold chains
could make them: and there was a large attendance of the
clergy in their white robes. The Bishop had come in from
Hartlebury, and was on his throne, and the service began.
The Rev. Mr. Wheeler chanted; the Dean read the lessons.
Of course the music was all right; they put up fine services
on Assize Sundays now: and the sheriff's chaplain went up
in his black gown to preach the sermon. Three-quarters of an
hour, if you'll believe me, before that sermon came to an end!

Ere the organ had well played its Amen to the Bishop's
blessing, the crowd began to push out. We pushed with the
rest, and took up our places in the long cathedral body to see
the procession pass back again. It came winding down
between the line of javelin-men. Just as the judges were
passing, Tod touched me to look opposite. There stood a
young boy in dreadful clothes, patched all over, but otherwise
clean: with great dark wondering eyes riveted on the judges,
as if they had been peacocks on stilts; on their wigs, on their
solemn countenances, on their held-up scarlet trains.

Where had I seen those eyes, and their brilliant brightness?
Recollection flashed over me before Tod's whisper; "Jake's
boy; the youngster we saw in the tent."

To get across the line was impossible: good manners would
not permit it, let alone the javelin-guard. And when the procession had passed, leaving nothing but a crowd of shuffling
feet and the dust on the white cathedral floor, the boy was
gone.

"I say, Johnny, it is rather odd we should come on those
tent-people, just as the woman has turned up," exclaimed
Tod, as we go clear of the cathedral.

"But you don't think they can be connected, Tod!"

"Well, no; I suppose not. It's a queer coincidence, though."

This we also carried to the Squire, as we had the other news. He was standing in the Star gateway.

"Look here, you boys," said he, after a pause of thought; "keep your eyes open; you may come upon the lad again, or some of his folks. I should like to do something for that poor man; I've wished it ever since he brought home Lena, and that confounded Molly drove him out by way of recompense."

"And if they should be confederates, sir?" suggested Tod.

"Who confederates? What do you mean, Joe?"

"These people and the female-stripper. It seems strange they should both turn up again in the same spot."

The notion took away the Pater's breath. "If I thought that; if I find it is so," he broke forth, "I'll—I'll—transport the lot."

Mrs. Todhetley arrived with Lena on Sunday afternoon. Early on Monday, the Squire and Tod took her to the governor's house at the county prison, where she was to see the woman, as if accidentally, nothing being said to Lena.

The woman was brought in: a bold jade with a red face: and Lena nearly went into convulsions at the sight of her. There could be no mistake: the woman was the same: and the Pater became red-hot with anger; especially to think he could not punish her in Worcester.

As the fly went racing up Salt Lane after the interview, on its way to leave the Squire at the county courts, a lad ran past. It was Jake's boy; the same we had seen in the cathedral. Tod leaped up and called to the driver to stop, but the Pater roared out an order to go on. His appearance at the court could not be delayed, and Tod had to stay with Lena. So the clue was lost again. Tod brought Lena to the Star, and then he and I went to the criminal court, and bribed a fellow for places. Tod said it would be a sin not to hear the kidnapper tried.

It was nearly the first case called on. Some of the lighter cases were taken first, while the grand jury deliberated on their bills for the graver ones. Her name, as given in, was Nancy Cole, and she tried to excite the sympathies of the judge and jury by reciting a whining account of a deserting husband and other ills. The evidence was quite clear. The two children (little shavers in petticoats) set up a roar in court at sight of the woman, just as Lena had in the governor's house; and a dealer in marine stores produced their clothes, which he had bought of her. Tod whispered to me that he should go about Worcester after this in daily dread of seeing Lena's blue-silk frock and open-worked stockings hanging in a shop window. Some allusion was spoken during the trial to the raid the prisoner had also recently made on the little daughter of Mr. Todhetley, of Dyke Manor, Warwickshire, and of Crabb Cot, Worcestershire, "one of the gentlemen of the grand jury at present sitting in deliberation in an adjoining chamber of the court." But, as the judge said, that could not be received in evidence.

Mrs. Cole brazened it out: the testimony was too strong to attempt denial. "And if she *had* took a few bits o' things, cause she was famishing, she didn't hurt the children. She'd never hurt a child in her life; couldn't do it. Just conterairy to that; she gave 'em sugar plums—and candy—and a piece of a wig,* she did. What was she to do? Starve? Since her wicked husband, that she hadn't seen for this five year, deserted of her, and her two boys, fine grown lads both of 'em, had been accused of theft and got put away from her, one into prison, t'other into a 'formitory, she hadn't got no soul to care for her nor help her to a bit o' bread. Life was hard, and times was bad; and—there it was. No good o' saying more."

"Guilty," said the foreman of the jury, without turning round. "We find the prisoner guilty, my lord."

The judge sentenced her to six months' imprisonment with hard labour. Mrs. Cole brazened it still.

---

* A sort of plain bun sold in Worcester.

2*

"Thank you," said she to his lordship, dropping a curtsey
as they were taking her from the dock; "and I hope you'll sit
there, old gentleman, till I come out."

When the Squire was told of the sentence that evening, he
said it was too mild by half, and talked of bringing her also
to book at Warwick. But Mrs. Todhetley said, "No; forgive
her." After all, it was but the loss of the clothes.

Nothing whatever had come out during the trial to connect
Jake with the woman. She appeared to be a stray waif without friends. "And I watched and listened closely for it, mind
you, Johnny," remarked Tod.

It was a day or two after this—I think, on the Wednesday
evening. The Squire's grand jury duties were over, but he
stayed on, intending to make a week of it; Mrs. Todhetley and
Lena had left for home. We had dined late, and Tod and I
went for a stroll afterwards; leaving the Pater, and an old
clergyman, who had dined with us, to their wine. In passing
the cooked-meat shop in High-street, we saw a little chap looking in, his face flattened against the panes. Tod laid hold of
his shoulder, and the boy turned his brilliant eyes and their
hungry expression upon us.

"Do you remember me, Dor?" You see, Tod had not forgotten his name.

Dor evidently did remember. And whether it was that he
felt frightened at being accosted, or whether the sight of us
brought back to him the image of the dead child sister lying
on the rushes, was best known to himself; but he burst out
crying.

"There's nothing to cry for," said Tod; "you need not be
afraid. Could you eat some of that meat?"

Something like a shiver of glad surprise broke over the
boy's face at the question; just as though he had had no food
for weeks. Tod gave him a shilling, and told him to go in
and buy some. But the boy looked at the money doubtingly

"A whole shilling! They'd think I stole it."

Tod took back the money, and went in himself. He was as proud a fellow as you'd find in the two counties, and yet he would do all sorts of things that many another glanced askance at.

"I want half a pound of beef," said he to the man who was carving, "and some bread, if you sell it. And I'll take one of those small pork pies."

"Shall I put the meat in paper, sir?" asked the man: as if doubting whether Tod might prefer to eat it there.

"Yes," said Tod. And the customers, working men and a woman in a drab shawl, turned and stared at him.

Tod paid; took it all in his hands, and we left the shop. He did not mind to be seen carrying the parcels; but he would have minded letting them know that he was feeding a poor boy.

"Here, Dor, you can take the things now," said he, when we had gone a few yards. "Where do you live?"

Dor explained in a fashion. We knew Worcester well, but failed to understand. "Not far from the big church," he said ; and at first we thought he meant the cathedral.

"Never mind," said Tod; "go on, and show us."

He went skimming along, Tod keeping him within arm's length, lest he should try to escape. Why Tod should have suspected he might, I don't know ; nothing, as it turned out, could have been farther from Dor's thoughts. The church he spoke of proved to be All Saints' ; the boy turned up an entry near to it, and we found ourselves in a regular rookery of dirty, miserable, tumble-down houses. Loose men stood about, pipes in their mouths; women, in tatters, had their hair hanging down.

Dor dived into a dark den that seemed to be reached through a hole you had to stoop under. My patience! what a close place it was, with a smell that nearly knocked you backwards. There was not an earthly thing in the room that we could see, except some straw in a corner, and on that Jake was lying. The boy appeared with a piece of lighted candle, which he had been upstairs to borrow.

Jake was thin enough before; he was a skeleton now. His eyes were sunk, the bones of his thin face stood out, the skin glistening on his shapely nose, his voice was weak and hollow. He knew us, and smiled.

"What's the matter?" asked Tod, speaking gently. "You look very ill."

"I be very ill, master; I've been getting worse ever since."

His history was this. The same night that we had seen the tent at Cookhill, some travelling people of Jake's fraternity happened to encamp close to it for the night. By their help, the dead child was removed as far as Evesham, and there buried. Jake, his wife, and son, went on to Worcester, and there the man was taken worse; they had been in this room since; the wife had found a place of washing to go to twice a week, earning her food and a shilling each time. It was all they had to depend upon, these two shillings weekly; and the few bits o' things they had, to use Jake's words, had been taken by the landlord for rent. But to see Jake's resignation was something curious.

"He was very good," he said, alluding to the landlord and the seizure; "he left me the straw. When he saw how bad I was, he wouldn't take it. We had been obliged to sell the tent, and there was a'most nothing for him."

"Have you had no medicine? have you had no advice?" cried Tod, speaking as if he had a lump in his throat.

Yes, he had had medicine; the wife went for it to the free place (he meant the dispensary) twice a week, and a young doctor had been to see him.

Dor opened the paper of meat, and showed it to his father. "The gentleman bought it me," he said; "and this, and this. Couldn't you eat some?"

I saw the eager look that arose for a moment to Jake's face at sight of the meat: three slices of nice cold boiled beef, better than what we got at school. Dor held out one in his fingers; the man broke off a morsel, put it into his mouth, and had a choking fit.

"It's of no use, Dor."

"Is his name 'Dor'?" asked Tod.

"His name is James, sir; same as mine," answered Jake, panting a little from the exertion of swallowing the meat. The wife, she has called him 'Dor' for 'dear,' and I've felt into it. She has called me Jake all along."

Tod felt something ought to be done to help him, but he had no more idea what than the man in the moon. I had less. As Dor piloted us to the open street, we asked him where his mother was. It was one of her working days out, he answered; she was always kept late.

"Could he drink wine, do you think, Dor?"

"The gentleman said he was to have it," answered Dor, alluding to the doctor.

"How old are you, Dor?"

"I'm a nigh ten." He did not look it.

"Johnny, I wonder if there's any place where they sell beef-tea?" cried Tod, as we went up Broad Street. "My goodness! lying there in that state, with no help!"

"I never saw anything so bad before, Tod."

"Do you know what I kept thinking of all the time? I could not get it out of my head."

"What?"

"Of Lazarus at the rich man's gate. Johnny, lad, there seems an awful responsibility lying on some of us."

To hear Tod say such a thing was stranger than all. He set off running, and burst into our sitting-room in the Star, startling the Pater, who was alone and reading one of the Worcester papers with his spectacles on. Tod sat down and told him all.

"Dear me! dear me!" cried the Pater, growing red as he listened. "Why, Joe, the poor fellow must be dying!"

"He may not have gone too far for recovery, father," was Tod's answer. "If we had to lie in that close hole, and had nothing to eat or drink, we should probably soon become skeletons also. He may get well yet with proper care and treatment."

"It seems to me that the first thing to do is to get him into the Infirmary," remarked the Pater.

"And it ought to be done early to-morrow morning, sir; if it's too late to-night."

The Pater got up in a bustle, put on his hat, and went out. He was going to his old friend, the great surgeon, Henry Carden. Tod ran after him up Foregate Street, but was sent back to me. We stood at the door of the hotel, and in a few moments saw them coming along, the Pater arm-in-arm with Mr. Carden. He had come out as readily to visit the poor helpless man as he would to visit a rich one. Perhaps more so. They stopped when they saw us, and Mr. Carden asked Tod some of the particulars.

"You can get him admitted to the Infirmary at once, can you not?" said the Pater, impatiently, who was all on thorns to have something done.

"By what I can gather, it is not a case for the Infirmary," was the answer of its chief surgeon. "We'll see."

Down we went, walking fast: the Pater and Mr. Carden in front, I and Tod at their heels; and found the room again with some difficulty. The wife was in then, and had made a handful of fire in the grate. What with the smoke, and what with the other agreeable accompaniments, we were nearly stifled.

If ever I wished to be a doctor, it was when I saw Mr. Carden with that poor sick man. He was so gentle with him, so cheery and kind. Had Jake been a duke, I don't see that he could have been treated differently. There was something superior about the man, too, as though he had seen better days.

"What is your name?" asked Mr. Carden.

"James Winter, sir, a native of Herefordshire. I was on my way there when I was taken ill in this place."

"What to do there? To get work?"

"No, sir; to die It don't much matter, though; God's here as well as there."

"You are not a gipsy?"

"Oh dear no, sir. From my dark skin, though, I've been taken for one. My wife's descended from a gipsy tribe."

"We are thinking of placing you in the Infirmary, Jake," cried the Pater. "You will have every comfort there, and the best of attendance. This gentleman——"

"We'll see—we'll see," interposed Mr. Carden, breaking in hastily on the promises. "I am not sure that the Infirmary will do for him."

"It is too late, sir, I think," said Jake. quietly, to Mr. Carden.

Mr. Carden made no reply. He asked the woman if she had such a thing as a tea-cup or wine-glass. She produced a cracked cup with the handle off and a notch in the rim. Mr. Carden poured something into it that he had brought in his pocket, and stooped over the man. Jake began to speak in his faint voice.

"Sir, I'd not seem ungrateful, but I'd like to stay here with the wife and boy to the last. It can't be for long now."

"Drink this; it will do you good," said Mr. Carden, holding the cup to his lips.

"This close place is a change from the tent," I said to the woman, who was stooping over the bit of fire.

Such a look of regret came upon her countenance as she lifted it: just as if the tent had been a palace of gold. "When we got here, master, it was after that two days' rain, and the ground was sopping. It didn't do for *him*"—glancing round at the straw. "He was getting mighty bad then, and we just put our heads into this place—bad luck to us!"

The Squire gave her some silver, and told her to get anything in she thought best. It was too late to do more that night. The church clocks were striking ten as we went out.

"Won't it do to move him to the Infirmary?" were the Pater's first words to Mr. Carden.

"Certainly not. The man's hours are numbered."

"There is no hope, I suppose?"

"Not the least. He may be said to be dying now."

No time was lost in the morning. When Squire Todhetley took a will to heart he carried it out, and speedily. A decent room with an airy window was found in the same block of buildings. A bed and other things were put in it; some clothes were redeemed; and by twelve o'clock in the day Jake was comfortably lying there. The Pater seemed to think that this was not enough: he wanted to do more.

"His humanity to my child kept him from seeing the last moments of his," said he. "The little help we can give him now is no return for that."

Food and clothes, and a dry, comfortable room, and wine and proper things for Jake—of which he could not swallow much. The woman was not to go out to work again while he lasted, but to stay at home and attend to him.

"I shall be at liberty by the hop-picking time," she said, with a sigh. "Ah, poor creature! long before that."

When Tod and I went in later in the afternoon, she had just given Jake some physic, ordered by Mr. Carden. She and the boy sat by the fire, tea and bread-and-butter on the deal table between them. Jake lay in bed, his head raised on account of his breathing. I thought he was better; but his thin white face, with the dark earnest, glistening eyes, was almost painful to look upon.

"The reading-gentleman have been in," cried the woman suddenly. "He's coming again, he says, the night or the morning."

Tod looked puzzled, and Jake explained. A good young clergyman, who had found him out a day or two before, had been in each day since with his Bible, to read and pray. "God bless him!" said Jake.

"Why did you go away so suddenly?" Tod asked, alluding to the hasty departure from Cookhill. "My father was intending to do something for you."

"I didn't know that, sir. Many thanks all the same. I'd

like to thank *you* too, sir," he went on, after a fit of coughing "I've wanted to thank you ever since. When you gave me your arm up the lane, and said them pleasant things to me about having a little child in heaven, you knew she was gone."

"Yes."

"It broke the trouble to me, sir. My wife heard me coughing afar off, and came out o' the tent. She didn't say at first what there was in the tent, but began telling how you had been there. It made me know what had happened; and when she set on a-grieving, I told her not to: Carry was gone up to be an angel in Heaven."

Tod touched the hand he put out, not speaking.

"She's waiting for me, sir," he continued, in a fainter whisper. "I'm as sure of it as if I saw her. The little girl I found and carried to the great house has got rich friends and a fine home to shelter her; mine had none, and so it was for the best that she should go. God has been very good to me. Instead of letting me fret after her, or murmur at lying helpless like this, He only gives me peace."

"That man must have had a good mother," cried out Tod as we went away down the entry. And I looked up at him, he spoke so queerly.

"Do you think he will get better, Tod? He does not seem as bad as he did last night."

"Get better!" retorted Tod. "You'll always be a muff, Johnny. Why, every breath he takes threatens to be his last. He is miles worse than he was when we found him. This is Thursday; I don't believe he can last out longer than the week; and I think Mr. Carden knows it."

He did not last so long. On the Saturday morning, just as we were going to start for home, the wife came to the Star with the news. Jake had died at ten the previous night.

"He went off quiet," said she to the Squire. "I asked if he'd not like a dhrink; but he wouldn't have it: the good gentleman had been there giving him the bread and wine, and he said he'd take nothing, he thought, after that. 'I'm going, Mary,' he suddenly says to me about ten o'clock, and he called Dor up and shook hands with him, and bade him be good to me, and then he shook hands with me. 'God bless ye both,' says he, 'for Christ sake; and God bless the friends who have been kind to us!'　And with that he died."

That's all, for now.　And I hope no one will think I invented the account of Jake's death, for I should not like to do it. The wife related it to us in the exact words written.

"And I able to do so little for him!" broke forth the Squire, suddenly, when we were about half way home; and he lashed up Bob and Blister regardless of their tempers. Which the animals did not relish.

And so that assize week ended the matter.　Bringing imprisonment to the kidnapping woman, and to Jake death.

III.

WOLFE BARRINGTON'S TAMING.

THIS is an incident of our school life; one that I never care to look back upon. All of us have sad remembrances of some kind living in the mind; and we are apt in our painful regret to say, "If I had but done this, or had but done the other, things might have turned out differently."

The school was a large square house, built of rough stone, gardens and playgrounds and fields extending around it. It was called Worcester House: a title of the fancy, I suppose, since it was some miles away from Worcester. The master was Dr. Frost, a tall, stout man, in white frilled shirt, knee-breeches and buckles; stern on occasion, but a gentleman to the backbone. He had several under masters. Forty boys were received; we wore the college cap and Eton jacket. Mrs. Frost was delicate: and Hall, a sour old woman of fifty, was manager of the eatables.

Tod and I must have been in the school two years, I think, when Archie Hearn entered. He was eleven years old. We had seen him at the house sometimes before, and liked him. A regular good little fellow was Archie.

Hearn's father was dead. His mother had been a Miss Stockhausen, sister to Mrs. Frost. The Stockhausens had a name in Worcestershire: chiefly, I think, for dying off. There had been six sisters; and the only two now left were Mrs. Frost and Mrs. Hearn; the other four quietly decayed away one after another, not living to see thirty. Mr. Hearn

died (from an accident) when Archie was only a year old.
He left no will, and there ensued a sharp dispute about his
property. The Stockhausens said it all belonged to the little
son; the Hearn family considered a portion of it ought to go
back to them. The poor widow was the only quiet spirit
amidst them, willing to be led either way. What the disput-
ants did was to put it into Chancery; and I don't much think
it ever came out again.

It was the worst move they could have made for Mrs. Hearn.
For it reduced her to a very slender income, indeed, and the
world wondered how she got on at all. She lived in a cottage
about three miles off the Frosts, with one servant and the little child Archibald. In the course of years people seemed
to forget all about the property in Chancery, and to ignore
her as quite a poor woman.

Well, we—I and Tod—had been at Dr. Frost's two years
or so, when Archibald Hearn entered the school. He was a
slender little lad with bright brown eyes, a delicate face and
red cheeks, very sweet-tempered and pleasant in manner. At
first he used to go home at night, but when the winter weather
set in he got a cough, and he then came into the house altogether. Some of the big ones felt sure that old Frost took
him for nothing: but as little Hearn was Mrs. Frost's
nephew and we liked *her*, no talk was made over it. The
lad did not much like coming into the house: we could see
that. He seemed always to be hankering after his mother
and old Betty the servant. Not in words: but he'd stand
with his arms on the play-yard gate, and his eyes gazing out
to the quarter where the cottage was; as if he'd like his sight
to leap the wood and the two or three miles of distance,
and take a look at it. When any of us said to him as
a bit of chaff, " You are staring after old Betty," he would
say Yes, he wished he could see her and his mother; and
then tell no end of tales about what Betty had done for him
in his illnesses. Any way, Hearn was a straightforward little chap, and a favourite in the school.

He had been with us about a year when Wolfe Barrington came. Quite another sort of pupil. A big strong fellow who Lad never had a mother: rich and overbearing, and cruel enough. He was in black from head to foot for his father, who had just died: a rich Irishman, given to company and strong living. Wolfe came in for all the money; so that he had a fine career before him and might be expected to set the world on fire. Little Hearn's stories had been of home; of his mother and old Betty. Wolfe's were different. He had had the run of his father's stables and knew more about horses and dogs than the animals themselves. Curious things, too, he'd tell of men and women, who had stayed at old Barrington's place: and what he said of the public school he had been at might have made old Frost's hair stand on end. Why he quitted the public school we did not find out: some said he had run away from it, and that his father, who'd indulged him awfully, would not send him back to be punished; others said the public masters would not receive him back. In the nick of time the father died; and Wolfe's guardians put him at Dr. Frost's.

"I shall make you my fag," said Barrington, the day he entered, catching hold of little Hearn in the playground, and twisting him round by the arm.

"What's that?" asked Hearn, rubbing his arm — for Wolfe's grasp had not been a light one.

"What's that!" repeated Barrington, scornfully. "What a precious young fool you must be, not to know. Who's your mother?"

"She lives over there," answered Hearn, taking the question literally, and nodding beyond the wood.

"Oh!" said Barrington, twisting his mouth. "What's her name? And what's yours?"

"Mrs. Hearn. Mine's Archibald."

"Good, Mr. Archibald. You shall be my fag. That is, my servant. And you'll do every earthly thing that I order you to do. And mind you do it smartly, or maybe that girl's face of yours will show out rather green sometimes."

"I shall not be anybody's servant," returned Archie, in his mild, inoffensive way.

"Won't you! You'll tell me another tale before this time to-morrow. Did you ever get licked into next week?"

The child made no answer. He began to think the new fellow might be in earnest, and gazed up at him in questioning doubt.

"When your two eyes can't see out for the swelling round them, and your back's stiff with smarting and aching—*that's* the kind of licking I mean," went on Barrington. "Did you ever taste it?"

"No, sir."

"Good again. It will be the sweeter when you do. Now look you here, Mr. Archibald Hearn. I appoint you my fag in ordinary. You'll fetch and carry for me: you'll black my boots and brush my clothes; you'll sit up to wait on me when I go to bed, and read me to sleep; you'll be dressed before I am in the morning, and be ready with my clothes and hot water. Never mind whether the rules of the house are against hot water, *you'll have to provide it*, though you boil it on sticks in the bed-room grate, or out in the nearest field. You'll attend me at my lessons; look out words for me; copy my exercises in a fair hand—and if you were old enough to *do* them, you'd have *to*. That's a few of the items; but there are a hundred other things, that I've not time to detail. If I can get a horse for my use, you'll have to groom him. And if you don't put out your mettle to serve me in all these ways, and don't hold yourself in readiness to fly and obey me at any minute or hour, you'll get one of the lickings I've told you of every day, until you are licked into shape."

Barrington meant what he said. Voice and countenance alike wore a carelessly determined look, as if his words were law. Lots of the fellows, attracted by the talking, had gathered round. Hearn, honest and straightforward himself, did not altogether understand what evil might be in store for him, and grew seriously frightened.

The captain of the school walked up—John Whitney. "What is that you say Hearn has got to do?" he asked.

"*He* knows now," answered Barrington. "That's enough. They don't allow servants here: I must have a fag in place of one."

In turning his fascinated eyes from Barrington, Hearn saw Blair standing by, our mathematical master—of whom you will hear more later. Blair must have caught what passed: and little Hearn appealed to him.

"Am I obliged to be his fag, sir?"

Mr. Blair put us leisurely aside with his hands, and confronted the new fellow. "Your name is Barrington, I think," he said.

"Yes, it is," said Barrington, staring at him defiantly.

"Allow me to tell you that 'fags' are not permitted here. The system would not be tolerated by Dr. Frost for a moment. Each boy must wait on himself, and be responsible for himself: seniors and juniors alike. You are not at a public school now, Barrington. In a day or two, when you shall have learnt the in-door customs and rules here, I daresay you will find yourself quite sufficiently comfortable, and see that a fag would be an unnecessary appendage."

"Who is that man?" cried Barrington, as Blair turned away.

"Mathematical master. Sees to us out of hours," answered Bill Whitney.

"And what the devil did you mean by making a sneaking appeal to *him?*" continued Barrington, seizing Hearn roughly.

"I did not mean it for sneaking; but I could not do what you wanted," said Hearn. "He had been listening to us."

"I wish to goodness that confounded fool, Taptal, had been sunk in his horse-pond before he put me to such a place as this," cried Barrington, passionately. "As to you, you sneaking little devil, it seems I can't make you do what I wanted, fags being forbidden fruit here, but it shan't serve you much. There's to begin with"

Hearn got a shake and a kick that sent him flying. Blair was back on the instant.

"Are you a coward, Mr. Barrington?"

"A coward!" retorted Barrington, his eyes flashing. "You had better try whether I am or not."

"It seems to me that you act like one, in attacking a lad so much younger and weaker than yourself. Don't let me have to report you to Dr. Frost the first day of your arrival. Another thing—I must request you to be a little more careful in your language. You have come amidst gentlemen here, not blackguards."

The matter ended at this; but Barrington looked in a frightful rage. It was unfortunate that it should have occurred the day he entered; but it did, word for word, as I have written it. It set some of us rather against Barrington, and it set *him* against Hearn. He didn't "lick him into next week," but he gave him many a blow that the boy did nothing to deserve.

Barrington won his way, though, as the time went on. He had a large supply of money, and was open-handed with it; and he'd often do a generous turn for one and another. The worst of him was his savage roughness. At play he was always rough, and, when put out, savage as well. His strength and activity were something remarkable; he would not have minded hard blows himself, and he showered them out on others with no more care than if we had been made of pumice-stone.

It was Barrington who introduced the new system at football. We had played it before in a rather mild manner, speaking comparatively, but he soon changed that. Dr. Frost got to know of it in time, and he appeared amongst us one day when we were in the thick of it, and stopped the game with a sweep of his hand. They play it at Rugby now very much as Barrington made us play it then. The Doctor—standing with his face unusually red, and his shirt and necktie unusually white, and his knee-buckles shining—asked whether we were a pack of African cannibals, that we should kick at one another in that dangerous manner. If we ever attempted it again, he said, football should be interdicted.

So we went back to the old way. But we had tried the new, you see: and the consequence was that undue roughness would creep into it now and again. Barrington led it on. No African cannibal (as old Frost put it) could have been more incautiously furious at it than he. To see him with his sallow face in a steam, and his keen black eyes shining, his hat off, and his straight hair flung behind, was not the pleasantest sight to my mind. Snepp said one day that he looked just like the devil at these times. Wolfe Barrington overheard, and kicked him right over the hillock. I don't think he was ill-intentioned; but his powerful frame had been untamed; it required a vent for its superfluous strength: his animal spirits led him away, and he had never been taught to put a curb on himself or his inclinations. One thing was certain—that the name, Wolfe, for such a nature as his, was singularly appropriate. Some of us told him so. He laughed in answer; never saying that it was only so shortened from Wolfrey, which was his real name, as we learnt later. He could be as good a fellow and comrade as any of them when he chose, and on the whole we liked him a great deal better than we had thought we should at first.

As to the animosity against little Hearn, it was wearing off. The lad was too young to retaliate, and Barrington got tired of knocking him about: perhaps a little ashamed of it when there was no return. In a twelvemonth's time it had quite subsided, and, to the surprise of many of us, Barrington (coming back from a visit to his guardian, old Taptal) brought Hearn a handsome knife of three blades as a present.

And so it would have gone on but for an unfortunate occurrence. I shall always say and think so. But for that, it might have been peace between them to the end and the end. Barrington, who was defiantly independent, had betaken himself to Evesham, one half-holiday, without leave. He walked straight into some mischief there, and broke a street boy's head. Dr. Frost was appealed to by the boy's father, and of course there was a row. The Doctor forbade Barrington ever to stir beyond bounds again without first obtaining permission; and Blair had orders that for a fortnight to come Barrington was to be confined to the play-ground in after hours.

Very good. A day or two after—on the next Saturday afternoon—the school went to a cricket-match; Doctor, masters, boys, and all; Barrington only being left behind.

Was he one to stand this? No. He coolly walked away to the high road, saw a public conveyance passing, hailed it, mounted it and was carried to Evesham. There he disported himself for an hour or so, visited the chief fruit and tart shops; and then chartered a gig to bring him back to within half a mile of the school's entrance.

The cricket-match was not over when he got in, for it lasted up to the dark of the summer evening, and nobody would have known of the escapade but for one miserable misfortune— Archie Hearn happened to have gone that afternoon to Evesham with his mother. They were passing along the street, and he saw Barrington amid the sweets.

"There's Wolfe Barrington!" said Archie, in the surprise of the moment, and would have halted at the tart-shop door; but Mrs. Hearn, who was in a hurry, did not stop. On the Monday, she brought Archie back to school: he had been at home, sick, for more than a week, and knew nothing of Barrington's punishment. Archie came amidst us at once, but Mrs. Hearn stayed to take tea with her sister and Dr. Frost. Without the slightest intention to create mischief, quite unaware that she was doing it, Mrs Hearn mentioned incidentally that they had seen one of the boys—Barrington—at Evesham on the Saturday. Dr. Frost pricked up his ears at the news; not believing it, however: but Mrs. Hearn said yes, for Archie had seen him eating tarts at the confectioner's. The Doctor finished his tea, went to his study, and sent for Barrington. Barrington denied it. He was not in the habit of telling lies, was too fearless of consequences to do anything of the kind; but he denied it now to the Doctor's face; perhaps he began to think he might have gone a little too far. Dr. Frost rang the bell and ordered Archie Hearn in.

"Which shop was Barrington in when you saw him on Saturday?" questioned the Doctor.

"The pastry cook's," said Archie, innocently.

"What was he doing?" blandly went on the Doctor.

"Oh! no harm, sir; only eating tarts," Archie hastened to say.

Well—it all came out then, and though Archie was entirely innocent of wilfully telling tales; would have cut out his tongue rather than have said a word to harm Barrington, he got the credit of it now. Barrington took his punishment without a word; the hardest caning old Frost had given for many a long day, and heaps of work besides, and a promise of certain expulsion if he ever went off surreptitiously in coaches and gigs again. But Barrington thrashed Hearn worse when it was over, and branded him with the name of Tell-tale Sneak.

"He will never believe otherwise," said Archie, the tears of pain and mortification running down his cheeks, fresh and delicate as a girl's. "But I'd give the world not to have gone that afternoon to Evesham."

A week or two later we went in for a turn at "Hare and Hounds." Barrington's term of punishment was over then. Snepp was the hare; a fleet wiry fellow who could outrun most of us. But the hare this time came to grief. After doubling and turning, as Snepp used to like to do, thinking to throw us off the scent, he sprained his foot, trying to leap a hedge and dry ditch beyond it. We were on his trail, whooping and halloaing like mad; he kept quiet, and we passed on and never saw him. But there was no more scent to be seen (little pieces of white paper that Snepp had to let fall as he ran), and we found we had lost it, and went back. Snepp showed himself then, and the sport was over for the day. Some went home one way, and some another; all of us were as hot as Jupiter, and thirsting for water.

"If you'll turn down here by the great oak tree, we shall

come to my mother's house, and you can have as much **water** as you like," said little Hearn, in his good-nature.

So we turned down. There were but six or seven of us, for Snepp and his damaged foot made one, and most of them had gone on at a quicker pace. Tod helped Snepp on one side, Barrington on the other; he limping along between them.

It was a narrow red-brick house, a parlour window on each side the door, and three windows above; small altogether, but very pretty, with the jessamine and clematis climbing up the walls. Archie Hearn opened the door, and we trooped in, without any regard to ceremony. Mrs. Hearn—she had the same delicate face that Archie had, the same rose-pink colour and bright brown eyes—came out of the kitchen to stare. As well she might. Her cotton gown sleeves were turned up to the elbows, her fingers were stained red, and she had a coarse kitchen cloth pinned round her. She was pressing black currants for jelly.

We had plenty of water, and Mrs. Hearn made Snepp sit down, and looked at his foot, and put a wet bandage round kneeling before him to do it. I thought I had never seen so nice a face as hers; very placid, with a kind of sad look in it. Old Betty, that Hearn used to talk about, appeared in a short olue petticoat and a sort of jacket of brown print. I have seen homely servants in France, since dressed very similarly. Snepp thanked Mrs. Hearn for giving his foot relief, and we took off our hats to her as we went away.

The same night, before Blair called us in for prayers, Archie Hearn heard Barrington giving a sneering account of the visit to some of the fellows in the playground.

"Just like a cook, you know. Might be taken for one. Some coarse bunting tied round her middle, and hands steeped in red kitchen stuff."

"My mother could never be taken for anything but a lady," spoke up Archie bravely. "A lady may make jelly. A great many ladies prefer to do it themselves."

"Now you be off," cried Barrington, turning on him sharply "Keep at a distance from your betters."

"There's nobody in the world better than my mother," returned the boy, standing his ground, and flushing a painful flush: for, in truth, the small way they were obliged to live in, through Chancery retaining hold of the property, made a sore place in a corner of Archie's heart. "Ask Joseph Todhetley what he thinks of her. Ask John Whitney. *They* recognize her for a lady."

"But then they are gentlemen, themselves."

It was I put in that. I couldn't help having a fling at Barrington. A bit of applause followed, and stung him.

"If you shove in your oar, Johnny Ludlow, or presume to interfere with me. I'll pummel you to powder. There."

Barrington kicked out on all sides of him, sending us back. The bell rang for prayers then, and we had to go in.

The game the next evening was football. We went out to it as soon as tea was over, to the field by the river towards Vale Farm. I can't tell much about its progress, save that the play seemed rougher and louder than usual. Once there was a regular scrimmage: scores of feet kicking out at once; great struggling and pushing and shouting: and when the ball got off, and the tail after it in full hue and cry, one was left behind lying on the ground.

"I don't know why I turned my head back; it was the merest chance that I did turn it: and I saw Tod kneeling on the grass, raising a boy's head.

"Holloa!" said I, running back. "Anything amiss? Who is it?"

It was little Hearn. He had his eyes shut. Tod did not speak.

"What's the matter, Tod? Is he hurt?"

"Well, I think he's hurt a little," was Tod's answer. "He has had a kick here."

Tod touched the left temple with the point of his finger, drawing the finger down as far as the back of the ear, to indi

cate the part he meant.   It must have been a good wide kick,
I thought.

"It has stunned him, poor little fellow.   Can you get some
water from the river, Johnny?"

"I could if I had anything to bring it in.   It would leak
out of my hat long before I got here."   For the hat was of
straw.

But little Hearn made a move then, and opened his eyes.
Presently he sat up, putting his hands to his head.   Tod was
as tender with him as a mother.

"How do you feel, Archie?"

"Oh, I'm all right, I think.   A bit giddy."

Getting on his feet, he looked from me to Tod in a bewil
dered manner.   I thought it odd.   He said he'd not join the
game again, but would go in and rest.   Tod went with him,
ordering me to keep with the players.   Hearn walked all right,
and did not seem to be much the worse for it.

"What's the matter now?" asked Mrs. Hall, in her cranky
way; for she happened to be in the yard when they entered,
Tod marshalling little Hearn by the arm.

"He has had a blow at football," answered Tod.   "Here"
—showing the place he had shown me.

"A kick, I suppose you mean," said Mother Hall.

"Yes, if you like to call it so.   It was a blow with a foot."

"Did you do it, Master Todhetley?"

"No I did not," retorted Tod.

"I wonder the Doctor allows that football to be played?"
she went on, grumbling.   "I wouldn't, if I kept a school; I
know that.   It is a barbarous, cruel game, fit only for bears."

"I am all right," put in Hearn.   "I needn't have come in
but for feeling giddy."

But he was not quite right yet.   For without the slightest
warning, before he had time to stir from where he stood, he
became frightfully sick.   Hall ran for a basin and some warm
water.   Tod held his head.

"This is through having gobbled down your tea in such a

mortal hurry, to be off to that precious football," decided Hall resentfully. "The wonder is, that the whole crew of you are not sick, swallowing your food at the rate you do."

"I think I'll lie on the bed for a bit," said Archie, when the sickness had passed. "I shall be up again by supper time."

They went with him to his room. Neither of them had the slightest notion that he was hurt seriously, or that there could be any danger. Archie took off his jacket, and lay down in his other clothes. Mrs Hall offered to bring him up a cup of tea; but he said it might make him sick again, and he'd rather be quiet. She went down, and Tod sat on the edge of the bed. Archie shut his eyes and kept still. Tod thought he was dropping off to sleep, and began to creep out of the room. The eyes opened then, and Archie called to him.

"Todhetley?"

"I am here, old fellow. What is it?"

"You'll tell him I forgive him," said Archie, speaking in an earnest whisper. "Tell him I know he didn't think to hurt me."

"Oh, I'll tell him," answered Tod lightly.

"And be sure give my dear love to mamma."

"So I will."

"And now I'll go to sleep, or I sha'n't be down to supper. You will come and call me if I am not, won't you?"

"All right," said Tod, tucking the counterpane about him. "Are you comfortable, Archie?"

"Quite. Thank you."

Tod came on to the field again, and joined the game. It was a little less rough, and there were no more mishaps. We got home later than usual, and the supper stood on the table.

The suppers at Worcester House were always the same. Bread and cheese. And not too much of it. Half a round off the loaf, with a piece of cheese, for each fellow; and a small drop of beer or water. Our other meals were good and plentiful; but the Doctor waged war with heavy suppers. If old Hall had had her way, we should have had none. Little Hearn did not appear; and Tod, biting at his bread and cheese, went up to look after him. I followed.

Opening the door without noise, we stood listening and looking. Not that there was much good in looking, for the room was in darkness then.

"Archie," whispered Tod.

No answer. No sound.

"Are you asleep, old fellow?"

Not a word still. The dead might be there, for all the sound there was.

"He's asleep, for certain," said Tod, groping his way towards the bed. "So much the better, poor little chap. I'll not wake him."

It was a small room, two beds in it; Archie's was the one at the end by the wall. Tod groped his way to it: and, in thinking of it afterwards, I wondered that Tod did go up to him. The most natural thing would have been to come away, and shut the door. Unconscious instinct must have guided him—as it guides us all. Tod bent over him, touching his face, I think. I stood close behind. Now that our eyes were accustomed to the darkness, it seemed a bit lighter.

Something like a shout from Tod made me start. It was but a kind of suppressed cry. But in the dark, and holding the breath, one is startled easily.

"Get a light, Johnny. A light!—quick! for the love of heaven."

I believe I leaped the stairs at a bound. I believe I knocked over Mother Hall at the foot. I know I snatched the candle that was in her hand: and she screamed after me as if I had murdered her.

"Here it is, Tod."

He was at the door waiting for it, every atom of colour gone clean out of his countenance. Carrying it to the bed, he let its light fall full on Archie Hearn. The face was white and cold; the mouth covered with froth.

"Oh Tod! What is it that's the matter with him?"

"Hush, Johnny! I fear he's dying. Good Lord! to think we should have been such ignorant fools as to leave him by himself!—as not to have sent for Featherstone!"

We were down again in a moment. Hall stood scolding still at the top of her breath, demanding her candle. Tod said a word that stopped her. She backed against the wall, staring at him.

"Don't you play your tricks on me, Mr. Todhetley."

"Go and see," said Tod.

She took the light from his hand quietly, and went up. Just then, the Doctor and Mrs. Frost, who had been walking all the way home from Sir John Whitney's, where they had spent the evening, came in; and learnt what had happened.

Featherstone was there in no time, so to say, and shut himself in the bedroom with the Doctor and Mrs. Frost and Hall, and I don't know how many more. Nothing could be done for Archibald Hearn: he was not quite dead, but close upon it. He was dead before anybody thought of sending to Mrs. Hearn. It came to the same. Had there been telegraph wires to send and bring her upon, she would have come too late.

When I look back upon that evening—and a good many years have gone by since, as if it had been in the beginning of the world—nothing arises in my mind but a picture of confusion, tinged with a feeling of dreadful sorrow; ay, and of horror. If a death happens in a school, it is generally kept from the pupils, so far as may be; at any rate they are not allowed to see any of the attendant stir and details. But this was different. Upon masters and boys, upon mistress and household, it came with the like startling shock. Dr. Frost said feebly that the boys ought to go up to bed, and then Blair told us to go; but the boys stayed on where they were. Hanging about the passages, stealing up stairs and peeping into the room, questioning Featherstone (when we could get the chance to come upon him), whether Hearn would get well. Nobody checked us.

I went in once. Mrs. Frost was alone, kneeling by the bed; I thought she must have been saying a prayer. Just then

she lifted her head to look at him. As I backed away again she
began to speak aloud—and oh! what a sad tone she said it in!

"The only son of his mother, and she was a widow!"

There had to be an inquest. It did not come to much. The
most that could be said was, that he died from a kick at football. "A most unfortunate but accidental kick," quoth the
coroner. Tod had said that he saw the kick given: that is, had
seen some foot come flat down with a bang on the side of little
Hearn's head; and when Tod was asked if he recognized the
foot, he replied No; for boots looked much alike, and a vast
many were thrust out in the scrimmage, all kicking together.

Not one would own to having given it. For the matter of
that, the fellow might not have been conscious of what he did.
No end of thoughts glanced towards Barrington: both because
he was so ferocious at the game, and that he had a spite
against Hearn.

"I never touched him," said Barrington when this leaked
out; and his face and voice were fearlessly defiant. "It
wasn't me. I never so much as saw that Hearn was down."

And as there were others quite as brutal at football as Barrington, he was believed.

We could not get over it any way. It seemed so dreadful
that he should have been left alone to die. Hall was chiefly
to blame for that; and it cowed her.

"Look here," said Tod to us, "I have got a message for
one of you. Whichever the cap fits may take it to himself.
When Hearn was dying he told me to say that he forgave the
fellow who kicked him."

This was the evening of the inquest-day. We had all
gathered in the porch by the stone bench, and Tod took the
opportunity to relate what he had not related before. He repeated every word that Hearn had said.

"Did Hearn know who it was, then?" asked John Whitney.

"I think so."

"Then why didn't you ask him to name!"

"Why didn't I ask him to name," repeated Tod, in a fume

"Do you suppose I thought he was going to die, Whitney?—or that the kick was to turn out a serious one? Hearn was getting big enough to fight his own battles: and I never thought but he would be up again at supper time."

John Whitney pushed his hair back, in his quiet, thoughtful way, and said no more. He was to die himself the following year,—but that has nothing to do with the present matter

I was standing away at the gate after this, looking at the sunset, when Tod came up and put his arms on the top bar.

"What are you gazing at, Johnny?"

"At the sunset. How red it is! I was thinking that if Hearn's up there now he is better off. It is very beautiful."

"I would not like to have been the one to send him there, though," was Tod's answer. "Johnny, I am certain Hearn knew who it was," he went on in a low tone. "I am certain he thought the fellow, himself knew, and that it had been done for the purpose. I think I know also."

"Tell us," I said. And Tod glanced over his shoulders, to make sure nobody was within hearing before he replied.

"Wolfe Barrington."

"Why don't you accuse him, Tod?"

"It wouldn't do. And I am not absolutely sure. What I saw, was this. In the rush, one of them fell: I saw his head lying on the ground sideways. Before I could shout out to the fellows to take care, a boot with a grey trouser over it came stamping down (not kicking) on the side of the head. If ever anything was done deliberately, that stamp seemed to be; it could hardly have been accidental. I know no more than that: it all passed in a moment of time. I didn't *see* that it was Barrington. But—what other fellow is there among us who would have wilfully harmed little Hearn? It is that thought that brings me conviction."

I looked round to where a lot of them stood at a distance "Wolfe has got on grey trousers, too."

"That does not tell much," returned Tod. "Half of us wear the same. Yours are grey; mine are grey. It's just this: While I am convinced in my own mind that it was Barrington, there's no sort of proof that it was, and he denies it. So it must rest, and die away. Keep counsel, Johnny."

The funeral took place from the school. All of us went to it. In the evening, Mrs. Hearn, who had been staying at the house, surprised us by coming into the tea-room. She looked very small in her black gown. Her thin cheeks were more flushed than usual, and her eyes had a mournful sadness in them.

"I wish to say good-bye to you; and to shake hands with you before I go home," she began, in a kind tone, and we all got up from the table to face her.

"I thought you would like me to tell you that I feel sure it must have been an accident; that no harm was intended My dear little son said this to Joseph Todhetley when he was dying—and I fancy that some prevision of death must have lain then upon his spirit and caused him to say it, though he himself might not have been quite conscious of it. He died in love and peace with all; and, if he had anything to forgive —he forgave freely. I wish to let you know that I do the same. Only try to be a little less rough at play—God bless you all. Will you shake hands with me?"

John Whitney, a true gentleman always, went up to her first, meeting her offered hand.

"If it had been anything but an accident, Mrs. Hearn," he began in a tone of deep feeling, "if any one of us had done it wilfully, I think, standing to hear you now, we should shrink to the earth in our shame and contrition. You cannot regret Archibald much more than we do."

"In the midst of my grief, I know one thing: that God has taken him from a world of care to peace and happiness; I try to *rest* in that. Thank you all. Good-bye."

Catching up her breath, she shook hands with us one by one, giving each a smile; but did not say more.

And the only one of us who did not feel her visit as it was meant, was Barrington. But he had no feeling: his body was too strong for it, his temper too fierce. He would have thrown a sneer of ridicule after her, but Whitney hissed it down.

Before another day had gone over, Barrington and Tod had a row. It was about a crib. Tod could be as overbearing as Barrington when he pleased, and he was cherishing a bad feeling towards him. They went and had it out in private—but it did not come to a fight. Tod was not one to keep in matters till they rankled, and he openly told Barrington that he believed it was he had caused Hearn's death. Barrington denied it out-and-out; first of all swearing passionately that he had not, and then calming down to talk about it quietly. Tod felt less sure of it after that: as he confided to me in the bedroom.

Dr. Frost forbid football. And the time went on.

What I have to relate further may be thought a made-up story, such as we read in fiction. It is so very like a case of retribution. But it is all true, and happened as I shall put it. And somehow I never care to dwell long upon the calamity.

It was as nearly as possible a year after Hearn died. Jessup was captain of the school, for John Whitney was too ill to come. Jessup was nearly as rebellious as Wolfe; and the two would ridicule Blair audaciously, and call him " Baked pie" to his face. One morning, when they had given no end of trouble to old Frost over their Greek, and laid the blame upon the hot weather, the Doctor said he had a great mind to keep them in till dinner-time. However, they eat humble-pie, and were allowed to escape. Blair was taking us for a walk. Instead of keeping with the ranks, Barrington and Jessup fell out, and sat down on the gate of a field, where the wheat was being carried. Blair said they might sit there if they pleased, but forbid them to cross the gate. Indeed, there was a general and standing interdiction against our entering any field while the crops were being gathered. We went on and left them.

Half an hour afterwards, before we got back, Barrington had been carried home, dying.

Dying, as was supposed. He and Jessup had disobeyed Blair, disregarded orders, and rushed into the field, shouting and leaping like two mad fellows—as the labourers said afterwards. Making for the waggon, laden high with wheat, they mounted it, and started-on the horses. In some way Barrington lost his balance, slipped over the side, and the hind wheel went over him.

I shall never forget the house when we got home. Jessup, in his terror, had made off for his home, running all the way—seven miles. He was in the same boat as Wolfe, except that he escaped injury—had gone over the stile in defiance of orders, and got on the waggon. Barrington was lying in the blue-room; and Mrs. Frost, frightened out of bed, stood on the landing in her night-cap, a shawl wrapped round her loose white dressing-gown. She was ill at the time. Featherstone came striding up the road wiping his hot face.

"Lord bless me!" cried Featherstone when he had looked at Wolfe and touched him. "I can't deal with this by myself, Dr. Frost."

The Doctor had guessed that. And Roger was already away on a galloping horse, flying to fetch another. It was little Pink he brought: a shrimp of a man, with a fair reputation in his profession. But the two were more accustomed to treat rustic ailments than grave cases, and Dr. Frost knew that. Evening drew on, and the dusk was gathering, when a carriage with post horses came thundering in at the front gates, bringing Mr. Carden.

They did not explain to us boys the particulars of the injuries; and I don't know them to this day. The spine was hurt; the right ankle smashed: we heard that much. Taptal, Barrington's guardian, came over, and an uncle from London. Altogether it was a miserable time. The masters seized upon it to be doubly stern, and read us lectures upon disobedience and rebellion—as though we had been the offenders! As to Jessup, his father handed him back again to Dr. Frost, saying that in his opinion a taste of birch would much conduce to his benefit.

Barrington did not seem to suffer as keenly as some might; perhaps his spirits kept him up, for they were untamed. On the very day after the accident, he asked for some of the fellows to go in and sit with him, because he was dull. By-and-by, the doctors said. And the next day but one, Dr. Frost sent in me. Me! The paid nurse sat at the end of the room.

"Oh, it's you, is it, Ludlow? Where's Jessup?"

"Jessup's under punishment."

His face looked the same as ever, and that was all of him that could be seen. He lay on his back, covered over. As to the low bed, it might have been a board, to judge by the flatness. And perhaps was.

"I'm very sorry about it, Barrington. We all are. Are you in much pain?"

"Oh, I don't know," was his impatient answer. "One has to grin and bear it. The cursed idiots had stacked the wheat sloping to the sides, or it would never have happened. What do you hear about me?"

"Nothing but regret that it——"

"I don't mean that stuff. Regret, indeed! regret won't undo it. I mean as to my getting about again. Will it be ages first?"

"We don't hear a word."

"If they were to keep me here a month, Ludlow, I should go mad. Rampant. You shut up, old woman."

For the nurse had interfered, telling him he must not excite himself.

"My ankle's hurt; but I believe it is not half so bad as a regular fracture: and my back's bruised. Well, what's a bruise? Nothing. Of course there's pain and stiffness, and all that; but so there is after a bad fight, or a thrashing. And they talk about my lying here for three or four weeks! Catch me."

One thing was evident: that they had not allowed Wolfe to suspect the gravity of the case. Down stairs we had an inkling, I don't remember whence gathered, that it might possibly end in death. There was a suspicion of some injury that we could not get to know of; inward I think; and it is said that even Mr. Carden, with all his surgical skill, could not get to it either. Any way, the prospect of recovery for Barrington was supposed to be of the scantiest; and it put a gloom upon us.

A sad mishap was to occur. Of course nobody in their senses would have let Barrington learn the danger he was in; especially while there was just a chance that the peril would be surmounted. I read a book lately—I, Johnny Ludlow—where a little child met with an accident; and the first thing the people around him did, father, doctors, nurses, was to inform him that he would be a cripple for the rest of his days. That was common sense with a vengeance: and about as likely to occur in real life as that I could turn myself into a Dutch man. However, something of the kind did happen in Barrington's case, but through inadvertence. Another uncle came over from Ireland; an old man; and in talking with Featherstone spoke out too freely. They were outside Barrington's door, and besides that, supposed he was asleep. But he had woke then; and heard more than he ought. That blue-room always seemed to have an echo in it.

"So it's all up with me, Ludlow?"

I was by his bedside when he suddenly said this, in the gathering dusk of the summer's evening. He had been lying quite silent since I entered, and his face had a white, still look on it, never before noticed there.

"What do you mean, Barrington?"

"None of your shamming here. I know; and so do you, Johnny Ludlow. I say, though, it makes one feel queer to find the world's slipping away. I had looked for so much jolly *life* in it."

"Barrington, you may get well yet; you may, indeed. Ask Pink and Featherstone, else, when they next come; ask Mr Carden. I can't think what idea you have been getting hold of."

"There, that's enough," he answered. "Don't bother. **I want to be quiet.**"

He shut his eyes; and the dusk grew greater as the minutes passed. Presently some one came into the room with a gentle step: a lady in a black-and-white gown that didn't rustle. It was Mrs. Hearn. Barrington looked up at her.

"I am going to stay with you for a day or two," she said in a low sweet voice, bending over him and touching his forehead with her cool fingers. "I hear you have taken a dislike to the nurse: and Mrs. Frost is really too weakly just now to get about."

"She's a sly cat," said Barrington, alluding to the nurse; "she watches me out of the tail of her eye. Hall's as bad. They are in league together."

"Well, they shall not come in more than I can help. I will nurse you my myself."

"No; not you," said Barrington, his face looking red and uneasy. "I'll not trouble *you*."

She sat down in my chair, just pressing my hand in token of greeting. And I left them.

In the ensuing days his life trembled in the balance . and even when part of the more immediate danger was surmounted, part of the worst of the pain, it was still a toss-up. Barrington had no hope whatever: I don't think Mrs. Hearn had, either.

She hardly left him. At first he seemed to resent her presence; to wish her away; to receive what she did for him unwillingly: but, in spite of himself, he grew to look round for her, and to let his hand lie in hers whenever she chose to take it.

Who can tell what she said to him? Who can know how she softly and gradually awoke the good feelings within him, and won his heart from its brazen hardness? She did do it, and that's enough. The way was paved for her. What the accident had not done, the fear of death had. Tamed him.

One evening when the sun had sunk, leaving only its light fading in the western sky, and Barrington had been watching it from his bed, he suddenly burst into tears. Mrs. Hearn, busy amidst the physic bottles, was by his side in a moment.

"Wolfe!"

"It's very hard to have to die."

"Hush, my dear, you are not worse: a little better. I think you may be spared; I do indeed. And—in any case—you know what I read to you this evening: that to die is gain."

" es, for some. I've never had my thoughts turned that way."

"They are turned now. That is quite enough."

"It is such a little while to have lived," went on Barrington, after a pause. "Such a little while to have enjoyed earth. What are my few years compared to the ages that have gone by, to the ages and ages that are to come? Nothing. Not as much as a single drop of water to the wide ocean."

"Wolfe, dear, if you live out the allotted years of man, three score and ten, what would even that be in comparison? As you say—nothing. It seems to me that our well-being or ill-being here need not much concern us; the days, whether short or long, will pass as a dream. Eternal life lasts for ever; soon we must all be departing for it."

Wolfe made no answer. The clear sky was assuming its pale tints, blue, green, orange, shading off one into another, a beautiful opal, and his eyes were looking out at it. But as if he saw nothing.

"Listen, my dear. When Archibald died, *I* thought I should have died; died of grief and aching pain. I grieved to think how short had been his span of life on this fair earth; how cruel his fate in being taken from it so early. But, oh, Wolfe, God has shown me my mistake. I would not have him back if I could."

Wolfe put up his hand to cover his face. Not a word spoke he.

"I wish you could see things as I see them, now that they have been cleared for me," she resumed. "It is so much better to be in heaven than on earth. We, who are here, have to battle with many cares and crosses; and shall have to the end. Archie has thrown all care off. He is in happiness amidst the redeemed."

The room was getting darker; the sky's opal tints came out brighter. Wolfe's face was one of intense pain.

"Wolfe, dear, do not mistake me; do not think me hard if I say that you would be happier there than here. There is nothing to dread, dying in Christ. Believe me, I would not for the world have Archie back again: how could I then make sure what the eventual ending would be? You and he will know each other up there."

"Don't," said Wolfe.

"Don't what?"

Wolfe pulled her hand close to his face, and she knelt down to catch his whisper.

"I killed him."

A pause: and a kind of sob in her throat. Then, drawing away her hand, she laid her cheek to his.

"My dear, I think I have known it."

"You—have—known—it?" stammered disbelieving Wolfe.

"Yes. I thought it was likely. I felt nearly sure. Don't let it trouble you now. Archie forgave, you know, and I forgave; and God will forgive."

"How could you come here to nurse me—knowing that?"

"It made me the more anxious to come. You have no mother."

"No." Wolfe was sobbing bitterly. "She died when I was born. I've never had anybody. I've never had a chapter read to me, or a prayer prayed."

"No, no, dear. And Archie—oh, Archie had all that. From the time he could speak, I tried to train him for heaven. It has seemed to me, since, just as though I had foreseen he would go early, and was preparing him for it."

"I never meant to kill him," sobbed Wolfe. "I saw his head down there, and I sent my foot upon it without a moment's thought. If I had taken thought, or known it would hurt him seriously, I'd not have done it."

"He is better off, dear," was all she said. "You have that comfort."

"Any way, I am paid out for it. At the best, I suppose I shall go upon crutches for life. That's bad enough: but dying's worse. Mrs. Hearn, I am not ready to die."

"Be you very sure God will not take you until you are ready, if you only wish and hope to be made so from your very heart," she whispered. "I am praying to Him often for you, Wolfe."

"I think you must be one of heaven's angels," said Wolfe, with a burst of emotion.

"No, dear; only a weak woman. I have had so much sorrow and care, trial upon trial, one disappointment after another, that it has left me nothing but heaven to lean upon. Wolfe, I am trying to show you a little bit of the way thither; and I think—I do indeed—that this accident, which seems, and is, so dreadful, may have been sent by God in mercy. Perhaps, else, you might never have found Him: and where would you have been in all that long, long eternity that has to come? A few years here: millions of never-ending ages hereafter!—oh, Wolfe! bear up bravely for the little span, even though the cross may be heavy. Fight on manfully for the real life."

'If you will help me."

"To be sure I will."

Wolfe got about again, and came out upon crutches. After awhile they were discarded, first one, then the other, and he took to a stick permanently. He would never go without that. He would never run or leap again, or kick much either. The doctors looked upon it as a wonderful cure—and old Featherstone was apt to talk to us boys as if it were he who had pulled him through. But not in Henry Carden's hearing.

The uncles and Taptal said he would be better now at a private tutor's. But Wolfe would not leave Dr. Frost's. A low pony carriage was bought for him, and all his spare time he would go driving over to Mrs. Hearn's. He was as a son to her. His great animal spirits had been taken out of him, you see; and he had to find his happiness in quieter grooves. One

Saturday afternoon he drove me over. Mrs. Hearn had asked me to stay with her until the Monday morning. Barrington generally stayed.

It was in November. Considerably more than a year after the accident. The guns of the sportsmen were heard in the wood; a pack of hounds and their huntsmen rode past the cottage at a gallop, in full chase after a late find. Barrington looked and listened, a sigh escaping him.

"These pleasures are barred to me now."

"But a better one has been opened to you," said Mrs. Hearn, with a meaning smile, as she took his hand to hold.

And on Wolfe's face, when he glanced at her in answer, there sat a look of satisfied rest, that I am sure had never been seen on it before he fell off the wagon.

IV.

MAJOR PARRIFER.

E was one of the worst magistrates that ever sat upon the bench of justices. Strangers were given to wonder how he got his commission. But, you see, men are fit or unfit for a post according to their doings in it; and, generally speaking, people cannot tell what the doings will be beforehand.

They called him Major: Major Parrifer: but he only held rank in a militia regiment, and everybody knows what that is. He had bought the place he lived in some years before, and christened it Parrifer Hall. The worst title he could have hit upon; seeing that the good old Hall, with the good old family in it, was only a mile or two distant. Parrifer Hall was only a stone's throw, so to say, beyond our village, Church Dykely.

They lived at a high rate; money was not lacking; the Major, his wife, six daughters, and a son who did not come home much. Mrs. Parrifer was stuck up: it is one of our country sayings, and it applied to her well. When she called on people her silk gowns rustled as if buckram lined them; her voice was loud, her manner patronising; the Major's voice and manner were the same; and the girls took after them.

Close by, at the corner of Piefinch Lane, was a cottage that belonged to me. To me, Johnny Ludlow. Not that I had control yet awhile over that, or any other cottage I might possess George Reed rented the cottage. It stood in a good large garden which touched Major Parrifer's side fence. On the

other side the garden, a high hedge divided it from the lane ;
but it had only a low hedge in front, with a low gate in
the middle. Well-kept trim edges: George Reed took care
of that.

There was quite a history attaching to him. His father had
been indoor servant at the Court ; when he married and left it,
my grandfather gave him a lease of this cottage, renewable
every seven years. George was the only son, had been very
decently educated, but turned out wild when he grew up and
got out of everything ; the result was, that he was only a day-
labourer, and never likely to be anything else. He took to the
cottage after old Reed's death. and worked for Mr. Sterling ;
who had the Court now. George Reed was civil in ordinary,
but uncommonly independent. His first wife had died, leaving a daughter, Cathy ; later he married again. Reed's wild
oats had been sown years ago ; he was thoroughly well-con-
ducted and industrious now, working in his own garden early
and late.

When Cathy's mother died, she was taken to by an aunt,
who lived near Worcester. At fifteen she came home again,
for the aunt had died. Her ten years' training there had done
very little for her, except make her into a pretty girl. Cathy
had been trained to idleness, but to very little else. She could
sing ; self-taught of course ; she could embroider handkerchiefs
and frills and petticoat-tails ; she could write a tolerable letter
without many mistakes, and was great at reading, especially
when the literature was of the half-penny kind issued weekly.
The acquirements (except the last) were not bad things in
themselves, but entirely unsuited to Cathy Reed's condition
and her future prospects in life. The best that she could as-
pire to be, the best her father expected for her, was that of
entering on a light respectable service, and later to become,
perhaps. a labourer's wife.

The second Mrs. Reed, a quiet kind of young woman, had
one little girl only when Cathy came home. She was nearly
struck dumb when she found what had been Cathy's acquire-

ments in the way of usefulness; or rather what were her non-acquirements: the facts unfolding themselves by degrees.

" Your father thinks he'd like you to get a service with some of the gentlefolks, Cathy," her stepmother said to her. " Perhaps at the Court, if they could make room for you; or over a' Squire Todhetley's. Meanwhile you'll help me with the work at home for a few weeks first; won't you, dear? When another little one comes, there'll be a good deal on my hands."

"Oh, I'll help," answered Cathy, who was a good-natured, ready-speaking girl.

" That's right. Can you wash?"

" No," said Cathy, with a very decisive shake of the head.

" Not wash?"

" Oh dear, no."

" Can you iron ?"

" Pocket-handkerchiefs."

" Your aunt was a seamstress: can you sew well?"

" I don't like sewing."

Mrs. Reed looked at her, but said no more then, rather leaving it to practice instead of theory to develop Cathy's capabilities. But when she came to put her to the test, she found Cathy could not, or would not, do any kind of useful work whatever. Cathy could not wash, or iron, or scour, or cook, or sweep; or even sew coarse plain things, such as are required in labourers' families. Cathy could do several kinds of fancy work. Cathy could idle away her time at the glass, oiling her hair, and dressing herself to the best advantage; Cathy had a smattering of history and geography and chronology; and of polite literature, as comprised in the pages of the aforesaid half-penny and penny weekly romances. The aunt had sent Cathy to a cheap day-school where such learning was supposed to be taught: had let her run about when she ought to have been cooking and washing; and of course Cathy had acquired a distaste for work. Mrs. Reed sat down aghast, her hands falling helpless on her lap, and a kind of fear at what might be Cathy's future stealing into her heart.

"Child, what is to become of you?"

Cathy had no qualms upon the point herself. She gave a laughing kiss to the little child, toddling round the room by the chairs, and took out of her pocket one of those halfpenny serials, whose enthrilling stories of brigands and captive damsels she had learnt to take her chief delight in.

"I shall have to teach her everything," sighed disappointed Mrs. Reed. "Catherine, I don't think the kind of useless things your aunt has let you learn are good for poor folks like us."

Good! Mrs. Reed might have gone a little farther. She began her instruction, but Cathy would not learn. Cathy was good-humoured always; but of work she would do none. If she attempted it, Mrs. Reed had to do it over again.

"Where on earth will the gentlefolks get their servants from, if the girls are to be like you?" cried honest Mrs. Reed.

Well, time went on; a year or two. Cathy Reed tried two or three services, but did not keep them. Young Mrs. Sterling at the Court at length took her. In three months Cathy was back home as usual. "I do not think Catherine will be kept anywhere," Mrs. Sterling said to her stepmother. "When she ought to have been minding the baby, the nurse would find her with a strip of embroidery in her hand, or else buried in the pages of some bad story that can only do her harm."

Cathy was turned seventeen when the warfare set in between her father and Major Parrifer. The Major suddenly cast his eyes on the little cottage outside his own land and coveted it. Before this, young Parrifer (a harmless young man with no whiskers, and sandy hair parted down the middle) had struck up an acquaintance with Cathy. When he left Oxford (where he got plucked twice, and at length took his name off the books) he would often be seen leaning over the cottage-gate, talking to Cathy in the garden, with her two little half-sisters that she pretended to mind. There was no harm: but perhaps Major Parrifer feared it might grow into it; and he badly wanted the plot of ground to be his, that he might pull the cottage down and extend his own boundaries to Piefinch Lane.

One fine day in the holidays, when Tod and I were indoors making flies for fishing, our old servant, Thomas, appeared, and said that George Reed had come over and wanted to speak to me. Which set us wondering. What could he want with me?

"Show him in here," said Tod.

Reed came in: a tall and powerful man of forty; with dark curling hair, and a determined, good-looking face. He began saying that he had heard Major Parrifer was after his cottage, wanting to buy it; so he had come over to beg me to interfere and stop the sale.

" Why, Reed, what can I do?" I asked. "You know I have no power."

" You'd not turn me out of it yourself, I know, sir."

" That I'd not."

Neither would I. I liked George Reed. And I remembered that he used to have me in his arms sometimes when I was a little fellow at the Court. Once he carried me to my mother's grave in the churchyard, and told me she had gone to live in heaven.

" When a rich gentleman sets his mind on a poor man's bit of a cottage, and says, 'That shall be mine,' the poor man has not got much chance against him, sir, unless he that owns the cottage will be his friend. I know you have got no power at present, Master Johnny; but if you'd speak to Mr. Brandon, perhaps he would listen to you."

" Sit down, Reed," interrupted Tod, putting his catgut out of his hand. " I thought you had the cottage on a lease."

"And so I have, sir. But the lease will be out at Michaelmas next, and Mr. Brandon can turn me from it if he likes. My father and mother died there, sir; my wife died there; my children were born there; and the place is as much like my homestead as if it was my own."

" How do you know old Parrifer wants it?" continued Tod.

"I have heard it from a sure source. I've heard, too, that

his lawyer and Mr. Brandon's lawyer have settled the matter between their two selves, and don't intend to let me as much as know I'm to go out till the time has come, for fear I should make a row over it. Nobody upon earth can stop it except Mr. Brandon," added Reed with energy.

"Have you spoken to Mr. Brandon, Reed?"

"No, sir. I was going up to him; but the thought took me that I'd better come off at once to Master Ludlow; his word might be of more avail than mine. There's no time to be lost. If once the lawyers get Mr. Brandon's consent, he may not be able to recall it."

"What does Parrifer want with the cottage?"

"I fancy he covets the bit of garden, sir; he sees the good order I've brought it into. If it's not that, I don't know what it can be. The cottage can be no eyesore to him; he can't see it from his windows."

"Shall I go with you, Johnny?" said Tod, as Reed went home, after drinking the ale old Thomas gave him. "We will circumvent that Parrifer, if there's law or justice in the Brandon land."

We went off to Mr. Brandon's in the pony-carriage, Tod driving. He lived near Alcester, and had the management of my property while I was a minor. As we went along who should ride past, meeting us, but Major Parrifer.

"Looking like the bull-dog that he is," cried Tod, who could not bear the man. "Johnny, what will you lay that he has not been to Mr. Brandon's? The negotiations are becoming intricate."

Tod did not go in. On second thought, he said it might be better to leave it to me. The Squire must try, if I failed. Mr. Brandon was at home; and Tod drove on into Alcester by way of passing the time.

"But I don't think you can see him," said the housekeeper when she came to me in the drawing-room. "This is one of his bad days. A gentleman called just now, and I went in to the master, but it was of no use."

"I know; it was Major Parrifer. We thought he might have been calling here."

Mr. Brandon was little and thin, with a shrivelled face. He lived alone, except for three or four servants, and always fancied himself ill with one ailment or another. When I went in, for he said he'd see me, he was sitting in an easy chair, with a geranium-coloured Turkish cap on his head, and two bottles of medicine at his elbow.

"Well, Johnny, an invalid as usual, you see. And what is it you so particularly want?"

"I want to ask you a favour, Mr. Brandon, if you'll please to grant it me."

"What is it?"

"You know that cottage, sir, at the corner of Piefinch Lane. George Reed's."

"Well?"

"I am come to ask you to please not to let it be sold."

"Who wants to sell it?" asked he, after a pause.

"Major Parrifer wants to buy it; and to turn out Reed. The lawyers are going to arrange it."

Mr. Brandon pushed the Turkish cap up on his brow and gave the purple tassel over his ear a twirl as he looked at me. People thought him incapable; but it was only because he had no work to do that he seemed so. He would get a bit irritable sometimes; very rarely though; and he had a squeaky voice: but he was a good and just man.

"How did you hear this, Johnny?"

I told him all about it. What Reed had said, and of our having met the Major on horseback as we drove along.

"He came here, but I did not feel well enough to see him," said Mr. Brandon. "Johnny, you know that I stand in place of your father, as regards your property; to do the best I can with it."

"Yes, sir. And I am sure you do it."

"If Major Parrifer—I don't like the man," broke off Mr. Brandon, "but that's neither here nor there. At the last

magistrates' meeting I attended he was so overbearing as to
shut us all up. My nerves were unstrung for four-and-twenty
hours afterwards."

"And Squire Todhetley came home swearing," I could not
help putting in.

"Ah," said Mr. Brandon. " Yes; some people can throw
bile off in that way. I can't. But, Johnny, all that goes for
nothing, in regard to the matter in hand: and I was about to
point out to you that if Major Parrifer has set his mind upon
buying Reed's cottage and the bit of land attached to it, he is
no doubt prepared to offer a large price; more, probably, than
it is worth. If so, I should not, in your interests, be justified
in refusing this."

I could feel my face flush with the sense of injustice, and
the tears come into my eyes. They called me a muff for many
things.

"I would not touch the money myself, sir. And if you
used it for me I'm sure it would never bring any good."

" What's that, Johnny ? "

" Money got by oppression or injustice never does. There
was a fellow at school——"

" Never mind the fellow at school. Go on with your own
arguments."

" To turn Reed out of the place where he has always lived,
out of the garden he has done so well by, just because a rich
man wants to get it into his possession, would be fearfully
unjust, sir. It would be as bad as the story we heard read
in church last Sunday, for the First Lesson, of Naboth's vine
yard. Tod said so as we came along."

" Whose Tod ? "

" Joseph Todhetley. If you turned Reed out, sir, for the
sake of benefiting me, I should be ashamed to look people in
the face when they talked of it. If you please, sir, I do not
think my father would allow it if he were alive. Reed says
the place is like his homestead."

Mr. Brandon measured two tablespoonfuls of medicine into

a glass, drank it, and ate a French plum afterwards. The
plums were in a paper, and he handed them to me. I ate
one, and tried to crack the stone.

"You have taken up a strong opinion upon this matter,
Master Johnny."

"Yes, sir. I like Reed. And if I did not, he has no more
right to be turned out of his home than Major Parrifer has
out of his. How would *he* like it, if some great rich powerful man came down on his place and turned him out?"

"Major Parrifer can't be turned out of his, Johnny. It is
his own."

"And Reed's place is mine, sir—if you'll not be angry with
me for saying it. Please don't let it be done, Mr Brandon."

The pony-carriage came rattling up at this juncture, and we
saw Tod look at the windows impatiently. I got up, and Mr.
Brandon shook hands with me.

"What you have said is all very good, Johnny, right in
principle; but I cannot let it entirely outweigh your interest.
When this proposal shall be put before me—as you say it will
be—it must have my full consideration."

I stopped when I got to the door and turned to look at him.
If he would but have given me an assurance! He read in
my face what I wanted.

"No, Johnny, I can't do that. You may go home easy for
the present, however; for I will promise not to accept the offer
to purchase without first seeing you again and showing you my
reasons."

"I may have gone back to school, sir."

"I tell you I will see you again if I decide to accept the
offer," he repeated emphatically. And I went out to the
pony-chaise.

"Old Brandon means to sell," said Tod when I told him.
And he gave the pony an angry cut, that made him fly off
with a leap.

Will anybody believe that I never heard another word upon
the subject?—except what people said in the way of gossip.

It was soon known that Mr. Brandon had declined to sell the cottage; and when his lawyer wrote him word that the sum offered for it was increased to quite an unprecedented amount, considering the small value of the cottage and garden in question, Mr. Brandon only sent a peremptory note back again, saying he was not in the habit of changing his decisions, an*
the place *was not for sale.* Tod threw up his hat.

"Bravo, old Brandon! I thought he'd not go quite over to the enemy."

George Reed wanted to thank me for it. One evening in passing his cottage on my way home from the Court, I leaned over the gate to speak to his little ones. He saw me and came running out. The rays of the setting sun shone on the children's white corded bonnets.

"I have to thank you for this, sir. They are going to renew my lease."

"Are they? All right. But you need not thank me; I know nothing about it."

George Reed gave a sort of decisive nod. "If you had not got the ear of Mr. Brandon, sir, I know what box I'd have been in now. Look at them girls!"

It was not a very complimentary mode of speech, as applied to the Misses Parrifer. Three of them were passing, dressed outrageously in the fashion as usual. I lifted my straw hat, and one of them nodded in return, but the other two only looked out at the tail of their eyes.

"The Major has been trying it on with me now," remarked Reed, watching them out of sight. "When he found he could not buy the place, he thought he'd try and buy out me. He wanted the bit of land for a kitchen-garden, he said; and he'd give me a bank-note of five pounds to go out of it. Much obliged, Major, I said; but I'd not go for fifty."

"As if he had not got heaps of land himself to make kitchen-gardens of!"

"But don't you see, Master Johnny, to a man like Major Parrifer, who thinks the world was made for him, there's

nothing so mortifying as being balked. He set his mind
upon this place; he can't get it; and he is just boiling over.
He'd poison me if he could. Now then, what's wanted?"

Cathy had come up, with her pretty dark eyes, whispering
some question to her father. I ran on; it was getting late,
and the Manor ever-so-far off.

From that time the feud grew between Major Parrifer and
George Reed. Not openly; not actively. It could not well
be either when the relative positions in life were so different.
Major Parrifer was a wealthy proprietor, a county magistrate
(and an awfully overbearing one); and George Reed was a
poor cottager who worked for his bread as a day-labourer.
But that the Major grew to abhor and hate Reed; that the
man, inhabiting the place at his very gates in spite of him,
and looking at him independently, as if to say he knew it,
every time he passed, had become an eyesore; was easy to be
seen.

The Major resented it on us all. He was rude to Mr.
Brandon when they met; he struck out his whip once when
he was on horseback, and I passed him, as if he would like to
strike me. I don't know whether he was aware of my visit
to Mr. Brandon; but the cottage was mine, I was friendly
with Reed, and that was enough. Months, however, went on,
and nothing came of it.

One Sunday morning in winter, when our church bells
were going for service, Major Parrifer's carriage turned out
with the ladies all in full fig. The Major himself turned out
after it, walking, one of his daughters with him, a young
man who was on a visit there, and a couple of servants. As
they passed George Reed's, the sound of work being done in
the garden at the back of the cottage caught the Major's
quick ears. He turned softly down Piefinch Lane, stole to
the high hedge on tiptoe, and stooped to peep through it.

Reed was doing something to his turnips; hoeing them, the

Major said. He called the gentleman to him and the two servants, and bade them look through the hedge. Nothing more. The party came on to church then.

On Tuesday, the Major rode out to take his place on the magisterial bench at Alcester. It was bitterly cold January weather, and only one magistrate besides himself was on it a *clergyman*. Two or three petty offenders were brought before them, who were severely sentenced—as prisoners always were when Major Parrifer was the presiding judge. Another magistrate came in afterwards.

Singularly to say, Tod and I had gone to the town that day about a new saddle for his horse; singular on account of what happened. In saying we were there I am telling the truth; it is not an invented fiction to give colour to the tale. Upon turning out of the saddler's, which is near the justice-room, old Jones the constable was coming along with a hand-cuffed prisoner, a tail trailing after him.

"Halloa!" cried Tod. "Here's fun!"

But I had seen what Tod did not, and rubbed my eyes, wondering if they saw double.

"*Tod!* It is George Reed!"

Reed's face was as white as a sheet, and he walked along, not to say unwillingly, but as one in a state of sad shame, of awful rage. Tod made only one bound to the prisoner; and old Jones knowing us, did not push him back again.

"As I'm a living man, I do not know what this is for, or why I am paraded through the town in disgrace," spoke Reed in answer to Tod's question. "If I'm charged with doing wrong, I am willing to appear and answer for it, without being made into a felon in the face and eyes of folks, beforehand."

"Why do you bring Reed up in this manner—with the hand-cuffs on?" demanded Tod of the constable.

"Because the Major telled me to, young Mr. Todhetley."

Be you very sure Tod pushed after them into the justice-room: the police saw him, but he was magistrate's son. The crowd would have liked to push in also, but were ignominiously

4*

sent to the right-about. I waited, and was presently admitted surreptitiously. Reed was standing before Major Parrifer and the other two, handcuffed still; and I gathered what the charge was.

It was preferred by Major Parrifer, who had his servants there and a gentleman as witnesses. George Reed had been working in his garden on the previous Sunday morning—which was against the law. Old Jones had gone to Mr. Sterling's and taken him on the Major's warrant, as he was thrashing corn.

Reed's answer was to the following effect.

He was *not* working. His wife was ill—her little boy being but four days old—and Dr. Duffham ordered her some mutton broth. He went to the garden to get the turnips to put in it. It was only on account of her illness that he didn't go to church himself, he and Cathy. They might ask Dr. Duffham.

"Do you dare to tell me you were not hoeing turnips?" cried Major Parrifer.

"I dare to say I was not doing it as work," independently answered the man. "If you looked at me, as you say, major, through the hedge, you must have seen the bunch of turnips I had got up, lying near. I took the hoe in my hand, and I did use it for two or three minutes. Some dead weeds had got thrown along the bed, by the children, perhaps, and I pulled them away. I went indoors directly: before the clock struck eleven the turnips were on, boiling with the scrag of mutton. I peeled them and put them in myself."

"I see the bunch of turnips," cried one of the servants. "They was lying——"

"Hold your tongue, sir," roared his master; "if your further evidence is wanted, you'll be asked for it. As to this defence"—and the Major turned to his brother magistrates with a scornful smile—"it is quite ingenious; one of the clever excuses we usually get here. But it will not serve your turn, George Reed. When the sanctity of the Sabbath is violated——"

"Reed is not a man to say he did not do a thing if he did," interrupted Tod.

The Major glared at him for an instant, and then put out of hand a big gold pencil he was waving majestically.

"Clear the room of spectators," said he to the policeman.

Which was all Tod got for interfering. We had to go out: and in a minute or two Reed came out also, handcuffed as before: not in charge of old Jones, but of the county police. He had been sentenced to a month's imprisonment Major Parrifer had wanted to make it three months; he said something about six; but the other two thought they saw some slightly extenuating circumstances in the case. A solicitor who was intimate with the Sterlings, and knew Reed very well, had been present towards the end.

"Could you not have spoken in my defence, sir?" asked Reed, as he passed this gentleman in coming out.

"I would had I been able. But you see, my man, when the law gets broken——"

"The devil take the law," said Reed savagely. "What I want is justice."

"And the administrators of it are determined to uphold it, what can be said?" went on the solicitor equably, as if there had been no interruption.

"You would make out that I broke the law, just doing what I did; and I swear it was no more? That I can be legally punished for it?"

"Don't, Reed; it's of no use. The Major and his witnesses swore you were at work. And it appears you were."

"I asked them to take a fine—if I must be punished. I might have found friends to advance it for me."

"Just so. And for that reason of course they did not take it," said the candid lawyer.

"What is my wife to do while I am in prison? And the children? I may come out to find them starved. A month's long enough to starve them in such weather as this."

Reed was allowed time for no more. He would not have been allowed that, but for having been jammed by the crowd

at the doorway He caught my eye as they were getting
clear.

"Master Johnny, will you go to the Court for me—your own
place, sir—and tell the master that I swear I am innocent?
Perhaps he'll let a few shillings go to the wife weekly; tell him
with my duty that I'll work it out as soon as I am released.
All this is done out of revenge, sir, because Major Parrifer
couldn't get me from my cottage. May the Lord repay him!"

It caused a commotion, I can tell you, this imprisonment of
Reed; the place was ringing with it between the Court and
Dyke Manor. Our two houses seemed to have more to do
with it than other people's; first because Reed worked at the
Court; secondly, because I, who owned both the Court and
the cottage, lived at the Manor. People took it up pretty
warmly, and Mrs. Reed and the children were cared for. Mr
Sterling paid her five shillings a week; and Mr. Brandon and
the Squire helped her on the quiet, and there were others.
In small country localities gentlemen don't like to say openly
that their neighbours are in the wrong: at any rate, they
rarely *do* anything by way of remedy. Some spoke of an
appeal to the Secretary of State, but it came to nothing, and
no steps were taken to liberate Reed. Bill Whitney, who was
staying a week with us, wrote and told his mother about it;
she sent back a sovereign for Mrs. Reed; we three took it to
her, and went about saying old Parrifer ought to be kicked,
which was a relief to our feelings.

But there's something to tell about Cathy. On the day that
Reed was taken up, it was not known at his home immediately.
The neighbours, aware that the wife was ill, said nothing to
her—for old Duffham thought she was going to have a fever
and ordered her to be kept quiet. For one thing, they did not
know what there was to tell; except that Reed had been
marched off from his work in handcuffs by Jones the constable.
In the evening, when news came of his committal, it was
agreed that an excuse should be made to Mrs. Reed that
her husband had gone out on a business job for his master;

and that Cathy—who could not fail to hear the truth from one or another—should be warned not to say anything.

"Tell Cathy to come out here," said the woman, looking over the gate. It was the little girl they spoke to; who could talk well: and she answered that Cathy was not there. So Ann Perkins, Mrs. Reed's sister, was called out.

"Where's Cathy?" cried they.

Ann Perkins answered in a passion—that she did not know where Cathy was, but should uncommonly like to know, and she only wished she was behind her—keeping her there with her sister when she ought to be at her own home? Then the women told Ann Perkins what they had been intending to tell Cathy, and looked out for the latter.

She did not come back. The night passed, and the next day passed, and Cathy was not seen or heard of. The only person who appeared to have met her was Goody Picker. It was about two o'clock in the afternoon, Tuesday, and Cathy had her best bonnet on. Mother Picker remarked upon her looking so smart, and asked where she was going to. Cathy answered that her uncle (who lived at Evesham) had sent to say she must go over there at once. "But when she came to the two roads, she turned off quite on the conterairy way to Evesham, and I thought the young woman must be daft," concluded Mrs. Picker.

The month passed away, and Reed came out; but Cathy had not returned. He got home on foot, in the afternoon; with his hair cut close, and seemed as quiet as a lamb. The man had been daunted. It was an awful insult to put upon him; a slur on his good name for life; and some of them said George Reed would never hold up his head again. Had he been cruel or vindictive, he might have revenged himself on Major Parrifer, personally, in a manner the Major would have found it difficult to forget.

The wife was about again, but sickly: the little ones did not at first know their father. One of the first people he asked after was Cathy. The girl was not at hand to welcome him, and he took it in the light of a reproach. When men come for the first time out of jail, they are sensitive.

"Mr. Sterling called in yesterday, George, to say you were to go to your work again as soon as ever you came home," said the wife, evading the question about Cathy. "Everybody has been so kind; they know you didn't deserve what you got."

"Ah," said Reed, carelessly. "Where's Cathy?"

Mrs. Reed felt herself obliged to tell. No diplomatist, she brought out the news abruptly: Cathy had not been seen or heard of since the afternoon he was sent to prison. That aroused Reed: nothing else seemed to have done it: and he got up from his chair.

"Why, where is she? What's become of her?"

The neighbours had been indulging in sundry speculations on the same question, which they had obligingly favoured Mrs. Reed with; but she did not think it necessary to impart them to her husband.

"Cathy was a good girl on the whole, George; putting aside that she'd do no work, and spent her time reading good-for-nothing books. What I think is this—that she heard of your misfortune after she left, and wouldn't come home to face it. She is eighteen now, you know."

"Come home from where?"

Mrs. Reed had to tell the whole truth. That Cathy, dressed up in her best things, had left home without saying a word to anybody, stealing out of the house unseen; she had been met in the road by Mrs. Picker, and told her what has already been said. But the uncle at Evesham had seen nothing of her.

Forgetting his shorn hair—as he would have to forget it, or, at least, to ignore it until it should grow again—George Reed went tramping off, there and then, the nearly two miles of way to Mother Picker's. She could not tell him much more than he already knew. "Cathy was all in her best, her curls 'iled, and her pink ribbons as fresh as her cheeks, and said in answer to questions that she had been sent for sudden to her uncle's at Evesham: but she had turned off quite the conterairy road." From thence Reed walked on to his brother's at Evesham; and learnt that Cathy had not been sent for, and had not come.

When Reed got home, he was dead-beat. How many miles the man had walked that bleak February day, he did not stay to think—perhaps twenty. When excitement buoys up the spirit, the body does not feel fatigue. Mrs. Reed put supper before her husband, and he ate a bit mechanically, lost in thought.

"It fairly 'mazes me," he said, presently, in the local phraseology. "But for going out in her best things, I should think some bad accident had come to her. There's ponds about, and young girls might slip in unawares. But the putting on her best things shows she was going somewhere."

"She put 'em on, and went off unseen," repeated Mrs. Reed, snuffing the candle. "*I* should have thought she'd maybe gone off to some wake—only there wasn't one agate within range."

"Cathy had no bad acquaintance to lead her astray," he resumed. "The girls about here are decent, and mind their work."

Which Cathy didn't, thought Mrs. Reed. "Cathy held her head above 'em," she said, aloud: "it's my belief she used to fancy herself one o' them fine ladies in her halfpenny books. She didn't seem to make acquaintance with nobody but that young Parrifer. She'd talk to him by the hour together, and I couldn't get her indoors."

Reed lifted his head. "Young Parrifer!—what—*his* son?" turning his thumb in the direction of Parrifer Hall. "Cathy talked to him?"

"By the hour together," reiterated Mrs. Reed. He'd be on that side the gate, a-talking, and laughing, and leaning on it; and Cathy, she'd be in the path by the tall hollyhocks, talking back to him, and fondling the children."

Reed rose up, a strange look on his face. "How long was that going on?"

"Ever so long; I cannot remember just. But young Parrifer is only at the Hall by fits and starts."

"And you never told me, woman!"

"I thought no harm of it. I don't think harm of it now," emphatically added Mrs. Reed. "The worst of young Parrifer, that I've seen, is that he's as soft as a tomtit."

Reed put on his hat without another word, and walked out. Late as it was, he was going to the Hall. He rang a peal at it, more like a lord, than a labourer just let out of prison. There was some delay in opening the door: the household had gone upstairs; but a man came at last.

"I want to see Major Parrifer."

The words were so authoritative; the man's appearance so strange, with his tall figure and his clipped hair, as he pushed forward into the hall, that the servant momentarily lost his wits. A light, in a room on the left, guided Reed; he entered it, and found himself face to face with Major Parrifer, who was seated in an easy chair before a good fire, spirits on the table, and a cigar in his mouth. What with the curling smoke from that, what with the faint light—for all the candles had been put out but one—the Major did not at first distinguish his late visitor's face. When the bare head and the resolute eyes met his, he certainly paled a little, and the cigar fell on the carpet.

"I want my daughter, Major Parrifer."

To hear a demand made for a daughter when the Major had possibly been thinking the demand might be for his life, was undoubtedly a relief. It brought back his courage.

"What do you mean, fellow?" he growled, stamping out the fire of the cigar. "Are you out of your mind?"

"Not quite. You might have driven some men out of theirs, though, by what you've done. *We'll let that part be,* Major. I have come to-night about my daughter. Where is she?"

They stood looking at each other. Reed stood just inside the door, his hat in his hand; he did not forget his good manners even in the presence of his enemy; they were a habit with him. The Major, who had risen in his surprise, stared at him: he really knew nothing whatever of the matter, not even that the girl was missing; and he did think Reed's imprisonment must have turned his brain. Perhaps Reed saw that he was not understood.

"I come home from prison, into which you put me, Major Parrifer, to find my daughter Catherine gone. She went away the day I was taken up. Where she went, or what she's doing, heaven knows; but you or yours are answerable for it, which ever way it may be."

"You have been drinking," said Major Parrifer.

"*You* have, maybe," returned Reed, glancing at the spirits.

"Either Cathy went out on a harmless jaunt, and is staying away because she can't face the shame at home which you have put there; or else she went out to meet your son, and has been taken away by him. I think it must be the last; my fears whisper it to me; and, if so, you can't be off knowing something of it. Major Parrifer, I must have my daughter."

Whether the hint given about his son alarmed the Major, causing him to forget his bluster for once, and answer civilly he certainly did it. His son was in Ireland with his regiment, he said; had not been at the Hall for weeks and weeks; he could answer for it that Lieutenant Parrifer knew nothing of the girl.

"He was here at Christmas," said George Reed. "I saw him."

"And left two or three days after it. How dare you, fellow, charge him with such a thing? He'd wring your neck for you if he were here."

"Perhaps I might find cause to wring his first. Major Parrifer, I want my daughter."

"If you do not get out of my house, I'll have you brought before me to-morrow for trespassing, and give you a second month's imprisonment," roared the Major, gathering bluster and courage. "You want another month of it: this one does not appear to have done you the good it ought. Now—go!"

"I'll go," said Reed, who began to see the Major really did not know anything of Cathy—and it had not been very probable that he did. "But I'd like to leave a word behind me. You have succeeded in doing me a great injury, Major Parrifer. You are rich and powerful, I am poor and lowly. You set your mind on my bit of a home, and because you could not drive me from it, you took advantage of your magistrate's post to sentence me to prison, and so be revenged. It has done me a great deal of harm. What good has it done you?"

Major Parrifer could not speak for rage.

"It will come home to you, sir; mark me if it does not. God has seen my trouble, and my wife's trouble, and I don't believe He ever let such a wrong pass by unrewarded. *It will come home to you, Major Parrifer.*"

George Reed went out, quietly shutting the hall-door behind him, and walked home through the thick flakes of snow that had begun to fall.

V.

COMING HOME TO HIM.

THE year was getting on. Summer fruits were ripening. It had been a warm spring, and hot weather was upon us early.

One fine Sunday morning, George Reed came out of his cottage and turned up Piefinch Lane. His little girls were with him, one in either hand, in their clean cotton frocks and pinafores, and straw hats. People had gone into church, and the bells had ceased. Reed had not been constant in attendance since the misfortune in the winter, when Major Parrifer put him into prison. The month's imprisonment had altered him; his daughter Cathy's mysterious absence had altered him more: he seemed not to like to face people, and any trifle was made an excuse to himself to keep away from service. To-day it was afforded by the baby's illness. Reed said to his wife that he would take the little girls out a bit to keep the place quiet.

Rumors were abroad that he had heard once from Cathy; that she told him she should come back some day and surprise him and the neighbours, that she was " all right, and he had no call to fret after her." Whether this was true or pure fiction, Reed did not say: he was a closer man than he used to be.

Lifting the children over a stile in Piefinch Lane, just beyond his garden, Reed strolled along the cross path of the field. It brought him to the high hedge that skirted the premises of Major Parrifer. The man had taken it by chance, because it was a quiet walk. He was passing along slowly, the children running about the field, on which the second crop of grass was beginning to grow, when voices on the other side the hedge struck on his ear. Reed gently put some of the foliage aside, and looked through; just as Major Parrifer had looked through the hedge in Piefinch Lane at him, that Sunday morning some few months before.

Major Parrifer had been suffering from a slight temporary indisposition. He did not consider himself sufficiently recovered to attend service, but neither was he ill enough to lie in bed. With the departure of his family for church, the Major had come strolling out in the garden in an airy dressing-gown, and there saw his gardener picking peas.

"Halloa, Hotty! This ought to have been done before."

"Yes, sir, I know it; I'm a little late," answered Hotty; "I shall have done in two or three minutes. The cook makes a fuss if I pick 'em too early; she says they don't eat so well."

The peas were for the delectation of the Major's own palate, so he found no more fault. Hotty went on with his work, and the Major gave a general look round. On a wall near, at right angles with the hedge through which Reed was then peering, some fine apricots were growing, green yet.

"These apricots want thinning, Hotty," observed the Major.

"I have thinned 'em some, sir."

"Not enough. Our apricots were not as fine last year as they ought to have been. I said then they had not had sufficient room to grow. Green apricots are always useful; they make the best tart known."

Major Parrifer walked to the greenhouse, outside which a small basket was hanging, brought it back, and began to pick some of the apricots where they looked too thick. Reed, outside, watched the process—not alone. As luck had it, a man appeared in the field path, who proved to be Gruff Blossom, the Jacobsons' groom, coming home to spend Sunday with his friends. Reed made a sign to Blossom for silence, and caused him to look on also.

With the small basket half full, the Major desisted, thinking possibly he had plucked enough, and turned away carrying it. Hetty came out from the peas then, his task finished. They strolled slowly down the path by the hedge; the Major first, Hetty a step behind, talking about late and early peas, and whether Prussian blues or marrowfats were the best eating.

"Do you see those weeds in the onion-bed?" suddenly asked the Major, stopping as they were passing it.

Hetty turned his head to look. A few weeds certainly had sprung up. He'd attend to it on the morrow, he told his master; and then said something about the work accumulating almost beyond him, since the under gardener had been at home ill.

"Pick them out now," said the Major; "there's not a dozen of them."

Hetty stooped to do as he was bid. The Major made no more ado but stooped also, he himself uprooting quite half of the weeds. Not much more, in all, than the dozen he had spoken of: and then they went on with their baskets to the house.

Never had George Reed experienced so much gratification since the day he came out of prison. "Did you see the Major, at it?—thinning his apricots and pulling up his weeds? he asked of Gruff Blossom. And Blossom's reply, gruff as usual, was to ask what might be supposed to ail his eyes that he shouldn't see it.

"Very good," said Reed.

One evening in the following week, when we were sitting out on the lawn, the Squire smoking, Mrs. Todhetley nursing her face in her hand, with tooth-ache as usual, Tod teazing Hugh and Lena, and I up in the beech-tree, a horseman rode in. It proved to be Mr. Jacobson. Giles took his horse, and he came and sat down on the bench. The Squire asked him what he'd take, and he chose cider, being thirsty. Which Thomas brought.

"Here's a go," began Mr. Jacobson. "Have you heard what's up?"

"I've not heard anything," answered the Squire.

"Major Parrifer has got a summons served on him for working in his garden on a Sunday, and is to appear before the magistrates at Alcester to-morrow," continued old Jacobson, drinking off a glass of cider at a draught.

"No!" cried Squire Todhetley.

"It's a fact. Blossom, our groom, has also a summons served on him to give evidence."

Mrs. Todhetley lifted her face; Tod left Hugh and Lena to themselves: I slid down from the beech-tree; and we listened for more.

But Mr. Jacobson could not give particulars, or say much else than he had already said. All he knew was, that on Monday morning George Reed had appeared before the magistrates and made a complaint. At first they were unwilling to grant a summons; laughed at it; but Reed, in a burst of reproach, civilly delivered, asked why there should be a law for the poor and not for the rich, and in what lay the difference between himself and Major Parrifer; that the one should be called to account and punished for doing wrong, and the other was not even to be accused when he had done it.

"Brandon happened to be on the Bench," continued Jacobson. "He appeared struck with the argument, and signed the summons."

The Squire nodded.

"My belief is," continued old Jacobson, with a wink over the rim of the cider glass, "that the granting of that summons was as good as a play to Brandon and the rest. I'd as lieve, though, that they'd not brought Blossom into it."

"Why?" asked Mrs. Todhetley, who had been grieved at the time at the injustice done to Reed.

"Well, Parrifer is a disagreeable man to offend. And he is sure to visit Blossom's part in this on me."

"Let him," said Tod, with enthusiasm. "Well done, George Reed!"

Be you very sure we went over to the fight. Squire Todhetley did not appear: at which Tod exploded a little: he only wished *he* was a magistrate, wouldn't he take his place and judge the Major! But the Pater said that when people had lived to his age, they liked to be at peace with their neighbours—not but what he hoped Parrifer would "get it," for having been so cruelly hard upon Reed.

Major Parrifer came driving to the Court-house in his high carriage with a great bluster, and his iron-grey hair sticking up, two grooms attending him. Only the magistrates who had granted the summons sat. The news had gone about like wild-fire, and several of them were in the town and about, but did not take their places. I don't believe there was one would have lifted his finger to save the Major from a month's imprisonment; but they did not care to sentence him to it.

It was a regular battle. Major Parrifer was in an awful passion all the time; asking, when he came in, how they dared summons him. *Him!* Mr. Brandon, cool as a cucumber, answered in his squeaky voice, that when a complaint of breaking the law was preferred before them and sworn to by witnesses, they could only act upon it.

First of all, the Major denied the facts. *He* work in his garden on a Sunday!—the very supposition was preposterous! Upon which George Reed, who was in his best clothes, and looked every bit as good as the Major, and far pleasanter, testified to what he had seen.

Major Parrifer, dancing with temper when he found he had been looked at through the hedge, and that it was Reed who looked, gave the lie direct. He called his gardener, Richard Hotty, ordering him to testify whether he, the Major, ever worked in his garden, either on Sundays or week-days.

"Hotty was working himself, gentlemen," interrupted

George Reed. "He was picking peas; and he helped to weed the onion-bed? But it was done by his master's orders, so it would be unjust to seek to punish him."

The Major turned on Reed as if he would strike him, and demanded of the magistrates why they permitted the fellow to interrupt. They ordered Reed to be quiet, and told Hotty to proceed.

But Hotty was one of those slow men to whom anything like evasion is difficult. His master had thinned the apricot tree that Sunday morning; he had helped to weed the onion-bed; Hotty, conscious of the fact, but not liking to admit it, stammered and stuttered, and made a poor figure of himself. Mr. Brandon thought he would help him out.

"Did you see your master pick the apricots?"

"I see him pick—just a few; green uns," answered Hotty, shuffling from one leg to the other in his perplexity. "'Twarn't to be called work, sir."

"Oh! And did he help you to weed the onion-bed?"

"There warn't a dozen weeds in it in all, as the Major said to me at the time," returned Hotty. "He see 'em, and stooped down on the spur o' the moment, and me too. We had 'em up in a twinkling. 'Twarn't work, sir; couldn't be called it nohow? The Major, he never do work at no time."

Blossom had not arrived, and it was hard to tell how the thing would terminate: the Major had this witness, Hotty, such as he was, protesting that nothing to be called work was done. Reed had no witness, as yet.

"Old Jacobson is keeping Blossom back, Johnny," whispered Tod. "It's a sin and a shame."

"No, he is not," I said. "Look there!"

Blossom was coming in. He had walked over, and not hurried himself. Major Parrifer cast daggers upon him, if looks could do it, but it made no difference to Blossom.

He gave his evidence in his usual surly manner. It was clear and straightforward. Major Parrifer had thinned the apricot tree for its own benefit; and had weeded the onion bed, Hotty helping at the weeds by order.

"What brought *you* spying at the place, James Blossom?" demanded a lawyer on the Major's behalf.

"Accident," was the short answer.

"Indeed! You didn't go there on purpose, I suppose?—and skulk under the hedge on purpose?—and peer into the Major's garden on purpose?"

"No, I didn't," said Blossom. "The field is open to walk in, and I was crossing it on my way to old father's. George Reed made me a sign afore I came up to him, to look in, as he was doing; and I did so, not knowing what there might be to see. It would be nothing to me if the Major worked in his garden of a Sunday from sunrise to sunset; he's welcome to do it; but if you summon me here and ask me, did I see him working, I say yes, I did. Why d'you send me a summons if you don't want me to tell the truth? Let me be, and I'd ha' said nothing to mortal man."

Evidently nothing favourable to the defence could be got out of James Blossom. Mr. Brandon began saying to the Major that he feared there was no help for it; they should be obliged to convict him: and he was met by a storm of reproach.

Convict him! roared the Major. For having picked two or three green apricots—and for stooping to pull up a couple or so of worthless weeds? He would be glad to ask which of them, his brother magistrates sitting there, would not pick an apricot, or a peach, or what not, on a Sunday, if he wanted to eat one. The thing was utterly preposterous.

"And what was it *I* did?" demanded George Reed, drowning interfering voices that would have stopped him. "I went to the garden to get up a bunch of turnips for my sick wife, and seeing some withered weeds flung on the bed I drew them off with the hoe. What was that I ask? And it was no more. No more, gentlemen, in the sight of heaven."

No particular answer was given to this; perhaps the justices had not any ready. Mr. Brandon was beginning to confer with the other two in an under tone, when Reed spoke again.

"I was dragged up here in handcuffs, and told I had broken the law; Major Parrifer said to me himself that I had violated the sanctity of the Sabbath (those were the words), and therefore I must be punished; there was no help for it. What has he done? I did not do as much as he has."

"Now you know, Reed, this is irregular," said one of the justices. "You must not interrupt the court."

"You put me in prison for a month, gentlemen," resumed Reed, paying no attention to the injunction. "They cut my hair close in the prison, and they kept me to hard labour for the month, as if I did not have enough of hard labour out of it. My wife was sick and disabled at the time, my three little children are helpless: it was no thanks to the magistrates who sentenced me, gentlemen, or to Major Parrifer, that they did not starve."

"Will you be quiet, Reed?"

"If I deserved one month of prison," persisted Reed, fully bent on saying what he had to say, "Major Parrifer must deserve two months, for his offence is larger than mine. The law is the same for both of us, I suppose. He——"

"Reed, if you say another word, I will order you at once from the room," interrupted Mr. Brandon, his thin voice sharp and determined. "How dare you persist in addressing the bench when told to be quiet?"

Reed fell back and said no more. He knew that Mr. Brandon had a habit of carrying out his own authority, in spite of his nervous health and querulous way of speaking. The justices spoke a few words together, and then said they found the offence proved, and inflicted a fine on Major Parrifer.

He dashed the money down on the table, in too great a rage to do it politely, and went out to his carriage. No other case was on, that day, and the justices got up and mixed with the crowd. Mr. Brandon, who felt chill in the hottest summer's

day, and was afraid of showers, buttoned on a light over-
coat.

"Then there are *two* laws, sir?" said Reed to him, quite
civilly, but in a voice that everybody might hear. "When
the law was made against Sabbath-breaking, those that made
it passed one for the rich and another for the poor!"

"Nonsense, Reed."

"*Nonsense*, sir? I don't see it. *I* was put in pri-on; Major
Parrifer has only got to pay a bit of money, which is of no
more account to him than dirt, and that he can't feel the loss
of. And my offence—if it was an offence—was less than his."

"Two wrongs don't make a right," said Mr. Brandon, dropping his voice to a low key. You ought not to have been put
in prison, Reed; had I been on the bench it should not have
been done."

"But it was done, sir, and my life got a blight on it. It's on
me yet; will never be lifted off me."

Mr. Brandon smiled one of his quiet smiles, and spoke in a
whisper. "He has got it too, Reed, unless I mistake. He'll
carry that fine about with him always. Johnny, are you
there? Don't go and repeat what you've heard me say."

Mr. Brandon was right. To have been summoned before the
the bench, where he had pompously sat to summon others, and
for working on a Sunday above all things, to have been found
guilty and fined, was the bitterest potion to Major Parrifer.
The bench would never be to him the seat it had been; the
remembrance of the day when he was before it would, as Mr.
Brandon expressed it, be carried about with him always.

They projected a visit to the sea-side at once. Mrs. Parrifer,
with three of the Misses Parrifer, came dashing up to people's
houses in the carriage finer and louder than ever; she said that
she had not been well, and was ordered to Aberystwith for six
weeks. The next day they and the Major were off; and heaps
of cards were sent round with "P.P.C." in their corner. I
think Mr. Brandon must have laughed when he got his.

The winter holidays came round again. We went home for Christmas, as usual, and found George Reed down with some sort of illness. There's an old saying, "When the mind's at ease the body's delicate," but Mr. Duffham always maintained that though that might apply to a short period of time, in the long run mind and body sympathised together. George Reed had been a very healthy man, and as free from care as most people; this last year care and trouble and mortification had lain on his mind, and at the beginning of winter his health broke down. It was quite a triumph (in the matter of opinion) for old Duffham.

The illness began with a cough and a low fever, neither of which can labourers afford time to lie by for. It went on to greater fever, and to inflammation on the chest or lungs, or both. There was no choice then, and Reed took to his bed. For the most part, when our poor people got ill, they had to get well again without notice being taken of them; but events had drawn attention to Reed, making him into a conspicuous character. His illness was talked of, and so he received help. Ever since the prison affair I had felt sorry for Reed, as had Mrs. Todhetley.

"I have had some nice strong broth made for Reed, Johnny," she said to me one day in January; "it's as good and nourishing as beef-tea. If you want a walk, you might take it to him."

Tod had gone out with the Squire; I felt dull, as I generally did without him, and put on my coat and hat. Mrs. Todhetley had the broth put into a bottle, and brought it me wrapped in paper.

"I would send him a drop of wine as well, Johnny, if you'd take care not to break the bottles, carrying two."

No fear. I put the one bottle to lodge in my breast-pocket, and took the other in my hand. It was a cold afternoon, the sky nearly of a steel-blue, the sun bright, the ground hard. Major Parrifer and two of his daughters, coming home from a ride, were cantering into the gates as I passed, their groom riding behind. I lifted my hat to the girls, but they only tossed their heads.

Reed was getting over the worst then, and I found him sitting by the kitchen fire, muffled in a bed-rug. Mrs. Reed took the bottles from me in the back'us—as they called the back place where washing and the like was done—for Reed was sensitive, and did not like things to be sent to him.

"Please God, I shall be at work next week," said Reed, with a groan: and I saw he knew I had brought something.

He had been saying that all along; four or five weeks now. I sat down opposite to him, and took up the boy, Georgy. The little shaver had come round to me, holding by the chairs.

"It's going to be a hard frost, Reed."

"Is it, sir? Out-o'-door weather don't seem to be of much odds to me now."

"And a fall o' some sort's not far off, as my wrist tells me," put in Mrs. Reed. Years ago she had broken her wrist, and felt it always on change of weather. "Maybe some snow's coming."

I gave Georgy a biscuit; the two little girls, who had been standing still against the press, began to come slowly forward. They guessed there was a supply in my pocket. I had dipped my hand into the biscuit-basket at home before coming away. The two put out a hand each without being told, and I dropped a biscuit into them.

It had taken neither time nor noise, and yet there was some one standing inside the door when I looked up again, who must have come in stealthily; some one in a dark dress, and a black and white plaid shawl. Mrs. Reed looked and the children looked; and then Reed turned his head to look.

I think I was the first to know her; she had a thick black veil before her face, and the room was not light. Reed's illness had left him thin, causing his eyes to appear very large: they assumed a sort of frightened stare.

"Father! you are sick!"

Before he could answer, she ran across the brick floor and

had her arms round his neck. Cathy! The two girls were frightened and flew to their mother; one began to scream and the other followed suit. Altogether there was noise and commotion; Georgy, like a brave little man, sucking his biscuit through it all with great composure.

What Reed said or did, I had not noticed; I think he went to fling Cathy from him—to avoid suffocation perhaps. She burst out laughing in her old light manner, and took something out of the body of her gown, under the shawl.

"No need, father: I am as honest as anybody," said she. "Look at this."

Reed's hand shook so that he could not open the paper, or understand it at first when he had opened it. Cathy flung off her bonnet and caught the children to her. They began to know her then and ceased their cries. Presently Reed held the paper across to me, his hand trembling worse than before, and his face, that illness had left white, turning ghastly with emotion.

"Please read it, sir."

I did not understand it at first either, but the sense came to me soon. It was a certificate of the marriage of Spencer Gervoise Daubeney Parrifer and Catherine Reed. They had been married at Liverpool the very day after Cathy disappeared from home; now just a year ago.

A sound of sobbing broke the stillness. Reed had fallen back in his chair in a sort of hysterical fit. Defiant, hard, strong-minded Reed! But the man was three parts dead from weakness. It lasted but a minute or two; he roused himself as if ashamed, and swallowed down his sobs.

"How came he to marry you, Cathy?"

"Because I would not go with him without it, father. We have been staying in Ireland."

"And be you a repenting of it yet?" asked Mrs. Reed, in an ungracious tone.

"Pretty near," answered Cathy, with candour.

It appeared that Cathy had made her way direct to Liver

pool when she left home the previous January, travelling all night. There she met young Parrifer, who had preceded her and made arrangements for the marriage. They were married that day, and afterwards went on to Ireland, where he had to join his regiment.

To hear all this, sounding like a page out of a romance, would be something wonderful for our quiet place when it came to be told. You meet with marvellous stories in towns now and then, but they are almost unknown with us.

"Where's your husband?" asked Reed.

Cathy tossed her head. "Ah! Where! That's what I've come home about," she answered: and it struck me at once that something was wrong.

What occurred next we only learnt from hearsay. I said good-day to them, and came away, thinking to myself it might have been better if Cathy had not married and had not left home. It was a fancy of mine, and I don't know why it should have come to me, but it proved to be a right one. Cathy put on her bonnet again to go to Parrifer Hall: and the particulars of her visit were known abroad later.

It was getting rather dusk when she approached it; the sun had set, the grey of evening was drawing on. Two of the Misses Parrifer were at the window and saw her coming, but Cathy had her veil down and they did not recognise her. The actions and manners and air of a lady do not come on a sudden to one who has been bred differently; and the Misses Parrifer supposed the visitor to be for the servants.

"Like her impudence!" said Miss Jemima. "Coming to the front entrance!"

For Cathy, whose year's experience in Ireland had widely changed her, had no notion of taking up her old position. She meant to hold her own; and was capable of doing it, not being deficient in the quality just ascribed to her by Miss Jemima Parrifer.

"What next?" cried Miss Jemima, as a ring and a knock

resounded through the house, waking up the Major: who had been dozing over the fire amidst his daughters.

The next was, that a servant came to the room and told the Major a lady wanted him. She had been shown into the library.

"What name?" asked the Major.

"She didn't give none, sir. I asked, but she said never mind the name."

"Go and ask it again."

The man went and came back. "It is Mrs. Parrifer, sir."

"Mrs. who?"

"Mrs. Parrifer, sir."

The Major turned and stared at his servant. They had no relatives. Consequently the only Mrs. Parrifer within his knowledge was his wife.

Staring at the man would not bring any elucidation. Major Parrifer went to the library, and there saw the lady standing at one side of the fender, holding her foot to the fire. She had her back to him, did not turn, and so the Major went round to the other side of the hearth-rug where he could see her.

"My servant told me a Mrs. Parrifer wanted me. Did he make a mistake in the name?"

"No mistake at all, sir," said Cathy, throwing up her thick veil, and drawing a step or two back. "I am Mrs. Parrifer."

The Major recognised her then. Cathy Reed! He was a man whose bluster rarely failed, but he had none ready at that moment. Three-parts astounded, various perplexities tied his tongue.

"That is to say, Mrs. Spencer Parrifer," continued Cathy "And I have come over from Ireland on a mission to you, sir, from your son."

The Major thought that of all the audacious women it had ever been his lot to meet, this one was the worst: at least as much as he could think anything, for his wits were a little confused just then. A moment's pause, and then the storm burst forth.

Cathy was called various agreeable names, and ordered out of the room and the house. The Major put up his hands to "hurrish" her out—as we say in Worcestershire by the cows, though I don't think you would find the word in the dictionary. But Cathy stood her ground. He then went screaming towards the door, calling for the servants to come and put her forth. Cathy, quicker than he, gained it first and turned to face him, her back against it. "You needn't call me those names, Major Parrifer. Not that I care—as I might if I deserved them. I am your son's wife, and have been such ever since I left father's cottage last year; and my baby, your grandson, sir, which it's seven weeks old he is, is now at the Red Lion, a mile off. I've left it there with the landlady."

He could not put her out of the room unless by force; he looked ready to kick and strike her; but in the midst of it a horrible dread rose up in his heart that the calm words were true. Perhaps from the hour when Reed had presented himself at the house to ask for his daughter, the evening of the day he was discharged from prison, up to this time, Major Parrifer had never thought of the girl. It had been said in his ears now and again that Reed was grieving for his daughter; but the matter was altogether too contemptible for Major Parrifer to take note of. And now to hear that the girl had been with his son all the while, his wife! But that utter disbelief came to his aid, the Major might have fallen into a fit on the spot. For young Mr. Parrifer had cleverly contrived that neither his father away at home nor his friends near should know anything about Cathy. He had been with his regiment in quarters; she had lived privately in another part of the town. Mrs. Reed had once called Lieutenant Parrifer as soft as a tom-tit. He was a vast deal softer.

"Woman! if you do not quit my house with your shameless lies, you shall be flung out of it."

"I'll quit it as soon as I have told you what I came over the sea to tell. Please to look at this first, sir?"

Major Parrifer snatched the paper that she held out, carried it to the window, and put his glasses across his nose. It was a copy of the certificate of marriage. His hands shook as he read it, just as Reed's had shaken a short while before; and he tore it passionately in two.

"It is only the copy," said Cathy calmly, as she picked up the pieces. "Your son—if he lives—is about to be tried for his life, sir. He is in custody for wilful murder!"

"How dare you!" shrieked Major Parrifer.

"It is what they have charged him with. I have come all the way to tell it you, sir."

Major Parrifer, brought to his senses by a shock of fright, could but listen. Cathy, her back against the door still, gave him the heads of the story.

Young Parrifer was so soft that he had been made a butt of by sundry of his brother officers. They might not have tolerated him at all, but for winning his money. He drank, and played cards, and bet upon horses; they encouraged him to drink, and then made him play and bet, and altogether cleared him out : not of brains, he had none to be cleared of : but of money. Ruin stared him in the face: his available cash had been parted with long ago; his commission (it was said) was mortgaged : how many promissory notes, bills, IOU's he had signed could not even be guessed at. In a quarrel a few nights before, after a public-house supper, when some of them were the worse for drink, young Parrifer, who could go on rare occasions into frighful passions, flung a carving-knife at one of the others, a lieutenant named Cook ; it entered a vital part and killed him. Mr. Parrifer was arrested by the police at once ; he was in plain clothes, and there was nothing to show that he was an officer. They had to strap him down to carry him to prison : between drink, rage, and fever, he was as a maniac. The next morning he was lying in brain fever, and when Cathy left he had been put into a strait-waistcoat.

She gave the heads of this account in as few words as it is written. Major Parrifer stood like a helpless man. Taking one thing with another, the blow was horrible. Parents don't often see the defects in their own childen, especially if they are only sons; far from having thought his son soft, unfit (as he was nearly) to be trusted about, the Major had been proud of him as his heir, and told the world he was perfection. Soft as young Parrifer was, he had contrived to keep his ill-doings from his father.

Of course it was only natural that the Major's first relief should be abuse of Cathy. He told her all that had happened to his son *she* was the cause of, and called her a few more genteel names in doing it.

"Not at all," said Cathy; "you are wrong there, sir. His marriage with me was a little bit of a stop-gap and served to keep him straight for a month or two; but for that, he would have done for himself before he has. Do you think I've had a bargain in him, sir? No. Marriage is a thing that can't be undone, Major Parrifer: but I wish to my heart that I was at home again in father's cottage, light-hearted Cathy Reed."

The Major made no answer. Cathy went on.

"When the news was brought to me by his servant, that he had killed a man and was lying raving, I thought it time to go and see about him. They would not let me into the lock-up house where he was lying—and you might have heard his ravings outside: *I* did. I said I was his wife; and then they told me I had better see Captain Williams. I went to head-quarters and saw Captain Williams. He seemed to doubt me; so I showed him the certificate, and told him my baby was at home, turned six weeks old. He was very kind then, sir; he took me to see my husband; and he advised me to come over here at once and give you the particulars. I told him what was the truth—that I had no money, and the lodgings were owing for. He said the lodgings must wait: and he would lend me enough money for the journey."

"Did you see him?" growled Major Parrifer.

Cathy knew that he alluded to his son, though he would not speak the name.

"I saw him, sir; I told you so. He did not know me or anybody else; he was raving mad, and shaking so that the bed shook under him."

"How is it that they have not written to me?" demanded Major Parrifer.

"I don't think anybody liked to do it. Captain Williams said the best plan would be for me to come. He asked me if I'd like to hear the truth of the past as regarded my husband; or if I would just come here and tell you the bare facts that were known, about his illness and the charge against him. I said I'd prefer to hear the truth—that it couldn't be worse than I suspected. Then he went on to the drinking and the gambling and the debts, just as I have repeated to you, sir. He was very gentle; but he said he thought it would be mistaken kindness not to let me fully understand the state of things. He said Mr. Parrifer's father, or some other friend, had better go over to Ireland."

In spite of himself, a groan escaped Major Parrifer. The blow was the worst that could have fallen upon him. He had not cared much for his daughters; his ambition was centred in his son. Visions of a sojourn at Dublin, and of figuring off at the Vice-Regal Court, himself, his wife, and his son, had floated occasionally in rose-coloured clouds before his brain, poor pompous old simpleton. And now—to picture the visit he must set out upon ere the night was over, nearly drove him wild with pain. Cathy unlatched the door, but waited to speak again before she opened it.

"I'll rid the house of me now that I have broke it to you, sir. If you want me I shall be found at father's cottage; I suppose they'll let me stay there: if not, you can hear of me at the place where I've left my baby. And if your son should ever wake out of his delirium, Major Parrifer, he will be able to tell you that if he had listened to me and heeded me, o even only come to spend his evenings with me—which it's months since he did—he would not have been in this plight now. Should they try him for murder; and nothing can save him from it if he gets well; I——"

A succession of screams cut short what Cathy was about to add. In her surprise she drew wide the door, and was confronted by Miss Jemima Parrifer. That young lady, curious upon the subject of the visit and visitor, had thought it well to put her ear to the library door. To no effect, however, until Cathy unlatched it. And then she heard more than she had thought for.

"Is it *you!*" roughly cried Miss Jemima, recognizing her for the ill-talked of Cathy Reed, the daughter of the Major's enemy. "What do you want here?"

Cathy did not answer. She walked to the hall-door and let herself out. Miss Jemima went on into the library.

"Papa, what was it she was saying about Spencer, that vile girl? What did she do here? Why did she send in her name as Mrs. Parrifer?"

The Major might have heard the questions, or he might not; he didn't respond to them. Miss Jemima, looking closely at him in the dusk of the room, saw a grey, worn, terror-stricken face, that looked as her father's had never looked yet.

"Oh, papa! what is the matter? Are you ill?"

He walked towards her in the quietest manner possible, took her arm and pushed her out at the door. Not rudely; softly, as one might do who is in a dream.

"Presently, presently," he muttered in quite an altered voice, low and timid. And Miss Jemima found the door bolted against her.

It must have been an awful moment with him. Look on what side he would, there was no comfort. Spencer Parrifer was ruined past redemption. He might die in this illness, and then, what of his soul? Not that the Major was given to that kind of reflection. Escaping the illness, he must be tried—for his life, as Cathy had phrased it. And, escaping that, if the miracle were possible, there remained the miserable debts and the miserable wife he had clogged himself with.

Curious enough, as the miserable Major, most miserable in that moment, pictured these things, there suddenly rose up before his mind's eye another picture. A remembrance of Reed, who had stood in that very room less than twelve months ago, in the dim light of late night, with his hair cut close, and his semi-threat: "*It will come home to you, Major Parrifer.*" *Had* it come home to him? Home to him already? The drops of agony broke out on his face as he asked the question. It seemed to him, in that moment of excitement, so very like some of Heaven's own lightning.

One grievous portion of the many ills had perhaps not fallen, but for the putting of Reed in prison—the marriage; and that one was more humiliating to Major Parrifer's spirit than all the rest. Had Reed been at liberty, Cathy might not have made her escape untracked, and the bitter marriage might, in that case, have been avoided.

A groan, and now another, broke from the Major. How it had come home to him! not his selfishness and his barbarity and his pride, but this blow of sorrow. Reed's month of prison, compared to this, was a drop of water to the wide waves of the ocean. As to the girl—when Reed had come asking for tidings of her, it had seemed to the Major not of the least moment whither she had gone or what ill she had entered on: was she not a common labourer's daughter, and that labourer George Reed? Even then, at that very time, she was his daughter-in-law, and his son the one to be humiliated. Major Parrifer ground his teeth, and only stopped when he remembered that something must be done about that disgraceful son.

He started that night for Ireland. Cathy, affronted at some remark made by Mrs. Reed, took herself off from her father's cottage. She had a little money left yet from her journey, and could spend it.

Spencer Gervoise Daubeney Parrifer (the Major and his wife had bestowed upon him the fine names in pride at his baptism) died in prison. He lived but a day after Major

Parrifer's arrival, and never recognized him. It of course saved the trial, when he would probably have been convicted of manslaughter. It saved the payment of his hundreds of debts too: post-obits and all; he died before his father. But it could not save exposure; it could not save the facts from the world. Major and Mrs. Parrifer, so to say, would never lift up their heads again; the sun of their life had set.

Neither would Cathy lift hers yet awhile. She contrived to quarrel with her father; the Parrifers never took the remotest notice of her; she was nearly starved and her baby too. What little she earned was by hard work: but it would not keep her, and she applied to the parish. The parish in turned applied to Major Parrifer, and forced from him as much as the law allowed, a few shillings a week. The having to apply to the parish was, for Cathy, a humiliation never to be forgotten. The neighbours made their comments.

"Cathy Reed have brought her pigs to a fine market!"

So she had; and she felt it more than the loss of her baby, who died soon after. Better that she had married an honest day-labourer: and Cathy knew it now.

VI.

LEASE, THE POINTSMAN.

IT happened when we were staying at our house, Crabb Cot. In saying "we" were staying at it, I mean the family, for Tod and I were at school.

Crabb Cot lay beyond the village of Crabb. Just across the road, a few yards higher up, was the large farm of Mr. Coney; and his house and ours were the only two that stood there. Crabb Cot was a smaller and more cosy house than Dyke Manor; and, when there, we were not so very far from Worcester: less than half way, comparing it with the Manor.

Crabb was a large and straggling parish. North Crabb, which was nearest to us, had the church and schools in it, but very few houses. South Crabb, further off, was more populous. Nearly a mile beyond South Crabb, there was a regular junction of rails. Lines, crossing each other in a most bewildering manner, led off in all directions; and it required no little manœuvring to send the trains away right at busy times. Which of course was the pointsman's affair.

The busiest days had place in summer, when excursion trains were in full swing: but they would come occasionally at other periods, driving the South Crabb station people off their heads with bother before night.

The pointsman was Harry Lease. I dare say you have noticed how certain names seem to belong to certain places. At North Crabb and South Crabb, and in the district round about, the name of Lease was as common as are blackberries in a hedge; and if the different Leases had been cousins in the days gone by, the relationship was lost now. There might be seven-and-twenty Leases, in and out, but Harry Lease was not, so far as he knew, akin to any of them.

South Crabb was not much of a place at best. A part of it, Crabb Lane, branching off towards Massock's brick-fields, was crowded as a London street. Poor dwellings were huddled together, and children jostled each other on the door-steps. Squire Todhetley said he remembered it when it really was a lane, hedges on either side and a pond that was never dry. Harry Lease lived in the last house, a thatched hut with three rooms in it. He was a steady, hardworking, civil man, superior to some of his neighbours, who were given to reel home at night and beat their wives on arrival. His wife, a nice kind of woman to talk to, was a poor manager; but the five children were better behaved and better kept than the other grubbers in the gutter.

Lease was the pointsman at South Crabb Junction, and aided also in the general business there. He walked to his work at six in the morning, carrying his breakfast with him; went home to dinner at twelve, the slack part of the day at the station, and had his tea taken to him at four; leaving in general at nine. Sometimes his wife arrived with the tea; sometimes the eldest child, Polly, an intelligent girl of six. But, one afternoon in September, a crew of mischievous boys from the brick-fields espied what Polly was carrying. They set upon her, turned over the can of tea in fighting for it, ate the bread and butter, tore her pinafore in the scrimmage, and frightened her nearly to death. After that, Lease said that the child should not be sent with the tea: so, when his wife could not take it, he went without tea. Polly and her father were uncommonly alike, too quiet to do much battle with the world: sensitive, in fact: though it sounds odd to say that.

During the month of November one of the busy days occurred at South Crabb Junction. There was a winter meeting on Worcester race-course, a cattle and pig show in a town larger than Worcester, and two or three markets and other causes of increased traffic, all falling on the same day. What with eat the trains, and ordinary and special trains, and good trains and the grunting of ill-conditioned pigs, Lease had plenty to do to keep his points in order.

How it fell out he never knew. Between eight and nine o'clock, when a train was expected in on its way to Worcester, Lease forgot to shift the points. A goods train had come in ten minutes before, for which he had had to turn the points, and he never turned them back again. On came the train, almost as quickly as though it had not to pull up at South Crabb Junction. Watson, the station-master, came out to be in readiness.

"The engine has got her steam on to-night," he remarked to Lease as he watched the red lights, like two great eyes, come tearing on. "She'll have to back."

She did something worse than back. Instead of slackening along on the near lines, she went flying off at a tangent to some outer ones on which the goods train stood, waiting until the passenger train should pass. There was a sound from the whistle, a great collision, a noise of hissing steam, a sense of dire confusion: and for one minute afterwards a dead lull, as if everybody and thing were paralysed.

"You never turned the points!" shrieked the station-master to Lease.

Lease made no rejoinder. He backed against the wall like a helpless man, his arms stretched out, his face and eyes wild with horror. Watson thought he was going to have a fit, and shook him roughly.

"*You've* done it nicely, you have!" he added, as he flew off to the scene of disaster, from which the steam was beginning to clear away. But Lease reached it before him.

"God forgive me! God have mercy upon me!"

A porter, running side by side with Lease, heard him say it. In telling it afterwards the man described the tone as one of piteous agony.

The Squire and Mrs. Todhetley, who had been a few miles

off to spend the day, were in the train with Lena. The child did nothing but cry and sob; not with damage, but fright. Mr. Coney also happened to be in it; and Massock, who owned the brick-fields. They were not hurt at all, only a little shaken, and (as the Squire put it afterwards) mortally scared. Massock, an under-bred man, who had grown rich by his brick-fields, was more pompous than a lord. The three seized upon the station-master.

"Now then, Watson," cried Mr. Coney, "what was the cause of all this?"

"If there have been any negligence here—and I know there have—you shall be transported for it, Watson, as sure as I'm a living man," roared Massock.

"I'm afraid, gentlemen, that something was wrong with the points," acknowledged Watson, willing to shift the blame from himself, and too confused to consider policy. "At least that's all I can think."

"With the points!" cried Massock. "Them's Harry Lease's work. Was he on to-night?"

"Lease is here as usual, Mr. Massock. I don't say this lies at his door," added Watson, hastily. "The points might have been out of order; or something else wrong totally different. I should like to know, for my part, what possessed Roberts to bring up his train at such speed."

Darting in and out of the heap of confusion like a mad spirit; now trying by his own effort to lift the broken parts of carriages off some sufferer, now carrying a poor fellow away to safety, but always in the thick of danger; went Harry Lease. Braving the heat and steam as though he felt them not, he flew everywhere, himself and his lantern alike shaking with agitation.

"Come and look here, Harry; I'm afraid he's dead." said a porter, holding his light down to a man's face. The words arrested Mr. Todhetley, who was searching for Lease to let off a little of his explosive anger. It was Roberts, the driver of the passenger train, that lay there, his face white and still

Somehow the sight made the Squire still, too. Raising Roberts's head, the men put a drop of brandy between his lips, and he moved. Lease broke into a low glad cry.

"He is not dead! he is not dead!"

The angry reproaches died away on the Squire's tongue: it did not seem quite the time to speak them. By-and-by he came upon Lease again. The man had halted to lean against some palings, feeling unaccountably strange, much as though the world around were closing to him.

"Had you been drinking to-night, Lease?"

The question was put quietly: which was, so to say, a feather in the hot Squire's cap. Lease only shook his head by way of answer. He had a pale, gentle kind of face, with brown eyes that always wore a sad expression. He never drank, and the Squire knew it.

"Then how came you to neglect the points, Lease, and cause this awful accident?"

"I don't know, sir," answered Lease, rousing up from his lethargy, but speaking like one in a dream. "I can't think but what I turned them as usual."

"You knew the train was coming? It was the ordinary train."

"I knew it was coming," assented Lease. "I watched it come along, standing by the side of Mr. Watson. If I had not set the points right, why, I should have thought surely of them then; it stands to reason I should. But never such a thought came into my mind, sir. I waited there, just as if all was right; and I believe I *did* shift the points."

Lease did not put this forth as a false excuse: he only spoke aloud the problem that was working in his mind. Having shifted the points regularly for five years, it seemed just impossible that he could have neglected it now. And yet the man could not *remember* to have done it this evening.

"You can't call it to mind?" said Squire Todhetley, repeating his last words.

"No I can't, sir: and no wonder, with all this confusion

around me and the distress I'm in. I may be able to do so to-morrow."

"Now look ye heere, Lease," said the Squire, getting just a little cross, "if you had put the points right you couldn't fail to remember it. And what causes you to be in distress, I'd like to ask, but the knowledge that you *didn't*, and that all this carnage is owing to you?"

"There is such a thing as doing things mechanically, sir, without the mind being conscious of it."

"Doing things wilfully," roared the Squire. "Do you want to tell me I am a fool to my face?"

"It has often happened, sir, that when I have wound up the mantel-shelf clock at night in our sleeping-room, I'll not know the next minute whether I've wound it or not, and I have to try it again, or else ask my wife," went on Lease, his eyes look-ing straight out in the darkness, as if he could see the mantel-shelf clock then. "I can't think but what it must have been just in that way that I put the points right to-night."

Squire Todhetley, in his anger, which was growing hot again, felt that he should like to give Lease a sound shaking. He had no notion of such talk as this.

"I don't know whether you are a knave or a fool, Lease. Killing men and women and children; breaking arms and shins and bones; putting a whole trainful into mortal fright; smashing goods and property and engines to atoms; turning the world, in fact, upside down, so that people don't know whether they stand on their heads or their heels! You may think you can do this with impunity perhaps, but the law will soon teach you better. I should not like to go to bed with human lives upon my soul."

The Squire disappeared in a whirlwind. Lease—who seemed to have taken a leaf out of his own theory, and listened mechanically—closed his eyes and put his head back against the top ledge of the palings, like one who has had a shock. He went home when there was nothing more to do. Not down the frequented highway, but choosing the field path, where he would not be likely to meet a soul. Crabb Lane, accustomed to put itself into a state of commotion for nothing at all, had got something at last, and was up in arms. All the men employed at the station lived in Crabb Lane. The wife and children of Bowen, the stoker of the passenger train,— dead—also inhabited a room in that screaming locality. So that when Lease came in view of the place, he saw a noisy multitude, though it was then long after ordinary bed-time. Groups stood in the highway; heads, thrust forth at upstairs windows, were shrieking remarks across the street and back again. Keeping on the far side of the hedge, Lease got in by the back door unperceived. His wife was sitting by the fire, shaking all over. She started up.

"Oh, Harry! what is the truth of this?"

He did not answer. Not in rough neglect; Lease was as civil indoors as out, which can't be said of everybody; but as if he did not hear it. The supper—bread and half a cold red herring—was on the table. Generally he was hungry enough for supper, but he never glanced at it this evening.

Sitting down, he looked into the fire and remained still, listening perhaps to the hubbub outside. His wife, half dead with fear and apprehension, could keep silence no longer, and asked again.

"I don't know," he answered then. "They say that I never turned the points; I'm trying to remember doing it, Mary. My senses have been scared out of me."

"But *don't* you remember doing it?"

He put his hands to his temples, and the eyes took that far-off, sad look, often seen in eyes when the heart is troubled. With all his might and main, the man was trying to recall to mind the occurrence which would not come into it. A dread conviction began to dawn within him that it never would or could come; and Lease's head and face grew wet with cold drops of agony.

"I turned the points for the down goods train," he said presently; "I remember that. When the goods came in, I know I was in the signal house. Then I took a message to Hoar; and next I stepped across with some oil for the engine of an up train that dashed in; they called out that it wanted some. I helped to do it, and took the oil back again. It would be then that I went to put the points right," he added after a pause. "I *hope* I did."

"But, Harry, don't you remember doing it?"

"No, I don't; there's where it is."

"You always put the points straight at once after the train has passed?"

"Not if I'm called off by other work. It ought to be done. A pointsman should stand while the train passes, and then step off to right the points at once. But when you are called off half a dozen ways to things crying out to be done, you can't spend the time in waiting for the points. We've never had a harder day's work at the station than this has been, Mary; trains in, trains out; the place has hardly been free a minute together. And the extra telegraphing!—half the passengers that stopped seemed to want to send messages. When six o'clock came I was worn out; done up; fit to drop."

Mrs. Lease gave a start. An idea flashed into her mind, causing her to ask mentally whether *she* could have had indirectly a hand in the calamity. For that had been one of the days when her husband had no tea taken to him. She had been very busy washing, and the baby was sick and cross: that had been quite enough to fill incapable Mrs. Lease's hands, without bothering about her husband's tea. And, of all days in the year, it seemed that he had, on this one, most needed tea. Worn out! done up!

The noise in Crabb Lane was increasing, voices sounded louder, and Mrs. Lease put her apron over her ears. Just then a sudden interruption occurred. Polly, supposed to be safe asleep above stairs, burst into the kitchen in her night-gown, and flew into her father's arms, sobbing and crying.

"Oh father, is it true?—is it true?"

"Why— Polly!" cried the man, looking at her in astonishment, "what's this?"

She hid her face on his waistcoat, her hands clinging round him. Polly had awoke and heard the comments outside. She was too nervous and excitable for Crabb Lane

"They are saying you have killed Kitty Bowen's father. It isn't true, father! Go out and tell them that it isn't true!"

His own nerves were unstrung; his strength had gone out of him; it only needed something of this kind to finish up Lease; and he broke into sobs nearly as loud as the child's. Holding her to him with a tight grasp, they cried together. If Lease had never known agony before in his life, he knew it then.

The days went on. There was no longer holding-out on Lease's part on the matter of points: all the world said he had been guilty of neglecting to turn them; and he supposed he had. He accepted the fate meekly, without resistance, his manner strangely still, like one who has been subdued. When talked to, he freely avowed that it remained a puzzle to him how he could have forgotten the points, and what made him forget them. He shrank neither from reproach nor abuse; listening patiently to all who chose to attack him, as if he had no more any right to claim a place in the world.

He was not spared. Coroner and jury, friends and foes, alike went on at him, painting his sins in flaring colours, and calling him names to his face. "Murderer" was one of the politest of them. Four had died in all; Roberts was not expected to live; the rest were getting well. There would have been no trouble over the inquest (held at the "Bull," between Crabb Lane and the station), it might have been finished in a day, and Lease committed for trial, but that one of those who had died was a lawyer; and his brother (also a lawyer) and other of his relatives (likewise lawyers) chose to raise a commotion. Mr. Massock helped them. Passengers must be examined; rails tried; the points tested; every conceivable obstacle was put in the way of a conclusion. Fifteen times had the jury to go and take a look at the spot, and see the working of the points tested. And so the inquest was adjourned from time to time, and might get finished perhaps under a year.

The public were like so many wolves, all howling at Lease; from the relatives aforesaid and Brick-field Massock, down to the men and women of Crabb Lane. Lease was home on bail, surrendering himself at every fresh meeting of the inquest. A few ill-conditioned malcontents had begun to hiss him as he passed in and out of Crabb Lane.

When we got home for the Christmas holidays, nothing met us but tales of Lease's wickedness, in having sent the one train upon the other. The Squire grew hot in talking of it. Tod, given to be contrary, said he should like to have Lease's own version of the affair. A remark that affronted the Squire.

"You can go off and get it from him, sir. Lease won't refuse it; he'd give it to the dickens, for asking. He likes nothing better than to talk of it."

"After all, it was but a misfortune," said Tod. "It was not done willingly."

"Not done willingly!" stuttered the Pater in his rage. "When I, and Lena, and her mother were in the train, and might have been smashed to atoms! When Coney, and Massock (not that I like the fellow), and scores more were put in jeopardy, and some were killed; yes, sir, killed. A misfortune! Johnny, if you stand there with a grin across your mouth, like an idiot, I'll send you back to school: you shall both pack off this very hour. A misfortune, indeed! Lease deserves hanging."

The next morning we came upon Lease accidentally in the fields. He was leaning over the gate amid the trees, as Tod and I crossed the rivulet bridge—which was nothing but a plank. Two bounds, and we were up with him.

"Now for it, Lease!" cried Tod. "Let us hear a bit about the thing.'

Was not Lease altered! His cheeks were thin and white, his eyes had nothing but gloom in them. Standing up he touched his hat respectfully.

"Ay, sir, it has been a sad time," answered Lease, in a low, patient voice, as if he felt worn out with weariness. "I little thought when I last shut you and Mr. Johnny into the carriage the morning you left, that misfortune was so close at hand." For, just before it happened, we had been at home for a day's holiday.

"Well, tell us about it."

Tod stood with his arm round the trunk of a tree, and I sat down on an opposite stump. Lease had very little to say; nothing, except that he must have forgotten to change the points.

And that made Tod stare. I, watching him, saw his brow go in and his lips go out, a sure sign of displeasure. Tod, like the Pater, was hasty by nature. Knowing Lease's good character, he had not supposed him guilty; and to hear the man quietly admit that he *was*, excited Tod's ire.

"What do you mean, Lease?"

"Mean, sir?" returned Lease, meekly.

"Do you mean to say that you did *not* attend to the points?—that you just let one train run on to the other?"

"Yes, sir; that is how it must have been. I didn't believe it, sir, for a long while afterwards: not for several hours."

"A long while, that," said Tod, an unpleasant sound of mockery in his tone.

"No, sir; I know it's not much, counting by time," answered Lease patiently. "But nobody can ever picture how long those hours seemed to me. They were like years. I couldn't get the idea into me at all that I had not set the points as usual; it seemed a thing unbelievable; but, try as I would, I was unable to call to mind the having done it."

"Well, I must say that is a nice thing to confess to, Lease! And there was I, yesterday afternoon, taking your part and quarrelling with my father,"

"I am sorry for that, sir. I am not worth having my part taken in anything, since that happened."

"But how came you to *do* it?"

"It's a question that I shall never be able to answer, sir. We had a busy day, were on the run from morning till night, and there was a great deal of confusion at the station: but it was no worse than many a day that went before it."

"Well, I shall be off," said Tod. "This has shut me up. I thought of going in for you, Lease, finding everybody else was dead against you. A misfortune is a misfortune, but wilful carelessness is sin: and my father and his wife and my little sister were in the train. Come along, Johnny."

"Directly, Tod. I'll catch you up. I say, Lease, how will it end?" I asked, as Tod went on.

"It can't end better than two years' imprisonment for me, sir; and I suppose it may end worse. It is not *that* I think of."

"What else, then?"

"Four dead already, sir; four—and one soon to follow them, making five," he answered, his voice hushed nearly to a whisper. "Master Johnny, it lies on me always, a dreadful weight never to be got rid of. When I was young, I had a kind of low fever, and used to see in my dreams some dreadful task too big to attempt, and yet I had to do it; and the weight on my mind was awful. I didn't think, till now, such a weight could fall in real life. Sleeping or waking, sir, I see those four before me dead. Squire Todhetley told me that I had their lives on my soul. And it is so."

I did not know what to answer.

"So you see, sir, I don't think much of the imprisonment; if I did, I might be wanting to get the suspense over. It's not any term of imprisonment, no, not though it were for life, that can wash out the past. I'd give my own life, sir, twice over if that could undo it."

Lease had his arm on the gate as he spoke, leaning forward. I could not help feeling sorry for him.

"If people knew how I'm punished within myself, Master Johnny, they'd perhaps not be so harsh. I have never had a proper night's rest since it happened, sir. I have to get up and walk about in the middle of the night because I can't lie. The sight of the dawn makes me sick, and I say to myself, How shall I get through the day? When bed-time comes, I wonder how I shall lie till morning. Often I wish it had pleased God to take me before that day had happened."

"Why don't they get the inquest over, Lease?"

"There's something or other always brought up to delay it, sir. I don't see the need of it. If it would bring the dead back, why they might delay it; but it won't. They might as well let it end, and sentence me, and have done with it. Each time when I go back home through Crabb Lane the men and women call out, What, put off again! what, ain't he in gaol yet! Which is the place they say I ought to have been in all along."

"I suppose the coroner knows you'll not run away, Lease."

"Everybody knows that, sir."

"Some would, though, in your place."

"I don't know where they'd run to," returned Lease. "They couldn't run away from their own minds—and that's the worst part. Sometimes I wonder whether I shall ever get it off mine, sir, or if I shall have it on me, like this, to the end of my life. The Lord knows what it is to me; nobody else does."

You cannot always make things fit into one another. I was thinking so as I left Lease and went after Tod. It was an awful carelessness not to have set the points; causing death, and sorrow, and distress to many people. Looking at it from their side, the pointsman was detestable: only fit, as the Squire said, for hanging. But looking at it side by side with Lease, seeing his sad face, and his self-reproach, and his patient suffering, it seemed altogether different; and the two sides would not by any means fit in together.

Christmas week, and the absence of a juror who had gone

out visiting, made another excuse for putting off the inquest to the next week. When that came, the coroner was ill. There seemed to be no end to the delays, and the public steam was getting up in consequence. As to Lease, he went about dazed, like a man who is looking for something that he has lost and cannot find.

One day when the ice lay in Crab Lane, and I was taking the slides on my way through it to join Tod, who had gone rabbit-shooting, a little girl ran across my feet, and was knocked down. I fell too; and the child began to cry. Picking her up, I saw it was Polly Lease.

"You little stupid! why did you run into my path like that?"

"Please, sir, I didn't see you," she sobbed, "I was running after father. Mother saw him in the field yonder, and sent me to tell him we'd got a bit o' fire."

Polly had grazed both her knees; they began to bleed just a little, and she went into convulsions nearly at the sight of the blood. I carried her in. There was about a handful of fire in the grate,—I'm sure I could have put it into my two hands. The mother sat on a low stool, close into it, nursing one of the children, and the rest sat on the floor.

"I never saw such a child as this in all my life, Mrs. Lease. Because she has hurt her knees a bit, and sees a drop of blood, she's going to die of fright. Look here."

Mrs. Lease put down the boy and took Polly, who was shaking all over with her deep low sobs.

"It was always so, sir," said Mrs. Lease; "always since she was a baby. She is the timorest-natured child possible. We have tried everything; coaxing and scolding too; but we can't get her out of it. If she pricks her finger her face turns white."

"I'd be more of a woman than to cry at nothing, if I were you, Polly," said I, sitting on the window-ledge, while Mrs. Lease washed the knees; which were hardly damaged at all when they came to be looked into. But Polly only clung to her mother, with her face hidden, and gave a deep sob now and then.

"Look up, Polly. What's this?"

I put it into her hand as I spoke; a bath bun that I had been carrying with me, in case I did not get home to luncheon. Polly looked round, and at the sight dried the tears on her swollen face. You never saw such a change all in a moment, or such eager, glad little eyes as hers.

"Divide it, mother," said she. "Leave a bit for father."

Two of them came flocking round like a couple of young wolves; the youngest couldn't get up, and the one Mrs. Lease had been nursing stayed on the floor where she put him. He had a sickly face, with great bright grey eyes and hot, red lips.

"What's the matter with him, Mrs. Lease?"

"With little Tom, sir? I think it's a kind of fever. He never was strong; none of them are: and of course these bad times can but tell upon us."

"Don't forget father, mother," said Polly. "Leave the biggest piece for father."

"Now I tell you all what it is," said I to the children, when Mrs. Lease began to divide it into five hundred pieces, "that bun's for Polly, because she has hurt herself: you shall not take any of it from her. Give it to Polly, Mrs. Lease."

Of all the uproars ever heard, those little cormorants set up the worst. Mrs. Lease looked at me.

"They must have a bit, sir: they must indeed. Polly wouldn't eat all herself, Master Ludlow; you couldn't get her to."

But I was determined Polly should have it. It was through me she got hurt; and besides, I liked her.

"Now just listen, you little pigs. I'll go to the baker's, Ford's, and bring you all a penny plum-bun a piece, but Polly must have this one. They have got lots of currants in them, for children that don't squeal. How many are there of you? One, two, three,——four."

Catching up my cap, I was going out when Mrs. Lease touched me. "Do you really mean it, sir?" she asked in a whisper.

"Mean what? That I am going to bring the buns? Of course I mean it. I'll be back with them directly."

"Oh, sir—but do forgive me for making free to ask such a thing—if you would but let it be a half-quartern loaf instead?"

"A half-quartern loaf!"

"They've not had a bit within their lips this day, Master Ludlow," she said, catching up her breath, as her face, which had flushed, turned pale again. "Last night I divided between the four of them a piece of bread half the size of my hand; Tom, he couldn't eat."

I stared for a minute. "How is it, Mrs. Lease? can you not get enough food?"

"I don't know where we should get it from, sir. Lease has not broken his fast since yesterday at midday."

Dame Ford put the loaf in paper for me, wondering what on earth I wanted with it, as I could see by her inquisitive eyes, but not liking to ask; and I carried it back with the four buns. They were little wolves and nothing else when they saw the food.

"How has this come about, Mrs. Lease?" I asked, while they were eating the bread she cut them, and she had taken Tom on her lap again.

"Why, sir, it is eight weeks now, or hard upon it, since my husband earned anything. They didn't even pay him for the last week he was at work, as the accident happened in it. We had nothing in hand; people with only eighteen shillings a week and five children, can't save; and we have been living on our things. But there's nothing left now to make money of—as you may see by the bare room, sir."

"Does not anybody help you?"

"Help us!" returned Mrs. Lease. "Why, Master Ludlow, people, for the most part, are so incensed against my husband, that they'd take the bread out of our lips, instead of putting a bit into them. All their help goes to poor Nancy Bowen

and her children: and Lease is glad it should be so. When I
carried Tom to Mr. Cole's yesterday, he said that what the
child wanted was nourishment."

"This must try Lease."

"Yes," she said, her face flushing again, but speaking very
quietly. · "Taking one thing with another, I am not sure but
it is killing him."

After this break, I did not care to go to the shooting, but
turned back to Crabb Cot. Mrs. Todhetley was alone in the
bow-windowed parlour, so I told her of the state the Leases
were in, and asked if she would not help them.

"I don't know what to say about it, Johnny," she said, after
a pause. "If I were willing, you know Mr. Todhetley would
not be. He can't forgive Lease for his carelessness. Every
time Lena wakes up from sleep in a fright, fancying it is another accident, his anger returns. We hear her crying out,
you know, down here in an evening."

"The carelessness was no fault of Lease's children that they
should suffer for it."

"When you get older, Johnny, you will find that the consequences of people's faults fall more on others than on themselves. It is very sad the Leases should be in this state; I am
sorry for them."

"Then you'll help them a bit, good mother."

Mrs. Todhetley was always ready to help any one, not needing to be urged; on the other hand, she liked to bend impli-
citly to the opinions of the Squire. Between the two, she went
into a dilemma.

"Suppose it were Lena, starving for want of food and
warmth?" I said. "Or Hugh sick with fever, as that young
Tom is? Those children have done no more harm than ours."

Mrs. Todhetley put her hand up to her face, and her mild
eyes looked nearly as sad as Lease's.

"Will you take it to them yourself, Johnny, in a covered basket, and not let it be seen? That is, make it your own doing?"

"Yes."

"Go to the kitchen then, and ask Molly. There are some odds and ends of things in the larder that will not be particularly wanted. You see, Johnny, I do not like to take an active part in this; it would seem like opposing the Squire."

Molly was stooping before the big fire, basting the meat, and in one of her vile humours. If I wanted to rob the larder, I must do it, she cried; it was my business, not hers; and she dashed the iron basting spoon across the table by way of chorus.

I gave a good look round the larder, and took a raised pork pie that had a piece cut out of it, and a leg of mutton three parts eaten. On the shelf were a dozen mince-pies, just out of their patty-pans; I took six and left six. Molly, screwing her face round the kitchen door, caught sight of them as they went into the basket, and rushed after me out of the house, shrieking out for her mince-pies.

The race went on. She was a woman not to be daunted. Just as we turned round by the yellow barn, I first, she raving behind, redder than a turkey-cock, the Squire pounced upon us, asking what the uproar meant. Molly told her tale, I was a thief, and gone off with the whole larder, more particularly with her mince-pies.

"Open the basket, Johnny," said the Squire: which was the one Tod and I used when we went fishing.

No sooner was it done than Molly marched off with the pies in triumph. The Pater regarded the pork pie and the meat with a curious gaze.

"This is for you and Joe, I suppose. I should like to know for how many more."

I was one of the worst to conceal things, when taken to like this, and he got it all out of me in no time. And then he put his hand on my shoulder and ordered me to say *who* the things were for. Which I had to do.

Well, there was a row. He wanted to know what I meant by being wicked enough to give food to Lease. I said it was for the children. I'm afraid I cried a little, for I did not like him to be angry with me, but I know I promised not to eat

any dinner at home for three days if he would let me take
the meat.   Molly's comments, echoing through the house, betrayed to Mrs. Todhetley what had happened, and she came
down the road with a shawl over her head.   She told the
Squire the truth then: that she had sanctioned it.   She said
she feared the Leases were quite in extremity, and begged him
to let the meat go.

"Be off for this once, you young thief," stamped the Squire,
"but don't let me catch you at anything of this sort again."

So the meat went to the Leases, and two loaves that Mrs.
Todhetley whispered me to order for them at Ford's.   When
I reached home with the empty basket, they were going in to
dinner.   I took a book and stayed in the parlour.   In a minute or two the Squire sent to ask what I was doing that for.

"It's all right, Thomas.   I don't want any dinner to-day."

Old Thomas went away and returned again, saying the
master ordered me to go in.   But I wouldn't do anything of
the sort.   If he forgot the bargain, I did not.

Out came the Squire, his face red, his napkin in his hand,
and laid hold of me by the shoulders.

"You obstinate young Turk!   How dare you defy me?
Come along."

"But it is not to defy you, sir.   It was a bargain, you know;
I promised."

"What was a bargain?"

"That I should not eat dinner for three days.   Indeed I
meant it."

The Squire's answer was to propel me into the dining-room.
"Move down, Joe," he said, "I'll have him by me to-day.
I'll see whether he is to starve himself out of bravado."

"Why, what's up?" asked Tod, as he went to a lower seat.
"What have you been doing, Johnny?"

"Never mind," said the Squire, putting enough mutton on
my plate for two.   "You eat that, Mr. Johnny."

It went on so through the dinner.   Mrs. Todhetley gave
me a big share of apple pudding; and, when the macaroni

came on, the Squire heaped my plate. And I know it was all done to show he was not really angry with me for having taken the things.

Mr. Cole, the surgeon, came in after dinner, and was told of my wickedness. Lena ran up to me and said might she send her new sixpence to the poor little children who had no bread to eat.

"What's that Lease about, that he does not go to work?" asked the Squire, in a loud tone. "Letting folks hear that his young ones are starving!"

"The man can't work," said Mr. Cole. "He is out on probation, you know, waiting for the verdict, and the sentence on him that is to follow."

"Then why don't they return their verdict and sentence him?" demanded the Squire in his hot way.

"Ah!" said Mr. Cole, "it's what they ought to have done long ago."

"What will it be? Transportation?"

"I should take care it was *not*, if I were on the jury. The man had too much work on him that day, and had had nothing to eat or drink for too many hours."

"I won't hear a word in his defence," growled the Squire.

When the jury met for the last time, Lease was ill. A day or two before that, some one had brought Lease word that Roberts, who had been lingering all that while in the infirmary at Worcester, was going at last. Upon which Lease started to see him. It was not the day for visitors at the infirmary, but he gained admittance. Roberts was lying in the accident ward, with his head low and a blue look in his face; and the first thing Lease did, when he began to speak, was to burst out crying. The man's strength had gone down to nothing and his spirit was broken. Roberts made out that he was speaking of his distress at having been the cause of the calamity, and asking to be forgiven.

"Mate," said Roberts, putting out his hand that Lease might take it, "I've never had an ill thought to ye. Mishaps come to all of us that have to do with rail-travelling; us drivers get more nor you pointsmen. It might have happened to me to be the cause, just as well as to you. Don't think no more of it."

"Say you forgive me," urged Lease, "or I shall not know how to bear it."

"I forgive thee with my whole heart and soul. I've had a spell of it here, Lease, waiting for death, knowing it must come to me, and I've got to look for it kindly. I don't think I'd go back to the world now if I could. I'm going to a better. It seems just peace, and nothing less. Shake hands, mate."

They shook hands.

"I wish ye'd lift my head a bit," Roberts said, after awhile. "The nurse she come and took away my pillow, thinking I might die easier, I suppose: I've seen her do it to others. Maybe I was a'most gone, and the sight of you woke me up again like."

Lease sat down on the bed and put the man's head upon his breast in the position that seemed most easy to him; and Roberts died there.

It was one of the worst days we had that winter. Lease had a night's walk home of many miles, the sleet and the wind beating at him all the way. He was not well clad either, for his best things had been pawned.

So that when the inquest assembled two days afterwards, Lease did not appear at it. He was in bed with inflammation of the chest, and Mr. Cole told the coroner that it would be dangerous to take him out of it. Some of them called it bronchitis; but the Squire never went in for new names, and never would.

"I tell you what it is, gentlemen," broke in Mr. Cole, when they were quarrelling whether there should be another adjournment or not, "you'll put off and put off, until Lease slips through your fingers."

"Oh, will he though!" blustered old Massock. "He had better try at it! We'd soon fetch him back again."

"You'd be clever to do it," said the doctor.

Any way, whether it was this or not, they thought better of the adjournment, and gave their verdict. "Manslaughter against Henry Lease." And the coroner made out his warrant of committal to Worcester county prison: where Lease would lie until the March assizes.

"I am not sure but it ought to have been returned Wilful Murder," remarked the Squire, as he and the doctor turned out of the Bull, and picked their the way over the slush towards Crabb Lane.

"It might make no difference, one way or the other," answered Mr. Cole.

"Make no difference! What d'ye mean? Murder and manslaughter are two opposite crimes, Cole, and punished accordingly. You see, Johnny, what your friend Lease has come to!"

"What I meant, Squire, was this: that I don't much think Lease will live to be tried at all."

"Not live!"

"I fancy not. Unless I am much mistaken, his life will have been claimed by its Giver long before March."

The Squire stopped and looked at Cole. "What's the matter with him? This inflammation—that you went and testified to?"

"That will be the cause of death, as returned to the registrar."

"Why, you speak just as if the man were dying now, Cole!"

"And I think he is. Lease has been very low in frame for a long while," added Mr. Cole; "half clad, and not a quarter fed. But it is not that, Squire: the heart and spirit are alike broken: and when this cold caught him, he had no stamina to withstand it; and so it has laid hold of a vital part."

"Do you mean to tell me to my face that he will die of it?" cried the Squire, holding on by the middle button of old Cole's great coat. "Nonsense, man! you must cure him. We—we did not want him to die, you know."

"His life or his death, as it may be, are in the hands of One higher than I, Squire."

"I think I'll go in and see him," said the Squire, meekly.

Lease was lying on a bed close to the floor when we got to the top of the creaky stairs, which had threatened to come down with the Squire's weight and awkwardness. He had dozed off, and little Polly, sitting on the boards, had her head upon his arm. Her starting up awoke Lease. I was not in the habit of seeing dying people; but the thought struck me that Lease must be dying. His pale weary face wore the same hue that Jake's had worn when he was dying: if you have not forgotten him.

"God bless me!" exclaimed the Squire.

Lease looked up with his sad eyes. He supposed they had come to tell him officially about the verdict—which had already reached him unofficially.

"Yes, gentlemen, I know it," he said, trying to get up out of respect, and falling back. "Manslaughter. I'd have been present if I could. Mr. Cole knows I wasn't able. I think God is taking me instead."

"But this won't do, you know, Lease," said the Squire. "We don't want you to die."

"Well, sir, I'm afraid I am not good for much now. And there'd be the imprisonment, and then the sentence, so that I could not work for my wife and children for some long years. When people come to know how I repented of that night's mistake, and that I have died of it, why they'll perhaps befriend them and forgive me. I think God has forgiven me: He is very merciful."

"I'll send you in some port wine and some jelly and some beef-tea and some blankets, Lease," cried the Squire quickly, as if he felt flurried. "And Lease, poor fellow, I am sorry for having been so angry with you."

"Thank you for all favours, sir, past and present. But for

the help from your house my little ones would have starved. God bless you all, and forgive me! Master Johnny, God bless you."

"You'll rally yet, Lease; take heart," said the Squire.

"No, sir, I don't think so. The great dark load seems to have been lifted off me, and light to be breaking. Don't sob, Polly! Perhaps father will be able to see you from up there as well as if he stayed here."

The first thing the Squire did when we got out, was to attack Mr. Cole, telling him he ought not to have let Lease die. As he was in a way, Cole excused it, quietly saying it was no fault of his.

"I should like to know what it is that has killed him, then?"

"Grief," said Mr. Cole. "The man has died of what we call a broken heart. Hearts don't actually sever, you know, Squire, like a china basin, and there's always some ostensible malady that serves as a hold to talk about. In this case it will be bronchitis. Which, in point of fact, is the final end, because Lease could not rally against it. He told me yesterday that his heart had ached so keenly since November, it seemed to have dried up within him."

"We are all a pack of hard-hearted sinners," groaned the Squire, in his repentance. "Johnny, why could you not have found them out sooner? Where was the use of your doing it at the eleventh hour, sir, I'd like to know?"

Harry Lease died that night. And Crabb Lane, in a fit of repentance as sudden as the Squire's, took the cost of the funeral off the parish (giving some abuse in exchange) and went in a body to the grave. I and Tod followed.

VII.

AUNT DEAN.

TIMBERDALE was a small place on the other side of Crabb Ravine. Its rector was the Rev. Jacob Lewis. Timberdale called him Parson Lewis when not on ceremony. He had married a widow, Mrs. Tanerton: she had a good deal of money and two boys, and the parish thought the new lady might be above them. But she proved kind and good; and her boys did not ride roughshod over the land or break down the farmers' fences. She died in three or four years, after a long illness.

Timberdale talked about her will, deeming it a foolish one. She left all she possessed to the rector, " in affectionate confidence," as the will worded it, " knowing he would do what was right and just by her sons." As Parson Lewis was an upright man with a conscience of his own, it was supposed he would do so; but Timberdale considered that for the boys' sake she should have made it sure herself. It was eight hundred a year, good measure.

Parson Lewis had a sister, Mrs. Dean, a widow also, who lived near Liverpool. She was not left well off at all; could but just make a living of it. She used to come on long visits to the parsonage, which saved her cupboard at home; but it was said that Mrs. Lewis did not like her, thinking her deceitful, and they did not get on very well together. Parson Lewis, the meekest man in the world and most easily led, admitted to his wife that Rebecca had always been a little given to scheming, but he thought her true at heart.

When poor Mrs. Lewis was out of the way for good in Timberdale church-yard, Aunt Dean had the field to herself, and came and stayed as long as she pleased, with her child, Alice. She was a little woman with a mild face and fair skin, and had a sort of purring manner with her. Hardly speaking above her breath, and saying "dear" and "love" at every sentence, and caressing people to their faces, the rule was to fall in love with her at once. The boys, Herbert and Jack, had taken to her without question from the first, and called her "Aunt." Though she was of course no relation whatever to them.

Both the boys made much of Alice—a bright-eyed, pretty little girl with brown curls and timid, winsome ways. Herbert, who was very studious himself, helped her with her lessons: Jack, who was nearer her age, but a few months older, took her out on expeditions, haymaking and blackberry ing and the like, and would bring her home with her frock torn and her knees damaged. He told her that brave little girls never cried with him; and the child would ignore the smart of the grazed knees and show herself as brave as a martyr. Jack was so brave and fearless himself and made so little of hurts, that she felt a kind of shame at giving way to her natural timidity when with him. What Alice liked best was to sit indoors by Herbert's side while he was at his lessons, and read story books and fairy tales. Jack was the opposite of all that, and a regular renegade in all kinds of study. He would have liked to pitch the books into the fire, and did not even care for fairy tales. They came often enough to Crabb Cot when we were there, and to our neighbours the Coneys, with whom the parsonage was intimate. I was only a little fellow at the time, years younger than they were, but I remember I liked Jack better than Herbert. As did Tod also for the matter of that. Herbert was too clever for us, and he was to be a parson besides. He chose the calling for himself. More than once he was caught muffled in the parson's white sur- plice, preaching to Jack and Alice a sermon he had composed

Aunt Dean had her plans and her plots. One great plot was always at work. She made it into a dream, and peeped into it night and day, as if it were a kaleidoscope of rich colours. Herbert Tanerton was to marry her daughter and succeed to his mother's property as eldest son: Jack must go adrift, and earn his own living. She considered it was already three parts as good as accomplished. To see Herbert and Alice poring over books together side by side and to know that they had the same tastes, was welcome to her as the sight of gold. As to Jack, with his roving propensities and his climbing and his daring, she thought it little matter if he came down a tree head-foremost some day, or pitched neck over heels into the depths of Crabb Ravine, and so threw away his life. Not that she really wished any cruel fate for the boy; but she did not care for him; and he might be terribly in the way, when her foolish brother, the parson, came to apportion out the money. And he *was* foolish in some things; soft, in fact: she often said it.

One summer day when the fruit was ripe and the sun shining Mr. Lewis had gone into his study to write his next Sunday's sermon. He did not get on very quickly, for Aunt Dean was in there also, and it disturbed him a little. She was of a restless habit, everlastingly dusting books, and putting things in their places without need.

"Do you wish to keep out all *three* of these inkstands, Jacob! It is not necessary, I should think. Shall I put one up?"

The parson took his eyes off his sermon to answer. "I don't see that they do any harm, Rebecca. The children are using two sometimes. Do as you like, however."

Mrs. Dean put one of the inkstands inside the book-case, and then looked round the room to see what else she could do. A letter caught her eye.

"Jacob, I do believe you have never answered the note old Mullet brought this morning! There it is on the mantelpiece."

The parson sighed. To be interrupted in this way he took quite as a matter of course, but it teased him a little.

"I must see the churchwardens, Rebecca, before I answer it. I want to know, you see, what would be best approved of by the parish."

"Just like you, Jacob," she caressingly said. "The parish must approve of what you approve."

"Yes, yes," he hastily said; "but I like to live at peace with everybody."

He dipped his pen into the ink, and wrote a line in his sermon. The open window looked on the kitchen-garden. Herbert Tanerton had his back against the walnut-tree, doing nothing. Alice sat near on a stool, her head buried in a book that by its canvas cover Mrs. Dean knew to be "Robinson Crusoe." Just then Jack came out of the raspberry bushes with a handful of fruit, which he held out for Alice to eat. "Robinson Crusoe" fell to the ground.

"Oh, Jack, how good they are!" said Alice. And the words came distinctly to Aunt Dean's ears in the still day.

"They are as good again when you pick them off the trees for yourself," cried Jack. "Come along and get some, Alice."

With the taste of the raspberries in her mouth, the temptation was not to be resisted; and she ran after Jack. Aunt Dean put her head out at the window.

"Alice, my love, I cannot have you go amidst those raspberry bushes; you would stain and tear your frock."

"I'll take care of her frock, aunt," called back Jack.

My darling Jack, it cannot be. That is her new muslin frock, and she must not go where she might hurt it."

So Alice sat down again to "Robinson Crusoe," and Jack went his way amid the raspberry bushes, or whither he would.

"Jacob, have you begun to think of what John is to be?" resumed Aunt Dean, as she shut down the window.

The parson pushed his sermon from him in a kind of patient hopelessness, and turned round on his chair. "To be?—in what way, Rebecca?"

"In profession," she answered. "I fancy it is time it was thought of."

"Do you? I'm sure I don't know. The other day when something was being mentioned about it, Jack said he did not care what he was to be, provided he had no books to trouble him."

"I only hope you will not have trouble with him, Jacob, dear," observed Mrs. Dean, in an ominous tone, that plainly intimated she thought the parson would.

"He has a good heart, though he is not so studious as his brother. Why have you shut the window, Rebecca? It is very warm."

Mrs. Dean did not say why. Perhaps she wished to guard against the conversation being heard. When any question not quite convenient to answer was put to her, she had a way of passing it by in silence; and the parson was too yielding or too inert to ask again.

"*Of course*, Brother Jacob, you will make Herbert the heir."

The parson looke 1 surprised. "Why should you suppose that, Rebecca? I think the two boys ought to share and share alike."

"My dear Jacob, how *can* you think so? Your dead wife left you in charge, remember."

"That's what I do remember, Rebecca. She never gave me the slightest hint that she should wish a difference to be made: she was as fond of one boy as of the other."

"Jacob, you must do your duty by the boys," returned Mrs. Dean, with affectionate solemnity. "Herbert must be his mother's heir; it is right and proper it should be so: Jack must be trained to earn his own livelihood. Jack—dear fellow!—is, I fear, of a roving, random disposition: were you to leave any portion of the money to him, he would squander it it in a year."

"Dear me, I hope not! But as to leaving all to his brother—or even a larger portion than to Jack—I don't know that it would be right. A heavy responsibility lies on me in this charge, don't you see, Rebecca?"

"No doubt it does. It is full eight hundred a year. And *you* must be putting something by, Jacob."

"Not much. I draw the money yearly, but expenses seem to swallow it. What with the ponies kept for the boys, and the cost of the masters from Worcester, and a hundred a year out of it that my wife desired the poor old nurse should have till she died, there's not a great deal left. My living is a poor one, you know, and I like to help the poor freely. When the boys go to the university it will be all wanted."

Help the poor freely!—just like him! thought Aunt Dean

"It would be waste of money and waste of time to send Jack to college. You should try and get him some appointment abroad, Jacob. In India, say."

The clergyman opened his eyes at this, and said he should not like to see Jack go out of his own country. Jack's mother had not had any opinion of foreign places. Jack himself interrupted the conversation. He came flying up the path, put down a cabbage leaf of raspberries on the window-sill, and flung open the window with his stained fingers.

"Aunt Dean, I've picked these for you," he said, introducing the leaf, his handsome face and his good-natured eyes sparkling. "They've never been so good as they are this year. Father, you just taste them."

Aunt Dean smiled sweetly, and called him her darling, and Mr. Lewis tasted the raspberries.

"We were just talking of you, Jack," cried the unsophisticated man—and Mrs. Dean knitted her brows slightly. "Your aunt says it is time you began to think of some profession."

"What, yet awhile?" returned Jack.

"That you may be suitably educated for it, my boy."

"I should like to be something that won't want education," cried Jack, leaning his arms on the window-sill, and jumping up and down. "I think I'd rather be a farmer than anything, father."

The parson drew a long face. It had never entered into his calculation.

"I fear that would not do, Jack. I should like you to choose something higher than that; some good profession by which you may rise in the world. Herbert will go into the Church: what should you say to the Bar?"

Jack's jumping ceased all at once. "What, to be a barrister, father? Like those be-wigged fellows that come circuit twice a year to Worcester?"

"Like that, Jack."

"But they have to study all their lives for it, father; and read up millions of books before they can pass! I couldn't do it; I couldn't indeed."

"What do you think of being a high-class lawyer, then? I might place you with some good firm, such as ——"

"Don't, there's a dear father!" interrupted Jack, all the sunshine leaving his face. "I'm afraid if I were at a desk I should kick it over without knowing it: I must be running out and about.—Are they all gone, Aunt Dean? Give me the leaf to throw away, and I'll pick you some more."

The years went on. Jack was fifteen; Herbert eighteen and at Oxford: the advanced scholar had gone to college early. Aunt Dean spent quite half her time at Timberdale, from Easter till autumn, and the parson never rose against it. She let her house during her absence: it was situated on the banks of the river a little way from Liverpool, near the place they call New Brighton now. It might have been called New Brighton then for all I know. One family always took the house for the summer months, glad to get out of hot Liverpool.

As to Jack, nothing had been decided in regard to his future, for opinions about it differed. A little Latin and a little history and a great deal of geography (for he liked that) had been drilled into him: and there his education ended. But he was the best climber and walker and leaper, and withal the best-hearted young fellow that Timberdale could boast: and he knew about land thoroughly, and possessed a great stock of general and useful practical information. Many a day when some of the poorer farmers were in a desperate hurry to get in their hay or carry their wheat on account of threatening weather, has Jack Tanerton turned out to help, and toiled as hard and as long as any of the labourers. He was hail-fellow-well-met with everybody, rich and poor.

Mrs. Dean had worked on always to accomplish her ends. Slowly and imperceptibly, but surely: Herbert must be the heir; John must shift for himself. The parson had had this dinned into him so often now, in her apparently frank and reasoning way, that he began to lend an ear. What with his strict sense of innate justice, and his habit of yielding to his sister's views, he felt mostly in a kind of pickle. But Mrs. Dean had come over this time determined to get something settled, one way or the other.

She arrived before Easter this year. The interminable Jack (as she often called him in heart) was at home; Herbert not. Jack and Alice did not seem to miss him, but went out on their rambles together as they did when children. The morning before Herbert was expected, a letter came from him to his stepfather, saying he had been invited by a fellow-student to spend the Easter holidays at his home near London and had accepted it.

Mr. Lewis took it as a matter of course in his easy way; but it disagreed with Aunt Dean. She said all manner of things to the parson, and incited him to write for Herbert to return at once. Herbert's answer to this was a courteous intimation that he could not alter his plans; and he hoped his father, on consideration, would fail to see any good reason why he should. Herbert Tanerton had a will of his own.

"Neither do I see any reason, good or bad, why he should not pay the visit, Rebecca," confessed the rector. "I'm afraid it was foolish of me to object at all. Perhaps I have not the right to deny him, either, if I wished it. He is getting on for nineteen, and I am not his own father."

So Aunt Dean had to make the best and the worst of it; but she felt as cross as two sticks.

One day when the parson was abroad on parish matters, and the Rectory empty, she went out for a stroll, and reached the high steep bank where the primroses and violets grew. Looking over, she saw Jack and Alice seated below; Jack's arm round her waist.

"You are to be my wife, you know, Alice, when we are grown up. Mind that."

There was no answer, but Aunt Dean certainly thought she heard the sound of a kiss. Peeping over again, she saw Jack taking another.

"And if you don't object to my being a farmer, Alice, I should like it best of all. We'll keep two jolly ponies and ride about together. Won't it be good!"

"I don't object to farming, Jack. Anything you like. A successful farmer's home is a very pleasant one."

Aunt Dean drew away with noiseless steps. She was too calm and callous a woman to turn white; but she did turn angry, and registered a vow in her heart. That presuming, upstart Jack! They were but two little fools, it's true; no better than children; but the nonsense must be stopped in time.

Herbert went back to Oxford without coming home. Alice, to her own infinite astonishment, was despatched to school till midsummer. The parson and his sister and Jack were left alone; and Aunt Dean, with her soft smooth manner and her false expressions of endearment, ruled all things; her brother's better nature amid the rest.

Jack was asked what he would be. A farmer, he answered. But Aunt Dean had somehow caught up the most bitter notions possible against farming in general; and Mr. Lewis, not much liking the thing himself, and yielding to the undercurrent ever gently flowing, told Jack he must fix on something else.

"There's nothing I shall do so well at as farming, father," remonstrated Jack. "You can put me for three or four years to some good agriculturist, and I'll be bound at the end of the

ı ime I should be fit to manage the largest and best farm in
the country Why, I am a better farmer now than some of
them are."

"Jack, my boy, you must not be self-willed. I cannot let
you be a farmer."

"Then send me to sea, father, and make a sailor of me,"
returned Jack, with undisturbed good humour.

But this startled the parson. He liked Jack, and he had a
horror of the sea. "Not that, Jack, my boy. Anything but
that."

"I'm not sure but I should like the sea better than farming,"
went on Jack, the idea full in his head. "Aunt Dean lent
me 'Peter Simple' one day. I know I should make a first-
rate sailor."

"Jack, don't talk so. Your poor mother would not have
liked it, and I don't like it; and I shall never let you go."

"Some fellows run away to sea," said Jack, laughing.

The parson felt as though a bucket of cold water was thrown
down his back. Did Jack mean that as a threat?

"John," said he, in as solemn a way as he had ever spoken,
"disobedience to parents sometimes brings a curse with it.
You must promise me that you will never go to sea."

"I'll not promise that, off hand," said Jack. "But I will
promise never to go without your consent. Think it over well,
father; there's no hurry."

It was on the tip of Mr. Lewis's tongue to withdraw his
objection to the farming scheme there and then: in comparison with the other it looked quite fair and bright. But he
thought he might compromise his judgment to yield thus
instantly: and, as easy Jack said, there was no hurry.

So Jack went rushing out of doors again to the uttermost
bounds of the parish, and the parson was left to Aunt Dean.
When he told her he meant to let Jack be a farmer, she laughed
till the tears came into her eyes, and begged him to leave
matters to her. *She* knew how to manage boys, without ap-
pearing directly to cross them: there was this kind of trouble

7

with most boys, she had observed, before they settled satisfactorily in life but it all came right in the end.

So the parson said no more about farming: but Jack talked a great deal about the sea. Mr. Lewis went over in his gig to Worcester, and bought a book he had heard of, "Two Years before the Mast." He wrote Jack's name in it and gave it him, hoping its contents might serve to sicken him of the sea.

The next morning the book was missing. Jack looked high and low for it, but it was gone. He had left it on the sitting-room table when he went up to bed, and it mysteriously disappeared during the night. The servants had not seen it, and declared it was not on the table in the morning.

"It could not—I suppose—have been the cat," observed Aunt Dean, in a doubtful manner, her eyes full of wonder as to where the book could have got to. "I have heard of cats doing strange things."

"I don't think the cat would make away with a book of that size, Rebecca," said the parson. And if he had not been the least suspicious parson in all the Worcester Diocese, he might have asked his sister whether *she* had been the cat, and secured the book lest it should serve to dissipate Jack's fancy for the sea.

The next thing she did was to carry Jack off to Liverpool. The parson objected at first: Liverpool was a seaport town, and might put Jack more in mind of the sea than ever. Aunt Dean replied that she meant him to see the worst sides of a sea life, the dirty boats in the Mersey, the wretchedness of the crews, and the real discomfort and misery of a sailor's life. That would cure him, she said: what he had got in his head now was the romance picked up from books. The parson thought there was reason in this, and yielded. He was dreadfully anxious about Jack.

She went straight to her house near New Brighton, Jack with her, and a substantial sum in her pocket from the rector to pay Jack's keep. The old servant, Peggy, who took care of it, was thunderstruck to see her mistress come in. It was not

yet occupied by the Liverpool people, and Mrs. Dean sent
them word they could not have it this year: at least not for
the present.   While she got matters straight, she supplied Jack
with all Captain Marryat's novels to read.   The house looked
on the river, and Jack would watch the fine grand vessels
starting on their long voyages, their trim white sails glowing
fair in the sunshine, or hear the joyous shouts from the sailors
of a homeward bound, ship as Liverpool hove in view; and he
grew to think there was no sight so pleasant to the eye as
these beauteous ships; no fate so desirable as to sail in them.

But Aunt Dean had entirely changed her tactics.   Instead
of sending Jack on to the dirtiest and worst managed boats in
the docks, where the living was hard and the sailors were dis-
contented, she allowed him to roam at will on the finest ships,
and make acquaintance with their enthusiastic young officers,
especially with those who were going to sea for the first time
with just such notions as Jack's.   Before Midsummer came,
Jack Tanerton had got to think that he could never be happy
on land.

There was a new ship just launched, the Rose of Delhi; a
magnificent vessel.   Jack took rare interest in her.   He was
for ever on board; was for ever saying to her owners—friends
of Aunt Dean's, to whom she had introduced him—how much
he should like to sail in her.   The owners thought it would
be an advantageous thing to get so active, open, and ready a
lad into their service, although he was somewhat old for
entering, and they offered to article him for four years as
"midshipman" on the Rose of Delhi.   Jack went home with
his tale, his eyes glowing; and Aunt Dean neither checked
him nor helped him.

Not *then*.   Later, when the ship was all but ready to sail,
she told Jack she washed her hands of it, and recommended
him to write and ask his stepfather whether he might sail in
her, or not.

Now Jack was no letter writer; neither, truth to tell, was
the parson.   He had not once written home; but had con-

tented himself with sending affectionate messages in Aunt Dean's letters. Consequently, Mr. Lewis only knew what Aunt Dean had chosen to tell him, and had no idea that Jack was getting the real sea fever. But at the suggestion Jack sat down now, and wrote a long letter.

Its purport was this. That he was longing and hoping to . go to sea; was sure he should never like anything else in the world so well; that the Rose of Delhi, Captain Druce, was the most magnificent ship ever launched; that the owners bore the best character in Liverpool for liberality, and Captain Druce for kindness to his middies; and that he hoped, oh he hoped, his father would let him go; but that if he still refused, he (Jack) would do his best to be content to stay on shore, for he did not forget his promise of never sailing without consent.

"Would you like to see the letter, Aunt Dean, before I shut it up?" he asked.

Aunt Dean, who had been sitting by, took the letter, and privately thought it was as good a letter and as much to the purpose as the best scribe in the land could have written. She disliked it, for all that.

"Jack, dear, I think you had better put a postscript," she said. "Your father detests writing, as you know. Tell him that if he consents he need not write any answer: you will know what it means,—that you may go,—and it will save him trouble."

"But, Aunt Dean, I should like him to wish me good-bye and God-speed."

"He will be sure to do the one in his heart and the other in his prayers, my boy. Write your postscript."

Jack did as he was bid: he was as docile as his stepfather. Exactly as Mrs. Dean suggested, wrote he: and he added that if no answer arrived within two posts, he should take it for granted that he was to go, and should see about his outfit. There was no time to lose, for the ship would sail in three or four days.

"I will post it for you, Jack," she said, when it was ready. "I am going out."

"Thank you, Aunt Dean, but I can post it myself. I'd rather; and then I shall know it's off. Oh, sha'n't I be on thorns till the time for an answer comes and goes!"

He snatched his cap and vaulted off with the letter before he could be stopped. Aunt Dean had a curious look on her face, and sat biting her lips. She had not intended the letter to go.

The first post that could possibly bring an answer brought one. Jack was not at home. Aunt Dean had sent him out on an early commission, watched for the postman, and hastened to the door herself to receive what he might bring. He brought two letters—as it chanced. One from the Rector of Timberdale; one from Alice Dean. Mrs. Dean locked the one up in her private drawer above stairs: the other she left on the breakfast table.

"Peggy says the postman has been here, aunt!" cried the boy, all excitement, as he ran in.

"Yes, dear. He brought a letter from Alice."

"And nothing from Timberdale?"

"Well, I don't know that you could quite expect it by this post, Jack. Your father might like to take a little time for consideration. You may read Alice's letter, my boy: she comes home this day week for the summer holidays."

"Not till this day week!" cried Jack, in frightful disappointment. "Why, I shall have sailed then, if I go, Aunt Dean! I shall not see her."

"Well, dear, you will see her when you come home."

Aunt Dean had no more commissions for Jack after that, and each time the postman was expected, he posted himself outside the door to wait for him. The man brought no other letter. The reasonable time for an answer went by, and there came none.

"Aunt Dean, I suppose I may get my outfit now," said

Jack, only half satisfied. "But I wish I had told him to write in any case: just a line."

"According to what you said, you know, Jack, silence must be taken to give consent."

"Yes, I know. I'd rather have had a word, and made certain. I wish there was time for me just to run over to Timberdale and see him!"

"But there's not, Jack, more's the pity: you would lose the ship. Get a piece of paper and make out a list of the articles the second mate told you you would want."

The Rose of Delhi sailed out of port for Calcutta, and John Tanerton with her, having signed articles to serve in her for four years. The night before his departure he wrote a short letter of farewell to his stepfather, thanking him for his tacit consent, and promising to do his best to get on, concluding it with love to himself and to Herbert, and to the Rectory servants. Which letter somehow got put into Aunt Dean's kitchen fire, and never reached Timberdale.

Aunt Dean watched the Rose of Delhi sail by; Jack, in his bran-new uniform, waving his last farewells to her with his gold-banded cap. The sigh of relief she heaved when the fine vessel was out of sight seemed to do her good. Then she bolted herself into her chamber, and opened Mr. Lewis's letter, which had lain untouched till then. As she expected, it contained a positive interdiction, written half sternly, half lovingly, for John to sail in the Rose of Delhi, or to think more of the sea. Moreover, it commanded him home at once, and it contained a promise that he should be placed to learn the farming without delay. Aunt Dean tripped to Peggy's fire and burnt that too.

There was a dreadful fuss when Jack's departure became known at Timberdale. It fell upon the parson like a thunderbolt. He came striding through the ravine to Crabb Cot, and burst out crying while telling the news to the Squire. He feared he had failed somehow in bringing John up, he said, or he never would have repaid him with this base disobedience and ingratitude. For, you see, the poor man thought Jack had received his letter, and gone off in defiance of it. The Squire agreed with him that Jack deserved the cat-o'-nine tails, and all other boys who traitorously decamped to sea.

Before the hay was all got in, Aunt Dean was back at Timberdale, bringing Alice with her and the bills for the outfit. She let the parson think what he would about Jack, ignoring all knowledge of the letter, and affecting to believe that Jack could not have had it. But the parson argued that Jack must have had it, and did have it, or it would have come back to him. The only one to say a good word for Jack was Alice. She persisted in an opinion that Jack could not be either disobedient or ungrateful, and that there must have been some strange mistake somewhere.

Aunt Dean's work was not all done. She took the poor parson under her wing, and proved to him that he had no resource now but to disinherit Jack, and make Herbert the entire heir. To leave money to Jack would be wanton waste, she urged, for he would be sure to squander it: better bequeath all to Herbert, who would of course look after his brother in later life, and help him if he needed help. So one of the Worcester solicitors, Mr. Hill, was sent for to Timberdale to receive instructions for making the parson's will in Herbert's favour, and to cut off Jack.

That night, after Mr. Hill had gone back again, was one of the worst the parson had ever spent. He was a just man and a kind one, and he felt racked with fear lest he had taken too severe a measure, and one that his late wife, the true owner of the money and John's mother, would never have sanctioned. His bed was as a fever, his pillow a torment; up he got, and walked the room in his night-shirt.

" My Lord and God knoweth that I would do what is right," he groaned. " I am sorely troubled. Youth is vain and desperately thoughtless; perhaps the boy, in his love of adventure never looked at the step in the light of ingratitude. I cannot cut him quite off, I should never find peace of mind if I did.

He shall have a little; and perhaps if he grows into a steady fellow and comes back what he ought to be, I may alter the will later and leave them equal."

The next day the parson wrote privately to Mr. Hill, saying he had reconsidered his determination and would let Jack inherit to the extent of a hundred and fifty pounds a year.

Herbert came home for the long vacation; and he and Alice were together as they had been before that upstart Jack stepped in. They often came to the Squire's and oftener to the Coneys. Grace Coney, a niece of old Coney, had come to live at the farm; she was a nice girl, and she and Alice liked each other. You might see them with Herbert strolling about the fields any hour in the day. At home Alice and Herbert seemed never to care to separate. Mrs. Dean watched them quietly, and thought how beautifully her plans had worked.

Aunt Dean did not go home till October. After she left, the parson had a stroke of paralysis. Charles Ashton, then just ordained to priest's orders, took the duty. Mrs. Dean came back again for Christmas. As if she would let Alice stay away from the parsonage when Herbert was at home!

The Rose of Delhi did not come back for nearly two years. She was what is called a free ship, and took charters for any place she could make money by. One day Alice Dean was leaning out of the windows of her mother's house, gazing wistfully on the sparkling sea, when a grand and stately vessel came sailing homewards, and some brown-faced young fellow on the quarter-deck set on to swing his cap violently by way of hailing her. She looked to the flag which happened to be flying, and read the name there, "The Rose of Delhi." It must be Jack who was saluting. Alice burst into tears of emotion.

He came up from the docks the same day. A great brown handsome fellow, with the old single heart and open manners. And he clasped Alice in his arms and kissed her ever so many times before she could get free. Being a grown-up young lady now, she did not approve of unceremonious kissing, and told Jack so. Aunt Dean was not present, or she might have told him so more to the purpose.

Jack had given satisfaction, and was getting on. He told Alice privately that he did not like the sea so much as he anticipated, and could not believe how any other fellow did ; but as he had chosen it as his calling, he meant to stand by it. He went to Timberdale, in spite of Aunt Dean's advice and efforts to keep him away. Herbert was absent, she said ; the rector ill and childish. Jack found it all too true. Mr. Lewis's mind had failed and his health was breaking. He knew Jack and was over-affectionate with him, but seemed not to remember anything of the past. So never a word did Jack hear of his own disobedience, or of any missing letters.

One person alone questioned him ; and that was Alice. It was after he got back from Timberdale. She asked him to tell her the history of his sailing in the Rose of Delhi, and he gave it in detail, without reserve. When he spoke of the postscript that Aunt Dean had bade him add to his letter, arranging that silence should be taken for consent, and that as no answer had come, he of course had so taken it, the girl turned sick and faint. She saw the treachery that had been at work and where it had lain ; but for her mother's sake she hushed it up and let the matter pass. Alice had not lived with her mother so many years without detecting her propensity for deceit.

Some years passed by. Jack got on well. He served as third mate on the Rose of Delhi long before he could pass, by law, for second. He was made second mate as soon as he had passed for it. The Rose of Delhi came in and went out, and Jack stayed by her, and passed for first mate in course of time. He was not sent back in any of his examinations, as most young sailors are, and the board once went the length of complimenting him on his answers. The fact was, Jack held to his word of doing his best ; he got into no mischief and was the smartest sailor afloat. He was in consequence a favourite with the owners, and Captain Druce took pains with him and

7*

brought him on in seamanship and navigation, and showed him how to take observations, and all the rest of it. There's no end of difference in merchant-captains in this respect: some teach their junior officers nothing. Jack finally passed triumphantly for master, and hoped his time would come to get a command. Meanwhile he went out again as first mate on the Rose of Delhi.

One spring morning there came news to Mrs. Dean from Timberdale. The rector had had another stroke and was thought to be near his end. She started off at once, with Alice. Charles Ashton had had a living given to him; and Herbert Tanerton was now his stepfather's curate. Herbert had passed as shiningly in mods and divinity and all the rest of it as Jack had passed before the Marine Board. He was a steady, thoughtful, serious young man, did his duty well in the parish, and preached better sermons than ever the rector had. Mrs. Dean, who looked upon him as Alice's husband as surely as though they were married, was as proud of his success as though it had been her own.

The rector was very ill and unable to leave his bed. His intellect was quite gone now. Mrs. Dean sat with him most of the day, leaving Alice to be taken care of by Herbert. They went about together just as always, and were on the best of confidential terms; and came over to the Coneys, and to us when we were at Crabb Cot.

"Herbert," said Mrs. Dean one evening when she had all her soft, sugary manner upon her and was making the young parson believe she had nobody's interest at heart in the world but his: "my darling boy, is it not almost time you began to think of marriage? None know the happiness and comfort brought by a good wife, dear, until they experience it."

Herbert looked taken to. He turned as red as a school-girl, and glanced half a moment at Alice, like a detected thief.

"I must wait until I get a living to think of that, Aunt Dean."

"Is it necessary, Herbert? I should have thought you might bring a wife home to the Rectory here."

Herbert turned off the subject with a jesting word or two, and got out of his redness. Aunt Dean was eminently satisfied: his confusion and his impromptu glance at Alice had told tales; and she knew it was only a question of time.

The rector died. When the grass was long and the May flowers were in bloom and the cuckoo was singing in the trees he passed peacefully to his rest. Just before death he recovered speech and consciousness; but the chief thing he said was that he left his love to Jack.

After the funeral the will was opened. It had not been touched since that far past year when Jack had gone away to sea. Out of the eight hundred a year descended from their mother, Jack had a hundred and fifty; Herbert the rest. Aunt Dean made a hideous frown for once in her life; a hundred and fifty pounds a year for Jack, was only, as she looked upon it, so much robbery on Herbert and Alice. Out of the little money saved by the rector, five hundred pounds were left to his sister, Rebecca Dean; the rest was to be divided equally between Herbert and Jack; and his furniture and effects went to Herbert. On the whole, Aunt Dean was tolerably satisfied.

She was a woman who liked to keep up appearances strictly, and she made a move to leave the young parson at the end of a week or two's time, and go back to Liverpool. Herbert did not detain her. His own course was uncertain until a fresh rector should be appointed. The living was in the gift of a neighbouring baronet, and it was fancied by some that he might give it to Herbert. One thing did surprise Mrs. Dean; angered her too: that Herbert had not made his offer to Alice before their departure. Now that he had his own fortune at command, there was no necessity for him to wait for a living.

News greeted them on their arrival. The Rose of Delhi was on her way home once more, with John Tanerton in command. Captain Druce had been left behind at Calcutta, dangerously ill. Alice's colour came and went. She looked out for the homeward-bound vessels passing inwards, and felt quite sick with anxiety lest Jack should fail in any way, and never bring home the ship.

"The Rose of Delhi, Captain Tanerton." Alice Dean cast her eyes on the ship news in the morning paper, and read the announcement amidst the arrivals. Just for an instant her sight left her.

"Mamma," she presently said, quietly passing over the newspaper, "the Rose of Delhi is in."

"The Rose of Delhi, Captain Tanerton," read Mrs. Dean. "The idea of their sticking in Jack's name as captain! He will have to go down again as soon as Captain Druce returns. A fine captain I daresay he has made!"

"At least he has brought the ship home safely and quickly," Alice ventured to say. "It must have passed after dark last night."

"Why after dark?"

Alice did not reply—Because I was watching till daylight faded—which would have been the truth. "Had it passed before, some of us might have seen it, mamma."

The day was waning before Jack came up. Captain Tanerton. Jack was never to go back again to his chief-mateship, as Aunt Dean had surmised, for the owners had given him the permanent command of the Rose of Delhi. The last mail had brought news from Captain Druce that he should never be well enough for the command again, and the owners were only glad to give it to the younger and more active man. The officers and crew alike reported that never a better master sailed, than Jack had proved himself on this homeward voyage.

"Don't you think I have been very lucky on the whole, Aunt Dean? Fancy a young fellow like me getting such a beautiful ship as that!"

"Oh, very lucky," returned Aunt Dean.

Jack looked like a captain too. He was broad and manly, with an intelligent, honest, handsome face, and the quick keen eye of a sailor. Jack was particular in his attire too: and some sailors are not: he dressed as a private gentleman when on shore.

"Only a hundred and fifty left to me!" cried Jack, when he was told the news. "Well, perhaps Herbert may require more than I, poor fellow," he added in his good nature: "he may not get a good living, and then he'll be glad of it I shall be sure to do well now I've got the ship."

"You'll be at sea always, Jack, and will have no use for money," said Mrs. Dean.

"Oh, I don't know about having no use for it, Aunt Anyway, my father thought it right to leave it so, and I am content. I wish I could have said farewell to him before he died!"

A few days more, and Aunt Dean was thrown on her beam-ends at a worse angle than the Rose of Delhi hoped to be. Jack and Alice discussed matters between themselves, and the result was disclosed to her. They were going to be married.

It was Alice who told. Jack had just left, and she and her mother were sitting together in the summer twilight. At first Mrs. Dean thought Alice was joking: she was like a mad woman when she found it true. Her great dream had never foreshadowed this.

"How dare you to attempt to think of so monstrous a thing, you wicked girl? Marry your own brother-in-law!—it would be no better. It is Herbert that is to be your husband."

Alice shook her head with a smile. "Herbert would not have me, mamma; nor would I have him. Herbert will marry Grace Coney."

"Who?" cried Mrs. Dean.

"Grace Coney. They have been in love with one another ever so many years. I have known it all along. He will marry her as soon as his future is settled. I had promised to be one of the bridesmaids, but I suppose I shall not get the chance now."

" Grace Coney—that beggarly girl!" shrieked Mrs. Dean. " But for her uncle's giving her shelter she must have turned out in the world when her father died and got her living how she could. She is not a lady. She is not Herbert's equal.'

" Oh, yes, she is, mamma. She is a nice girl and will make him a perfect wife. Herbert would not exchange her for the richest lady in the land."

" If Herbert chooses to make a spectacle of himself, you never shall!" cried poor Mrs. Dean, all her golden visions fast melting into air. " I would see that wicked Jack Tanerton at the bottom of the sea first."

" Mother, dear, listen to me. Jack and I have cared for each other for years and years, and we should neither of us marry anybody else. There is nothing to wait for; Jack is as well off as he will be for years to come: and—and we have settled it so, and I hope you will not oppose it."

It was a cruel moment for Aunt Dean. Her love for other people had been all pretence, but she did love her daughter. Besides that, she was ambitious for her.

" I can never let you marry a sailor, Alice. Anything but that."

" It was you who made Jack a sailor, mother, and there's no help for it," said Alice, in a low tone. " I would rather he had been anything else in the world. I would have liked him to have had land and farmed it. We should have done well. Jack had his four hundred a year clear, you know. At least, he ought to have had it. Oh, mother, don't you see that while you have been plotting against Jack you have plotted against me?"

Aunt Dean felt sick with the memories that were crowding upon her. The mistake she had made was a frightful one.

" You cannot join your fate to Jack's, Alice," she repeated, wringing her hands. " A sailor's wife is too liable to be made a widow."

"I know it, mother. I shall share his danger, for I am
going out in the Rose of Delhi. The owners have consented,
and Jack is fitting up a lovely little cabin for me that is to
be my own saloon."

"My daughter sailing over the seas in a merchant ship!"
gasped Aunt Dean. "Never!"

"I should be no true wife if I could let my husband sail
without me. Mother, it is you alone who have carved out
our destiny. Better have left it to God."

In a startled way, her heart full of remorse, she was beginning to see it; and sat down, half fainting, on a chair.

"It is a miserable prospect, Alice."

"Mother, we shall get on. There's the hundred and fifty
a year certain, you know. That we shall put by; and, as
long as I sail with him, a good deal more besides. Jack's
pay is fixed at twenty pounds a month, and he will make
more by commission: perhaps as much again. Have no fear
for us on that score. Jack has been deprived unjustly of his
birth-right; and I think sometimes that perhaps as a recompense Heaven will prosper him."

"But the danger, Alice! The danger of a sea-life!"

"Do you know what Jack says about the danger, mother?
He says God is over us on the sea at well as on the land, and
will take care of those who put their trust in Him. In the
wildest storm I will try to let that great truth help me to feel
peace."

Alas for Aunt Dean! The arguments slipped away from
her hands just as her plans had slipped. In her bitter repentance, she lay on the floor of her room that night and
asked God to have pity upon her, for her trouble seemed
greater than she could bear.

The morning's post brought news from Herbert. He was
made rector of Timberdale. Aunt Dean wrote back, telling
him what had taken place, and asking, nay, almost command-
ing, that he should restore an equal share of the property to
Jack. Herbert replied that he should abide by his step

father's will. The living of Timberdale was not a rich one,
and he wished Grace, his future wife, to be comfortable.
" Herbert was always intensely selfish," groaned Aunt Dean.
Look on which side she would, there was no comfort.

The Rose of Delhi, Captain Tanerton, sailed out of port
again, carrying also with her Mrs. Tanerton, the captain's
wife. And Aunt Dean was left to bemoan her fate, and
wish she had never meddled to shape out other people's des-
tinies. Better, as Alice said, that she had left that to God.

VIII.

GOING THROUGH THE TUNNEL.

WE had to make a rush for it. And making a rush did not suit the Squire, any more than it does other people who have come to an age when the body's big and the breath nowhere. He reached the train, pushed head-foremost into a carriage, and then remembered the tickets. "Bless my heart!" he exclaimed, as he jumped out again and nearly upset a lady who had a little dog in her arms, and a great big mass of fashionable hair on her head, that the Squire, in his hurry, mistook for tow.

"Plenty of time, sir," said a guard who was passing. "There's three minutes to spare."

Instead of saying he was obliged to the man for his civility, or relieved to find the tickets might be had still, the Squire snatched out his old watch, and began abusing the railway clocks for being slow. Had Tod been there he would have told him to his face that it was the watch that was fast, braving all retort, for the Squire believed in his watch as he did in himself, and would rather have been told that *he* could go wrong than that the watch could. But there was only me: and I'd not have said it for anything.

"Keep two back-seats there, Johnny," said the Squire.

I put my coat on the corner-seat furthest from the door, and the rug on the one next to it, and followed him into the station. When the Squire was late in starting, he was apt to get into the greatest flurry conceivable; and the first thing I saw was himself blocking up the ticket-place, and undoing his pocket-book with twitching fingers. He had some loose gold about him, silver, too, but the pocket-book met his hand first, so he pulled out that. These flurried moments of the Squire's amused Tod beyond telling; he was so cool himself.

"Can you change this?" said the Squire, drawing out one from a roll of five-pound notes.

"No, I can't," was the answer, in the surly tone put on by ticket-clerks.

How the Squire crumpled up the note again, and searched in his breeches pocket for the gold, and came away with the two tickets and the change, I'm sure he never knew. There was a crowd gathered round, wanting to take their tickets in turn, and the knowledge that he was keeping them flurried him all the more. He stood at the back a moment, put the roll of notes into his case, fastened it and returned it to the breast of his over-coat, sent the change down into another pocket without counting it, and went out with the tickets in his hand. Not to the carriage; but to take a stare at the big clock in front.

"Don't you see, Johnny? exactly four minutes and a half difference," he cried, holding out his watch to me. "It is a strange thing they can't keep these railway clocks in order."

"My watch keeps good time, sir, and mine is with the railway. I think it is right."

"Hold your tongue, Johnny. How dare you! Right? You send your watch to be regulated the first opportunity, sir; don't *you* get into the habit of being too late or too early."

When we went finally to the carriage there were some people in it, but our seats were left. Squire Todhetley sat down by the further door, and settled himself and his coats and his things comfortably, which he had been too flurried to do before. Cool as a cucumber was he, now the bustle was over; cool as Tod could have been. At the other door, with his face to the engine, sat a dark, gentlemanly-looking man of forty, who had made room for us to pass him as we got in. He had a large signet-ring on one hand, and a lavender glove on the other The other three seats opposite to us were vacant.

Next to me sat a little man with a fresh colour and gold spectacles, who was already reading; and beyond him, in the corner, face to face with the dark man, was a lunatic. That's to to speak of him politely. Of all the restless, fidgety, worrying, hot-tempered passengers that ever put themselves into a carriage to travel with people in their senses, he was the worst. In fifteen moments he had made fifteen darts; now after his hat-box and things above his head; now calling the guard and the porters to ask senseless questions about his luggage; now treading on our toes, and trying the corner seat opposite the Squire, and then darting back to his own. His hair was a wig, and had a decided green tinge, the effect of keeping, perhaps, and his skin was dry and shrivelled as an Egyptian mummy's.

A servant, in undress livery, came to the door, and touched his hat, which had a cockade in it. as he spoke to the dark man.

"Your ticket, my lord."

Lords are not travelled with every day, and some of us looked up. The gentleman took the ticket from the man's hand and slipped it into his waiscoat pocket.

"You can get me a newspaper, Wilkins. The *Times*, if it is to be had."

"Yes, my lord."

"Yes, there's room here, ma'am," interrupted the guard, sending the door back with a click, for a lady who stood at it. "Make haste, please."

The lady who stepped in was the same the Squire had bolted against. She sat down in the seat opposite me, and looked at every one of us by turns. There was a kind of violet bloom on her face and some soft white powder, seen plain enough through her veil. She took the longest gaze at the dark gentleman, bending a little forward to do it; for, as he was in a line with her, and had his head turned from her as well, her curiosity could only get a view of his side-face. Mrs. Todhetley might have said she had not put on her company manners. In the midst of this, the servant-man came back again.

"The *Times* is not here yet, my lord. They are expecting the papers in by the next down train."

"Never mind, then. You can get me one at the next station, Wilkins."

"Very well, my lord."

Wilkins must certainly have had a scramble for his carriage, for we started before he had well left the door. It was not an express train, and we should have to stop at several stations. Where the Squire and I had been staying does not matter; it has nothing to do with what I have to tell. It was a long way from our own home, and that's enough to say.

"Would you mind changing seats with me, sir?"

I looked up, to find the lady's face close to mine; she had spoken in a half-whisper. The Squire, who carried his old-fashioned notions of politeness with him when he went travelling, at once got up to offer her the corner. But she declined it, saying she was subject to face-ache, and did not care to be next the window. So she took my seat, and I sat down in the one opposite Mr. Todhetley.

"Which of the peers is that?" I heard her ask him in a loud whisper, as the lord put his head out at his window.

"Don't know at all, ma'am," said the Squire. "Don't know many of the peers myself, except those of my own county: Lyttelton, and Beauchamp, and——"

Of all snarling barks, the worst was given that moment in the Squire's face, stopping the list suddenly. The little dog, an ugly, hairy, vile-tempered Scotch terrier, had been held in concealment under the lady's jacket, and now struggled himself free. The Squire's look of consternation was good! You see, he had not known any animal was there.

"Be quiet, Wasp. How dare you bark at the gentleman; He will not bite, sir: he——"

"Who has got a dog in the carriage?" shrieked out the luna tic, starting up in a passion. "Dogs don't travel with passengers. Here! Guard! Guard!"

To call out for the guard when a train is going at full speed is generally useless. The lunatic had to sit down again; and the lady defied him, so to say, coolly avowing that she had hid the dog from the guard on purpose, staring him in the face while she said it.

After this there was a lull, and we went speeding along, the lady talking now and again to the Squire. She seemed to want to get confidential with him; but the Squire did not seem to care for it, though he was quite civil. She held the dog in her lap amidst her clothes, so that nothing but his head peeped out.

"Halloa! How dare they be so negligent? There's no lamp in this carriage."

It was the lunatic again, and we all looked at the lamp. It had no light in it; but that it *had* when we first reached the carriage was certain; for, as the Squire went stumbling in, his head nearly touched the lamp, and I had noticed the flame. It seems the Squire had also.

"They must have put it out while we were getting our tickets," he said.

"I'll know the reason why when we stop," cried the lunatic, fiercely. "After passing the next station, we dash into the long tunnel. The idea of going through it in pitch darkness! It would not be safe."

"Especially with a dog in the carriage," spoke the lord, in a chaffing kind of tone, but with a good-natured smile. "We will have the lamp lighted, however."

As if to reward him for interference, the dog barked up loudly, and tried to make a spring at him; upon which the lady smothered the animal up, head and all.

Another minute or two, and the train began to slacken its speed. It was but an insignificant station, one not likely to be halted at for above a minute. The lunatic twisted his body out at the window, and shouted for the guard long before we were at a standstill.

"Allow me to manage this," said the lord, quietly putting him down. "They know me on the line. Wilkins!"

The man came rushing up at the call. He must have

been out already, though we were not quite at a standstill yet.

"Is it for the *Times*, my lord? I am going to get it."

"Never mind the *Times*. This lamp is not lighted, Wilkins. See the guard, and *get it done*. At once."

"And ask him what the mischief he means by his carelessness," roared out the lunatic in the wake of Wilkins, who went flying off. "Sending us on our road without a light?—and that dangerous tunnel close at hand."

The emphatic authority laid upon the words "Get it done," seemed an earnest that the speaker was accustomed to be obeyed at will, and would be this time. For once the lunatic sat quiet, watching the lamp, and for the light that was to be dropped into it from the top; and so did I, and so did the lady. We were all deceived, however, and the train went puffing on. The lunatic shrieked, the lord put his head out of the carriage and shouted for Wilkins.

No good. Shouting after a train is off never is much good. The lord sat down on his seat again, an angry frown crossing his face, and the lunatic got up and danced on his legs.

"I do not know where the blame lies," observed the lord. "Not with my servant, I think; he is attentive, and has been with me some years."

"I'll know where it lies," retorted the lunatic. "I am a director on the line, though I don't often travel on it. This *is* management, this is! A few minutes more and we shall be in the dark tunnel."

"Of course it would have been satisfactory to have a light, but it is not of so much consequence," said the nobleman, wishing to soothe him. "There's no danger in the dark."

"No danger! No danger, sir! I think there is danger. Who's to know that dog don't spring out and bite us? Who's to know there won't be an accident in mid-tunnel? A light is a protection against having our pockets picked, if it's a protection against nothing else."

"I fancy our pockets are pretty safe to day," said the lord

glancing round at us with a good-natured smile; as much as to say that none of us looked like thieves. "And I certainly trust we shall get through the tunnel in safety."

"And I'll take care the dog does not bite you in the dark," spoke up the lady, pushing her head forward to give the lunatic a nod or two that you'd hardly have matched for defiant impudence. "You'll be good, won't you, Wasp! But I should like the lamp lighted myself. You will perhaps be so kind, my lord, as to see that there's no mistake made about it at the next station!"

He slightly raised his hat to her and bowed in answer, but did not speak. The lunatic buttoned up his coat with fingers that were either nervous or angry, and then disturbed the little gentleman next him, who had read his big book throughout the whole commotion without once lifting his eyes by hunting everywhere for his pocket-handkerchief.

"Here's the tunnel!" he cried out resentfully, as we dashed with a shriek into pitch darkness.

It was all very well for her to say she would take care of the dog, but the first thing the young beast did was to make a spring at me and then at the Squire, barking and yelping frightfully. The Squire pushed it away in a commotion. Though well accustomed to dogs, he always fought shy of strange ones. The lady chattered and laughed, and did not seem to try to get hold of him, but we couldn't see, you know; the Squire hissed at him, the dog snarled and growled; altogether there was noise enough to deafen anything but a tunnel.

"Pitch him out at the window," cried the lunatic.

"Pitch yourself out," answered the lady. And whether she propelled the dog, or whether he went of his own accord, the beast sprang to the other end of the carriage, and was seized upon by the nobleman.

"I think, madam, you had better put him under your mantle and keep him there," said he, bringing the dog back to her and speaking quite civilly, but in the same tone of authority he had used to his servant about the lamp. "I have not the slightest objection to dogs myse'f, but many people have, and it is not altogether pleasant to have them loose in a railway carriage. I beg your pardon; I cannot see; is this your hand?"

It was her hand, I suppose, for the dog was left with her, and he went back to his seat again. When we emerged out of the tunnel into the light of day, the lunatic's face was blue.

"Ma'am, if that miserable brute had laid hold of me by so much as the corner of my great-coat tail, I'd have had the law of you. It is perfectly monstrous that anybody, putting themselves into a first-class carriage, should attempt to outrage railway laws, and upset the comfort of travellers with impunity. I shall complain to the guard."

"He does not bite, sir; he never bites," she softly answered, as if sorry for the escapade, and wishing to conciliate him. The poor little bijou is frightened at darkness, and leaped from my arms unawares. There! I'll promise that you shall neither see nor hear him again."

She had tucked the dog so completely out of sight, that no one could have suspected one was there, just as it had been on first entering. The train was drawn up to the next station; when it stopped, the servant came and opened the carriage-door for his master to get out.

"Did you understand me, Wilkins, when I told you to get this lamp lighted?"

"My lord, I'm very sorry; I understood your lordship perfectly, but I couldn't see the guard," answered Wilkins. "I caught sight of him running up to his van-door at the last moment, but the train began to move off, and I had to jump in myself, or else be left behind."

The guard passed as he was explaining this, and the nobleman drew his attention to the lamp, curtly ordering him to "light it instantly." Lifting his hat to us by way of farewell, he disappeared; and the lunatic began upon the guard as if he were commencing a lecture in Bedlam to a deaf audience

The guard seemed not to hear it, so lost was he in astonishment at there being no light.

"Why, what can have douted it?" he cried aloud, staring up at the lamp. And the Squire smiled at the familiar word, so common in our ears at home, and had a great mind to ask the guard whence he came.

"I lighted all these here lamps myself afore we started, and I see 'em all burning," said he. There was no mistaking the home accent now, and the Squire looked down the carriage with a beaming face.

"You are from Worcestershire, my man."

"From Worcester itself, sir. Leastways from St. John's, which is the same thing."

"Whether you are from Worcester, or whether you are from Jericho, I'll let you know that you can't put dark lamps into first-class carriages on this line without being made to answer for it!" roared the lunatic. "What's your name? I am a director."

"My name is Thomas Brooks, sir," replied the man, respectfully touching his silver-banded cap. "But I declare to you, sir, that I've told the truth in saying the lamps were all right when we started: how this one can have got douted, I can't think. There's not a guard on the line, sir, more particular in seeing to the lamps than I am."

"Well, light it now; don't waste time excusing yourself," growled the lunatic. But he said nothing about the dog, which was surprising.

In a twinkling the lamp was lighted, and we were off again. The lady and her dog were quiet now: he was out of sight: she leaned back to go to sleep. The Squire put his head against the curtain, and shut his eyes to do the same; the little man, as before, never looked off his book; and the lunatic frantically shifted himself every two minutes between his own seat and that of the opposite corner. There were no more tunnels, and we went smoothly on to the next station. Five minutes allowed there.

The little man, putting his book in his pocket, took up a

black leather bag from above his head, and got out; the lady. her dog hidden still, prepared to follow him, wishing the Squire and me, and even the lunatic, with a forgiving smile, a polite good morning. I had moved to that end, and was watching the lady's wonderful back hair as she stepped out, when all in a moment the Squire sprang up with a shout and a cry, and jumped out nearly upon her, calling out that he had been robbed. She dropped the dog, and I thought he must have caught the lunatic's disorder and become frantic.

It is of no use attempting to describe exactly what followed. The lady, snatching up her dog, shrieked out that perhaps she had been robbed too; she had laid hold of the Squire's arm, and went with him into the station-master's room. And there we were: us three; and the guard, and the station-master, and the lunatic, who had come pouncing out too at the Squire's cry. The man in spectacles had disappeared for good.

The Squire's pocket-book was gone. He gave his name and address at once to the station-master: and the guard's face lighted with intelligence when he heard it, for he knew Squire Todhetley by reputation. The pocket-book had been safe just before we entered the tunnel; the Squire was certain of that, having felt it. He had sat in the carriage with his coat un-buttoned, rather thrown back; and nothing could have been easier than for a practised thief to draw it cleverly out, under cover of the darkness.

" I had fifty pounds in it," he said; "fifty pounds in five-pound notes. And some memoranda besides."

" Fifty pounds!" cried out the lady, quickly. " And you could travel with all that about you, and not button up your coat! You ought to be rich!"

" Have you been in the habit of meeting thieves, madam, when travelling?" suddenly demanded the lunatic, turning upon her without warning, his coat whirling about on all sides with the rapidity of his movements, as if the wind took it.

"No, sir, I have not," she answered, in an indignant tone. " Have you?"

"I have not, madam. But then, you perceive I see no risk in travelling with a coat unbuttoned, although it may have bank-notes in its pockets."

She made no reply : was too much occupied in turning out her own pockets and purse, to ascertain that they had not been rifled. Reassured on the point, she sat down on a low box against the wall, nursing her dog ; which had begun his snarling barks again.

" It must have been taken from me in the darkness as we went through the tunnel," affirmed the Squire to the room in general and perhaps the station-master in particular. " I am a magistrate, and have some experience in these things. I sat completely off my guard, a ready prey to anybody, my hands stretched out before me, grappling with that dog, that seemed —why, goodness me ! yes he *did*, now that I think of it—that seemed to be held about fifteen inches off my nose on purpose to attack me. That's when the thing must have been done But now—which of them could it have been ?"

He meant of the passengers. As he looked hard at us in rotation, especially at the guard and station-master, who had not been in the carriage, the lady gave a shrill shriek, and threw the dog into the middle of the room.

" I see it all," she said, faintly. He has a habit of snatching at things with his mouth. He must have snatched the case out of your pocket, sir, and dropped it from the window. You will find it in the tunnel."

" Who has ? " asked the lunatic, while the Squire stared in wonder.

" My poor little Wasp. Ah, villain ! beast ! it is he that has done all this mischief."

" He might have taken the pocket-book," I said, thinking it time to speak, " but he could not have dropped it out, for I put the window up as we went into the tunnel."

It seemed a nonplus, and her face fell again. " There was the other window," she said in a minute. " He might have dropped it there. I heard his bark quite close to it."

"*I* pulled up that window, madam," said the lunatic. "If the dog did take it out of the pocket it may be in the carriage now."

The guard rushed out to search it ; the Squire followed, but the station-master remained where he was, and closed the door after them. A thought came over me that he was staying to keep the two passengers in view.

No; the pocket-book could not be found in the carriage. As they came back, the Squire was asking the guard if he knew who the nobleman was who had got out at the last station with his servant. But the guard did not.

"He said they knew him on the line."

"Very likely, sir. I have not been on this line above a month or two."

"Well, this is an unpleasant affair," said the lunatic impatiently, "and the question is—What's to be done? It appears pretty evident that your pocket-book was taken in the carriage, sir. Of the four passengers, I suppose the one who left us at the last station must be held exempt from suspicion, being a nobleman. Another got out here, and has disappeared; the other two are present. I propose that we should both be searched."

"I'm sure I am quite willing," said the lady, and she got up at once.

I think the Squire was about to disclaim any wish so to act; but the lunatic was resolute, and the station-master agreed with him. There was no time to lose, for the train was in a hurry to go, her minutes were up, and the lunatic was turned out. The lady went into another room with two women, called by the station-master, and *she* was turned out. Neither of them had the pocket-book.

"Here's my card, sir," said the lunatic, handing one to Mr. Todhetley. "You know my name, I daresay. If I can be of any future assistance to you in this matter, you may command me."

"Bless my heart!" cried the Squire, as he read the name on the card. "How could you allow yourself to be searched, sir?"

"Because, in such a case as this, I think it only right and

fair that everybody who had the misfortune to be mixed up in it *should* be searched," replied the lunatic, as they went out together. "It is a satisfaction to both parties. Unless you offered to search me, you could not have offered to search that woman; and I suspected her."

"Suspected *her!*" cried the Squire, opening his eyes.

"If I didn't suspect, I doubted. Why on earth did she cause her dog to make all that row the moment we got into the tunnel? It must have been done then. I should not be startled out of my senses if I heard that that silent man by my side and hers was in league with her."

The Squire stood in a kind of maze, trying to recall what he could of the little man in spectacles, and see if things would fit into one another.

"Don't you like her look?" he suddenly asked.

"No, I *don't*," said the lunatic, turning himself about recklessly. "I have a prejudice against painted women: they put me in mind of Jezebel. Look at her hair. It's awful."

He went out in a storm, and took his seat in the carriage, not a moment before it puffed off.

"*Is* he a lunatic?" I whispered to the Squire.

"He a lunatic!" he roared. "You must be a lunatic for asking it, Johnny. Why, that's—that's——"

Instead of saying more, he showed me the card, and the name nearly took my breath away. He is a well-known London man, of science, talent, and position, and of world-wide fame.

"Well, I thought him nothing better than an escaped maniac."

"*Did* you?" said the Squire. "Perhaps he returned the compliment on you, sir. But now—Johnny, who has got my pocketbook?"

As if it was any use asking me! As we turned back to the station-master's room, the lady came into it, evidently resenting the search, although she had seemed to acquiesce in it so readily.

"They were rude, those women. It is the first time I ever had the misfortune to travel with men who carry pocket-books to lose them, and I hope it will be the last," she pursued, in scornful passion, meant for the Squire. "One generally meets with *gentlemen* in a first-class carriage."

The emphasis came out with a sort of shriek, and it told on him. Now that she was proved innocent, he was as vexed as she for having listened to the advice of the scientific man — but I can't help calling him a lunatic still. The Squire's apologies might have disarmed a cross-grained hyena; and she came round with a smile.

"If anybody *has* got the pocket-book," she said, as she stroked her dog's ears, "it must be that silent man with the gold spectacles. There was nobody else, sir, who could have reached you without getting up to do it. And I declare on my honour, that when that commotion first arose through my poor little dog, I felt for a moment something like a man's arm stretched out across me. It could only have been his. I hope you have the numbers of the notes."

"But I have not," said the Squire.

The room was being invaded by this time. Two stray passengers, a friend of the station-master's, and the porter who took the tickets, had crept in. All thought the lady's opinion must be correct, and said the spectacled man had got clear off with the pocket-book. There was nobody else to pitch upon.

A nobleman travelling with his servant would not be likely to commit a robbery; the lunatic was really the man his card represented him to be, for the station-master's friend had seen and recognized him; and the lady was proved innocent by practical search. Wasn't the Squire in a passion!

"That close reading of his was all a blind," he said, in sudden conviction. "He kept his face down that we should not know him in future. He never looked at one of us! he never said a word! I shall go and find him."

Away went the Squire, as fast as he could run, but came back in a moment to know which was the way out, and where it led to. There was quite a lot of us by this time. Some fields lay beyond the outlet of the station at the back; and a boy affirmed that he had seen a little gentleman in spectacles, with a black bag in his hand, making over the first stile.

"Now look you here, boy," said the Squire. "If you catch that same man, I'll give you five shillings."

Tod could not have flown faster than the boy did. He took the stile at a kind of leap; it was high and awkward; and the Squire tumbled over it after him. Some boys and men joined in the chase; and a cow, feeding in the field, trotted after us and brought up the rear.

Such a shout from the boy. It came from behind the op posite hedge of the long field. I was over the gate first; the Squire came next.

On the edge of the dry ditch sat the passenger, his legs hanging down, his neck imprisoned in the boy's arms. I knew him at once. His hat and his gold spectacles had fallen off in the scuffle; the black bag was wide open, and had a tall bunch of something green sticking up from it; some tools lay on the ground.

"Oh, you wicked hypocrite!" spluttered the Squire, not in the least knowing what he said in his passion. "Are you not ashamed to have played upon me such a vile trick? How dare you go about to commit robberies!"

"I have not robbed you, at any rate," said the man, his voice shaking a little and his face pale, while the boy loosed the neck but pinioned the arms behind.

"Not robbed me!" cried the Squire. "Good heavens! Whom do you suppose you have robbed, if not me? Here Johnny, lad, you are a witness. He says he has not robbed me."

"I did not know it was yours," said the man meekly. "Loose me, boy; I'll not attempt to run away."

"Halloa! here! what's to do?" roared a big fellow, swing-ing himself over the gate. "Any tramp been trespassing?—anybody wanting to be took up? I'm the parish constable."

If he had said he was the parish engine, ready to let loose buckets of water on the offender, he could not have been more welcome. The Squire's face was rosy with satisfaction.

"Have you got your handcuffs with you, my man?"

"I've not got them, sir; but I fancy I'm big enough and strong enough to take *him* without 'em. Something to spare, too."

"There's nothing like handcuffs for safety," said the Squire, rather damped, for he believed in them as one of the country's institutions. "Oh, you villain! Perhaps you can tie him with cords?"

The thief floundered out of the ditch and stood upon his feet. He did not look an ungentlemanly thief, now you came to see him and hear him; and his face, though scared and white, might have been thought an honest one. He picked up his hat and glasses, and held them in his hand while he spoke, in a tone of earnest remonstrance.

"Surely, sir, you would not have me taken up for this slight offence. I did not know I was doing wrong, and I doubt if the law would condemn me: I thought it was public property!"

"Public property!" danced the Squire, turning red at the words. "Of all the impudent brazen-faced rascals that are cheating the gallows, you must be the worst. My bank-notes public property!"

"Your what, sir?"

"My bank-notes, you villain. How dare you repeat your insolent question?"

"But I don't know anything about your bank-notes, sir," said the man meekly. "I do not know what you mean."

They stood facing each other, a sight for a picture; the Squire with his hands under his coat, dancing a little in rage, his face crimson; the other quite still, holding his hat and gold spectacles, and looking at him in wonder.

"You don't know what I mean! When you confessed with **your** last breath that you had robbed me of my pocket-book!"

"I confessed—I have not sought to conceal—that I have

robbed the ground of this rare fern," said the man, handling carefully the green-stuff in the black bag. "I have not robbed you, or any one, of anything else."

The tone, simple, quiet, self-contained, put the Squire in amaze. He stood staring.

"Are you a fool?" he asked. "What do you suppose I have to do with your rubbishing ferns?"

"Nay, I supposed you owned them; that is, owned the land. You led me to believe so, in saying I had robbed you."

"What I've lost is a pocket-book, with ten five-pound bank-notes in it; I lost it in the train; it must have been taken as we came through the tunnel; and you sat next but one to me," reiterated the Squire.

The man put on his hat and glasses. "I am a geologist and botanist, sir. I came here after this plant to-day—having seen it yesterday, but I had not then my tools with me. I don't know anything about the pocket-book and bank-notes."

So that was another mistake, for the botanist turned out of his pockets a heap of letters directed to him, and a big book he had been reading in the train, a treatise on botany, to prove who he was. And, as if to leave no loophole of doubt, one stepped up who knew him and assured the Squire there was not a more learned man in his line, no, nor one more respected, in the three kingdoms. The Squire shook him by the hand in apologizing, and told him we had some valuable ferns near Dyke Manor, if he would come and see them.

Like Patience on a monument, when we got back, sat the lady, waiting to see the prisoner brought in. Her face would have made a picture too, when she discovered the upshot, and the hot Squire and the gold spectacles walking side by side in friendly talk.

"I think still he must have got it," she said sharply.

"No, madam," answered the Squire. "Whoever may have taken it, it was not he."

"Then there's only one man, and that is he whom you have let go in the train," she decisively returned. "I thought his

8*

fidgety movements were not put on for nothing. He had secured the pocket-book somewhere, and then made a show of offering to be searched. Ah, ha!"

And the Squire veered round again at this suggestion, and began to suspect he had been doubly cheated. First, out of his money, next out of his suspicions. One only thing in the whole bother seemed clear; and that was, that the notes and case had gone for good. As, in point of fact they had.

We were on the chain-pier at Brighton, Tod and I. It was about eight or nine months after. I had put my arms on the high rails at the end, looking at a pleasure-party sailing by. Tod, next to me, was bewailing his ill-fortune in not possessing a yacht and opportunities of cruising in it.

"I tell you No. I don't want to be made sea sick."

The words came from somebody behind us. It seemed almost as though they were spoken in reference to Tod's wish for a yacht to cruise in. But it was not *that* that made me turn sharply round; it was the sound of the voice, for I thought I recognized it.

Yes: there she was. The lady who had been with us in the carriage that day. The dog was not with her now, but her hair was more amazing than ever, enough of it hanging down behind to make a horse's tail. She did not see me. As I turned, she turned, and began to walk slowly back, arm-in-arm with a gentleman. And to see him—that is, to see them together—made me open my eyes. For it was the lord who had travelled with us.

"Look Tod!" I said, and told him in a word who they were.

"What the deuce do they know of each other?" cried Tod with a frown, for he felt angry every time the thing was referred to. Not for the loss of the money, but for what he called the stupidity of us all; saying always had *he* been there, he should have detected the thief at once.

I sauntered after them: why I wanted to learn which of the

lords he was, I can't tell, for lords are numerous enough, but I had had a curiosity upon the point ever since. They encountered some people and were standing to speak; three ladies, and a fellow in a black glazed hat with a piece of green ribbon round it.

"I was trying to induce my wife to take a sail," the lord was saying, "but she won't. She is not a very good sailor unless the sea has its calmest behaviour on."

"Will you go to-morrow, Mrs. Mowbray?" asked the man in the glazed hat, who spoke and looked like a gentleman. "I will promise you perfect calmness; I am weather-wise, and can assure you this little wind will have gone down before night, leaving us without a breath of air."

"I will go: on condition that your assurance shall prove correct."

"All right. You of course will come, Mowbray?"

The lord nodded. "Very happy."

"When do you leave Brighton, Mr. Mowbray?" asked one of the ladies.

"I don't know exactly. Not for some days."

"A muff as usual, Johnny," whispered Tod. "That man is no lord: he is a Mr. Mowbray."

"But, Tod, he *is* the lord. It is the one that travelled with us; there's no mistake about that. Lords can't put off their titles as parsons can: do you suppose his servant would have called him ' my lord,' if he had not been one?"

"At least there is no mistake that these people are calling him Mr. Mowbray now."

That was true. It was equally true that they were calling her Mrs. Mowbray. My ears had been as quick as Tod's, and I don't deny I was puzzled. They turned to come up the pier again with the people, and the lady saw me standing there with Tod. Saw me looking at her, too, and I think she did not relish it, for she took a step backward like one startled, and then stared me full in the face, as if asking who I might be. I lifted my hat

There was no response. In another moment she and her husband were walking quickly down the pier together, and the other party went on to the top quietly. A man in a tweed suit and brown hat drawn low on his eyes, was standing back with his arms folded, looking after the two with a queer smile upon his face. Tod marked it and spoke.

"Do you happen to know that gentleman?"

"Yes, I do," was the answer.

"Is he a peer?"

"On occasion."

"On occasion!" repeated Tod. "I have a reason for asking," he added; "do not think me impertinent."

"Been swindled out of anything?" asked the man, coolly.

"My father was, some months ago. He lost a pocket-book with fifty pounds in it in a railway carriage. Those people were both in it, but not then acquainted with each other."

"Oh, weren't they!" said the man.

"No, they were not," I put in, "for I was there. He was a lord then."

"Ah," said the man, "and had a servant in livery no doubt, who came up my-lording him without occasion every other minute. He is a member of the swell-mob; one of the cleverest of the *gentleman* fraternity of them, and the one who acts as servant is another."

"And the lady?" I asked.

"She is a third. They have been working in concert for two or three years now; and will give us trouble yet before their career is stopped. But for being cautiously clever, we should have had them long ago. And so they did not know each other in the train! I daresay not!"

The man spoke with quiet authority. He was a detective officer come down from London to Brighton that morning; whether for a private sanitary trip, or on business, he did not say. I related to him what had passed in the train.

"Ay," said he, after listening. "They contrived to put the lamp out before starting. The lady took the pocket-book during the commotion she caused the dog to make, and the lord received it from her hand when he gave her back the dog. Cleverly done! He had it about him, young sir, when he got out at the next station. *She* waited to be searched, and to throw the scent off. Very ingenious: but they'll be a little too much some fine day."

"Can't you take them up?" demanded Tod.

"No."

"I will accuse them of it," he haughtily said. "If I meet them again on this pier——"

"Which you won't do to-day," interrupted the man.

"I heard them say they were not going for some days."

"Ah, but they have seen you now. And I think—I'm not quite sure—that he saw me. They'll be off by the next train."

"Who are *they?*" asked Tod, pointing to the top of the pier.

"Unsuspicious people whose acquaintance they have casually made here. Yes, an hour or two will see Brighton quit of the pair."

And it was so. A train was starting within an hour, and Tod and I galloped to the station. There they were: in a first class carriage: not apparently knowing each other, I verily believe, for he sat at one door and she at the other, passengers dividing them.

"Lambs between two wolves," remarked Tod. "I have a great mind to warn the people of the sort of company they are in. Would it be actionable, Johnny?"

The train moved off as he was speaking. And may I never write another word, if I did not catch sight of the servant-man and his cockade in the carriage next behind them!

IX.

DICK MITCHEL.

DID not relate this story by my own wish. To my mind there's nothing much in it to relate. At the time it was written the newspapers were squabbling about farmers' boys and field labour and political economy. "And," says a gentleman to me, "as you were at the top and tail of the thing when it happened, and are well up in the subject generally, Johnny Ludlow, you may as well make a paper of it." That was no other than the surgeon—Duffham.

About two miles from Dyke Manor across the fields, but in the opposite direction to that of the Court where the Sterlings lived, Elm Farm was situated. Mr. Jacobson lived in it, as his father had lived before him. The property was not their own; they rented it: it was fine land, and Jacobson had the reputation of being the best farmer for miles around. Being a wealthy man, he had no need to spare money on house or land, and did not spare it. He and the Squire were about the same age, and had been cronies all their lives.

Not to go into extraneous matter, I may as well say at once that one of the labourers on Jacobson's farm was a man named John Mitchel. He lived in a cottage not far from us —a poor place of two rooms and a wash-house; but they call it back'us there—and had to walk nearly two miles to his work of a morning. Mitchel was a steady man of thirty-five, with a round head and not any great amount of brains inside it. Not but what he had as much brains as many labourers have, and quite enough for the kind of work his life was passed in. There were six children ; the eldest, Dick, ten years old ; and most of them had straw-coloured hair, the pattern of their father's.

Just before the turn of harvest one hot summer, John Mitchel presented himself at Mr. Jacobson's house in a clean smock frock, and asked a favour. It was, that his boy, Dick, should be taken on as ploughboy. Old Jacobson objected ; saying the boy was too young and little. Little he might be, Mitchel answered, but not too young—warn't he ten? The lad had been about the farm for some time as scarecrow : that is, employed to keep the birds away : and had a shilling a week for it. Old Jacobson stood to what he said, however, and little Dick did not get his promotion.

But old Jacobson got no peace. Every opportunity Mitchel could get, or dare to use, he began again, praying that Dick might be tried. The boy was "cute," he said, strong enough also, though little ; and if the master liked to pay him only fourpence a day, they'd be grateful for it; 'twould be a help, and was wanted badly. All of no use : old Jacobson still said No.

One afternoon during this time, we started to go to the Jacobsons' after a one o'clock dinner,—I and Mrs. Todhetley. She was fond of going over to an early tea there, but not by herself, for part of the near way across the fields was lonely. Considering that she had been used to the country, she was a regular coward as to lonely walks, expecting to see a tramp or a robber at every corner. In passing the row of cottages in Duck Lane, for that's the road we took, we saw Hannah Mitchel leaning over the footboard of her door to look after her children, who were playing near the pond in the sunshine with a lot more ; quite a heap of little reptiles, all badly clad and as dirty as pigs. Other labourers' dwellings stood within hail, and the children seemed to spring up in the place thicker than wheat ; Mrs. Mitchel's was quite a small family, reckoning by comparison, but how the six got clothed and fed was a mystery, out of Mitchel's wages of ten shillings a week. It was thought good pay. Old Jacobson was liberal, as farmers go. He paid the best wages; gave all his labourers a stunning big portion of home-fed fresh pork at Christmas, with fuel to cook it: and his wife was good to the women when they fell sick.

Mrs. Todhetley stopped to speak. "Is it you, Hannah Mitchel? Are you pretty well?"

Hannah Mitchel stood upright and dropped a curtséy. She had a covered-up bundle in her arms, which proved to be the baby, then not much above a fortnight old.

"Dear me! it's very early for it to be about," said Mrs Todhetley, touching its little red cheeks. "And for you too."

"It is, ma'am; but what's to be done?" was the answer. "When there's only a pair of hands for everything, one can't afford to lie by long."

"You seem but poorly," said Mrs. Todhetley, looking at her. She was a thin, dark-haired woman, with a sensible face. Before she married Mitchel, she had lived under-nurse in a gentleman's family, where she picked up some idea of good manners.

"I be feeling a bit stronger, thank you," said the woman. "Strength don't come back to one in a day, ma'am."

The Mitchel children were sidling up, attracted by the sight of the lady. Four young grubs in tattered garments.

"I can't keep 'em decent," said the mother, with a sigh of apology. "I've not got no soap nor no clothes to do it with. They come on so fast, and make such a many, one after another, that it's getting a hard pull to live anyhow."

Looking at the children; remembering that, with the father and mother, there were eight months to feed, and that the man's wages were the ten shillings weekly all the year round (but there were seasons when he did over-work and earned more), Mrs. Todhetley might well give her assenting answer with an emphatic nod.

"We was hoping to get on a bit better," resumed the wife; "but Mitchel he says the master don't seem to like to listen. A'most a three weeks it be now since Mitchel first asked it him."

"In what way better?"

" By a putting little Dick to the plough, ma am.   He gets a shilling a week now, he'd got two then, perhaps three, and 'twould be such a help to us.   Some o' the farmers gives fourpence half-penny a day to a ploughboy, some as much as sixpence.   The master he bain't one of the near ones ; but Dick be little of his age, he don't grow fast, and Mitchel telled the master he'd take fourpence a day and be thankful for't."

Thoughts were crowding into Mrs. Todhetley's mind—as she mentioned afterwards.   A child of ten ought to be learning and playing ; not working from twelve to fourteen hours a day.

" It would be a hard life for him."

" True, ma'am, at first ; but he'd get used to it.   I could have wished the summer was coming on instead o' the winter —'twould be easier for him to begin upon.   Winter mornings be so dark and cold."

" Why not let him wait until the next winter's over ? "

The very suggestion brought tears into Hannah Mitchel's eyes.   " You'd never say it ma'am, if you knew how bad his wages is wanted and the help they'd be.   The older children grows, the more they wants to eat ; and we've got six of 'em now.   What would you, ma'am ?—they don't bring food into the world with 'em ; they must help to earn it for themselves as quick as anybody can be got to let 'em earn it.   Sometimes I wonder why God should send such large families to us poor people."

Mrs. Todhetley was turning to go on her way, when the woman in a timid voice said, " Might she make bold to ask, if she or Squire Todhetley would say a good word to Mr. Jacobson about the boy ; that it would be just a merciful kindness."

" We should not like to interfere," replied Mrs. Todhetley. " In any case I could not do it with a good heart : I think it would be so hard upon the poor little boy."

" Starving's harder, ma'am."

The tears came running down her cheek with the answer ; and they won over Mrs. Todhetley.

Crossing the high, crooked, awkward stile—over which, in coming the other way, if people were not careful they generally pitched over with their noses into Duck Lane mud —we found ourselves in what was called the square paddock— a huge piece of land, ploughed last year. The wheat had been carried from it only this afternoon, and the gleaners in their cotton bonnets were coming in. On, from thence, across other fields and stiles; we went a little out of our way to call at Glebe Cottage—a small white house that lay back amidst the fields —and inquire after old Mrs. Parry, who had just had a stroke.

Who should be at Elm Farm, when we got in, but the surgeon, Duffham: come on there from paying his daily visit to Mrs. Parry. He and old Jacobson were in the green-house, looking at the grapes: a famous crop they had that year; not ripe yet. Mrs. Jacobson sat at the open window of the long parlour, making a new jelly-bag. She was a pleasant-faced old lady, with small flat silver curls and a net cap.

Of course they got talking about little Dick Mitchel. Duffham knew the boy; seeing that when a doctor was wanted at the Mitchels', it was he that attended. Mrs. Todhetley told exactly what had passed: and old Jacobson—a tall, portly man. with a healthy colour—grew nearly purple in the face, disputing.

Dick Mitchel would be of as good as no use for the team, he said, and the carters put shamefully upon those young ones. In another year the boy would be stronger and bigger. Perhaps he would take him then.

"For my part, I cannot think how the mothers can like their poor boys to go out so young," cried the old lady, looking up from her flannel bag. "A ploughboy's life is very hard in winter."

"Hannah Mitchel says it has to be one of two things—early work or starving," said Mrs. Todhetley. "And that's pretty true."

"Labourers' boys are born to it, ma'am, and so it comes easy to 'em: as skinning does to eels," cried Duffham quaintly.

"Poor things, yes. But it is very hard upon the children. The worst is, all the labourers seem to have no end of them. Hannah Mitchel has just said she sometimes wonders why God should send so many to poor people."

This was an unfortunate remark. To hear the two gentlemen laugh, you'd have thought they were at a Christmas pantomime. Old Jacobson brought himself up in a kind of passion.

What business, in the name of all that was imprudent, had these poor people to have their troops of children? he asked. They knew quite well they could not feed them; that the young ones would be three parts starved in their earlier years, and in their later ones come to the parish and be a burden on the community. Look at this same man, Mitchel. His grandfather, a poor miserable labourer, had a troop of children; Mitchel's father had a troop, twelve; *he*, Mitchel, had six, and seemed to be going on fair to have six more. There was no reason in it. Why couldn't they be content with a moderate number, three or four, that might get a chance of being found room for in the world? It was not much less than a crime for these men next door to paupers themselves, to launch their tens and their dozens of boys and girls into life, and then turn round and say, Why does God send them? Nice kind of logic that was!

And so he kept on, for a good half hour, Duffham helping him. *He* brought up the French peasantry: saying our folks ought to take a lesson from them. You don't see whole flocks of children over there, cried Duffham. One, or two, or at most three, would be found to comprise the number of a family. And why? Because the French were a prudent race. They knew there was no provision for superfluous children; no house-room at home, or food, or clothing; and no parish pay to fall back upon: they knew that however many children they had they must provide for them: they didn't set up, themselves, a regiment of little famishing mouths, and then charge it on heaven; they were not so reckless and wicked. Yes, he must repeat it, wicked; and the two ladies listening would endorse the word if they knew half the deprivation and the sufferings these poor small mortals were born to; he saw enough of it, having to be often amidst them.

"Why don't you tell the parents this, doctor?"

Tell them! returned Duffham. He *had* told them; told them till his tongue was tired.

Any way, the little things were grievously to be pitied, was what the two ladies made answer.

"I have often wished it was not a sin to drown the super fluous little mites as we do kittens," wound up Duff.

One of the ladies dropped the jelly-bag, the other shrieked out, "Oh!"

"For their sakes," he added. "It's true, upon my word and honour. Of all wrongs the world sees, never was there a worse wrong than the one inflicted on these inoffensive children by the parents, in bringing them into it. God help the little wretches! man can't do much."

And so they talked on. The upshot was, that old Jacobson stood to his word, and declined to make Dick Mitchel a ploughboy yet awhile.

We had tea at four o'clock—at which fashionable people may laugh; considering that it was the real tea, not the sham one lately come into custom. Mrs. Todhetley wanted to get home by daylight, and the summer evenings were shortening. Never was brown bread-and-butter so sweet as the Jacobsons': we used to say it every time we went; and the home-baked rusks were better than Shrewsbury cake. They made Mrs. Todhetley take two or three in her bag for Hugh and Lena.

Old Duff went with us across the first field, turning off there to take the short cut to his home. It was a warm, still, lovely evening, the yellow moon rising. The gleaners were busy in the square paddock: Mrs. Todhetley spoke to some as we passed. At the other end, near the crooked stile, two urchins stood fighting, the bigger one trying to take a small armful of wheat from the other. I went to the rescue, and the marauder made off as fast as his small bare feet would carry him.

"He haven't gleaned, hisself, and wants to take mine," said the little one, casting up his big grey eyes to us in appeal through the tears. He was a delicate-looking pale-faced boy of nine, or so, with light hair.

"Very naughty of him," said Mrs. Todhetley. "What's your name?"

"It's Dick, lady."

"Dick—what?"

"Dick Mitchel."

"Dear me—I thought I had seen the face," said Mrs. Todhetley to me. "But there are so many boys about here, Johnny; and they all look pretty much alike. How old are you, Dick?"

"I'm over ten," answered Dick, with an emphasis on the over. Children catch up ideas, and no doubt he was as eager as the parents coul! be to impress on the world his fitness, in years, to be a ploughboy.

"How is it that you have been gleaning, Dick?"

"Mother couldn't, 'cause o' the babby. They give me leave to come on since four o'clock: and I've got all this."

Dick looked at the stile and then at his bundle of wheat, so I took it while he got over. As we went on down the lane, Mrs. Todhetley inquired whether he wanted to be a ploughboy. Oh yes! he answered, his face lighting up, as if the situation offered some glorious prospect. It 'ud be two shilling a week; happen more; and mother said as he and Totty and Sam and the t'others 'ud get treacle to their bread on Sundays then. Apparently Mrs. Mitchel knew how to diplomatize.

"I'll give him one of the rusks, I think, Johnny," whispered Mrs. Todhetley.

But while she was getting it from the bag, he ran in with his wheat. She called to him to come back, and gave him one. His mother had taken the wheat from him; she looked out at the door with it in her hands. Seeing her, Mrs. Todhetley went up, and said Mr. Jacobson would not at present do anything. The next minute Mitchel appeared pulling at his straw hair.

"It is hard lines," he said, humbly, "when the lad's of a' age to be a earning, and the master can't be got to take him on. And me to ha' worked on the same farm, man and boy; and father afore me."

"Mr. Jacobson thinks the boy would not be strong enough for the work."

"Not strong enough, and him rising eleven!" exclaimed Mitchel, as if the words were some dreadful aspersion on Dick. "How can he be strong if he gets no work to make him strong, ma'am? Strength comes with the working—and nobody don't oughtn't to know that better nor the master. Anyhow, if he *don't* take him, it'll be cruel hard lines for us."

Dick was outside, dividing the rusk with a small girl and boy, all three seated in the lane, and looking as happy over the rusk as if they had been children in a fairy tale. " It's Totty," said he, pausing in the work of division to speak, "and that 'un's Sam." Mrs. Todhetley could not resist the temptation of finding two more rusks, which made one apiece.

" He is a good-natured little fellow, Johnny," she remarked as we went along. "Intelligent, too: in that he takes after his mother."

" Would it be wrong to let him go on the farm as plough-boy?"

" Johnny, I don't know. I'd rather not give an opinion," she added, looking right before her into the moon, as if seeking for one there. "Of course he is not old enough or big enough, practically speaking; but on the other hand, where there are so many mouths to feed, it seems hard not to let him earn money if he can earn it. The root of the evil lies in there being so many mouths—as was said at Mr. Jacobson's this afternoon."

It was winter before I heard anything more of the matter. Tod and I got home for Christmas. One day in January, when the skies were lowering, and the air cold with a raw coldness, but not frosty, I was crossing a field on old Jacobson's land then being ploughed. The three brown horses at the work were as fine as ye'd wish to see.

"You'll catch it smart on that there skull o' yourn, if ye doan't keep their yeads straight, ye young divil."

The salutation was from the man at the tail of the plough to the boy at the head of the first horse. Looking round, I saw little Mitchel. The horses stopped, and I went up to him. Hall, the ploughman, took the opportunity to beat his arms. I daresay they were cold enough.

"So your ambition is attained, is it Dick? Are you satisfied?"

Dick seemed not to understand. He was taller, but the face looked pinched, and there was never a smile on it.

"Do you like being a ploughboy?"

"It's hard and cold. Hard always; frightful cold of a morning."

"How's Totty?"

The face lighted up just a little. Totty weren't any better, but she didn't die; Jimmy did. Which was Jimmy?—Oh, Jimmy was after Nanny, next to the babby.

"What did Jimmy die of?"

Whooping-cough. They'd all been bad but him—Dick. Mother said he'd had it when he was no older nor the babby.

Whether the whooping-cough had caused an undue absorption of Mitchel's means, certain it was, Dick looked famished. His cheeks were thin, his hands blue.

"Have you been ill, Dick?"

No, he had not been ill. 'Twas Jimmy and the t'others.

"He's the incapablest little villain I ever had put me to do with," struck in the ploughman, stilling his arms to speak. "More lazy nor a fattening pig."

"Are you lazy, Dick?"

I think an eager disclaimer was coming out, but the boy

remembered in time who was present—his master, the plough-man.

"Not lazy wilful," he said, bursting into tears. "I does my best: mother tells me to."

"Take that, you young sniveller," said Hall, dealing him a good sound slap on the left cheek. "And now go on: ye know ye've got this lot to go through to-day."

He caught hold of the plough, and Dick stretched up his poor trembling hands to the first horse to guide him. I am sure the boy *was* trying to do his best; but he looked weak and famished and ill.

"Why did you strike him, Hall? He did nothing to deserve it."

"He don't deserve nothing else," was Hall's answer. "Let him alone, and the furrows 'ud be as crooked as a dog's leg. You dun' know what these young 'uns be for work, sir.—Keep 'em in the line, you fool!"

Looking back as I went down the field, I watched the plough going slowly up it, Dick seeming to have his hands full with the well-fed horses.

"Yes, I heard the lad was taken on, Johnny," Mrs. Todhetley said when I told her that evening. "Mitchel prevailed with his master at last. Mr. Jacobson is good-hearted, and knew the Mitchels were in sore need of the extra money the boy would earn. Sickness makes a difference to the poor as well as to the rich."

I saw Dick Mitchel three or four times during that January month. The Jacobsons had two nephews staying with them from Oxfordshire, and it caused us to go over often. The boy seemed a weak little mite for the place; but of course, having undertaken the work, he had to do it. He was no worse off than others. To be at the farm before six o'clock, he had to leave home at half-past five, taking his breakfast with him, which was mostly dry bread. As to the boy's work, it varied— as those acquainted with the executive of a busy farm can tell. Besides the ploughing, he had to pump, and carry water and

straw, and help with the horses, and go errands to the blacksmith's and elsewhere, and so on. Carters and ploughmen do
not spare their helping boys; and on a large farm like this
they are the immediate rulers, not the master himself. Had
Dick been under Mr. Jacobson's personal eye, perhaps it
might have been lightened a 'ittle, for he was a humane man.
There were three things that made it seem particularly hard for
Dick Mitchel, and those three were under nobody's control;
his natural weakliness, his living so far off the farm, and its being
winter weather. In summer the work is nothing like as hard
for the boys; and it was a great pity that Dick had not first
entered on his duties in that season to get inured to them
against the winter. Mr. Jacobson gave him the best wages
—three shillings a week. Looking at the addition it must
have seemed to Mitchel's ten, it was little wonder he had not
ceased to petition old Jacobson.

The Jacobsons were kind to the boy—as I can testify. One
cold day when I was over there with the nephews, shooting
birds, we went into the best kitchen at twelve o'clock for some
pea-soup. They were going to carry the basins into the parlour,
but we said we'd rather eat it there by the blazing big fire.
Mrs. Jacobson came in. I can see her now, with a soft white
woollen kerchief thrown over her shoulders to keep the cold off,
and her net cap above her silver curls. We were getting our
second basinfuls.

"Do have some, aunt," said Fred. "It's the best you ever
tasted."

"No, thank you, Fred. I don't care to spoil my dinner."

"It won't spoil ours."

She laughed a little, and stood looking from the window
into the fold-yard, saying presently that she feared the frost
was going to set in now in earnest, which would not be pleasant for their journey.—For this was the last day of the nephews' stay, and she was going home with them for a week.
There had been no very sharp cold all the winter; which was
a shame because of the skating; 'if the ponds got a thin

coating of ice on them one day, it would be all melted the
next.

"Bless me! there's that poor child sitting out in the cold!
What is he eating?—his dinner?"

Her words made us look from the window. Dick Mitchel
had stuck himself down by the far-off pig-sty, and seemed to
be eating something that he held in his hands. He was very
white—as might be seen even from where we stood.

"Mary," said she to one of the servants, "go and call that
boy in."

Little Mitchel came in; pinched and white and blue. His
clothes were thin, not half warm enough for the weather; an
old red woollen comforter was twisted round his neck. He
took off his battered drab hat, and put his bread into it.

"Is that your dinner?" asked Mrs. Jacobson.

"Yes 'm," said Dick, pulling the forelock of his light hair.

"But why did you not go home to-day?"

"Mother said there was nothing but bread for dinner to-day,
and she give it me to bring away with my breakfast."

"Well, why did you sit out in the cold? You might have
gone indoors somewhere to eat it."

"I were tired 'm," was all Dick answered.

To look at him, one would say the "tired" state was chronic.
He was shivering slightly all over with the cold; his teeth
chattered. Mrs. Jacobson took his hand, and put him to sit
on a low wooden stool close to the fire, and gave him a basin
of the pea-soup.

"Let him have more if he can eat it," she said to Mary when
she went away. So the boy for once got well warmed and fed.

Now, it may be thought that Mrs. Jacobson, being a kind
old lady, might have told him to come in for some soup every
cold day. And perhaps her will was good to do it. But it
would never have answered. There were boys on the farm
besides Dick, and no favour could be shown to one more than
to another. No, nor to the boys more than to the men. Nor
to the men on this farm more than to the men on that. Old

Jacobson would have had his brother farmers pulling at his ears. Those of you acquainted with the subject will know all this.

And there's another thing I had better say. In telling of Dick Mitchel, it will naturally sound like an exceptional or isolated case, because those who read have their attention directed to this one and not to others. But, in actual fact, Dick's was only one of a great many ; the Jacobsons had employed ploughboys and other boys always, lots of them ; some strong and some weak, just as the boys might happen to be. For a young boy to be out with the plough in the cold winter weather, seems to a farmer and a farmer's men nothing ; it lies in the common course of events. He has to get through as he best can ; he must work to eat ; and as a compensating balance there comes the genial warmth and the easy work of summer. Dick Mitchel was but one of the race ; the carter and ploughman, his masters, had begun life exactly as he did, had gone through the same ordeal, the hardships of a long winter's day and the frost and snow. Dick Mitchel was as capable of his duties as many another had been. Dick's father had been little and weakly in his boyhood, but he got over that and grew as strong as the rest of them. Dick might have got over it, too, but for some extraordinary weather that came in.

Mrs. Jacobson had been in Oxfordshire a week when old Jacobson started to fetch her home, intending to stay there two or three days. The weather since she left had been going on in the same stupid way ; a thin coating of snow to be seen one day, the green of the fields the next. But on the morning after old Jacobson started, the frost set in with a vengeance, and we got our skates out. Another day came in, and the Squire declared he had never felt anything to equal the cold. We had not had it as sharp for years: and then, you see, he was too fat to skate. The best skating was on a pond on old Jacobson's land, which they called the lake from its size.

It was on this second day that I came across Dick Mitchel.

Hastening home from the lake-pond after dark—for we had skated till we couldn't see and then kept on by moonlight—the skates in my hand and all aglow with heat, who should be sitting by the bank on this side the crooked stile instead of getting over it, but little Mitchel. But for the moon shining right on his face, I might have passed without seeing him.

"You are taking it airily, young Dick. Got the gout?"

Dick just lifted his head and stared a little; but didn't speak.

"Come! Why don't you go home?"

"I'm tired," murmured Dick. "I'm cold."

"Get up. I'll help you over the stile."

He did as he was bid at once. We had got well on down the lane, and I had my hand on his shoulder to steady him, for his legs seemed to slip about like Punch's in the show, when he turned suddenly back again.

"The harness."

"The what?" I said.

Something seemed the matter with the boy: it was just as if he had partly lost the power of ready speech, or had been struck stupid. I made out at last that he had left some harness on the ground, which he was ordered to take to the blacksmith's.

"I'll get over for it, Dick. You stop where you are."

It was lying where he had been sitting; a short strap with a torn buckle. Dick took it and we went on again.

"Were you asleep, just now, Dick?"

"No, sir. It were the moon."

"What was the moon?"

"I were looking into it. Mother says God's all above there: I thought happen I might see Him."

A long explanation for Dick to-night. The recovery of the strap seemed to have brightened up his intellect.

"You'll never see Him in this world, Dick. He sees you always."

"And that's what mother says. He sees I can't do more nor my arms'll let me. I'd not like Him to think I can."

"All right, Dick. You only do your best always: He won't fail to see it."

I had hardly said the last words when down went Dick without warning, face foremost. Picking him up, I took a look into his eyes by the moon's light.

"What did you do that for, Dick?"

"I don't know."

"Is it your legs?"

"Yes, it's my legs. I didn't mean it. I didn't mean it when I fell under the horses to-day, but Hall he beated of me and said I did."

After that I did not loose him; or I'm sure he would have gone down again. Arrived at his cottage, he was for passing it.

"Don't you know your own door, Dick Mitchel?"

"It's the strap," he said. "I ha' got to take it to Cawson's."

"Oh, I'll step round with that. Let's see what there is to do."

He seemed unwilling, saying he must take it back to Hall in the morning. Very well, I said, so he could. We went in at his door; and at first I thought I must have got into a black fog. The room was a narrow, poking place; but I couldn't see to the other end of it. Two children were coughing, one choking, one crying. Mrs. Mitchel's face, ornamented with blacks, gradually loomed out to view through the atmosphere.

"It be the chimbley, sir. I hope you'll please to excuse it. It don't smoke as bad as this except when the weather's cold beyond common."

"It's to be hoped it doesn't. I should call it rather miserable if it did."

"Yes, sir. Mitchel, he says he thinks the chimbley must have frozed."

"Look here, Mrs. Mitchel, I've brought Dick home; I found him sitting in the cold on the other side of the stile yonder, and my belief is, he thought he could not get over it. He is about as weak as a young rat."

"It's the frost, sir," she said. "The boys all feel it that has to be out and about. It'll soon be gone, Dick. This here biting cold don't never last long."

Dick was standing against her, bending his face on her old stuff gown. She put her arm about him kindly.

"No, it can't last long, Mrs. Mitchel. Could he not be kept indoors until it gives a bit—let him have a holiday? No Wouldn't it do?"

She opened her eyes wide at this, braving the cloud of flying blacks. Such a thing as keeping a ploughboy at home for a holiday had never entered her imagination at its widest range.

"Why, Master Ludlow, sir, he'd lose his place!"

"But, suppose he were ill, and had to stay at home?"

"Then the Lord help us, if it came to that! Please, sir, his wages might be stopped. I've heard of a master paying in illness, though it's not many of 'em as would, but I've never knowed 'em pay for holidays. The biting cold will go soon, Dick," she added, looking at him; "don't be down-hearted."

"I should give him a cup of hot tea, Mrs. Mitchel, and let him go to bed. Good-night; I'm off."

I would have liked to say beer instead of tea; it would have put a bit of strength into the boy; but I might just as well have suggested wine, for all they had of either. Leaving the strap at the blacksmith's—it was but a minute or two out of my road—I told him to send it up to Mitchel's as soon as it was done.

"I daresay!" was what I got in answer.

"Look here, Cawson: the lad's ill, and his father was not in the way. If you don't choose to let your boy run up with that, or take it yourself, you shall never have another job of work from the Squire if I can prevent it."

"I'll send it, sir," said Cawson, coming to his senses. Not that he had much from us: we mostly patronized Dovey, down in Piefinch Cut.

Now, all this happened: as Duffham and others could tes-

tify if necessary; it is not put in to make up a story. But I
never thought worse of Dick than that he was done over for
the moment with the cold.

Of all days in remembrance, the next was the worst. The
cold was more intense—though that had seemed impossible;
and a fierce wind was blowing that cut you in two. It kept
us from skating—and that's saying a good deal. We got
halfway to the lake-pond, and couldn't stand it, so turned
home again. Jacobson's team was out, braving the weather:
we saw it at a distance.

"What a fool that waggoner must be to bring out the team
to-day!" cried Tod. "He can't do any good on this hard
ground. He must be doing it for bravado. It is a sign his
master's not at home."

In the afternoon, when a good hot meal had put warmth
into us, we thought we'd be off again; and this time gained
the pond. The wind was like a rough knife: I never skated
in such before: but we kept on till dusk.

Going homewards, in passing Glebe Cottage, which lay
away on the left, we caught sight of three or four people
standing before it.

"What's to do there?" asked Tod of a man, expecting to
hear that old Mrs. Parry had a second stroke.

"Sum'at's wrong wi' Jacobson's ploughboy," was the answer.
"He has just been took in there."

"Jacobson's ploughboy! why, Tod, that must be Dick
Mitchel."

"And what if it is!" returned Tod, starting off again.
"The youngster's half frozen, I daresay. Let us get home,
Johnny. What are you stopping for?"

By saying "half frozen" he meant nothing. Not a thought
of real ill was in his mind. I went across to the house; and
met Hall the ploughman coming out of it.

"Is Dick M'tchel ill, Hall?"

"He ought to be, sir; if he ain't shamming," returned
Hall, crustily. "He have fell down five times since noon,

and the last time wouldn't get up upon his feet again nohow
Being close a nigh the old lady's I carried of him in."

Hall went back to the house with me. I don't think he
much liked the boy's looks. Dick had been put to lie on the
warm brick floor before the kitchen fire, a blanket on his legs,
and his head on a cushion. Mrs. Parry was ill in bed upstairs.
The servant looked a stupid young country girl, seemingly
born without wits.

"Have you given him anything?" I asked her.

"Please sir, I've put the kettle on to bile."

"Is there any brandy in the house?"

"*Brandy!*" the girl exclaimed with wonder. No. Her
missis never took nothing stronger nor tea and water gruel.

"Hall," I said, looking at the man, "somebody must go
for Mr. Duffham. And Dick's mother might as well be
told."

Bill Leet, a strapping young fellow standing by, made off
at this, saying he'd bring them both. Hall went away to his
waiting team, and I stopped over the boy.

"What is the matter, Dick? Tell me how you feel."
Except that Dick smiled a little, he made no answer. His
eyes, gazing up into mine, looked dim. The girl had taken
away the candle, but the fire was bright. As I took one of
his hands to rub it, his fingers clasped themselves round mine.
Then he began to say something, with a stop between each
word. I had to bend down close to catch it.

"He--brought—that—there—strap."

"All right, Dick."

"Thank—ee—sir."

"Are you in any pain, Dick?"

"No."

"Or cold?"

"No."

The girl came back with a candle and some hot milk in
a tea-cup. I put a teaspoonful into Dick's mouth. But
he could not swallow it. Who should come rushing in

then but old Jones the constable, wanting to know what was up.

"Well I never!—why, that's Mitchel's Dick!" cried Jones, peering down in the candle-light. "What's took *him?*"

"Jones, if you and the girl will rub his hands, I'll go and get some brandy. We can't let him lie like this and give him nothing."

Old Jones, liking the word brandy on his own score, knelt down on his fat gouty legs with a groan, and laid hold of one of the hands, the girl taking the other. I went leaping off to Elm Farm.

And went for nothing. Mr. and Mrs. Jacobson being out, the cellar was locked up, and no brandy could be got at. The cook gave me a bottle of gooseberry wine; which she said might do as well if hotted up.

Duffham was stooping over the boy when I got back, his face long, and his cane lying on the ironing-board. Bill Leet had met him half-way, so no time was lost. He was putting something into Dick's lips with a teaspoon—perhaps brandy. But it ran the wrong way; out instead of in. Dick never stirred, and his eyes were shut. The doctor got up.

"Too late, Johnny," he whispered.

The words startled me. "Mr. Duffham! No?"

He looked into my eyes, and nodded Yes. "The exposure to-day has been too much for him. He is going fast."

And just at that moment Hannah Mitchel came in. I have often thought that the extreme poor, whose lives are but one vast hardship from the cradle to the grave, who have to struggle always, do not feel strong emotion. At any rate, they don't show much. Hannah Mitchel knelt down, and looked quietly at the white and shrunken face.

"Dicky," she said, putting his hair gently back from his brow, which had now a damp moisture on it. "What's amiss, Dicky?"

He opened his eyes at the voice and feebly lifted one hand towards her. Mrs. Mitchel glanced round at the doctor's face;

9*

and I think she read the truth there. She gathered his poor head into her arms and let it rest on her bosom. Her old black shawl was on, her bonnet fell backwards and hung from her neck by the strings.

"Oh, Dicky! Dicky!"

He lay still, looking at her. She gave one sob and choked the rest down.

"Be he dying, sir?—ain't there no hope?" she cried to Mr. Duffham, who was standing in the blaze of the fire. And the doctor just moved his head for answer.

There was a still hush in the kitchen. Her tears began to fall down her cheeks slowly and softly.

"Dicky, wouldn't you like to say 'Our Father'?"

"I—'ve—said—it,—mother."

"You've always been a good boy, Dicky."

Old Jones blew his nose; the stupid girl burst into a sob. Mr. Duffham told them to hush.

Dick's eyes were slowly closing. The breath was very faint now, and came at long intervals. Presently Mr. Duffham took him from his mother, and laid him down flat, without the cushion.

Well, he died. Poor little Dicky Mitchel died. And I think, taking the wind and the work into consideration, that he was better off.

Mr. Jacobson got back the next day. He sharply taxed the ploughman with the death, saying he ought to have seen the state the boy was in on that last bitter day, and have sent him home. But Hall declared he never thought anything ailed the boy, except that the cold was cutting him more than ordinary, just as it was cutting everybody else.

The county coroner came over to hold the inquest. The jury, after hearing what Mr. Duffham had to say, brought it in that Richard Mitchel died from exposure to the cold during the recent remarkable severity of the weather, not having sufficient stamina to resist it. Some of the local newspapers took it up, being in want of matter that dreary season. They attacked the farmers; asking the public whether labourers' children were to be held as of no more value than this, in a free and generous country like England, and why they were made to work so young by such hard and wicked task-masters as the master of Elm Farm. That put the master of Elm Farm on his mettle. He retorted by a letter of sharp good sense; finishing it with a demand to know whether the farmers were expected to club together to provide meat and puddings gratis for the flocks of children that labourers chose to gather about them. The Squire read it aloud to everybody, as the soundest letter he'd ever seen written.

"I am afraid their view is the right one—that the children are too thick on the ground, poor things," sighed Mrs. Todhetley. "Any way, Johnny, it is very hard on the young ones to have to work as poor little Dick did; late and early, wet or dry: and I am glad for his sake that God has taken him."

X.

A HUNT BY MOONLIGHT.

THIS is another tale of our school life. It is not much in itself, you may say, but it was to lead to events that lasted. Curious enough it is, to sit down and trace out the beginning of things: when we *can* trace it; but it is often too remote for us.

Mrs. Frost died, and the summer holidays were prolonged in 'consequence. September was not far off when we met again, and gigs and carriages went bowling up with us and our boxes.

Sanker was in the large class room when we got in. He looked up for a minute, and turned his head away. Tod and I went up to him. He did shake hands, and it was as much as you could say. I don't think he was the sort of fellow to bear malice; but it took time to bring him round if once offended.

Sanker had gone home with us to Dyke Manor when the holidays began. He belonged to a family in Wales (very poor they were now), and was a distant cousin of Mrs. Todhetley's. Before he had been with us long, a matter occurred that put him out, and he betook himself away from the Manor there and then. But I do not intend to go into that history now.

Things had been queer at school towards the close of the past term. Petty pilferings took place: articles and money alike disappeared. A thief was among us, and no mistake but we did not know where to look for him. It was to be hoped that the same thing would not occur again.

"My father and Mrs. Todhetley are in the drawing-room," said Tod. "They are asking to see you."

Sanker hesitated; but he went at last. The interview softened things a little, for he was civil to us when he came back again.

"What's that about the plants?" he asked of me.

I told him what. They had been destroyed in some unaccountable manner. "Whether it was done intentionally, or whether the moving them into the hall and back again did it, is not positively decided; I don't suppose it ever will be. You ought to have come over to that ball, Sanker, after all of us writing to press it."

"Well," he said, coldly, "I don't care for balls. Monk was suspected, was he not?"

"Yes. Some of us suspect him still. He was savage at being accused of——but never mind that"—and I pulled myself up in sudden recollection. "Monk has left, and we have engaged another gardener. Jenkins is not good for much."

"Hallo! What, has *he* come back?"

Ned Sanker was looking at the door as he spoke. Two of them were coming in, who must have arrived at the same time—Vale and Lacketer. They were new ones, so to say, both having entered only the past Easter. Vale was a tall, quiet fellow, with a fair, good-looking face and mild blue eyes; his friends lived at Vale Farm, about two miles off. Lacketer had sleek black hair, and a sharp nose; he had only an aunt, and was from Oxfordshire. I didn't like him. He had a way of cringing to those of us who were born to position in the world; but any poor friendless chap, who had nothing but himself and his work to get on by, he put upon shamefully. As for him, we couldn't find out that he'd ever had any relations at all, except the aunt.

I looked at Sanker, to see which he spoke of; his eyes were

fixed on Vale with a stare. Vale had not been going to leave, that the school knew of.

"Why are you surprised that he has come back, Sanker?"

"Because I—didn't suppose he *would*," said Sanker, with a pause where I have put it, and an uncommonly strong emphasis on the "would."

It was just as though he had known something about Vale. Flashing across my memory came the mysterious avowal Sanker had made at our house about the discovery of the thief at school; and I now connected the one with the other. They call me a muff, I know, but I cannot help my thoughts.

"Sanker! was *he* the thief?"

"Hold your tongue, Ludlow," returned Sanker, in a fright. "I told you I'd give him a chance again, didn't I? But I never thought he would come back to take it."

"I would have believed it of any fellow rather than of Vale."

Sanker turned his face sharp, and looked at me. "Oh, would you?" said he, after a pause. "Well then, you'd *better* believe it of any other. Mind you do. It will be the safer line, Johnny Ludlow."

He walked away right into a group of them, as if afraid of my saying more. I turned out at the door leading to the playground, and came upon Tod in the porch.

"What was that you and Sanker were saying about Vale, Johnny?"

I was aware that I ought not to tell him; I knew I ought not: but I *did*. Tod read me always as one reads a book, and I had never attempted to keep from him any earthly thing.

"Sanker says it was Vale. About the things, lost last half. He told me, you know, that he had discovered who it was that took them."

"What, he the thief! Vale?"

"Hush, Tod. Give him another chance; as Sanker says."

Tod rushed out of the porch with a bound. He had heard

a movement on the other side of the trellis-work, but was only in time to catch a glimpse of the tassel of a cap disappearing round the corner.

We went in for noise at Worcester House just as much as they do at other schools; but not this afternoon. Mrs. Frost had been a favourite, and Sanker told us about her funeral. Things seemed to wear a mournful look. The servants were in black, the doctor was in jet black, even to his gaiters. He wore the old style of dress always, knee breeches and buckles: but I have mentioned this before. We used to call him old Frost; this afternoon we said "the Doctor."

"You can't think what it was like while the house was shut up," said Sanker. "Coal-pits are jolly to it. I never saw the Doctor until the funeral. Being the only fellow at school, was, I suppose, the reason they asked me to go to it. He cried so over the grave."

"Fancy old Frost crying!" interrupted Lacketer.

"I cried too," avowed Sanker, in a short sharp tone, as if he disappoved of the remark; and it silenced Lacketer. "She had been ailing a long while, as we all knew, but she only grew very ill at the last, she told me."

"When did you see her?"

"Two days before she died. Hall came to me, saying I was to go up. It was on Wednesday at sunset. The hot red sun was shining right into the room, and she sat back from it on the sofa in a white gown. It was very hot these holidays, and she felt at times fit to die of it: she never bore heat well."

To hear Sanker tell this was nearly as good as a play. A solemn play I mean. None of us made the least noise as we stood round him: it seemed as if we could see Mrs. Frost's room, and her nice placid face, drawn back from the rays of the red hot sun.

"She told me to reach a little Bible that was on the drawers, and sit close to her and read a chapter," continued Sanker. "It was the seventh of St. John's Revelation; where that verse is, that says there shall be no more hunger and thirst; neither shall the sun light on them nor any heat She held my hand while I read it. I had complained of the light for her, saying what a pity it was the room had no shutters. 'You see,' she said, when the chapter was read 'how soon all discomforts here will pass away. Give my dear love to the boys when they come back,' she went on 'Tell them I should like to have seen them all and said good-bye. Not good-bye for ever; be sure tell them that, Sanker: I leave them all a charge to come to me *there* in God's good time. Not one of them must fail.' And now I've told you, and it's off my mind," concluded Sanker, in a different voice.

"Did you see her again?"

"When she was in her coffin. She gave me the Bible."

Sanker took it out of his pocket. His name was written in it, "Edward Brooke Sanker, with Mary Frost's love." She had made him promise to read in it daily, if he began only with one verse. He did not tell us that then.

While we were looking at the writing, Bill Whitney came in. Some of them thought he had left at midsummer. Lacketer shook hands; he made much of Whitney, after the fashion of his mind and manners. Old Whitney was a baronet, and Bill would be Sir William some time: for his elder brother, John, whom we had so much liked, was dead. Bill was good-natured, and divided hampers from home liberally.

"*I* don't know why I am back," he said, in answer to questions; "you must ask Sir John. I shall be the better for another year or two of it, he says. Who likes grapes?"

He was beginning to undo a basket he had brought: it was filled with grapes, peaches, plums, and nectarines. Those of us who had plenty of fruit at home did not care to take much; but the others went in for it eagerly.

"Our peaches are finer than these, Whitney," cried Vale.

Lacketer gave Vale a push. "You big lout, mind your manners!" cried he. "Don't eat the peaches if you don't like 'em."

"So they were," said Vale, who never answered offensively.

"There! that's enough insolence from *you*."

Old Vale was Sir John Whitney's tenant. Of course, according to Lacketer's creed, Vale deserved putting down for only speaking to Whitney.

"He is right," said Whitney, who thought no more of being his father's son than he would of being a shopkeeper's.

"Mr. Vale's peaches were this year the finest in the county. He sent my mother some, and she said they ought to have gone up to a London fruit-show."

"I never saw such peaches as Mr. Vale's," put in Sanker, talking at Lacketer, and not kindly. "And the flavour was so good as the look. Mrs. Frost enjoyed those peaches to the last: it was nearly the only thing she took."

Vale's face shone. "We shall always be glad at home that they were so good this year, for her sake."

Altogether, Lacketer was shut up. He stood over Whitney, who was undoing a small desk he had brought. Amidst the things, that lay on the ledge inside, was a thin, yellow, old-fashioned looking coin.

"It's a guinea," said Bill Whitney. "I mean to have a hole bored in it and wear it to my watch-chain."

"I'd lock it up safely until then, Whitney," burst out Snepp, who came from Alcester. "Or it may go after the things that were lost last half-year."

Turning to glance at Sanker, I found he had left the room. Whitney was balancing the guinea on his finger.

"Fore-warned, fore-armed, Snepp," he said. "Who the thief was, I can't think; but I advise him not to begin his game again."

"Talking of warning, I should like to give one on my own score," said Tod. "By-gones may be by-gones; I don't wish to recur to them; but if I lose anything this half and can find the thief, I'll put him into the river."

"What, to drown him?"

"To duck him. I'll do it as sure as my name's Todhetley."

Vale dropped his handkerchief and stooped to pick it up again. It might have been accident; and the redness of his face might have come of stooping; but I saw Tod did not think so. Ducking is the favourite punishment in Worcester-shire for a public offender, as all the county knows. When a man misbehaves himself on the race-course at Worcester, they duck him in the Severn underneath.

"The guinea would not be of much use to anybody," said Lacketer. "You couldn't pass it."

"Oh, couldn't you, though!" answered Whitney. 'You'd better try. It's worth twenty-one shillings, and they might give a shiling or two in for the antiquity of the coin."

"Gentlemen."

We turned to see the Doctor, standing there in his deep mourning, with his subdued red face. He came in to introduce a new master.

The time went on. We missed Mrs. Frost; and Hall, the crabbed woman with the cross face, made a mean substitute. She had it all her own way now. The puddings had less jam in them, and the pies no fruit. Little Landon fell ill; and one day, after hours, when some of us went up to see him, we found him crying for Mrs Frost. He was only seven; the youngest in the school, and made a sort of plaything of; an orphan with no friends to see to him much. Illness had used to be Mrs. Frost's great point. Any of us that were laid by she'd sit with half the day, reading nice stories, and talking to us of good things, just as our mothers might do. I know mine would if she had lived However, we managed to get along in spite of Hall, hoping the Doctor would find her out and discharge her.

Matters went on quietly for some weeks. Nobody lost any-thing: and we had nearly forgotten there had been a doubt that we might lose, when it occurred. The loss was Tod's—rather curious, at first sight, that it should be, after his threat of what he would do. And Tod, as they all knew, was not one to break his word. It was only half-a-crown; but there could be no security that sovereigns would not go next. Not to speak of the disagreeable sense of feeling the thief was amidst us still, and taking to his tricks again.

Tod was writing to Evesham for some articles he wanted. Bill Whitney, knowing of this, got him to add an order for some stationery for himself: which came back in the parcel. The account, nine-and-tenpence, was made out to Tod ("Joseph Todhetley, Esquire!"), half-a-crown of it being Whitney's portion. Bill handed him the half-crown at once; and Tod, who was busy with his own things and had his hands full, asked him to put it on the mantel-piece.

The tea-bell rang, and they came away and forgot it. Only they two had been in the room. But others might have gone in afterwards. We were getting up from tea when Tod called to me to go and fetch him the half-crown.

"It is on the mantel-piece, Johnny."

I went through the passages and turned into the box-room; a place where knots of us gathered sometimes. But the mantel-piece had no half-crown on it, and I carried the news back to Tod.

"Did you take it up again, Bill!" he asked of Whitney.

"I didn't touch it after I put it down," said Whitney. "It was there when the tea-bell rang."

They said I had overlooked it, and both went to the box-room. I followed slowly; thinking they should search for themselves. Which they did; and were standing with blank faces when I got in.

"It has gone after my guinea," Whitney was saying.

"What guinea?"

"My guinea. The one you saw. That disappeared a week ago."

Bill was not a fellow to make much row over anything; but Tod—and I, too—wondered at his having taken it so easily. Tod asked him why he had not spoken.

"Because Lacketer—who was with me when I discovered the loss—asked me to be silent for a short while," said Whitney.

"He has a suspicion; and is looking out for himself."

"Lacketer has?"

"He says so. I am sure he has. He thinks he could put his finger any minute on the fellow; but it would not do to accuse him without proof; and he is waiting for it."

Tod glanced at me, and I at him, both of us thinking of Vale. "Yesterday Lacketer lost something himself," continued Whitney. "A shilling, I think it was. He went into a fine way over it, and said now he'd watch in earnest."

"Who is it he suspects?" asked Tod.

"He won't tell me; says it would not be fair."

"Well, I shall talk about my half-crown, if you and Lacketer choose to be silent over your losses," said Tod, decisively. "And I'll be as good as my word, and give the reptile a ducking if I can track him."

He went straight to the playground. It was a fine October evening, the daylight nearly gone, and the hunter's moon rising in the sky. Tod told about his half-crown, and the boys ceased their noise to listen to him. He talked himself into a passion, and said some stinging things. "He suspected who it was, and he heard that Lacketer suspected, and he fancied that another or two suspected, and one *knew;* and he thought, now that affairs were come to this pitch, when nothing, put for a minute out of hand, was safe, it might be better for them all to declare their suspicions, and hunt the animal as they'd hunt a hare."

There was a pause when Tod finished. He was about the biggest and strongest in the school; his voice was one of power, his manner ready and decisive; so that it was just as though a master spoke. Lacketer came out from amidst them, looking white. I could see that in the twilight.

"Who says I suspect? Speak for yourself, Todhetley. Don't bring up my name."

"Do you scent the fox, or don't you?" roared Tod back

again, not at all in a humour to be crossed. "If you *do*, you must speak, and not shirk it. Is the whole school to lie under doubt because of one black sheep?"

Tod's concluding words were drowned in noise; applause for him, murmurs for Lacketer. I looked round for Vale and saw him behind the rest, as if preparing to make a run for it. That said nothing : he was one of those quiet-natured fellows who liked to hold aloof from rows. When I looked back again, Sanker was standing a little forward, not far from Lacketer.

"As good speak as not, Lacketer," put in Whitney. "I don't mind telling now that guinea of mine has been taken ; and you know you lost a shilling yourself. You say you could put your finger on the fellow."

"Speak !" "Speak !" "Speak !" came the shouts from all quarters. And Lacketer turned whiter.

"There's no proof," he said. "I might have been mistaken in what I fancied. I *won't* speak."

"Then I shall say you are an accomplice," roared Tod, in his passion. "I intend to hunt the fellow to earth to-night, and I'll do it."

"I don't suspect any one in particular," said Lacketer, looking as if he were run to earth himself. "There."

Great commotion. Lacketer was hustled, but got away and disappeared. Sanker went after him. Tod had been turning on Sanker, saying why didn't *he* speak.

"Half-a-crown is half-a-crown, and I mean to get mine back again," avowed Tod. "If some of you are rich enough to lose your half-crowns, I'm not. But it isn't that. Sovereigns may go next. It isn't *that*. It is the knowing we have got a light-fingered, disreputable, sneaking rat amongst us, whose proper place would be a reformatory school, not one for honest men's sons."

"Name !" "Proofs !" "Proofs !" "Name !" It was as if a very torrent had been let loose. In the midst of the lull that ensued a voice was heard, and a name.

"*Vale*. Harry Vale."

Harding was the one to say it: a clever, first-class boy. You might have heard a pin drop in the surprise: and Harding went on after a minute.

"I beg to state that I do not accuse Vale myself. I know nothing whatever about the case. But I have reason to think Vale's name is the one that has been mentioned in connection with the losses last half."

"I know it is," cried Tod, who had only wanted the lead, not choosing to take it himself. "Now then, Vale, make your defence if you can."

I daresay you recollect how hotly you used to take up a cause when you were at school yourselves, not waiting to know whether it might be right or wrong. Mrs. Frost said to us on one of these occasions she wondered whether we should ever be as eager to take up heaven. They pounced upon Vale with an awful row. He stood with his arm round one of the trees behind, looking scared to death. I glanced back for Sanker, expecting his confirming testimony, but could not see him, and at that moment Lacketer appeared again, peeping round the trees. Whitney called to him.

"Here, Lacketer. Was it Vale you suspected?"

"As much as I did anybody else," doggedly answered Lacketer. It was taken as an affirmative. The boys believed the thief was found, and were mad against him. Vale spoke something, shaking and trembling like the leaves in the wind, but his words were drowned. He was not brave, and they looked ready to tear him to pieces.

"My half-crown, Vale," roared Tod. "Did you take it just now?"

Vale made no answer; I thought he could not. His face frightened me; the lips were blue and drawn back, the teeth chattered.

"Search his pockets."

It was a simultaneous thought, for a dozen said it. Vale was turned out, and half-a-crown found upon him; no other money. They boys yelled and groaned. Tod, with his great strength, pushed them aside, as the coin was flung to him.

"Shall I resume possession of this half-crown?" he asked of Vale, holding it before him in defiant mockery.

"If you like, I——"

Vale broke down with a gasp and a sob. His piteous aspect might have moved even Tod.

"Look here," said he, "I don't care in general to punish a coward; I regard him as an abject animal beneath me: but I cannot go from my word. Ducking is too good for you, Vale, but you shall have it. Be off to that further tree yonder; we'll give you so much grace. Let him start fair, boys, and then hound him on. It will be a fine chase."

Vale, seeming to be too confused and terror-stricken to do anything but obey, went to the tree, and then darted away *in the direction of the river*. It takes time to read all this; but scarcely a minute appeared to have passed since Tod first came out with Whitney, and spoke of the half-crown. Giving Vale the fair start, the boys sprang after him, like a pack of hounds in full cry. Tod, the swiftest runner in the school, was following, when he found himself seized by Sanker. I had stayed.

"Have you been accusing Vale? Are you going to duck him?"

"Well!" cried Tod, angry at being stopped.

"It was not Vale who took the things. Vale! He is as innocent as you are. You'll kill him, Todhetley; he cannot bear terror."

"Who says he is innocent?"

"I do. I say it on my honour. It was another fellow, whose name I've been suppressing. This is *your* work, Johnny Ludlow."

I felt a sudden rush of repentance. A conviction that Sanker spoke nothing but the truth.

"You said it was Vale, Sanker."

"I never did. *You* said it. I told you you'd better believe it was any other rather than Vale. And I meant it."

But that Sanker was not a fellow to tell a lie, I should have thought he told one then. The impression, resting on my memory, was that he acknowledged to its being Vale, if he had not exactly stated it.

"You know you told me to be quiet, Sanker: you said, give him a chance."

But I thought you were speaking of another then, not Vale. I swear it was not Vale. He is as honest as the day."

Tod, looking ready to strike me, waiting for no more explanation, was already off, shouting to the crew to turn, far more anxious now to save Vale than he had been to duck him.

How he managed to arrest them, I never knew. He did do it. But for being the fleetest runner and strongest fellow, he could never have overtaken, passed, and flung himself back upon them, with his arms stretched out, his word of explanation on his lips.

The river was more than a mile away, taking the straight course over the fields, as a bird flies, and leaping fences and ditches. Vale went panting on, *for it*. It was as if his senses were scared. Tod flew after him, the rest following on more gently. The school-bell boomed out to call us in for evening study, but none heeded it.

"Stop, Vale! Stop!" shouted Tod. "It has been a mistake. Come back and hear about it. It was not you; it was another fellow. Come back, Harry; come back!"

The more Tod shouted, the faster Vale went on. You should have seen the chase in the bright moonlight. It put us in mind of the fairy tales of Germany, where the phantom huntsman and his pack are seen coursing at midnight. Vale made for a part where the banks of the river are overshadowed by trees. Tod was only about thirty yards behind when he gained it; he saw him leap in, and heard the plunge.

But when he got close, there was no sign of Vale in the water. Had he suddenly sunk? Tod's breath and heart stood still with fear. The boys were coming up by ones and twos, and a great silence ensued. Tod stript ready to plunge in when Vale should rise.

"Here's his cap," whispered one, picking it up from the bank.

"He was a good swimmer; he must have been seized with the cramp."

"Look here; they say there are holes in the river, just above this bend. What if he has sunk into one?"

"Hold your row, all of you," cried Tod, in a hoarse whisper that betrayed his fear. "Who's to listen with that noise?"

He was listening for a sound, watching for the faintest ripple, that might give indication of Vale's rising. But none came. Tod stood there in his shirt till he shivered with cold. And the church clock struck seven, and then eight, and it was of no use waiting.

It was a horrible feeling. Somehow we seemed, I and Tod, to be responsible for Vale's death. I for having mistaken Sanker; Tod for entering upon the threatened ducking, and hounding the boys on.

The worst was to come: the going back to Dr. Frost and the masters with the tale; the breaking it to Mr. and Mrs. Vale at Vale Farm. While Tod was dressing himself, the rest went on slowly, nobody staying by him but me and Sanker.

"It's *your* doings more than mine," Tod said, turning to Sanker in his awful distress. "If you knew who the thief was last half, you should have disclosed it; not have given him the opportunity to resume his game. Had you done so this could not have happened."

"I promised him then I should proclaim him if he did resume it; I have told him to-night I shall do it," quietly answered Sanker. "It was Lacketer."

"Lacketer!"

"Lacketer. And since my eyes were opened, it has seemed to me that all yours must have been closed, not to find him out. His manner was enough to betray him: only, I suppose—you wanted the clue."

10

"But, Sanker, why did you let me think it was Vale?" I asked.

"*You* made the first mistake; I let you lie under it for Lacketer's sake; to give him the chance," said Sanker. "Who was to foresee you would go and tell it?"

It had never passed my lips, save those few words at the time when Tod questioned me. Harding was the one outside the porch who had overheard it; but he had kept it to himself until now, when he thought the time had come for speaking.

What was to be done?—oh, what was to be done? It seemed as if a great weight of darkness had suddenly fallen upon us, and could never again be lifted. We had a death upon our hands.

"There's just a chance," said Tod, dragging his legs along like so much lead, and beginning with a sort of groan. "Vale may have made for the land again as soon as he got in, and come out lower down. In that case he would run to his home probably."

Just a chance, as Tod said. But in the depth of despair chances are caught at. If we cut across to the left hand (the left, standing with our backs to the river), Vale Farm was not more than a mile off: and we turned to it. The absenting ourselves from school seemed as nothing. Tod went on with a bound, now there was an object, a ray of hope; I and Sanker after him.

"I can't go in," said Tod, when we came in front of the farm, a long, low house, with lights gleaming in some of the windows. "It's not cowardice; at least, I don't think it is. It's——never mind; I'll wait for you here."

"I say," said Sanker to me, "what excuse are we to make for going in at this time? We can't tell the truth."

I could not. Harry Vale stood alone; he had neither brother nor sister. I could not go in and tell his mother that he was dead. She was sitting in one of the front parlours, sewing by the lamp. We saw her through the window as we stole up to look in. But there was no time for plotting. Footsteps

approached, and we did but get back on the path when Mr.
Vale came up. He was a tall, fine man, with a fair face and
blue eyes like his son's. What we said I hardly know; some
thing about being close by, and thought we'd call on our way
home. Sanker had been there several times in the holidays

Mr. Vale took us in with a beaming face to his wife. They
were the kindest-hearted people, liberal and hospitable, as
most well-to-do farmers are. Mrs. Vale, rolling up her work,
said we must take something to help us on our way home, and
rang the bell We never said we could not stop; we never
said Tod was waiting outside. But there were no signs that
Vale had gone home half-drowned.

Two maids put the supper on the table, and Mrs. Vale helped
them; for Sanker had summoned courage to say it was late
for us to stop. About fifteen things. Cold ducks, and a ham
and collared-head, and a big dish of custard with nutmeg on
the top, and fruit and cake. I couldn't have swallowed a
morsel; the lump rising in my throat would have hindered it.
I don't think Sanker could, for he said resolutely we must not
sit down because of Dr. Frost.

"How is Harry?" asked Mrs. Vale.

"Oh, he is—very well," said Sanker, after waiting to see if
I'd answer. "Have you seen him lately?"

"Not since last Sunday week when he and Master Snepp
spent the day here. He was looking well, and seemed in
spirits. It was rather a hazard, the sending him to school at
all; Mr. Vale wanted to have him taught at home, as he has
been until this year. But I think it is turning out for the
best."

"He gets frightened, does he not?" said Sanker, who knew
what she meant.

"He did," replied Mrs. Vale; "but he is growing out of
it. Never was a braver little child born than he; but when
he was four years old, he strolled away from his nurse into a
field where a bull was at grass, a savage animal. What exactly
happened, we never knew; that Harry was chased across the

field by it was certain, and then tossed. The chief injury was
to the nerves, strange though that may seem for so young a
child. For a long while afterwards, the least alarm would
put him into a state of terrible fear, almost a fit. But he is
getting over it now.

She told this for my benefit; just as if she had divined the
night's work; Sanker knew it before. I felt sick with remorse
as I listened—and Tod called him a coward! Let us get away.

"I wish you could stay, my lads," cried Mr. Vale; "it
vexes me to turn you out supperless. What's this, Charlotte?
Ah yes, to be sure! I wish you could put up the whole table
for them."

For Mrs. Vale had been putting some tartlets into paper,
and gave them to us, a packet for each. "Eat them as you go
along," she said. "And give my love to Harry."

"And tell him that he must bring you both on Sunday, to
spend the day," added Mr. Vale. "Perhaps young Mr. Todhetley will come also. You might get here to breakfast, and
go with us to church. I'll write to Dr. Frost."

Outside at last; I and my shame. These good, nice, simple-
hearted people——oh, had we indeed, between us, made them
childless? "Young Mr. Todhetley," waiting amid the stubble
in the outer field, came springing to the fence, his white face
working in the bright light of the hunter's moon.

"What a long while you have been? Well?"

"Nothing," said Sanker, briefly. "No news! I don't think
we've been much above five minutes."

What a walk home it was! Mr. Blair, the out-of-school
master, came down upon us with his thunder, but Tod seemed
never to hear him. The boys, hushed and quiet as nature is
before an impending storm, had not dared to tell and provoke
it. I could not see Lacketer.

"Where's Vale?" roared Mr. Blair, supposing he had been
with us. "But that prayers are waiting, I'd cane all four of
you. Where are you going, Todhetley?"

"Don't stop me, Mr. Blair," said Tod, putting him aside

with a quiet authority and a pain in his voice that made Blair stare. We called Blair, Baked Pie, because of his name, Pye-finch.

"Read the prayers without me, please, Mr. Blair," went on Tod. "I must see Dr. Frost. If you don't know what has happened to-night, sir, ask the rest to tell you."

He went out to his interview with the Doctor. Tod was not one to shirk his duty. The seeing Vale's father and mother he had shrunk from; but the confession to Dr. Frost he made himself. What passed between them we never knew: how much contrition Tod spoke, how much reproach the Doctor. Roger and Miles, the man-servant and boy, were called into the library, and sent abroad: we thought it might be to search the banks of the river, or give notice for it to be dragged. The next of us called in, was Sanker. The next Lacketer.

But Lacketer did not answer the call. He had vanished. Mr. Blair went searching for him high and low, and could not find him. Lacketer had run away. He knew his time at Worcester House was over, and thought he'd save himself from dismissal. It was he who had been the thief, and whom Sanker suspected. As good mention here Dr. Frost got a letter from his aunt the next Saturday, saying the school did not agree with her nephew, and she had withdrawn him from it.

Whether the others slept that night, I can't tell; I did not. Harry Vale's drowned form was in my mind all through it; and the sorrow of Mr. and Mrs. Vale. In the morning Tod got up, looking more like one dead than alive: he had one of his frightful headaches. I felt ready to die myself; it seemed that never another happy morning could dawn in the world.

"Shall I ask if I may bring you some breakfast up here, Tod? And it's just possible, you know, that Vale——"

"Hold your peace, Johnny?" he snapped. "If ever you tell me a false thing of a fellow again, I'll thrash your life out of you."

He came down-stairs when he was dressed, and went out,

waiting neither for breakfast nor prayers. I went out to watch him away, knowing he must be going to Vale Farm.

Oh, I never shall forget it. As Tod passed round the corner by the railings, he ran against him. *Him*, Harry Vale.

My sight grew dim; I couldn't see; the field and the railings were reeling. But it only lasted for a moment or two. Tod's breath was coming in great gasps then from his heaving chest, and he had Vale's two hands grasped in his. I thought he was going to hug him; a loud sob broke from him like a cry.

"We have been thinking you were drowned!"

Vale smiled. "I am too good a swimmer for that."

"But you disappeared at once."

"I struck back out of the river the instant I got into it; I was afraid you'd come in after me; and crept around the alder trees lower down. When you were all gone I swam across in my clothes; see how they've shrunk!"

"Swam across! Have you not been home?"

"No, I went to my uncle's: it's nearer than home: and they made me go to bed, and dried my things, and sent to tell Dr. Frost. I did not say why I went into the water," added Vale, lifting his kind face. "But the Doctor came round the ferry late, and he knew all about it. They talked to me well, he and my uncle, about being frightened at nothing, and I've promised not to be so stupid again."

"God bless you, Vale!" cried Tod. "You know it was a mistake."

"Yes, Dr. Frost said so. The half-crown was my own. My uncle met us boys when we were out walking yesterday morning, and gave it me. I thought you might have seen him give it."

Tod linked his arm within Vale's and walked off to the breakfast-room. The wonder to me was how, with Vale's good honest face and open manners, we could have suspected him capable of theft. But when you once go in for a mistake it carries you on in for an instant when Vale went in, and then you'd have thought the roof was coming off with cheers. Tod stood looking from the window, and I vow I saw him rub his handkerchief across his eyes.

We went to Vale Farm on Sunday morning early: the four of us invited, and Harding. Mr. Vale shook hands twice with us all round so heartily, that we might see, I thought, they bore no malice; and Mrs. Vale's breakfast was a sight to do you good, with the jugs of cream and the home-made sausages.

After that, came church: it looked like a procession turning out for it. Mr. and Mrs. Vale, and the grandmother, an upright old lady with a China-crape shawl and white hair, us five and a man and maid servant. The river lay on the right, the church was in front of us; people dotted the fields on their way to it, and the bells were ringing as they do at a wedding.

"This is a different sort of Sunday from what we thought last Thursday it would be," I said in Tod's ear when we were together for a minute at the gate.

"Johnny, if I were older, and went in for that kind of thing, as perhaps I shall do some time, I should like to put up a public thanksgiving in church to-day."

"A public thanksgiving?"

"For mercies received."

I stared at Tod. He did not seem to heed it, but took his hat off and walked with it in his hand all across the church-yard.

XI

THE BEGINNING OF THE END.

PERHAPS this might be called the beginning of the end of the chain of events that I alluded to in that other paper. An end that terminated in distress, and death, and sorrow.

It was the half year following that hunt of ours by moonlight. Summer weather had come in, and we were looking forward to the holidays, hoping the heat would last.

The half-mile field, called so from its length, on Vale Farm was being mowed. Sunday intervened, and the grass was left to dry until the Monday. The haymakers had begun to put it into cocks. The river stretched past along the field on one side; a wooden fence bounded it on the other. It was out of all proportion, that field, so long and so narrow.

Tod and I and Sanker and Harry Vale were spending the Sunday at the farm. Since that hunt last autumn Mr. and Mrs. Vale often invited us. There was no evening service, and we went into the hay-field, and began throwing the hay at one another. It was rare fun; they might nearly have heard our shouts at Worcester House; and I don't believe but that every one of us forgot it was Sunday.

What with the sultry weather and the hay, some of us got into a tolerable heat. The river wore a tempting look; and Tod and Sanker, without so much as a thought, undressed themselves behind the trees, and plunged in. It was twilight then; the air had begun to wear its weird silence; the shadows were putting on their ghastliness; the moon, well up, sailed along under white clouds.

I and Vale were walking slowly back towards the Farm, when a great cry broke over the water,—a cry as of something in pain; but whether from anything more than a night-bird was uncertain. Vale stopped and turned his head.

A second cry: louder, longer, more distinct, and full of agony. It came from one of those two in the water. Vale flew back with his fleet foot—fleeter than any fellow's in the school except Tod's and Snepp's. As I followed, a startling recollection came over me, and I wondered how it was that all of us had been so senseless as to forget it: that one particular spot on the river was known to be dangerous.

"Bear up; I'm coming," shouted Vale. "Don't lose your heads."

A foot-passenger walking on the other side the fence, saw something was wrong: if he did not hear Vale's words, he heard the cry. He came cutting across the field, scattering the hay with his feet. And then I saw it was Baked Pie: which meant our mathematical master, Mr. Blair. They had given him at baptism the name of "Pyefinch," after some old uncle who had money to leave; no second name, nothing but that: and the school had converted him into "Baked Pie." But I don't think fathers and mothers have any right to put odd names upon helpless babies and send them out to be a laughing-stock to the world.

Blair was not a bad fellow, putting his name aside, and had gone in for honours at Cambridge. We got to the place together.

"What is amiss, Ludlow?"

"I don't know, sir. Todhetley and Sanker are in the water; and we've heard cries."

"In the water to-night! And *there*."

Vale, already in the middle of the river, was swimming back, holding up Sanker. But Tod was nowhere to be seen. Mr Blair looked up and down; and an awful fear came over me. The current led down to Mr. Charles Vale's mill—Vale's uncle. More than one man had found his death there.

"Oh, sir! Mr. Blair! where is he? What has become of him?"

"Hush!" breathed Blair. He was sliding off some of his things quietly, his eyes fixed on a particular part of the river. In he went, striking out for it without more splash than he could help, and reached it just as Tod's head appeared above the water. *The third time of rising.* I did not go in for such a girl's trick as to faint; but I never afterwards could trace the minutes as they had passed by until Tod was lying on the grass under the trees. *That* I remember always. The scene is before my eyes now as plainly as it was then, though more time has gone by since than perhaps you'd think for: the treacherous river flowing on calmly, the quivering leaves overhead, through which the moon was glittering, and Tod lying there white and motionless. Mr. Blair had saved his life: there could be no question of that, saved it only by a minute of time; and I thought to myself I'd never call him Baked Pie again.

"Instead of standing moon-struck, Ludlow, suppose you make a run to the Farm and see what you can get," spoke Mr. Blair. "Todhetley must be carried there, and put between hot blankets."

Help was got. Sanker walked to the Farm, Tod was carried; and a regular bustle set in when they arrived there. Both of them were put to bed; Tod had come-to then. Mrs. Vale and the servants ran up and down like wild Indians; and the good old lady with the white hair insisted upon sitting up by Tod's bed-side all night.

"No, mother," said Mr. Vale, "some of us will do that."

"My son, I tell you that I shall watch by him myself," returned the old lady; and as they deferred to her always, she did.

When the explanation of the accident was given—as much of it as ever could be given—it sounded rather strange. *Both* of them had been taken with cramp, and the river was not in fault, after all. Tod said that he had been in the water two or three minutes, when he was seized with what he supposed to be cramp in the legs, though he never had it before. He was turning to strike out for the bank, when he found himself caught hold of by Sanker. They loosed each other in a minute, but Tod's legs were helpless, and he sank.

Sanker's story was very much the same. He was seized with cramp, and in his fear caught hold of Tod for protection. Tod was an excellent swimmer, Sanker a poor one; but while Sanker's cramp got better, or at least no worse, Tod's disabled him. Most likely, as we decided when we heard this, Sanker, who never went below at all, would have got out of the water without help; Tod would have been drowned but for Blair. He had sunk twice when the good rescue came. Mr. Featherston, the man of pills who attended the school, said it was all through their having jumped into the water when they were in a white heat; the cold had struck to them. While Mrs. Hall, with her grave face, thought it was through their having gone bathing on a Sunday.

Whatever it was through, Old Frost made a commotion. He was not severe in general, but he raised enough noise over this. What with one thing and another, the school, he declared, was being perpetually upset.

Tod and Sanker came back from Mr. Vale's on the next day; Monday. The Doctor ordered them into his study, and sat there with his cane in his hand while he talked, rapping the table with it now and again as fiercely as if it had been their backs. And the backs would surely have got it but for having just escaped coffins.

All this would not have been much, but it was to lead to a great deal more. To quite a chain of events, as I have said; and to trouble and sorrow in the far-off end. Hannah, at home, was fond of repeating to Lena what she called the sayings of poor Richard, "For want of a nail the shoe was lost; for want of a shoe the horse was lost; for want of a horse the rider was lost; and all for the want of a little care about a horse-shoe nail." The horse-shoe nail and the man's loss seemed a great deal nearer each other than that Sunday night's accident, and what was eventually to come of it. A little insignificant mustard-seed, dropped into the ground, shoots forth and becomes in the end a great spreading tree.

On the Wednesday, who should come over but the Squire, clasping Pyefinch Blair's hand in his, and saying with tears in his good old eyes that he had saved his son's life. Old Frost, you see, had written the news to Dyke Manor. Tod, strong and healthy in constitution, was all right again, not a hair on his head the worse for it; but Sanker had not escaped so well.

As early as the Monday night, the first night of his returning home from Vale Farm, it began to come on; and the next morning the boys, sleeping in the same room, told a tale of Sanker's having been delirious. He had sat up in bed and woke them all up with his cries, thinking he was trying to swim out of deep water, and could not. Next he said he wanted some water to drink; they gave him one draught after another till the big water-jug was emptied, but his thirst kept on saying "More! more!" Sanker did not seem to remember anything of this. He came down with the rest in the morning, his face very white, except for a pinkish spot in the middle of his cheeks, and he thought the fellows must be chaffing him. The fellows told him they were not; and one, it was Bill Whitney, said they would not think of chaffing him just after his having been so nearly drowned.

It went on to the afternoon. Sanker ate no dinner, for I looked to see; he was but one amidst the many, and it was not noticed by the masters. And if it had been, they'd have thought that the ducking had taken away his appetite. The drawing-master, Wilson, followed suit with Hall, and said he was not surprised at their being nearly drowned, after making hay on the Sunday. But, about four o'clock when the first class was before Dr. Frost with their Greek books, Sanker suddenly let his fall. Instead of stooping for it, his eyes took a far-off look, as if they were seeking for it round the walls of the room.

"Lay hold of him," said Dr. Frost.

He did not faint, but seemed dull: it looked as much like a lazy fit as anything; and he was sensible. They put him to sit on one of the benches, and then he began to tremble.

"He must be got to bed," said the doctor. "Mr. Blair, kindly see Mrs. Hall, will you. Tell her to warm it. Stay. Wait a moment."

Dr. Frost followed Mr. Blair from the hall. It was to say that Sanker had better go at once to the blue-room. If the bed there was not aired, or otherwise ready, Sanker's own bedding could be taken to it. "I'll give Mrs. Hall the orders myself," said the Doctor.

The blue-room—called so from its blue-stained walls—was the one used on emergencies. When we found Sanker had been taken there, we made up our minds that he was going to have an illness. Featherston came and thought the same.

The next day, Wednesday, he was in a kind of fever, rambling in his speech every other minute. The Squire said he should like to see him, and Blair took him upstairs. Sanker lay with the same pink hue on his cheeks, only deeper; and his eyes were bright and glistening. Hall, who was addicted to putting in her word on all occasions when it could tell against us boys, said if he had stayed two or three days in the bed at Vale Farm, where he was first put, he'd have had nothing of this. Perhaps Hall was right. It had been Sanker's own doings to get up. When Mrs. Vale saw him coming down-stairs, she wanted to send him back to bed again, but he told her he was quite well, and came off to school.

Sanker knew the Squire, and put out his hand. The Squire took it, not saying a word. He told us later that to him Sanker's face looked to have death in it. When he would have spoken, Sanker's eyes had grown wild again, and he was talking nonsense about his class-books.

"Johnny, boy, you sit in this room a bit at times; you are patient and not rough," said the Squire, when he went out to his carriage, for he had driven over. "I have asked them to let you be up there as much as they can. The poor boy is very ill, and has no relatives near him."

Dwarf Giles, touching his hat to Tod and me, was at the horses' heads, Bob and Blister. The cattle knew us: I'm sure of it. They had had several hours' rest in Old Frost's stables while the Squire went on foot about the neighbourhood to call on people. Dr. Frost, standing out with us, admired the fine dark horse greatly; at which Giles was prouder than if the doctor had admired *him*. He cared for nothing in the world so much as those two animals, and groomed them with a will.

"You'll take care that he wants for nothing, Doctor," I heard the Squire say as he shook hands. Don't spare any care and expense to get him well; I wish to look upon this illness as my charge. It seems something like an injustice, you see, that my boy should come off without damage, and this poor fellow be lying there."

He took the reins and stepped up to his seat, Giles getting in beside him. As we watched the horses step off with the high spring that the Squire loved, he looked back and nodded to us. And it struck me that, in this care for Sanker, the Pater was trying to make some recompense for the suspicion cast on him a year before at Dyke Manor.

It was a sharp, short illness, the fever raging, but not infectious; I had never been with anybody in such a one before, and I did not wish to be again. To hear how Sanker's mind rambled, was marvellous; but some of us shivered when it came to ravings. Very often he'd be making hay; fighting against numbers that were throwing cocks at him, while he could not throw back upon them. Then he'd be in the water buffeting with high sea-waves, and shrieking out that he was drowning, and throwing his thin hot arms aloft in agony. Sometimes the trouble would be his lessons, hammering at Latin derivations and Greek roots; and next he was toiling through a problem in Euclid.   One night when he was at the worst Old Featherston lost his head, and the next day Mr. Carden came posting from Worcester in his carriage.   I wonder if he remembers it?*

There were medical men of repute nearer: but somehow in extremity we all turn to him.   And his skill did not fail here. Whether it might be any particular relief he was enabled to give, or that the disease had reached its crisis, I cannot tell, but from the moment Mr. Carden stood at his bed-side, Sanker began to mend.   Featherston said the next day that the worst of the danger had passed.   It seemed to us that it had just set in ; no rat was ever so weak as Sanker.

The holidays came then, and the boys went home : all but me.   Sanker couldn't lift a hand, but he could smile at us and understand, and he said he'd like to have me stay a bit with him ; so they sent word from home I might.   Mr. Blair stayed also ; Dr. Frost wished it.   The Doctor was subpœnaed to give evidence on a trial at Westminster, and had to hasten up to London.   Blair had no relatives at all, and did not care to go anywhere.   He told me in confidence that his staying saved his pocket.   Blair was strict in school, but over Sanker's bed he got as friendly with me as possible.   I liked him ; he was always gentlemanly, and I grew to dislike their calling him Baked Pie as much as he disliked it.

"You go out and get some air, Ludlow," he said to me the day after the school broke up, "or we may have you ill next."

Upon that I demanded what I wanted with air.   I had taken precious long walks with the fellows up to the day before yesterday.

"You go," said he, curtly.

"Go, Johnny," said Sanker, in his poor weak voice, which couldn't raise itself above a whisper.   "I'm getting well, you know."

My way of taking the air was to sit down at the school-room

<hr>

* Since these papers were written, Henry Carden has, alas ! died.—ED.

desk and write to Tod. In about five minutes somebody
walked round the house as if looking for an entrance, and then
stopped at the side-door. Putting my head out of the window,
I took a view of her. It was a young lady in a plain grey
dress, and straw bonnet, with a cloak over her arm, and an
umbrella put up against the sun. The back regions were
turned inside out, for they had begun the summer cleaning
that morning, and the cook came stalking along in pattens to
answer the knock.

"This is Dr. Frost's, I believe. Can I see him?"

It was a sweet, calm, gentle voice. The cook, who had no
notion of visitors coming at the cleaning season, when the boys
were just got rid of and the Doctor had gone, stared at her
for a moment, and then asked in her surly way whether she
had business with Dr. Frost. That cook and Molly at home
might have run in a curricle, they were such a match for temper.

"Business!—oh, certainly. I must see him, if you please."

The cook kicked off her pattens, and went up the back stairs,
leaving the young lady outside. As it was business, she sup
posed she must call Mr. Blair.

"Somebody wants Dr. Frost," was the announcement she
made to him. "A girl at the side door."

Which of course caused Blair to suppose it might be a child
from one of the cottages come to ask for help of some sort; as
they did come sometimes. He thought Hall might have been
called to her, but he went down at once; without his coat, and
his sick-room slippers on. Naturally, when he saw the young
lady, it took him aback.

"I beg your pardon, sir; I hope you will not deem me an
intruder. I have just got here."

Blair stared nearly as much as the cook. The face was so
pleasant, the voice so refined, that he inwardly called himself
a fool for showing himself to her in that trim. For once, his
speech failed him; a thing Blair's had never done at mathe-
matics, I can tell you; he had not the smallest notion who she

was or what she wanted. And it seemed that the silence frightened her.

"Am I too late?" she asked, her face growing white. "Has the—the worse happened?"

"Happened to what?" questioned Blair, for he never once thought of the sick fellow above, and was all at sea. "Pardon me, young lady, but I do not know what it is you are speaking of."

"Of my brother, Edward Sanker. Oh, sir! is he dead?"

"Miss Sanker! Truly I beg your pardon for my stupidity. He is out of danger; he is getting well."

She sat down for a minute on the old stone bench beyond the door, rough with the crowd of boys' names cut in it. Her lips were shaking just a little, and the soft brown eyes had tears in them; but the face was breaking into a glad smile.

"Oh, Dr. Frost, thank you, thank you! Somehow, I never thought of him as dead until this minute, and it startled me."

Fancy her taking him for Frost! Blair was a good-looking fellow under thirty, slender, and well made. The Doctor stood out an old guy of fifty, with a stern face and black knee-breeches.

"My mother had your letter, sir, but she was not able to come. My father is very ill, needing her attention every moment; she strove to see on which side her duty lay—to stay with him, or to come to Edward; and she thought it must lie remaining with papa. So she sent me. I left Wales last night."

"Is Mr. Sanker's a fever, too?" asked Blair, in wonder.

"No, an accident. He was hurt in the mine."

It was odd that it should be so; the two illnesses occurring at the same time! Mr. Sanker, it appeared, fell from the shaft; his leg was broken, and there were other hurts. At first they were afraid for him.

Blair was struck into a dilemma. He'd not have minded Mrs. Sanker; but he did not know much about young ladies, not being accustomed to them. She got up from the bench.

"Mamma bade me say to you, Dr. Frost——"

"I beg your pardon," interrupted Blair again. "I am not Dr. Frost; the Doctor went to London this morning. My name is Blair—one of the masters. Will you walk in?"

He shut her into the parlour on his way to call Hall, and to put on his boots and coat. Seeing me, he turned into the school-room.

"Ludlow, are not the Sankers connections of yours?"

"Not of mine. Of Mrs. Todhetley's."

"It's all the same. You go in and talk to her. I don't know what on earth to do. She is come to be with Sanker, but she'll not like to stay here with only you and me. If the Doctor were at home it would be different."

"She seems an uncommon nice girl, Mr. Blair."

"Good gracious!" went on Blair in his dilemma. "The Doctor told me he had written to Wales some days ago; but he supposed Mrs. Sanker could not make it convenient to come; and yesterday he wrote again, saying there was no necessity for it, as Sanker was out of danger. I don't know what on earth to do with her," repeated Mr. Blair, who had a habit of getting hopelessly bewildered on occasions. "Hall! Where's Mrs. Hall?"

As he went along the flagged passage calling out, a boy came whistling to the door, carrying a big carpet-bag; Miss Sanker's luggage. The coach which she had had to take, on leaving the rail, put her down half a mile off, and she walked up in the sun, leaving her bag to be brought.

It seemed that we were going in for mistakes. When I went to her, and began to say who I was, she mistook me for Tod. It made me laugh.

"Tod is a great, strong fellow, as tall as Mr. Blair, Miss Sanker. I am only Johnny Ludlow."

"Edward has told me all about you both," she said, taking my hands, and looking into my face with her nice eyes. "Tod's proud and overbearing, though generous; but you have ever been pleasant with him. I am afraid I shall begin to call you 'Johnny' at once.

"Nobody ever calls me anything else; except the masters here."

"You must have heard of me—Mary?"

"But you are not Mary?"

"Yes, I am."

That she was telling truth any fellow might see, and yet at first I hardly believed her. Sanker had told us his sister Mary was beautiful as an angel. *Her* face had no beauty in it, so to say; it was only kind, and nice, and loving. People called Mrs. Parrifer a beautiful woman; perhaps I had taken my notions of beauty from her; she had a Roman nose, and great big eyes that rolled about, and a gruff voice, and a lovely peach-and-white complexion (but people said it was paint), and looked three parts a fool. Mary Sanker was just the opposite to all this, and her cheeks were dimpled. But still she had not what people call beauty.

"May I go up and see Edward?"

"I should think so; Mr. Blair, I suppose, will be back directly. He is looking very bad: you will not be frightened at him?"

"After picturing him in my mind as dead, he will not frighten me, however ill he may look."

"I should say the young lady had better take off her bonnet afore going in. Young Mr. Sanker haven't seen bonnets of late, and might be scared."

The interruption came from Hall; we turned, and saw her standing there. She spoke in a resentful tone, as if Miss Sanker had offended her; and no doubt she had, by coming when the house was not in company order, and had nothing better to send in for dinner but cold mutton and the half of a rhubarb pie. Hall would have to get the mutton hashed now, which she'd never have done for me and Blair.

"Yes, if you please; I should much like to take my bonnet off," said Miss Sanker, going to Hall with a smile. "I think you must be Mrs. Hall. My brother has talked of you."

Hall took her to a room, and presently she came forth al

fresh and nice, the travelling dust gone, and her bright brown hair smooth and shining. Her grey dress was soft, one that would not disturb a sick-room; it had a bit of white lace round the throat and at the wrists, and a little pearl brooch in front. She was twenty-one last birthday, but she did not look as much.

Blair had been in to prepare Sanker, and his great eyes (only great since his illness) were staring out for her with a wild expectation. You never saw brother and sister less alike; the one so nice, the other ugly enough to frighten the crows. Sanker had got my hand clasped tight in his, when she stooped to kiss him. I don't think he knew of it; but I could not get away. In that minute I saw how fond they were of each other.

"Could not the mother come, Mary?"

"No, papa is—is not well," she said, for of course she would not tell him yet of any accident. "Papa wanted her there, and you wanted her here; she thought her duty lay at home, and she was not afraid but that God would raise up friends to take care of you."

"What is the matter with him?"

"Some complicated illness or other," Mary Sanker answered, in a careless tone. "He was a little better when I came away. You have been very ill, Edward."

He held up his wasted hand as proof, with a half smile; but it fell again.

"I don't believe I should have pulled through it at all, Mary, but for Blair."

"That's the gentleman I saw. The one without a coat. Has he nursed you?"

Sanker made a motion with his white lips. "Right well, too. He, and Hall, and Johnny here. Old Hall is as good as gold when any of us are ill."

"And pays herself out by being tarter than ever when we are well," I could not help saying: for it was the truth.

"Blair saved Todhetley's life," Sanker went on. "We used

to call him Baked Pie before, and give him all the trouble we could."

"Ought you to talk, Edward?"

"It is your coming that seems to give me strength for it," he answered. "I did not know that Frost had written home."

"There was a delay in the letters, or I might have been here three days ago," said Miss Sanker, speaking in a penitent tone, as if she were in the habit of taking other people's faults upon herself. "While papa is not well, the clerk down at the mine opens the business letters. Seeing one directed to papa privately, he neither spoke of it nor sent it up, and for three days it lay unopened."

Sanker had gone off into one of his weak fits before she finished speaking: lying with his eyes and mouth wide open, between sleep and wake. Hall came in, and said, with a tone that snapped Miss Sanker up, *it wouldn't do:* if people could not be there without talking, they must not be there at all. I don't say but what she was a capable nurse, or that when a fellow was downright ill, she spared the wine in the arrowroot, and the sugar in the tea. Mary Sanker sat down by the bed-side, her fingers on her lips to show that she meant to keep silent.

We had visitors later. Mrs. Vale came over, as she did most days, to see how Sanker was getting on; and Bill Whitney brought his mother. Mrs. Vale told Mary Sanker that she had better sleep at the farm, as the Doctor was away; she'd give her a nice room and make her comfortable. Upon that, Lady Whitney offered a spacious bed and dressing-room at the Hall. Mary thanked them both, saying how kind they were to be so friendly with a stranger; but thought she must go to the Farm, as it would be within a walk night and morning. Bill spoke up, and said the carriage could fetch and bring her; but Vale farm was fixed upon; and when night came I went with her to show her the way.

"That's the water they went into, Miss Sanker; and that's the very spot, behind the trees." She shivered just a little as she looked, but did not say much. Mrs. Vale met us at the door, and the old lady kissed Mary and told her she was a good girl to come fearlessly all the way alone from Wales to nurse her sick brother. When Mary came back the next morning, she said they had given her such a beautiful room, the dimity window and bed curtains whiter than snow, and the sheets sweet with lavender.

Her going out to sleep appeased Hall;—that, or something else. She was gracious all day, and sent us in two chickens for dinner. Mr. Blair cut them up and helped us. He had written to tell Dr. Frost in London of Miss Sanker's arrival, and while we were at table a telegram came back, saying Mrs. Hall was to take care of Miss Sanker, and make her comfortable.

It went on so for three or four days; Mary sleeping at the Farm, and coming home in the morning. Sanker got well enough to be taken to a sofa in the pretty room that poor Mrs. Frost sat in nearly to the last; and we were all four growing very jolly, as intimate as if we'd known each other as infants. I had taken to call her Mary, hearing Sanker do it so often ; and twice the name slipped accidentally out of Mr. Blair. The news from Wales was better and better. For visitors we had Mrs. Vale, Lady Whitney and Bill, and old Featherston. Some of them came every day. Dr. Frost was detained in London. The trial did not come on so soon as it was put down for; when it did, it lasted a week, and the witnesses had to stay. He had written to Mary, telling her to make herself quite happy, for she was in good hands. He also wrote to Mrs. Vale, and to Hall.

Well, it was either the fourth or fifth day. I know it was on Monday; and at five o'clock we were having tea for the first time in Sanker's sitting-room, the table drawn near the sofa, and Mary pouring it out. It was the hottest of hot weather, the window was up as high as it would go, but not a breath of air came in at it. Therefore, to see Blair begin to shake as if he were taken with an ague fit, was something inexplicable. His face looked grey, his ears and hands had turned a kind of bluish white.

"Halloa!" said Sanker, who was the first to see him. "What's the matter, sir?"

Blair got up, and sat down again, his limbs shaking, his teeth chattering. Mary Sanker hastily put some of the hot tea into a saucer, and held it to his lips. His teeth rattled against the china; I thought they'd bite a piece out of it; and in trying to take the saucer from Miss Sanker to hold it himself, the tea was shaken over on the carpet.

"Just you call Mrs. Hall, Johnny," said Sanker, who had propped himself up on his elbow to stare.

Hall came, and Mr. Featherston came; but they could not make anything out of it except that Blair had had a shaking-fit. He was soon all right again (except for a burning heat); but the surgeon, given naturally to croak (or he'd not have got so frightened about Sanker when Mr. Carden was telegraphed for), said he hoped the mathematical master had not set in for fever.

He had set in for something. That was clear. The shaking-fits took him now and again, giving place to spells of low fever. Featherston was not sure whether it had a "typhoid character," he said; but the suspicion was quite enough, and our visitors fell off. Mrs. Vale was the only one who came; she laughed at supposing she could be afraid of it. So there we were still, we four; prisoners, as may be said; with some fever amid us that perhaps might have a typhoid character. Mr. Featherston said (or Hall, I forget which) that it must have been smouldering within him ever since the Sunday night when he jumped into the river. And Blair thought so himself.

Do not imagine he was ill as Sanker had been. Nothing of the kind. He got up every morning, and was in Mrs. Frost's sitting-room with us till evening: but he grew nearly the rat Sanker was for weakness, and wanted pretty nigh as much waiting on. Sometimes his hands were like a burning firecoal; sometimes so cold that Mary would take them in hers to try and rub into their veins a little life. She was the gentlest nurse possible, and did not seem to think anything more of waiting on him than on her brother. Mrs. Hall would stand by and say there was nothing left for her to do.

One day Lady Whitney came over, braving the typhoid character, and asked to see Miss Sanker in the great drawing-room; where she stood snifling at a bottle of aromatic vinegar.

"My dear," she said, when Mary went to her, "I do not think this is at all a desirable position that you are placed in. I should not exactly like it for one of my own daughters. Mr. Blair is a very gentlemanly man, and all that, with quite proper feelings no doubt; but sitting with him in sickness is altogether different from sitting with your brother. Featherston tells me there's little or no danger of infection, and I have come to take you back to the Hall with me."

But Mary would not go. It was not the position she should have voluntarily chosen, but circumstances had led her into it, and she thought her duty lay in staying where she was at present, was the substance of her answer. Mr. Blair had nursed her brother through his dangerous illness, and it would be cruelly ungrateful to leave him, now that he was ill himself. It seemed a duty thrown expressly in her way, she added; and her mother approved of what she was doing.

So Lady Whitney went away (leaving the bottle of aromatic vinegar as a present for the sick room) three parts convinced. Any way, she said to them when she got home, that Mary Sanker was a sweet, good girl, trustworthy to her fingers' ends.

I'm sure she was like sunshine in the room, and read to us out of the Bible just as Harry Vale's fine old grandmother might have done. The first day that Sanker took a drive in a fly, he was tired afterwards, and went to bed and to sleep at tea-time. Towards sunset, before I walked with her to the Farm, Mary got the Book as usual; and then hesitated, as if in doubt whether to presume to read or not, Sanker being away.

"Oh yes; yes, if you please," said Mr. Blair.

She began the tenth chapter of St. John. It is a passably

long one, as everybody knows; and when she laid the Book down again, Blair had his eyes shut and his head resting on the back of the easy chair where he generally sat. His face never looked stiller or whiter. I glanced at Mary and she at me; we thought he was worse, and she went up to him.

"I ought not to have read so long a chapter," she gently said. "I fear you are feeling worse."

"No; I was only thinking. Thinking what an angel you are," he added in a low, impassioned, and yet reverent tone, as he bent forward to look up in her face, and took both her hands to hold for a moment in his.

She drew them away at once, saying, as she passed me, that she was going to put her bonnet on, and should be ready in a minute. Of course it might have been the reflection of the red sun-clouds, but I never saw any face so glowing in all my life.

The next move old Featherston made, was to decide that the fever had *not* a typhoid character; and visitors came about us again. It was something like the opening of a public-house after a tide of closing: all the Whitneys flocked in together, except Sir John, who was in town for Parliament. Mrs. Hall was uncommonly short with everybody. She had said from the first there was nothing infectious in the fever, told Featherston so to his face, and resented people's having stayed away I wrote home to tell them there. On the Saturday Dr. Frost arrived, and we were glad to see him. Blair was getting rather better then.

"Well, that Sunday night's plunge in the water has taken out its revenge!" remarked Dr. Frost. "It only wants Todhetley and Vale to follow suit."

But neither of them had the least intention of following. On the Monday Tod arrived to surprise us, strong as ever. The Squire had trusted him to drive the horses: you should have seen them spanking in at the gate of Worcester House, pawing the gravel, as Tod in the high carriage, the ribbons in his hands, and the groom beside him, brought them up beautifully to the door. Some people called Tom ugly, saying his features

11

were strong; but I know he promised to be the finest man in our two counties.

He conveyed an invitation for the sick and the well. When the two invalids were able to get to Dyke Manor, Mr. and Mrs. Todhetley expected to see them, for change of air. Mary Sanker and I were to go as soon as we liked. Which we did in a few days, and were followed by Sanker and Mr. Blair; both able to help themselves then, and getting well all one way.

It did not surprise people very much to hear that the mathematical master and Mary Sanker had fallen in love with one another. He (as Bill Whitney's mother had put in) was gentlemanly; a good-looking fellow to boot: and you have heard what *she* was. The next week but one after arriving at Dyke Manor, Blair took Mrs. Todhetley into his confidence, though he had said nothing to Mary. They would be sure to marry in the end, she privately told the Squire, for the likeness in their faces to each other struck her at first sight.

" Mary will not have a shilling, Mr. Blair; she will go to her husband (whenever she shall marry) with even a very poor outfit," Mrs. Todhetley explained, wishing Blair fully to understand things. " Her father, Philip Sanker, was a gentleman bred and born, but his patrimony was small. He was persuaded to embark it in a Welsh mine, and lost all. Report said some roguery was at work, but I don't know that it was. It ended in his becoming the overlooker on the very same mine, at a salary so small that they could hardly have reared their family anywhere but in Wales. Mary does not play, or draw, you see; she has no accomplishments."

" She has what is a great deal better; she does not want them," answered Blair, his pale face lighting up.

" In point of fact, the Sankers—as I fancy—have sacrificed the girls' interests to the boys; they of course must have a thorough education," remarked Mrs. Todhetley. " They are good people, both; you could not fail to like them. I sometimes think, Mr. Blair, that the children of these refined men and women (and Philip Sanker and his wife are that), compelled to live closely and to look at every sixpence before it is spent, turn out all the better for it."

"I am sure they do," answered Blair, earnestly. "It was my own case."

Taking Mrs. Todhetley into confidence meant as to his means as well as his love. He had saved a little money during the eight years he had been at work for himself—about two hundred pounds. It might be possible, he thought, to take to a school with this, and set up a tent at once: he and Mary. Mrs. Todhetley shook her head; she could make as much of small sums as anybody, but fancied this would be scarcely enough for what he wished.

"There would be the furniture," she ventured to say with some hesitation, not liking to damp him.

"I think that is often included in the purchase-money for the good-will," said Blair.

He had been acting on this notion before speaking to Mrs. Todhetley, and a friend of his in London, the Rev. M. Lockett, was already looking out for any schools that might be in the market. In a few days news came down of one to be disposed of in the neighbourhood of London. Mr. Lockett thought it was as desirable an investment as Blair was likely to find, he wrote word: only, the purchase-money, inclusive of furniture, was four hundred pounds instead of two.

"It is of no use to think of it," said Mr. Blair, pushing his curly hair (they used to say he was vain of it at Frost's) off his perplexed brow. "My two hundred pounds will not go far towards that."

"It seems to me that the first step will be to go up and see the place," remarked Mrs. Todhetley. "If what Mr. Lockett says of the school be true; that is, if the people who have the disposal of it are not deceiving him; it must be a very good thing."

"I suppose you mean that the half of the purchase-money

should remain on it as a mortgage, to be paid off later," cried Blair, seizing on the idea and brightening up.

"No; not exactly," said Mrs. Todhetley, getting as red as a rose, for she did not like to tell him what she did mean; it looked rather like a conspiracy.

"Look here, Blair," cried the Squire, laying hold of him in the garden by the button-hole, "*I* will see about the other two hundred. You go up and make inquiries on the spot; and perhaps I'll go too; I should like a run; and if the affair is worth your while, we'll pay the money down on the nail, and so have done with it."

It was Blair's turn to get red now. "Do you mean, sir, that you—that you—would advance the half of the money? But it would be too generous. I have no claim on you——"

"No claim on me!" burst forth the Squire, pinning him against the wall of the pigeon-house in a passion. "No claim on me! When you saved my son from drowning but a few weeks ago! And got an ague fever through it! No claim on me! What next will you say?"

"But that was nothing, sir. Any man, with the commonest feelingg of humanity, would jump into the water if he saw a fellow-creature sinking."

"Commonest fiddlestick!" roared the Squire. "If this school is one likely to answer your purpose, you put down your two hundred pounds, and I will see to the rest. There! we'll go up to-day."

"Oh, sir, I never expected this. Perhaps in a year or two I shall be able to pay the money back: but the goodness I never can repay."

"Don't you trouble your head about paying me back till you're asked to do it," retorted the Squire, mortally offended at the notion. "If you are too proud to take it and say nothing about it, I'll give it to Mary Sanker instead of you. I will, too. Mind, sir! that half shall be your wife's, not yours."

If you believe me, there were tears in old Blair's eyes. He

was but soft at times. The Squire gave him another thrust, which nearly sent Blair into the pigeon-house, and then walked off with his head up and his nankeen coat-skirts held out behind, to watch Drew give the green meat to the pigs Blair got over his push, and went to find Miss Mary, his thin cheeks alight with a spot as red as Sanker's had worn when his illness was coming on.

They went up to London that day. The Squire had plenty of sense when he chose to bring it out; and instead of trust-ing to his own investigation and Blair's (which would have been the likeliest thing for him to do in general) he took a lawyer to the spot.

It proved to be all right. The gentleman giving up the school had made some money at it, and was going abroad to his friends, who had settled in Queensland. Any efficient man, he said to the Squire, able to *keep* the pupils when once he had secured them, could not fail to do well at it. The clergyman, Mr. Lockett, had called on one or two of the parents, who confirmed what was asserted. Altogether it was a straightforward, fair thing; but they'd not bate a shilling of the four hundred pounds.

The Squire concluded the bargain on the spot, for other applicants were after it, and there was danger in delay. He came back to Dyke Manor; and the next thing he did was to accompany Mary Sanker home, and tell the news there.

Mr. Blair stayed in London to take possession, and get things in order. He had but time for a few days' flying visit to Mr. and Mrs. Sanker in Wales before opening his new school. There was no opposition there: people are apt to judge of prospects according to their own circumstances; and they seemed to think it a good offer for Mary.

There was no opposition anywhere. Dr. Frost got a new mathematical master without trouble, and sent Blair his best wishes and a full set of plated spoons and forks and things, engraved with the initials P. M. B. He was wise enough to lay out the sum he wished to give in useful things, instead of a silver tea-pot or any other grand article of that kind, which would not be brought to light once in a year.

Blair cribbed a week's holiday at Michaelmas, and went down to be married. We saw them at the week's end as they passed through Worcester station. Mary looked the same sweet girl as ever, in the same quiet grey dress (or another that was related to it); and Blair was jolly. He clasped hold of the Squire's hands as if he wanted to take them with him. We handed in a big basket of nectarines and grapes from Mrs. Todhetley; and Mary's nice face smiled and nodded her thanks to the last, as the train puffed on.

"Good luck to them!" said Tod.

Good luck to them. You will hear what luck they had.

For this is *not* the end of that Sunday night's work, or it would have hardly been worth relating, seeing that people get married every day, and nobody thinks cheese of it but themselves. The end has to come. And I knew from the first it could not all be got into one paper.

XII.

JERRY'S GAZETTE.

THE school, taken to by Mr. Blair, was in one of the suburbs of London. It may be as well not to mention which; but some of the families yet living there cannot fail to remember the circumstances when they read this. For what I am going to tell you of is true. It did not happen last year; nor the year before. When it did, is of no consequence to anybody.

When Pyefinch Blair got into the house, he found that it had some dilapidations, which had escaped his notice, and would have to be repaired. Not an uncommon case by any means. Mr. Blair paid the four hundred pounds for the school, including furniture and good-will, and that drained him of his money. It was not a bad bargain, as bargains go. He had then the house put into fair order, and bought in a little more furniture that seemed to him necessary, intending his boys should be comfortable, as well as the young wife he was soon to bring home.

The school did not profess to be one of those higher-class ones that charge a hundred a year and extras. It was of moderate terms and moderate size; the pupils being mostly sons of well-to-do tradesmen, some of them living on the spot. At first, Blair (bringing with him his Cambridge notions) entertained thoughts of raising the school to a higher price and standard. But it would have been a risk; almost like beginning a fresh-venture. And when he found that the school paid well, and masters and boys alike got on comfortably, he dropped the wish.

More than two years went by. One evening, early in February, Mrs. Blair was sitting by the parlour fire after tea, with a great boy on her lap, who was forward with his tongue, and could say pa-pa, ma-ma, and had just begun to walk in a totter. I don't think you could have seen much difference in *her* from what she was as Mary Sanker. She had the same neat kind of dress and quiet manner, the fresh gentle face and sweet eyes, and the pretty, smooth brown hair. Her husband told her sometimes that she would spoil the boys with kindness. If any one got into disgrace, she was sure to beg him off; it was wonderful what a good mother she was to them, and only twenty-four years old yet.

Mr. Blair was striding the carpet with his head down, like one in perplexed thought, a great scowl upon his brow. It was something unusual, for he was always bright. He was as slender and good-looking a fellow as he used to be. Mrs. Blair noticed him and spoke.

"Have you the headache, Pyefinch?" She had long ago got over the odd sound of his Christian name. Habit smoothes most things.

"No."

"What is it, then?"

He did not make any answer; seemed not to hear her. Mrs. Blair put the boy down on the hearth-rug. The child was baptized Joseph, after Squire Todhetley, whom they persisted in calling their best friend.

"Run to papa, Joe. Ask him what the matter is."

The young gentleman went swaying across the carpet, with some unintelligible language of his own. Mr. Blair had no resource but to pick him up: and he carried him back to his mother.

"What is the matter, Pyefinch?" she asked again, catching his hand. "I am sure you are not well."

"I am quite well," he said; "but I have got into a little

bother lately. What ails me this evening is, that I find I must tell you of it, and I don't like to. There, Mary, send the child away."

She knew the nursemaid was busy; would not ring, but carried him out herself. Mr. Blair was sitting down when she returned, staring into the fire.

"I had hoped you would never know it, Mary; I had not intended that you should. The fact is——"

Mr. Blair stopped. His wife glanced at him; a serenely earnest calm in her eyes, a firm reliance in her loving tone.

"Do not hesitate, Pyefinch. The greater the calamity, the more need there is that I should hear it."

"Nay, it is no such great mischief as to be called a calamity. When I took to this house and school, I incurred a debt, and I am suddenly called upon to pay it."

"Do you mean Mr. Todhetley's?"

A passing smile at the question crossed the schoolmaster's face. "Mr. Todhetley's was a present; I thought you understood that, Mary. When I would have spoken of returning it, you may remember that he went into a passion."

"What debt is it, then?"

"I paid four hundred pounds, you know, to take to the school; half of it I had saved; the other was given by Mr. Todhetley. Well and good so far. But I had not thought of one thing—the money that would be wanted for current expenses, and for the hundred and one odd things that stare you in the face upon taking to a new concern. Repairs had to be done, needful furniture to be got in; and not a penny coming in until the end of the quarter: not much then, for most of the boys pay half-yearly. Lockett, who was down here most days, saw that if I could not get some money to go on with, there'd be no resource but to re-sell the school. He bestirred himself, and got me the loan of a hundred and fifty pounds from a friend, at only five per cent. interest. This money I am suddenly called upon to repay."

"But why?"
11*

"Because he from whom I had it is dead, and the executors have called it in.   It was Mr. Wells."

She recognized the name as that of a gentleman with whom they had been slightly acquainted ; he had died suddenly, in the prime of life.

"Has any of it been paid off?"

"None.   I could have repaid a portion every half-year as it came round, but Mr. Wells would not let me.   'You had a great deal better use it in improving the school and getting things comfortable about you ; I am in no hurry,' was his invariable rejoinder.   Lockett thought he meant eventually to make me a present of the money, being a wealthy man, without near relatives.   Of course I never looked for anything of the sort ; but I was as easy as to the debt as though I had not contracted it."

"Will the executors not let you have the use of the money still?"

"You should see their curt note, ordering its immediate re payment!   Lockett seems more vexed at the turn affairs have taken than even I am.   He was here to-day."

Mrs. Blair sat in silent reflection wishing she had known of this.   Many an odd shilling that she had thought justified in spending, she would willingly have recalled now.   Not that they could have amounted to much in the aggregate. Presently she looked at her husband.

"Pyefinch, it seems to me that there's only one thing to do. You must borrow the sum from some one else, which of course will make us only as much in debt as we are now ; and we must pay it off by instalments as quickly as we possibly can."

"It is what Lockett and I have decided on already as the only course.   Why, Mary, this worry has been on our minds for a fortnight past," he added, turning quickly.   "But now that it has come to borrowing again, and not from a friend, I felt I ought to tell you.   Besides, there's another thing."

"Go on," she said.

"We have found a man to advance the money. Lockett and I picked him out from the *Times* advertisements. These fellows are awful rogues, for the most part; but this is not one of the worst. Lockett made inquiries of a parishioner of his who understands these things, and finds Gavity (that's his name) is tolerably fair for a professional money-lender. I shall have to pay him higher interest. And he wants me to give him a bill of sale on the furniture."

" A bill of sale on the furniture ! What is that ? "

"That is what I meant when I said there was another thing," replied Mr. Blair. " Wells was content with my note of hand; this man requires tangible security on my goods. It is a mere matter of form in my case, he says. As I am doing well, and there's no fear of my not keeping the interest paid up, I suppose it is. In two or three years from this, all being well, the debt itself will be wiped off."

"Oh, yes; I hope so. The school is quite prosperous."

Her tone was anxious, and Mr. Blair detected it. But for considering she ought to know it, he would rather have kept this trouble to himself. And he was not sure upon another point: whether, in giving this bill of sale upon the furniture, Mr. Gavity might deem it essential to come in and take a list, article by article, bed by bed, table by table. If so, it would not have been possible to conceal it from her. He mentioned this. She, with himself, could not understand the necessity of their furniture being brought into the transaction at all, seeing that there could be no doubt as to their ability to repay. The one knew just as much about bills of sale and the rights they gave, as the other: and that was nothing.

And now that the communication to his wife was off his mind—for in that had lain the weight—Mr. Blair was more at ease. As they sat talking together, discussing the future in all its aspects, the shade lifted itself, and things looked brighter. It did not seem to either of them so formidable a cloud after all. It was but the changing the one creditor for another, and the paying a little higher interest.

The transaction was accomplished. Gavity advanced the money, and took the bill of sale upon the furniture. He shot up the expenses—which money-lenders of his stamp mostly do—and made out the loan to be a hundred and eighty, instead of a hundred and fifty. Still, taking things for all in all, the position was perhaps as fair and hopeful a one as can be experienced under debt. It was but a temporary clog; Mr. and Mrs. Blair both knew that. The school was flourishing; their prospects were good; they were young, and healthy, and hopeful. And though Mr. Gavity would of course exact his rights to the uttermost farthing, he had no intention of playing the rogue. In all candour let it be avowed, the gentleman money-lender did not see that it was a case affording scope for it.

I had to tell that much as well as I could, seeing that it only came to me by hearsay in the future.

And now to go back a little while, and to ourselves at Dyke Manor.

After their marriage the Squire did not lose sight of Mr and Mrs. Blair. A basket of things went up now and then, and the second Christmas they were invited to come down; but Mary wrote to decline, on account of the baby—Joe. "Let them leave Joe at home," cried Tod; but Mrs. Todhetley, shaking her head, said that the dear little infant would come to sad grief without its mother. Soon after that, when the Squire was in London, he took the omnibus and went to see them, and told us how comfortably they were getting on.

Years went round to another Christmas, when the exacting Joe would be some months over two years old. In the passing of time you are apt to lose sight of interests, unless they are close ones; and for some months we had heard nothing of the Blairs. Mrs. Todhetley spoke of it one evening.

"Send them a Christmas hamper," said the Squire.

The Christmas hamper went. With a turkey and ham, and a brace of pheasants in it; some bacon and apples to fill up, and sweet herbs and onions. Lena put in her favourite doll, dressed as a little mother, for young Joe. It had a false arm; and no legs, so to say: Hugh cut the feet off one day, and Hannah had to sew the stumps up. We hoped they would enjoy it all, including the doll, and drank good luck to them on Christmas Day.

A week and a half went on, and no news came. Mrs. Todhetley grew uneasy about the hamper, feeling sure it had been confiscated by the railway. Mary Blair had always written so promptly to acknowledge everything sent.

One January day the letter came in by the afternoon post. We knew Mary's handwriting. The Squire and Madam were at the Sterlings', and it was nine o'clock at night when they drove in: Mrs. Todhetley's face ached, which was quite customary: she had a white handkerchief tied round it. When they were seated round the fire, I remembered the letter, and gave it to her.

"Now to hear the fate of the hamper!" she exclaimed, carrying it to the lamp. But, what with the face-ache, and what with her eyes, which were not so good by candle-light as they used to be, Mrs. Todhetley could not read the contents off readily. She looked at the writing, page after page, and then gave a short scream of dismay. Something was wrong.

"Those thieves have grabbed the hamper!" cried the Squire.

"No; I think the Blairs have had the hamper. I fear it is something worse," she said faintly. "Perhaps you will read it aloud."

The Squire put his spectacles on as he took the letter. We gathered round the table, waiting. Mrs. Todhetley sat with her head aside, nursing her cheek; and Tod, who had been reading, put his book down. The Squire hammered a good deal over the writing, which was not so legible as Mary's was in general. She appeared to have meant it for Mrs. Todhetley and the Squire jointly.

"'MY VERY DEAR FRIENDS,—If I have delayed writing to you it was not for want of in-ingredients'"——

"Ingredients!" Cried one of us.

"It must be gratitude," corrected the Squire. "Don't interrupt."

"'Gratitude for your most welcome and liberal present, but because my heart and hands have alike shrunk from the ex—ex—explanation it must entail. Alas! a series of very terrible misfortunes have overwormed—overwhelmed us. We have had to give up our school and our prospects together, and to turn out of our once happy dome.'"

"Dome!" put in Tod.

"I suppose it's home," said the Squire. "This confounded lamp is as dim as it can be to-night!" And he went on fractiously.

"'Through no fault of my husband's he had to borrow a hundred and fifty pounds nearly twelve months ago. The man he had it from was a money-lender, a Mr. Gavity; he charged a high rate of interest, and brought the costs up to about thirty pounds; but we have no reason to think he wished to act un—unfar—unfairly by us. He required security—which I suppose was only reasonable. The Reverend Mr. Lockett offered himself as such; but Gavity said parsons were slippers.'"

"Good gracious!" said Mrs. Todhetley.

"The word's slippery, I expect," cried the Squire with a frown. "One would think she had emptied the water-bottle into the ink-pot."

"'Gavity said parsons were slippery; meaning that they were often worth no more than their word. He took, as security, a bill of sale on the furnace. Stay,—furniture. Our school was quite prosperous; there was not the slightest doubt that in a short while the whole of the debt could be cleared off; so we had no hesitation in letting him have the bill of sale. And no harm would have come of it, but for one dreadful misfortune, which (as it seems) was a necessary part of the

attendant proceedings. My husband got put into Jer—Jer
· Jerry's Gazelle.' "

" Jerry's Gazelle ? "

" Jerry's Gazette," corrected the Squire.

" Jerry's Gazette ? "

The lot of us spoke at once. He stared at the letters and
then at us. We stared back again.

" It *is* Jerry's Gazette—as I think. Come and see, Joe."

Tod looked over the Squire's shoulder. It certainly looked
like " Jerry's Gazette," he said ; but the ink was pale.

" ' Jerry's Gazette.' Go on, father. Perhaps you'll find an
explanation further on."

" ' This Jerry's Gazette, it appears, is circulated chiefly (and
I think privately) amongst comical men—commercial men ;
merchants, and tradespeople. When they read its list of
names, they know at once who is in difficulties. Of course
they saw my husband's name there, Pyefinch Blair ; unfortunately a name so peculiar as not to admit of doubt. I did
not see the Gazette, but I believe the amount of the debt was
stated, and that Gavity (but I don't know whether he was mentioned by name) had a bill of sale on our household furniture.' "

" What the dickens is Jerry's Gazette ? " burst forth the
Squire, giving the letter a passionate fling. " I know but of
one Gazette, into which men of all conditions go, whether they
are made lords or bankrupts. What's this other thing ? "

He put up his spectacles, and stared at us all again, as if
expecting an answer. But he might as well have asked it of
the moon. Mrs. Todhetley sat with the most hopeless look
you ever saw on her face. So he took up the reading again.

" ' We knew nothing about Jerry's Gazette ourselves, or that
there was such a pub—pub—publication, or that the transaction had appeared in it ; and could not imagine why the
school began to fall off. Some of the pupils were taken away
at once, some at Lady-day ; and by midsummer nearly every
one had left. We used to lie awake night after night, grieving
and wondering what could be the matter, searching in vain

for any cause of offence, given unwittingly to the boys or their parents. Often and often we got up in the morning to go about our day's work, never having closed our eyes. At last, a gentleman, whose son had been one of the first renewed—removed, told Pyefinch the truth : that he had appeared in Jerry's Gazette. The fathers who subscribed to Jerry's Gazette had seen it for themselves ; and they informed the others.' "

" The devil take Jerry's Gazette," interrupted Tod, deliberately.

" This reads like an episode of the Secret Inquisition, sir, in the days of the French Revolution."

" It reads like a thing that an honest Englishman's ears ought to redden to hear of," answered the Squire, as he lifted the lamp nearer, for his outstretched arms were getting cramped.

" ' Pyefinch went round to every one of the boys' fathers. Some would not see him, some not hear him ; but to those who did, he imported—imparted—the whole circumstances ; showing how it was he had had to borrow the money (or rather to re-borrow it, but I have not time in this letter to go so far into detail), and that it could not by any possibility injure the boys or touch their interests. Most of them, he said, were very kind and sympathising, so far as words went, saying that in this case Jerry's Gazette appeared to have been the means of inflicting a cruel wrong ; but they would not agree to replace their sons with us. They either declined point-blank, or said they'd consider of it ; but you see the greater portion of the boys were already placed at other schools. All of them told Pyefinch one thing—that they were thoroughly satisfied with his treatment in every respect, and but for this interruption would probably have left their sons with him as long as they wanted intrusion—instruction. The long and short of it was this, my dear friends : they did not choose to have their sons educated by a man who was looked upon in the commercial world as next door to a bankrupt. One of them delicately hinted as much, and said Mr. Blair must be aware that he was liable to have his house topped—stripped—at any moment under the bill of sale. We said to ourselves that evening, as Pyefinch and I talked together, that we might have removed boys of our own from a school under the like circumstances.'"

"'That's true enough," murmured Mrs. Todhetley.

"'My letter has grown very long and I must hasten to conclude it. Just before the rent was due at Michaelmas (we paid it half-yearly, by agreement) Gavity put the bill of sale into force. One morning several men came in and swept off the furniture. We were turned out next: though indeed to have attempted to remain in that large house were folly. The landlord came in a passion, and told Pyefinch that he would put him in prison if he were worth it; as he was not, he had better go out of the pitch—place—forthwith, as another tenant was ready to take possession. Since then we have been staying here, Pyefinch vainly seeking to get some profitable employment. What we hoped was, that he would obtain an under-mastership to some public fool——'"

"Fool, sir!"

"'School. But it seems difficult. He sends his best regards to you, and bids me say that the reason you have not heard from us so long is, that we could not bear to tell you the ill news after your former kindness to us. The arrival of the hamper leaves us no resource.

"'Thank you for that. Thank you very truly. The people at the old house have our address, and re-directed it here. We received it early on Christmas Eve. How good the things were, you do not need to be told. I stuffed the turkey—I shall make a famous cook in time—and sent it to the backhouse—bakehouse. You should have seen the pill—picture—it was when it came home. Believe me, my dear friends, we are both of us grateful for all your kindness to us, present and past. Little Joe is so delighted with the doll; he scarcely puts it out of his arms. Our best love to all; including Hugh and Lena. Thank Johnny for the beautiful new book he put in. I must apologize in conclusion for my w iting; the ink we get in these penny bottles is pale; ar d baby has been on my lap all the time, never easy a minute. Do not say any thing of all this, please, should you be writing to Wales. Ever most truly yours,   "'MARY BLAIR.

"'13, Difford's Buildings, Paddington.'"

The Squire put the letter down and his spectacles on it, quite solemnly. You might have heard a pin drop in that room.

"This is a thing that must be inquired into. I shall go up to-morrow."

"And I'd go too, sir, but for my engagement to the Whitneys," said Tod.

"She must mean, in speaking of a baby, that there's another," spoke Mrs. Todhetley, in a frightened sort of whisper, "besides little Joe. Dear me!"

"I don't understand it," stamped the Squire, getting red.

"Turned out of house and home through Jerry's Gazette! Do we live in England, I'd like to ask?—under English laws? —enjoying English rights and freedom? Jerry's Gazette? What the deuce *is* Jerry's Gazette? Where does it come out of? What issues it? The Lord Chamberlain's Office?—or Scotland Yard?—or some Patent society that we've not heard of, down here? The girl must have been imposed upon: her statement won't hold water."

"It looks as though she had been, sir."

"*Looks* like it, Johnny! it must be so," said the Squire, getting warmer. "I have temporary need of a loan of money, and I borrow it in straightforward fairness, honestly proposing and undertaking to pay it back with good interest, but not exactly wanting my neighbours to know; and you'd like me to believe that there's some association, or publication, or whatever else it may be, that won't allow this to be done privately, but must pounce upon the transaction, and take it down in print, and send it round to the public, just as if it were a wedding or a burying!"

The Squire had grown redder than a roost-cock. He always

did when tremendously put out, and the matter would not admit of calling in old Jones the constable.

"Folly! Moonshine! Blair, poor fellow, has been slipping into some damaging disaster, had his furniture seized, and so invents this fable to appease his wife, not liking to tell her the truth. Jerry's Gazette! When I was a youngster, my father took me to see an exhibition in Worcester called 'Jerry's Dogs.' The worst damage you could get there was a cold, from the holes in the canvas roof, or a pitch over the front into the sawdust. But in Jerry's Gazette, according to this tale, you may be damaged for life. Don't tell me! Do we live in Austria, or France, or any of those places, where—as it's said—a man can't so much as put on a pair of clean stockings in a morning, but it's laid before high quarters in black and white at mid-day by the secret police! No, you need not tell me that."

"I never heard of Jerry's Gazette in all my life; I don't know whether it is a stage performance or something to eat: but I feel convinced Mary Blair would not write this without having some good grounds for it," said Tod, bold as usual.

And do you know—though you may be slow to believe it —the Squire had taken latterly to listen to him. He turned his old red face on him now, and some of its fierceness went out of it.

"Then, Joe, all I can say is this—that English honour and English notions have changed uncommonly from what they used to be. 'Live and let live' was one of our mottoes; and most of us tried to act up to it. I know no more of this," striking his hand on the letter, "than you know, boys; and I cannot think but that she must have been under some un-accountable mistake in writing it. Any way, I'll go up to London to-morrow: and if you like, Johnny, you can go with me."

We went up. I did not feel sure of it until the train was off, for Tod seemed three-parts inclined to give up the shooting at the Whitneys', and start for London instead; in which case the Squire might not have taken me. Tod and some more young fellows were invited to Whitney Hall for three days, to a shooting-match.

It was dusk when we reached London, and as cold as charity. The Squire turned into the railway hotel and had some chops served, but did not wait for a regular dinner. When once he was in for impatience, he *was* in for it.

"Difford's Buildings, Paddington," had been the address, so we thought it would not be far to go. The Squire held on in his way along the crowded streets, as if he were about to set things straight to rights, elbowing the people, and asking the road at every turn. Some did not know Difford's Buildings, and some directed us wrongly; but we got there at last. It was in a narrow, quiet street; a row of what Londoners call eight-roomed houses, with little gates opening to the square patches of smoky garden, and "Difford's Buildings" written up as large as life at the corner.

"Let's see," said the Squire, looking sideways at the windows. "Number thirteen, was it not, Johnny?"

"Yes, sir."

Difford's Buildings was not well lighted, and there was no seeing the numbers. The Squire stopped before the one he thought must be thirteen; when somebody came out at the house-door, shutting it behind him, and encountered us at the gate. A youngish clergyman in a white necktie. He and the Squire stood looking at each other in the semi-darkness.

"Can you tell me if Mr. Blair lives here?"

"Yes, he does," was the answer. "I think—I think I have the pleasure of speaking to Mr. Todhetley."

The Squire knew him then—the Rev. Mr. Lockett. They had met when Blair first took to the school.

"What *is* all this extraordinary history?" burst forth the Squire, seizing him by the button of his great-coat, and taking him a few gates further on. "Mrs. Blair has been writing us a strange rigmarole, which nobody can make head or tail of; about ruin, and sales, and something she calls Jerry's Gazette."

" Ay," quietly answered the clergyman in a tone of pain, as he put his arm inside the Squire's, and they paced slowly up and down. " It is one of the saddest histories my experience has ever had to do with."

The Squire was near coming to an explosion in the open street. " Will you be pleased to tell me, sir, whether there exists such a thing as Jerry's Gazette, or whether it is a fable? I have heard of Jerry's Performing Dogs; went to see 'em once: but I don't know what this other invention can be."

" Certainly there is such a thing," said Mr. Lockett. " It is, I fancy, a list of people who unfortunately get into difficulties; at least, people who fall into difficulties seem to get published in it. I am told it is meant chiefly for private circulation: which may imply, as I imagine (but here I may be wrong) what may be called secret circulation. Blair had occasion to borrow a little money, and *his* name appeared in it. From that moment he was a marked man, and his school fell off."

" Goodness bless my soul!" cried the Squire solemnly, completely taken aback at hearing Mary's letter confirmed. " Who gives Jerry's Gazette the right to do this?"

" I don't know about the right. It seems it has the power."

" It is a power I never heard of before, sir. We've got a parson, down our way, who tells us every Sunday the world's coming to an end. I think it must be. I know it's getting too clever for me to understand. If a man has the misfortune (perhaps after years of private struggle that nobody knows anything about but himself) to break up at last, he goes into the land's Gazette in a straightforward manner, and the public read it over their breakfast-tables, and there's nothing underhand about it. But as to this other thing—if I comprehend the matter rightly—Blair did not as much as know of its existence, or that his name was going into it."

" I am sure he did not; or I, either," said Mr. Lockett.

" I'd like its meaning explained, then," cried the Squire getting hotter and angrier. " Is it a fair, upright, honest thing; or is it a kind of Spanish Inquisition?"

"I cannot tell you," answered the parson, as they both stood still. "Mr. Blair was informed by the father of one of his pupils that he believed the sheet was first of all set up as a speculation, and was found to answer so well that it became quite an institution. I do not know whether this is true."

"I have heard of an institution for idiots, but I never heard of one for selling up men's chairs and tables," stormed the Squire "No, sir, and I don't believe it now. I might take up my standing to-morrow on the top of the Monument, and say to the public, 'Here I am, and I'll ferret out what I can about you, and whisper it to one another of you;' and so, bring a serpent's trail on the unsuspecting heads, and altogether play Old Gooseberry with the crowds below me. Do you suppose, sir, the Lord Chancellor would wink his eye at me, stuck aloft there at my work, and would tolerate such a spectacle?"

"I fear the Lord Chancellor has not much to do with it," said Mr. Lockett, smiling at the Squire's logic.

"Then suppose we say good men—public opinion—commercial justice and honour? Come!"

He shook the frail railings, on which his hand was resting, till they nearly came to grief. Mr. Lockett related the particulars of the transaction from the beginning; the original debt, which Blair was suddenly called upon to pay off, and the contraction of the one to Gavity. He said that he himself had had as much to do with it as Blair, in the capacity of friend and adviser, and felt almost as though he were responsible for the turn affairs had taken; which had caused him scarcely to enjoy an easy moment since. The Squire began to abuse Gavity, but Mr. Lockett said that the man did not appear to have had any ill intention. As to his having sold off the goods—if he had not sold them, the landlord would.

"And what's Blair doing now?" asked Mr. Todhetley.

"Battling with illness for his life," said the clergyman. "I have just been praying with him."

The Squire retreated to the lamp-post, as if somebody had knocked him backwards. Mr. Lockett explained further.

It was in September that they had left their home. His own lodging and the church of which he was curate were in Paddington, and he found rooms for Blair and his wife in the same neighbourhood—two parlours in Difford's Buildings. Blair (who had lost heart terribly, so as to be good for little) spared no time or exertion in seeking for something to do. He tried to get in at King's College; they liked his appearance and testimonials, but at present had no vacancy : he tried in private schools for an ushership; but he did not get one : nothing seemed to be vacant just then. Then he tried for a clerk's place. Day after day, sick or well, rain or fine, breakfastless or full of bread, he went tramping about London streets. At last, one of those who had had sons at his school, gave him some out-door employment—the making known a new invention from shop to shop, and soliciting customers for it : Blair to be paid on commission according to his success. Naturally, he did not let weather stop him, and would come home to Difford's Buildings at night, wet through. There had been a great deal of rain in November and December. But he got wet once too often, and was attacked with rheumatic fever. The fever was better now ; the weakness it had left was more dangerous.

"She did not say anything about this in her letter," interrupted the Squire resentfully, when Mr. Lockett had explained so far.

"Blair told her not to. He thought if their position were revealed to the friends who had once shown themselves so kind, it might look almost like begging for help again."

"Blair's a fool!" roared the Squire.

"Mrs. Blair has not made the worst of it to her family in Wales. It would only distress them, she says, for they could not help her. Mr. Sanker has been ill again for some time past, has not been allowed, I believe, to draw his full salary, and there's no doubt they want every penny of their means for themselves ; and more too."

"How have they lived here?' asked the Squire, as we went back slowly to the gate.

"Blair earned a little commission while he could get about; and his wife has been enabled to procure some kind of wool-work from a warehouse in the city, which pays her very well," said the clergyman, dropping his voice to a whisper, as if he feared to be heard through the shutters. "Unfortunately there's the baby to take up much of her time. It was born in October, soon after they got in there."

"And I should like to know what business there has to be a baby?" cried the Squire, who was like a man off his head. "Couldn't the baby have waited to come at a more convenient season?"

"It might have been better; it is certainly a troublesome, crying little thing," said the parson. "Yes, you can go straight in: the parlour door is on the right. I have a service this evening at seven, and shall be late for it. This is your son, I presume, sir?"

"My son! law bless you! My son is a strapping young fellow, six feet two in his stockings. This is Johnny Ludlow."

He shook hands pleasantly, and was good enough to say he had heard of me. The Squire went on, and I with him. There was no lamp in the passage, and we had to feel on the right for the parlour door.

"Come in," called out Mary, in answer to the knock. I knew her voice again.

We can't help our thoughts. Things come into the mind without leave or license; and it is no use saying they ought not to, or asking why they do. Nearly close opposite the door in the small room was the fire-place. Mary Blair sat on a low stool before it, doing some work with coloured wools with a big hooked needle, a baby, in white, lying flat on her lap, and the little chap, Joe, sitting at her feet. All in a moment it put me in mind of Mrs. Lease, sitting on her stool before the fire that day long ago (though in point of fact, as I discovered afterwards, hers had been a bucket turned upside down) with the sick child on her lap, and the other little ones round her. Why this, to-night, should have reminded me of that other, I cannot say, but it did; and in the light of an omen. You must ridicule me if you choose: it is not my fault; and I am telling nothing but the truth. Lease had died. Would Pye-finch Blair die?

The Squire went in gingerly, as if he had been treading on a spiked ploughshare. The candle stood on the mantel-piece, a table was pushed back under the window. Altogether the room was poor, and a small saucepan simmered on the hob by the fire. Mary turned her head, and got up with a flushed face, letting the work fall on the baby's white nightgown, as she held out her hand. Little Joe, a sturdy fellow in a scarlet frock, with big brown eyes, backed against the wall by the fire-place and stood staring, Lena's doll held for safety under his pinafore, its legs projecting upwards.

She lost her presence of mind. The Squire was the veriest old stupid, when he wanted to make-believe, that you'd see in a winter's day. He began saying something about "happening to be in town, and so called." But he broke down, and blurted out the truth. "We've come to see after you, my dear; and to learn what all this trouble means."

And then *she* broke down. Perhaps it was the sight of us, recalling the old time at Dyke Manor, when the future looked so fair and happy; perhaps it was the mention of the trouble. She spread her hands before her face, and the tears rained through her fingers.

"Shut the door for me, will you, Johnny," she whispered. "Very softly."

It was the other door she pointed to, one at the end of the room, and I latched it without noise. Save for a sob now and again, that she kept as silent as she could, the grief passed. Young Joe, frightened at matters, suddenly went at her, full butt, and hid his eyes in her petticoats with a roar. I took him on my knee and got him round again. Somehow children are never afraid of me. The Squire rubbed up his old red nose, and said he had a cold.

But, was she not altered! Now that the flush had faded,

and the emotion passed, the once sweet, fresh, blooming face stood out in its naked reality. Sweet, indeed, it was still; but the bloom and freshness had given place to a haggard look, and to dark circles round the soft brown eyes, weary now.

She had no more to tell of the past calamities than her letter and Mr. Lockett had told. Jerry's Gazette was the sore point with the Squire, but she seemed not to understand it better than we did.

"I want to know one thing," said he, quite fiercely. "How did Jerry's Gazette get at the transaction between your husband and Gavity? Did Gavity go to it, open-mouthed, with the news?"

Mary did not know. She had heard something about a register—that the bill of sale had to be registered somewhere, and thought Jerry's Gazette might have got at the information from that source.

"Heaven bless us all!" cried the Squire. "Can't a man borrow a bit of money but it must become known to his enemies, if he's got any, bringing them down upon him like a pack of wolves in full cry? This used to be the freest land on earth."

The baby began to scream. She put down the wool-work, and hushed it to her. I am sure the Squire had half a mind to tell her to give it a gentle shaking. He looked upon screaming babies as natural enemies: the truth is, with all his abuse, he was afraid of them.

"Has it got a name?" he asked gruffly.

"Yes—Mary: he wished it," she said, glancing at the end door. "I thought we should have to call it Polly, in contra-distinction to mine."

Polly! That was another coincidence. Lease's eldest girl was Polly. And what made her speak of things in the past tense? She caught me looking at her; she caught, I am afraid, the fear on my face. I told her in a hurry that little Joe must be a Dutchman, for not a word could I understand of the tale he was whispering about his doll.

What with Mary's work, and the little earned by Blair while he was about, they had not wanted for necessaries in a plain way. I suppose Lockett took care they should not: but he was only a curate.

The baby needed its supper, to judge by the squealing Mary poured the contents of the saucepan—some thin gruel —into a saucer, and began feeding the little mite by teaspoonfuls, putting each one to her own lips first to test its coolness.

" That's poor stuff for it," cried the Squire, in a half-pitying, half-cross tone, his mind divided between resentment against babies in general and sympathy with this one. As the baby was there, of course it had to be fed, but what he wanted to know was, why it need have come just when trouble was about. When put out, he had no reason at all. Mrs. Blair suddenly turned her face towards the end door, listening; and we heard a faint voice calling " Mary."

" Joe, dear, go and tell papa that I will be with him in one minute."

The little chap slid down, leaving me his doll to nurse, and went pattering across the carpet, standing on tiptoe to open the door. The Squire said he should like to go in and see Blair. Mary went on first to warn him of our advent.

My goodness! *That* Pyefinch Blair, who used to flourish his cane, and cock it over us boys at Frost's! I should never have known him for the same.

He lay in bed, too weak to raise his head from the pillow, the white skin drawn tightly over his hollow features; and the cheek-bones taking a tinge of colour as he watched us coming. And again I thought of Lease; for the same grey look was on his face that had been on his when he was dying.

" Lord bless us!" cried the Squire, in what would have been a solemn tone but for surprise. And Mr. Blair began faintly to offer a kind of apology for his illness, hoping he should soon get over it now.

It was nothing but the awful look, putting one unpleasantly in mind of death, that kept the Squire from breaking out with a storm of abuse all round. Why could they not have sent word to Dyke Manor, he wanted to know. As to asking particulars about Jerry's Gazette, which the Squire's tongue was burning for, Blair was too far gone. While we stood there the doctor came in; a little man in spectacles, a friend of Mr. Lockett's. He told Blair he was getting on all right, spoke to Mrs. Blair, and took his departure. The Squire, wishing good-night in a hurry, went out after the doctor, and collared him as he was walking up the street.

"Won't he get over it?"

"Well, sir, I am afraid not. His state of weakness is alarming."

The Squire turned on him with a storm, just as though he had known him for years: asking why on earth Blair's friends (meaning himself) had not been written to, and promising a prosecution if he let him die. The doctor took it sensibly, and was as cool as iced water.

"We medical men are gifted at best but with human skill, sir," he said, looking the Squire full in the face.

"Blair is young—not much turned thirty."

"The young die as well as the old, when it pleases Heaven to take them."

"But it doesn't please Heaven to take *him*," retorted the Squire, worked up to the pitch that he was not accountable for his words. "But that you seem in earnest, young man, probably meaning no irreverence, I'd ask you how you dare bring Heaven's name into such a case as this? Did Heaven fling him out of house and home into Jerry's Gazette, do you suppose? Or did man? Man did, sir: selfish, hard, unjust man. Don't talk to me, Mr. Doctor, about Heaven."

"All I wished to imply, sir, was, that Mr. Blair's life is not in my power, or in that of any human hands," said the doctor, when he had listened quietly to the end. "I will do my best to bring him round; I can do no more."

"You must bring him round."

"There can be no 'must' in regard to it: and I doubt if

he is to be brought round. Mr. Blair has not naturally a large amount of what we call stamina, and the illness has laid a very serious hold of him. It would be something in his favour if the mind were at ease: which of course it cannot be under his circumstances."

"Now look here—you just say outright he is going to die," stormed the Squire. "Say it and have done with it. I like people to be honest."

"But I cannot say he is. Possibly he may get well. His life and his death both seem to hang on the turn of a thread."

"And there's that squealing young image within ear-shot! Could Blair be got down to my place in the country? You might come with him if you liked. There's some shooting."

"Not yet awhile. It would kill him. What we have to fight against now is the weakness: and a fight it is."

The Squire's face was rueful. "This London has a reputation for clever physicians: you pick out the best, and bring him here with you to-morrow morning. Do you hear, sir?"

"I will bring one, if you wish it. It is not essential."

"Not essential!" wrathfully echoed the Squire. "If Blair's recovery is not essential, perhaps you'll tell me, sir, whose is! What is to become of his poor young wife if he dies?—and the little fellow with the doll?—and that cross-grained puppet in white? Who will provide for them? Let me tell you, sir, that I won't have him die—if doctors can keep him from it. He belongs to me sir, in a manner: he saved my son's life—as fine a fellow as you could set eyes on, six feet two without his boots. Not essential! What next?"

"It is not so much medical skill he requires now as care, and rest, and renovation," spoke the doctor in his calm way.

"Never mind. You take a physician to him, and let him attend him with you, and don't spare expense. In all my life I never saw anybody want patching up so much as he wants it."

The Squire shook hands with him, and went on round the

corner.　I was following, when the doctor touched me on the shoulder.

"He has a good heart, for all his hot speech," whispered he, nodding towards the Squire.　"In talking with him this evening, when you find him indulging hopes of Blair's recovery, *don't encourage them:* rather lead him, if possible, to look on the other side of the question."

The surgeon was off before I recovered my surprise.　But it was now my turn to run after him.

"Do you know that he will not get well, sir?"

"I do not know it; the sick and the well are alike in the hands of God; but I think it scarcely possible that he can," was the answer; and the voice had a solemn tone, the face a solemn aspect, in the street's uncertain light.　"And I would prepare friends always to meet the worst when in my power."

"Now then, Johnny!　You were going to take the wrong turning, were you, sir!　Let me tell you, you might get lost in London before knowing it."

The Squire had come back to the corner of the street, looking for me.　I walked on by his side in silence, feeling half dazed, the hopeless words playing pranks in my brain.

"Johnny, I wonder where we can find a telegraph office?　I shall telegraph to your mother to send up Hannah to-morrow. Hannah knows what the sick need: and that poor thing with her children ought not to be left alone."

But as to giving any hint to the Squire of the state of affairs, I should like the doctor to have tried at it himself.　Before I had finished the first syllable, he attacked me as if I had been a tiger; demanding whether those were my ideas of Christianity, and if I supposed there'd be any justice in a man's dying because he had got into Jerry's Gazette.

In the morning the Squire went on an expedition to Gavity's office in the city.　It was a dull place of two rooms, and a man to answer people.　We had not been a minute there when the Squire began to explode, going on like anything at the man for saying Mr. Gavity was engaged and could not be seen

The Squire demanded if he thought we were creditors, that he should deny Gavity.

What with his looks and his insistance, and his promise to bring in Sir Richard Mayne, he got to see Gavity. We went into a good room with a soft red carpet and marble-topped desk in it. Mr. Gavity politely motioned to chairs before the blaz ing fire, and I sat down.

Not the Squire. Out it all came. He walked about the room, just as he walked at home when he was in a way, and said all kinds of things; wanting to know who had ruined Pyefinch Blair, and what Jerry's Gazette meant. Gavity seemed to be used to explosions: he took it so coolly.

When the Squire calmed down, he nearly grew to see things in Gavity's own light—namely, that Gavity had not been to blame. To say the truth, I could not understand that he had. ·Except in selling them up. And Gavity said if he had not done it, the landlord would.

So nothing was left for the Squire to vent his wrath on but Jerry's Gazette. He no more understood what Jerry's Gazette really was, or whether it was a good or bad thing in itself, than he understood the construction of the planet Jupiter. It's well Dwarf Giles was not present. The day before we came to London, he overheard Giles swearing in a passion, and the Squire had pounced upon him with an indignant inquiry if he thought swearing was the way to get to Heaven. What he said about Jerry's Gazette caused Gavity's eyes to grow round with wonder.

"Lord love ye!" said Gavity, "Jerry's Gazette a thing that wants putting down! Why, it is the blessedest of institutions to us City men. It is a public Benefactor. The commercial world has had no boon like it. Did you know the service it does, you'd sing its praises, sir, instead of abusing it."

"How dare you tell me so to my face?" demanded the Squire.

"Jerry's Gazette's like a mine of gold, sir. It is making its fortune. A fine one, too."

"*I* shouldn't like to make a fortune out of my neighbours' tears, and blood, and homes, and hearths," was the wrathful answer. "If Pyefinch Blair dies in this illness, will Jerry's Gazette settle a pension from its riches on his widow and children? Answer me that, Mr. Gavity."

Mr. Gavity, to judge by his looks, thought the question nearly as unreasonable as he thought the Squire. He wanted to tell of the vast benefit Jerry's Gazette had proved in certain cases; but the Squire stopped his ears, saying Blair's case was enough for him.

"I do not deny that the Gazette may work mischief once in a way," acknowledged Mr. Gavity. "It is but a solitary instance, sir; and in all commercial improvements the units must suffer for the mass."

No good. The Squire went at him again, hammer and tongs, and at last dashed away without saying good morning, calling out to me to come on, and stop not a moment longer in a nest of thieves and casuists.

Difford's Buildings had us in the afternoon. The baby was in its basket, little Joe lay asleep before the fire, the doll against his cheek, and Mary was kneeling by the bed in the back room. She got up hastily when she saw us.

"I think he is weaker," she said in a whisper, as she came through the door and pushed it to. "There is a look on his face that I do not like."

There was a look on hers. A wan, haggard, patiently hopeless look, that seemed to say she could struggle no longer. It was not natural; neither was the calm, dead tone.

"Stay here a bit, my dear, and rest yourself," said the Squire to her. "I'll go in and sit with him."

There could be no mistake now. Death was in every line of his face. His head was a little raised on the pillow; and the hollow eyes tried to smile a greeting. The Squire was good for a great deal, but not for making believe with that sight before him. He broke down with a great sob.

"Don't grieve for me," murmured poor Blair. "Hard

though it seems to leave her, I have learnt to say, 'God's will be done.' It is all for the best—oh it is all for the best. We must through much tribulation enter into the Kingdom."

And then *I* broke down, and hid my face on the counter-pane. Poor old Blair! And we boys had called him Baked Pie!

I went to Paddington station to meet the train. Hannah was in it, and came bursting out upon me with a shriek that might have been heard at Oxford. Upon the receipt of the telegram, she and Mrs. Todhetley came to the conclusion that I had been run over, and was lying in some hospital with my legs off. That was through the Squire's wording of the message; he would not let me write it. "Send Hannah to London to-morrow by mid-day train, to nurse somebody that's in danger."

Blair lingered three days yet before he died, sensible to the last, and quite happy. Not a care or anxiety on his mind about what had so troubled him all along—the wife and children.

"Through God's mercy; He knows how to soothe the death-bed," said Mr. Lockett.

Whether Mary would have to go home to Wales with her babies, or stay and do what she could for them in London, depending on the wool-work, the clergyman said he did not know, when talking to us at the hotel. He supposed it must be one of the two.

"We'll have them down at the Manor, and fatten 'em up a bit, Johnny," spoke the Squire, a rueful look on his good old face. "Mercy light upon us!—and all through Jerry's Gazette!"

I must say a word for myself. Jerry's Gazette (if there is such a thing still in existence) may be, as Mr. Gavity expressed it to us then, the "blessedest of institutions to him and commercial men." I don't wish to deny it, and I could not if I wished; for except in this one instance (which may have been

12*

an exceptional case, as Gavity insisted) I know nothing of it
or its working.   But I declare on my honour I have told
nothing but the truth in regard to what it did for the schoolmaster. Pyefinch Blair.

XIII.

SOPHIE CHALK.

THE horses went spanking along the frosty road, the Squire driving, his red comforter wrapped round his neck. Mrs. Todhetley sat beside him; Tod and I behind. It was one of the jolliest days that early January ever gave us; dark blue sky, and icicles on the trees: a day to tempt people out. Mrs. Todhetley, getting to her work after breakfast, said it was a shame to stay indoors: and it was hastily decided to drive over to the Whitneys' place and see them. So the large phaeton was brought round.

I had not expected to go. When there was a probability of their staying anywhere sufficiently long for the horses to be put up, Giles was generally taken: the Squire did not like to give trouble to other people's servants. It would not matter at the Whitneys': they had a host of them.

"I don't know that I care about going," said Tod, as we stood outside, waiting for the others, Giles at the horses' heads.

"Not care, Tod! Anna's at home."

He flicked his glove at my face for the impudence. We laughed at him about Anna Whitney sometimes. They were great friends. The Squire, hearing some nonsense one day, took it seriously, and told Tod it would be time enough for him to get thinking about sweethearts when he was out of leading-strings. Which of course Tod did not like.

It was a long drive; I can tell you that. And as we turned in at the wide gravel sweep that led up to the house, we saw their family coach being brought round with some luggage on it, the postilion in his undress jacket, just laced on the seams with crimson. The Whitneys never drove from the box.

Whitney Hall was a long red-brick house with a good many windows and wide circular steps leading to the door, its park and grounds lying around it. Anna came running to meet us as we went in, dressed for a journey. She was seventeen; very fair; with a gentle face, and smooth, bright, dark auburn hair; one of the sweetest girls you could see on a sunshiny day. Tod was the first to shake hands with her, and I saw her cheeks blush crimson as Sir John's state liveries.

"You are going out, my dear," said Mrs Todhetley

"Oh, yes," she answered, the tears rising in her blue eyes, which were as blue as the dark blue sky. "We have had bad news. William——"

The dining-room door across the hall opened, and a lot of them came forth. Lady Whitney in a plaid shawl and the strings of her bonnet untied; Miss Whitney (Helen), Harry, and some of the young ones behind. Anna's quiet voice was drowned, for they all began to tell of it together.

Sir John and William were staying at some friend's house at Ombersley. Lady Whitney thought they would have been home at this day: instead of which the morning's post had brought a letter to say that an accident had occurred to William in hunting; some muff who couldn't ride had gone swerving right against Bill's horse, and he was thrown. Except that Bill was insensible, nothing further of the damage could be gathered from the letter; for Sir John, if put out, could write no more intelligibly than the Squire. The chief of what he said was—that they were to come off at once.

"We are going, of course; I with the two girls and Harry; the carriage is waiting to take us to the station," said poor Lady Whitney, her bonnet pushed off till it hung by one ear. "But I do wish John had explained further: it is such suspense. We don't think it can be extremely serious, or there would have been a telegram. I'm sure I have shivered at every ring that has come to the door this morning."

"And the post was never in, as usual, until nearly ten o'clock," complained Harry. "I wonder my father puts up with it."

"And the worst is that we had a visitor coming to-day," added Helen. "Mamma would have telegraphed to London for her not to start, but there was not time. It's Sophie Chalk."

"Who is Sophie Chalk?" asked Tod.

Helen told us, while Lady Whitney was finding places for everybody at the table. They had been taking luncheon in a scrambling fashion; sitting or standing: cold beef, mince-pies, and cheese.

"Sophia Chalk was a schoolfellow of mine," said Helen. ' It was an old promise—that she should come to visit us. Different things have caused it to be put off, but we have kept up a correspondence. At length I got mamma to say that she might come as soon as Christmas was turned; and to-day was fixed. We don't know what on earth to do."

"Let her come to us until you see how things turn out," cried the Squire, in his hearty good-nature, as he cut himself a slice of beef. "We can take her home in the carriage: one of these boys can ride back if you'll lend him a horse."

Mrs. Todhetley said he took the same words out of her mouth. The Whitneys were too flurried to pretend to make ceremony, and very glad to accept the offer. But I don't think it would ever have been made had the Squire and madam known what was to come of it.

"There will be her luggage," observed Anna; who usually remembered things for everybody. And Lady Whitney put down the mince-pie she was eating, and looked round in consternation.

"It must come to us by rail; we will send for it from the station," decided Tod, always ready at a pinch. "What sort of a damsel is this Sophie Chalk, Anna?"

"I never saw her," replied Anna. "You must ask Helen."

Tod whispered something to Anna that made her smile and blush. "I'll write you my sentiments about her to Ombersley,' he said aloud. "Those London girls are something to look at." And I knew by Tod's tone that he was prepared *not* to like Miss Sophie Chalk.

We saw them out to the carriage; the Squire putting in my lady; Tod, Helen and Anna. One of the housemaids, Lettice Lane, was running in and out wildly, bringing things to the carriage. She had lived with us once; but Hannah's temper and Letty's propensity to gossip did not get on together. Mrs. Todhetley, when they had driven away, asked her how she liked her place—which she had entered at Michaelmas. Oh, pretty well, Lettice answered: but for her old mother, she should emigrate to Australia. She used to be always saying at Dyke Manor, and it was one of the things that Hannah would not put up with, telling her decent girls could find work at home.

Tod went off next on horseback: and, before three, we drove to the station to meet the London train. The Squire stayed in the carriage, sending me and Mrs. Todhetley on to the platform.

Two passengers got out at the small station; a little lady in feathers, and a butcher in a blue frock, who had a calf in the open van. Mrs. Todhetley stepped up to the lady and inquired whether she was Miss Chalk.

"I am Miss Chalk. Have I the honour of speaking to Lady Whitney?"

While matters were being explained, I stood observing her. A very small, slight person, with pretty features white as ivory; and wide-open light blue eyes, that were too close together, and had a touch of boldness on their surface. It would take a great deal to daunt their owner, if I could read countenances: and that I was always doing it was no fault of mine, for the instinct, strong and irrepressible, lay within me —as old Duffham once said. I did not like her voice, it had no true ring in it; I did not much like her face. But the world in general no doubt found her charming, and the Squire thought her so.

She sat in front with him, a carpet-bag between them: and

r, behind, had a great black box filling up my legs. She could not do without that much of her luggage: the rest might come by rail.

"Johnny," whispered Mrs. Todhetley to me, "I am afraid she is very grand and fashionable. I don't know how we shall manage to amuse her. Do you like her?"

"Well—she has got a stunning lot of hair."

"Beautiful hair, Johnny!"

With the hair close before us, I could but say so. It was brown; rather darker than Anna Whitney's, but with a red tinge upon it, and about double in quantity. Nature or oil was giving it a wonderful gloss in the light of the setting sun as she turned her head about, laughing and talking with the Squire. Her dress was some bright purple stuff trimmed with white fur; her hands, lying in repose on her lap, had yellow gauntlets on.

"I'm glad I ordered a duck for dinner, in addition to the boiled veal and bacon, Johnny," whispered Mrs. Todhetley again. "The fish won't be much: it is only the cold cod done up in parsley sauce."

Tod, at home long before, was at the door ready for us when we got up. I saw her eyes staring at him in the dusk.

"Who was the gentleman that handed me out?" she asked me as we went in.

"Mr. Todhetley's son."

"I—think—I have heard Helen Whitney talk of him," she said in reflection. "He will be very rich, will he not?"

"Pretty well. He will have what his father has before him, Miss Chalk."

Mrs. Todhetley offered tea, but she said she would prefer a glass of wine; and went up to her chamber after taking it. Hannah and the housemaid were putting one hastily in order for her. Sleepy with the frosty air, I was nodding over the fire in the drawing-room when the rustle of silk awoke me.

It was Miss Chalk. She came in like a gleaming fairy, her dress shining in the fire-light; for they had not been in to light the candles It had a bright green-and-gold tinge, and was cut very low. Did she think we had a party?--or that dressing for dinner was the fashion in our plain country house —as it might have been at a duke's? Her shoulders and arms were white as snow; she wore a silver necklace, the like of which I never saw before, silver bracelets. and a thick cord of silver twisting in and out of the complications of her hair.

"I'm sure it is very kind of your people to take me in," she said, standing still on the hearth-rug in her beauty. "They have lighted a fire in my room; it is so comfortable. I do like a country house. At Lady Augustus Difford's——"

Her head went round at the opening of the door. It was Tod. She stepped timidly towards him, like a school-girl: dressed as now, she looked no older than one. Tod might have made up his mind not to like her; but he had to surrender. Holding out her hand to him, he could but yield to the attractive vision, and his heart shone in his eyes as he bent them upon her.

"I beg your pardon for having passed you without notice, I did not even thank you for lifting me down; but I was frozen with the cold drive," she said in a low tone. "Will you forgive me, Mr. Todhetley?"

Forgive her! as Tod stood there with her hand in his, he looked inclined to eat her. Forgiveness was not enough. He led her to the fire, speaking softly some words of gallantry.

"Helen Whitney has often talked to me about you, Mr. Todhetley. I little thought I should ever make your acquaintance; still less, be staying in your father's house."

"And I as little dreamt of the good fortune that was in store for me," answered Tod.

He was a tall, fine young fellow then, rising twenty, looking older than his age; she (as she looked to-night) a delicate, beautiful fairy, of any teens fancy might please to picture. As Tod stood over her, his manner took a gentle air, his eyes a shy light—quite entirely unusual with him. She did not look up, save by a modest glance now and again, dropping

her eyes when they met his own. He had the chance to take
out his fill of gazing, and used it.

Tod was caught. From that very first night that his eyes
fell on Sophie Chalk, his heart went out to her. Anna Whitney! What child's play had the joking about her been to this!
Anna might have been his sister, for all the regard he had for
her of a certain sort; and he knew it now.

A looker-on sees more than a player, and I did not like one
thing—she drew him on to love her. If ever a girl spread a
net to entangle a man's unconscious feet, that girl was Sophie
Chalk. She went about it artistically, too; in the sweetest,
most natural way imaginable; and Tod did not see or suspect
mortal atom of it.

No fellow in a similar case ever does. If their heart's not
engaged, their vanity is; and it blinds them utterly. I said a
word or two to him, and nearly got knocked over for my pains
At the fortnight's end—and she was with us nearly that length
of time—Tod's heart had made its choice for weal or for woe.

She took care that it should be so; she did, though he cut
my head off now for saying it. You shall judge. On that
first night when she came down in her gleaming silk, with the
silver on her neck and hair, she began. In the drawing-room
after dinner, she sat by him on the sofa, talking in a low
voice, her face turned to him, lifting her eyes and dropping
them again. My belief is, she must have been to a school
where they taught eye-play. Tod thought it was sweet, natural, modest shyness. I thought it was all artistic. Mrs. Todhetley was called from the room on domestic matters; the
Squire, gone to sleep in his dinner-chair, had not come in.
After tea when all were present, she went to the piano, which
nobody ever opened but me, and played and sang, keeping
Tod by her side to turn the music, and to talk to her at available moments. In point of execution, her singing was perfect,
but the voice was a rather harsh one—not a note of real

melody in it. After breakfast the next morning, when we
were away together, she came to us in her jaunty hat, all
feathers, and purple dress with its white fur. She lured him
off to show her the dyke and goodness knows what else, leaving
Lena, who had come out with her, to be taken home by me.
In the afternoon Tod drove her out in the pony-chaise; they
had settled the drive between them down by the dyke, and I
know she had contrived for it, just as surely as though I had
been behind the hedge listening. I don't say Tod was loth; it
was quite the other thing from the first. They took a two-
hours' drive, coming home at dusk; and then she laughed and
talked with him and me round the fire until it was time to get
ready for dinner. That second evening she came down in a
gauzy sort of dress, with a thin white body. Mrs. Todhetley
thought she would be cold, but she said she was used to it.
And so it went on; never were they apart for an hour—no,
nor scarcely for a minute in the day.

At first Mr. and Mrs. Todhetley saw nothing. Rather were
they glad Tod should be so attentive to a stranger; for special
politeness had not previously been amid Tod's virtues; but
they could but notice as the thing went on. Mrs. Todhetley
grew to have an uneasy look in her eyes, and one day the
Squire spoke out. Sophie Chalk had tied a pink woollen scarf
over her head to go out with Tod to see the rabbits fed: he
ran back for something, and the Squire caught his arm.

"Don't carry that on too far, Joe. You don't know who
the girl is."

"What nonsense, sir!" returned Tod, with a ready laugh;
but he turned the colour of a peony.

We did not know much about her, except that she seemed
to be on the high ropes, talking a good deal of great people,
and of Lord and Lady Augustus Difford, with whom she had
been staying for two months before Christmas. Her home in
London, she said, was at her sister's, who had married a
wealthy merchant, and lived fashionably in Torriana Square.
Mrs. Todhetley did not like to appear inquisitive, and would

not question. Miss Chalk was with us as the Whitneys' friend, and that was sufficient.

Bill Whitney's hurt turned out to be something complicated in the ribs. There was no danger after the first week, and they returned home during the second, bringing Bill with them. Helen Whitney wrote the same day for Sophie Chalk, and she said that her mamma would be happy also to see Tod and me for a short while.

We went over in the large phaeton, Tod driving, with Miss Chalk beside him ; I and Dwarf Giles behind. She had thanked Mrs. Todhetley in the prettiest manner ; she told the Squire, as he handed her into the carriage, that she should never forget his kindness, and hoped some time to find an opportunity of repaying it.

Such kissing between Helen and Sophie Chalk ! I thought they'd never leave off. Anna stood by Tod, while he looked on : a hungry light in his eyes, as if envying Helen the kisses she took. He had no eyes now for Anna. Lady Whitney asked if we would go upstairs to William : he was impatient to see us both.

" Halloa, old Johnny !"

He was lying on his back on a broad flat sofa, looking just as well as ever in the face. They had given him up the best bed-room and dressing-room because he was ill : nice rooms, both—with the door open between.

" How did it happen, Bill ?"

" Goodness knows ! Some fellow rode his horse pretty near over mine—don't believe he had ever been across anything but a donkey before. Where's Tod ?"

" Somewhere.—I thought he was close behind me."

" I'm so glad you two have come. It's awfully dull, lying here all day."

" Are you obliged to lie ?"

" Carden says so."

" Do you have Carden ?"

" As if our folks would be satisfied without him when it's a surgical case, and one of danger! he was telegraphed for on the spot and got over in less than an hour. It happened near the Ombersley station. He comes here every other day, and Featherston between whiles as his locum tenens."

Tod burst in with a laugh. He had been talking to the girls in the gallery outside. Leaving him and Bill Whitney to have out their own chaffer, I went through the door to the other room—the fire there was the largest. "How do you do, sir?"

Somebody in a neat brown gown and close white cap, sewing at a table behind the door, had got up to say this with a curtesy. Where had I seen her?—a woman of three or four and thirty, with a delicate, meek face, and subdued expression. She saw the puzzle.

"I am Harry Lease's widow, sir. He was pointsman at South Crabb."

Why, yes, to be sure! And she was not much altered either. But it was a good while now since he died, and she and the children had moved away at the time. I shook hands: the sight of her brought poor Harry Lease to my mind—and many other things.

"Are you living here?"

"I have been nursing young Mr. Whitney, sir. Mr. Carden sent me over from Worcester to the place where he was lying; and my lady thought I might as well come on here with them for a bit, though he don't want more done for him now than a servant could do. What a deal you have grown, sir!"

"Have I? You should see Joseph Todhetley. You knew me, though, Mrs. Lease?"

"I remembered your voice, sir. Besides, I heard Miss Anna say that you were coming here."

Asking after Polly, she gave me the family history since Lease's death. First of all, after moving to her mother's at Worcester, she tried to get a living at making gloves. Her two youngest children caught some disorder, and died; and then she took to go out nursing. In that she succeeded so

well—for it seemed to be her vocation, she said—as to be
brought under the notice of some of the medical gentlemen
of the town. They gave her plenty to do, and she earned an
excellent living, Polly and the other two being cared for by
the grandmother.

"After the scuffle, and toil, and sorrow of the old days,
nursing seems like a holiday for me, Master Ludlow," she concluded; "and I am at home with the children for a day or
two as often as I can be."

"Johnny!"

The call was Bill Whitney's, and I went into the other
room. Helen was there, but not Tod. She and Bill were
disputing.

"I tell you, William, I shall bring her in. She has asked
to come. You can't think how nice she is."

"And I tell you, Helen, that I won't have her brought in.
What do I want with your Sophie Chalks?"

"It will be your loss."

"So be it! I can't do with strange girls here."

"You will see that."

"Now look here, Helen—*I won't have it.* To-morrow is
Mr. Carden's day for coming, and I'll tell him that I can't be
left in peace. He will soon give you a word of a sort."

"Oh, well, if you are so serious as that, let it drop," returned
Helen, with good-humour. "I only thought to give you
pleasure—and Sophie Chalk did ask to come in."

"Who *is* this Sophie Chalk? That's about the nineteenth
time I have asked it."

"The sweetest girl in the world."

"Let that go. Who is she?"

"I went to school with her at Miss Lakon's. She used to
do my French for me, and touch up my drawings. We vowed
a lasting friendship, and I am not going to forget it. Everybody loves her. Lord and Lady Augustus Difford have just
had her staying with them for two months."

"Good souls!" cried Bill, satirically

"She is the loveliest fairy in the world, and dresses like an angel. Will you see her now, William?"

"No."

Helen went off with a flounce. Bill was half laughing, half peevish over it. The confinement made him fretful.

"As if I'd let them bring a parcel of girls in to bother me! You've had her for these past three weeks, I hear, Johnny."

"Pretty near it."

"Do you like her?"

"Tod does."

"What sort of a creature is the syren?"

"She'd fascinate the hair off your head, Bill; give her the chance."

"Then I'll be shot if she shall get the chance as far as mine goes! Lease!"—raising his voice—"keep all strange ladies out here. If they attempt to enter, tell them we've got rats."

"Very well, sir."

Other visitors were staying in the house. A Miss Deveen, and her companion Miss Cattledon. We saw them first at dinner. Miss Deveen sat by Sir John—an ancient lady, active and upright, with a keen, pleasant face and white hair. She had on a shirt-front of worked muslin, with three emerald studs in it that glittered more than diamonds. They looked beautiful. After dinner, when those four old ones began whist, and we were at the other end of the drawing-room in a group, somebody spoke of the studs.

"They are nothing compared to some of her jewellery," said Helen Whitney. "She has a whole set of diamonds, most beautiful! I hardly know what they are worth."

"But those emeralds which she has on to-night must be of value," cried Sophie Chalk. "See how they sparkle!"

It made us all turn. As Miss Deveen stirred with the movement of throwing down her cards, the rays from the wax-lights shone on the emeralds, bringing out the purest green ever imagined by a painter.

"I should like to steal them," said Sophie Chalk; "they'd look well on me."

It made us laugh. Tod had his eyes fixed on her, a strange love lying in their depths. Anna Whitney, kneeling on the ground behind me, could see it.

"I would rather steal a set of pink topaz studs that she has," spoke Helen; "and the opals, too. Miss Deveen is great in studs."

"Why in studs?"

"Because she always wears this kind of white body; it is her evening dress, with satin skirts. I know she has a different set of studs for every day in the week."

"Who is she?" asked Sophie Chalk.

"A cousin of mamma's. She has a great deal of money, and no one in particular to leave it to. Harry says he hopes she'll remember, in making her will, that he is only a poor younger son."

"Just you shut up, Helen," interrupted Harry, in a whisper. "I believe that companion has got ears behind her head."

Miss Cattledon glanced round from the whist-table, as though the ears were there and wide open. She was a wiry lady of middle age, quite forty, with a screwed-in waist and creaking stays, a piece of crimson velvet round her long thin neck, and scanty hair as light as ginger.

"It is she that has charge of the jewel-box," spoke Helen, when we thought it safe to begin again. "Miss Deveen is a wonderful old lady for sixty; she has come here without a maid this time, and dresses herself. I don't see what use Miss Cattledon's of to her, unless it is to act as a general refrigerator, but she gets a hundred a year salary and some of the old satins. Sophie, I'm sure she heard what we said—that we should like to steal the trinkets."

"Hope she relished it!" quoth Harry. "She'll put them under double lock and key, for fear we should break in."

It was all jesting nonsense. Amid the subdued laugh, Tod

bent his face over Sophie Chalk, his hand touching the lace on her sleeve. She had on blue to-night, with a pearl neck lace.

"Will you sing that song for me, Miss Chalk?"

She rose and took his arm. Helen jumped up and arrested them ere they reached the p'ano.

"We must not have any music just now. Papa never likes it when they are at whist."

"How very unreasonable of him!" cried Tod, looking fiercely at Sir John's old red nose and steel spectacles.

"Of course it is," agreed Helen. "If he played for guinea stakes instead of sixpenny, he could not be more particular about having no noise. Let us go into the study: we can do as we like there."

We all trooped off. It was a small square room with a shabby carpet and worn horse-hair chairs. Helen stirred up the fire; and Sophie sat down on a low stool and said she'd tell us a fairy tale.

We had been there just a week when it came out. The week was good. Long walks in the frosty air; a huge swing between the cedar trees; riding by turns on the rough Welsh pony for fun; bagatelle indoors, work, music, chatter; one dinner party, and a small dance. Half my time was spent in Bill's room. Tod seemed to find but little leisure to come up, or for anything else, except Sophie Chalk. It was a gone case with Tod: looking on, I could see that; but I don't think anybody else did, except Anna. He liked Sophie too well to make it conspicuous. Harry made open love to her; Sir John said she was the prettiest little lady he had seen for many a day. I daresay Tod told her the same in private.

And she? Well, I don't know what to say. That she kept Tod at her side, quietly fascinating him always, was certain; but her liking for him did not appear real. To me it seemed that she was *acting* it. "I can't make that Sophie Chalk out

Tod," I said to him one day by the beeches: "she seems child-
ishly genuine, but I believe she's just as sharp as a needle."
Tod laughed idly, and told me I was the simplest muff that
ever trod in shoe leather. She was no rider, and somebody
had to walk by her side when she sat on the Welsh pony, holding her on at all the turnings. It was generally Tod: she
made believe to be frightfully timid with *him*.

It was at the week's end the loss was discovered: Miss
Deveen's emerald studs were gone. You never heard such a
commotion. She, the owner, took it quietly, but Miss Cattledon made noise enough for ten. The girls were talking round
the study fire the morning after the dance, and I was writing
a note at the table, when Lettice Lane came in, her face white
as death.

"I beg your pardon, young ladies, for asking, but have any
of you seen Miss Deveen's emerald studs, please?"

They turned round in surprise.

"Miss Deveen's studs!" exclaimed Helen. "We are not
likely to have seen them, Lettice. Why do you ask?"

"Because, Miss Helen, they are gone—that is, Miss Cattledon says they are. But, with so much jewels as there is in
that case, it is very easy to overlook two or three little things."

Why Lettice Lane should have shaken all over in telling
this, was an unexplained marvel. Her very teeth chattered.
Anna inquired; but all the answer given by the girl was, that
it had "put her into a twitter." Sophie Chalk's countenance
was full of compassion, and I liked her for it.

"Don't let it trouble you, Lettice," she kindly said. "If the
studs are missing, I dare say they will be found. Just before
I came down here my sister lost a brooch from her dressing
table. The whole house was searched for it, the servants were
uncomfortable——"

"And was it found, miss?" interrupted Lettice, too eager
to let her finish.

"Of course it was found Jewels don't get hopelessly lost
in gentlemen's houses. It had fallen down; and, caught by

13

the lace of the toilette drapery, was lying hid within its folds."

"Oh, thank you, miss; yes, perhaps the studs have fallen too," said Lettice Lane as she went out. Helen looked after her in some curiosity.

"Why should the loss trouble *her*? Lettice has nothing to do with Miss Deveen's jewels."

"Look here, Helen, I wish we had never said we should like to steal the things," spoke Sophie Chalk. "It was all jest, of course, but this would not be a nice sequel to it."

"Why—yes—you did say it, some of you," cried Anna, who, till then, had seemed buried in thought; and her face flushed.

"What if we did?" retorted Helen, looking at her in some slight surprise.

Soon after this, in going up to Bill's room, I met Lettice Lane. She was running down stairs with a plate, and looked whiter than ever.

"Are the studs found, Lettice?"

"No, sir."

The answer was short, the manner scared. Helen had wondered why the loss should affect her; and so did I.

"Where's the use of your being put out over it, Lettice? You did not take them."

"No, Master Johnny, I did not; but—but—" looking all round and dropping her voice to a whisper, "I am afraid I know who did; and it was through me. I'm a'most mad."

This was rather mysterious. She gave no opportunity for more, but ran down as though the stairs were on fire.

I went on to Bill's chamber, and found Tod and Harry with him; they were laughing over a letter from some fellow at Oxford. Standing at the window close by the inner door, which was ajar, I heard Lettice Lane go into the dressing-room and speak to Mrs. Lease in a half whisper.

"I can't bear this any longer," she said. "If you have taken those studs, for heaven's sake put them back. I'll make some excuse—say I found them under the carpet, or slipped under the drawers—anything—only put them back!"

" I don't know what you mean,' replied Mrs. Lease, who always spoke as though she had but half a voice.

" Yes, you do. You have got the studs."

By the pause that ensued, Nurse Lease seemed to have lost the use of her tongue. Lettice took the opportunity to put it stronger.

" If you've got them about you, give them into my hand now, and I'll manage the rest. Not a living soul shall ever know of this if you will. Oh, do give them to me!"

Mrs. Lease spoke then. " If you say this again, Lettice Lane, I'll tell my lady all. And indeed I have been wanting to tell her ever since I heard that something was gone. It was for your sake I did not."

" For my sake!" shrieked Lettice.

" Well, and it was. I'm sure I'd not like to say it if I could help, Lettice Lane; but it did strike me that you might have been tempted to—to—you know."

So it was accusation and counter-accusation. Which of the two confessed first was uncertain; but in a short while the whole was known to the house, and to Lady Whitney.

On the previous night the upper housemaid was in bed with some temporary illness, and it fell to Lettice Lane to put the rooms to rights after the ladies had dressed. Instead of calling one of the other servants she asked Mrs. Lease to help her—which must have been for nothing but to gossip with the nurse, as Lady Whitney said. On Miss Deveen's dressing-table stood her case of jewels, the key in the lock. Lettice .ifted the lid. On the top tray glittered a heap of ornaments, and the two women feasted their eyes with the sight. Nurse Lease declared that she never put " a finger's end " on a single article. Lettice could not say as much. Neither (if they were to be believed) had observed the green studs; and the upper tray was not lifted to see what was underneath. Miss Cattledon, who made one at the uproar, put in her word at this, to say they were telling a falsehood, and her face had enough vinegar in it to pickle a salmon. Other people might like Miss Cattledon, but I did not. She was in a silent rage with Miss Deveen for having chosen to keep the jewel-case during their stay at Whitney Hall, and for carelessly leaving the key in it. Miss Deveen took the loss calmly, and was as cool as a water-melon.

" I don't know that the emerald studs were in the upper tray last night; I don't remember to have seen them," Miss Deveen said, as if bearing out the assertion of the two women.

" Begging your pardon, madam, they *were* there," stiffly corrected Miss Cattledon. " I saw them. I thought you would put them on, as you were going to wear your green satin gown, and asked if I should lay them out; but you told me you would choose for yourself."

Miss Deveen had worn diamonds; we noticed their lustre.

" I'm sure it is a dreadful thing to have happened ! " said poor Lady Whitney, looking as flurried as a scared cow. " I dare not tell Sir John; he would storm the windows out of their frames. Lease, I am astonished at *you*. How could you dare open the box ? "

" I never did open it, my lady," was the answer. " When I got round from the bed, Lettice was standing with it open before her."

" I don't think there need be much doubt as to the guilty party," struck in Miss Cattledon with intense acrimony, as her eyes went swooping down upon Lettice. And if they were not sly and crafty eyes, never you trust me again.

" I do not think there need be so much trouble," corrected Miss Deveen. " It's not your loss, Cattledon—it is mine : and my own fault too."

But Miss Cattledon would not take the hint. She stuck to it like a leech, and sifted evidence as subtly as an Old Bailey lawyer. Mrs. Lease carried innocence on the surface ; no one could doubt it : Lettice might have been taken for a seven-years' thief. She sobbed, and choked, and rambled in her tale, and grew as confused as a hunted hare, contradicting herself at every second word. The Australian scheme (though it might have been nothing but foolish talk) told against her now.

Things grew more uncomfortable as the day went on, the house being ransacked from head to foot. Sophie Chalk cried. She was not rich, she said to me, but she'd give every shilling of money she had with her for the studs to be found; and she thought it was very wrong to accuse Lettice, when so many strangers had been in the house. I liked Sophie better than I had liked her yet: she looked regularly vexed.

Sir John got to know of it: Miss Cattledon told him. He did not storm the windows out, but he said the police must come in to see Lettice Lane. Miss Deveen, hearing of this, went straight to Sir John, and assured him that if he took any serious steps while the affair was so doubtful, she would quit his house on the instant, and never put foot in it again. He retorted that it must have been Lettice Lane—common sense and Miss Cattledon could not be mistaken—and that it ought to be investigated.

They came to a compromise. Lettice was not to be given into custody at present; but she must quit the Hall. That, said Miss Deveen, was of course as Sir John and Lady Whitney pleased. To tell the truth, suspicion did seem strong against her.

She went away at eventide. One of the men was charged to drive her to her mother's, about five miles off. I and Anna, hastening home from our walk—for we had lost the others, and the stars were coming out in the cold sky—saw them as we passed the beeches. Lettice's face was swollen with crying.

" We are so sorry this has happened, Lettice," Anna gently said, going to the gig. " I do hope it will be cleared up soon. Remember one thing—I shall think well of you until it is. *I* do not suspect you."

" I am turned out like a criminal, Miss Anna," sobbed the girl. " They searched me to the skin; that Miss Cattledon standing on to see that the housekeeper did it properly; and they have searched my boxes. The only one to speak a kind word to me as I came away, was Miss Deveen herself. It's a disgrace I shall never get over."

"That's rubbish, Lettice, you know,"—for I thought I'd put in a good word, too. "You will soon forget it, once the right fellow is pitched upon. Good luck to you, Lettice."

Anna shook hands with her, and the man drove on, Lettice sobbing aloud. Not hearing Anna's footsteps, I looked round and saw she had sat down on one of the benches, though it was white with frost. I went back.

"Don't you go and catch cold, Anna."

"Johnny, you cannot think how this is troubling *me*."

"Why you—in particular?"

"Well—for one thing I can't believe that she is guilty. I have always liked Lettice."

"So did we at Dyke Manor. But if she is not guilty, who is?"

"I don't know, Johnny," she continued, her eyes taking a far-off, thoughtful look. "What I cannot help thinking, is this—though I feel half ashamed to say it. Several visitors were in the house last night; suppose one should have found her way into the room, and taken them? If so, how cruel this must be on Lettice Lane."

"Sophie Chalk suggested the same thing to me to-day. But a visitor would not do such a thing. Fancy a lady stealing jewels!"

"The open box might prove a strong temptation. People do things in such moments, Johnny, that they would fly from at other times."

"Sophie said that too. You have been talking together."

"I have not exchanged a word with Sophie Chalk on the subject. The ideas might occur naturally to any of us."

I did not think it at all likely to have been a visitor. How should a visitor know there was a jewel-box open in Miss. Deveen's room? The chamber, too, was an inner one, and therefore not liable to be entered accidentally. To get to it you had to go through Miss Cattledon's.

"The room is not easy of access, you know, Anna."

"Not very. But it might be reached."

"I say, are you saying this for any reason?"

She turned round and looked at me rather sharply.

"Yes. Because I do not believe it was Lettice Lane."

"Was it Miss Cattledon herself, Anna? I have heard oi such like curious things. Her eyes took a greedy look to-day when they rested on the jewels."

As if the suggestion frightened her—and I hardly know how I came to whisper it—Anna started up, and ran across the lawn to the house, never looking back or stopping.

XIV.

AT MISS DEVEEN'S.

THE end of the table was between us as we stood in the dining-room at Dyke Manor—I and Mrs. Todhetley —and on it lay a three-cornered article of soft geranium-coloured wool, which she called a "fichu." I had my great-coat on my arm ready for travelling, for I was going up to London on a visit to Miss Deveen.

It was Easter now. Soon after the break-up of pleasure, caused by the loss of the emerald studs at Whitney Hall in January, the party had dispersed. Sophie Chalk returned to London; Tod and I came home; Miss Deveen was going to Bath. The studs had not been traced—had never been heard of since; and Lettice Lane, after a short stay in disgrace at her mother's cottage, had suddenly disappeared. Of course there were not wanting people to affirm that she had gone off to her favourite land of promise, Australia, carrying the studs with her.

The Whitneys were now in London. They did not go in for London seasons; in fact, Lady Whitney hardly remembered to have had a season in London at all, and she quite dreaded this, saying she should feel like a fish out of water. Sir John occupied a bedroom when he went up for Parliament, and dined at his club. But Helen was nineteen, and they thought she ought to be presented to the Queen. So Miss Deveen was consulted about a furnished house for them, and she and Sir John took one for six weeks from just before Easter. They left Whitney Hall at once to take possession; and Bill Whitney and Tod, who got an invitation, joined them the day before Good Friday.

The next Tuesday I received a letter from Miss Deveen. We were very good friends at Whitney, and she had been polite enough to say she should be glad to see me in London. I never expected to go, for three-parts of those invitations do not come to anything. She wrote now to ask me to go up; it might be pleasant for me, she added, as Joseph Todhetley was staying with the Whitneys.

It is of no use going on until I have said a word about Tod. If ever a fellow was hopelessly in love with a girl, he was with Sophie Chalk. I don't mean hopeless as to the love, but as to getting out of it. On the day that we were quitting Whitney Hall—it was on the 26th of January, and the icicles were clustering on the tree-branches—they had taken along walk together. What Tod said I don't know, but I think he let her know how much he loved her, and asked her to wait until he should be of age and could put the question—would she be his wife? We went with her to the station, and the way Tod wrapped her up in the railway carriage was as good as a show (Pretty little Mrs. Hughes, who had been visiting old Featherston, went up by the same train and in the same carriage.) They corresponded a little, she and Tod. Nothing particular in her letters, at any rate—nothing but what the world might see, or that she might have written to Mrs. Todhetley, who got one from her on occasion—but I know Tod just lived on those letters and her remembrance; he could not hide it from me; and I saw without wishing to see or being able to help myself. Why, he had gone up to London now in one sole hope—that of meeting again with Miss Chalk!

Mrs. Todhetley saw it too—had seen it from the time when Sophie Chalk was at Dyke Manor—and it grieved and worried her. But not the Squire: he no more supposed Tod was going to take up seriously with Sophie Chalk, than with the pink-eyed lady exhibited the past year at Pershore Fair.

Well, that's all of explanation. This was Wednesday morn-

18*

ing, and the Squire was going to drive me to the station for the London train. Mrs. Todhetley at the last moment was giving me charge of the fichu, which she had made for Sophie Chalk's sister.

"I did not send it by Joseph; I thought it was well not," she observed, as she began to pack it up in the tissue paper. "Will you take it down to Mrs. Smith yourself, Johnny, and deliver it?"

"All right."

"I—you know, Johnny, I have the greatest dislike to any thing that is mean or underhanded," she went on, dropping her voice a little. "But I do not think it would be wrong, under the circumstances, if I ask you to take a little notice of what these Smiths are. I don't mean in the way of being fashionable, Johnny; I suppose they are all that; but whether they are nice, good people. Somehow I did not like Miss Chalk, with all her fascinations, and it is of no use to pretend I did."

"She was too fascinating for ordinary folk, good mother."

"Yes, that was it. She seemed to put the fascinations on. And, Johnny, though we were to hear that she had a thousand a year to her fortune, I should be miserable if I thought Joe would choose her for his wife."

"She used to say she was poor."

"But she seemed to have a whole list of lords and ladies for her friends, so I conclude she and her connections must be people of note. It is not that, Johnny—rich or poor—it is that I don't like her for herself, and I do not think she is the one to make Joe happy. She never spoke openly about her friends, you know, or about herself. At any rate, you take down this little parcel to Mrs. Smith, with my kind compliments, and then you'll see them for yourself. And in judgment and observation you are worth fifty of Joe, any day."

"Not in either judgment or observation; only in instinct."

"And that's for yourself," she added, slipping a sovereign into my pocket. "I don't know how much Mr. Todhetley has given you. Mind you spend your money in right things, Johnny. But I am not afraid; I could trust you all over the world."

Giles put my portmanteau in, and we drove off. The hedges were beginning to bud; the fields looked green. From observations about the young lambs, and a broken fence, that he went into a passion over, the Squire suddenly plunged into something else.

"You take care of yourself, sir, in London! Boys get into all kinds of pitfalls there, if they don't mind."

"But I do not call myself a boy, sir, now."

"Not call yourself a boy!" retorted the Squire, staring. "I'd like to know what else you are. Tod's a boy, sir, and nothing else, though he does count twenty years. I wonder what the world's coming to!" he added, lashing up Bob and Blister. "In my days, youngsters did not think themselves men before they had done growing."

"What I meant was, that I am old enough to take care of myself. Mrs. Todhetley has just said she could trust me all over the world."

"Just like her foolishness! Take care you don't get your pockets picked: there's sure to be a thief at every corner. And don't you pick them yourself, Master Johnny. I knew a young fellow once who went up to London with ten pounds in his pocket. He was staying at the Castle and Falcon Hotel, near the place where the mails used to start from—and a fine sight it was to see them bowl out, one after another, with their lamps lighted. Well, Johnny, this young fellow got back again in four days by one of these very mails, every shilling spent, and his fare down not paid. You'd not think that was steady old Jacobson; but it was."

I laughed. The Squire looked more inclined to cry.

"Cleaned out, he was; not a rap left! Money melts in London—that's a fact—and it is very necessary to be cautious. *His* went in seeing the shows; so he told his father. Don't you go in for too many of them, Johnny, or you may find yourself without funds to bring you home, and railways don't give trust. You might go to the Tower, now ; and St. Paul's ; and the British Museum ; they are steady places. I'd not advise a theatre, unless it's just once—some good, respectable play ; and mind you go home straight after it. Some young men slink off to singing-shops now, they say, but I am sure such places can bring no good."

"Being with Miss Deveen, sir, I don't suppose I shall have the opportunity of getting into much harm."

"Well, it is right in me to caution you, Johnny. London is a dreadful place, full of sharpers and bad people. It used to be in the old days, and I don't suppose it has improved in these. You have no father, Johnny, and I stand to you in the light of one, to give you these warnings. Enjoy your visit rationally, my boy, and come home with a true report and a good conscience. That's the charge my old father always gave to me."

Miss Deveen lived in a nice house, north-westward, away from the bustle of London. The road was wide, the houses were semi-detached, with gardens around and plenty of trees in view. Somehow I had hoped Tod would be at the Paddington terminus, and was disappointed, so I took a cab and went on. Miss Deveen came into the hall to receive me, and said she did not consider me too big to be kissed, considering she was over sixty. Miss Cattledon, sitting in the drawing-room, gave me a finger to shake, and seemed not to like my coming. Her waist and throat were thinner and longer than ever ; her stays creaked like parchment.

If I'd never had a surprise in my life, I got one before I was in the house an hour. Coming down from the bed-chamber to which they had shown me, a maid-servant passed me on the first-floor landing. It was Lettice Lane! I wondered—believe me or not, as you will—I wondered whether I saw straight, and stood back against the pillar of the banisters.

"Why, Lettice, is it you ?"

"Yes, sir."

"But—what are you doing *here?*"

"I am here in service, sir."

She ran on upstairs. Lettice in Miss Deveen's house! It was worse than a Chinese puzzle.

"Is that you, Johnny? Step in here?"

The voice—Miss Deveen's—came from a partially open door, close at hand. It was a small, pretty sitting-room, with light blue curtains and chairs. Miss Deveen sat by the fire, ready for dinner. In her white body shone studs of amethyst, quite as beautiful as the lost emeralds.

"We call this the blue-room, Johnny. It is my own exclusively, and nobody enters it but upon invitation. Sit down. Were you surprised to see Lettice Lane?"

"I don't think I was ever so much surprised in all my life. She says she is living here."

"Yes; I sent for her to help my housemaid."

I was thoroughly mystified. Miss Deveen put down her book and spectacles.

"I have taken to glasses, Johnny."

"But I thought you saw so well."

"So I do, for anything but very small type—and that book seems to have been printed for none but the youngest eyes. And I see people as well as things," she added significantly.

I felt sure of that.

"Do you remember, Johnny, the day after the uproar at Whitney Hall, that I asked you to pilot me to Lettice Lane's mother's, and to say nothing about it?"

"Yes, certainly. You walked the whole four miles of the way. It is five by road."

"And back again. I am good for more yet than some of the young folks are, Johnny; but I always was an excellent walker. Next day the party broke up; that pretty girl, Sophie Chalk, departed for London, and you and young Todhetley left later. When you reached your home in the evening, I don't suppose you thought I had been to Dyke Manor the same day."

"No. Had you really, Miss Deveen?"

"Really and truly. I'll tell you now the reason of those journeys of mine. As Lettice Lane was being turned out of the Hall, she made a remark in the moment of departure, accidentally I am sure, which caused me to be nearly certain she was not guilty of stealing the studs. Before, while they were all condemning her as guilty, *I* had felt doubtful of it; but of course I could not be sure, and Miss Cattledon reproaches me with thinking everybody innocent under every circumstance—which is a mistake of hers. Mind, Johnny, the few words Lettice said might have been used designedly, by one crafty and guilty, on purpose to throw me off the suspicion: but I felt nearly fully persuaded that the girl had spoken them in unconscious innocence. I went to her mother's to see them both; I am fond of looking into things with my own eyes; and I came away with my good opinion increased. I went next to Mrs. Todhetley's to hear what she said of the girl; I saw her and your old nurse, Hannah, making it my request to both of them not to speak of my visit. They gave the girl a good character for honesty; Mrs. Todhetley thought her quite incapable of taking the studs; Hannah could not say what a foolish girl with roving ideas of Australia in her head might do in a moment of temptation. In less than a fortnight I was back in London, having paid my visit to Bath. I had been reflecting all that while, Johnny, on the cruel blight this must be on Lettice Lane, supposing that she was innocent. I thought the probabilities were that she *was* innocent, not guilty; and I determined to offer her a home in my own house during the uncertainty. She seemed only too glad to accept it, and here she is. If the girl should eventually turn out to be innocent, I shall have done her a real service; if guilty, why I shall not regret having held out a helping hand to her, that may perhaps save her for the future."

"It was very kind and thoughtful of you, Miss Deveen!"

"My chief difficulty lay in keeping the suspicion on Lettice Lane a secret from my household. Fortunately I had taken no servants with me to Whitney Hall, my maid having been ill at the time; but Cattledon is outrageously virtuous, and of course proportionally bitter against Lettice. You saw that at Whitney."

"She would have been the first to tell of her."

"Yes. I had to put the thing rather strongly to Miss Cattledon—'Hold your tongue or leave me.' It answered, Johnny. Cattledon likes her place here, and acts accordingly. She picks up her petticoats from contamination when she meets the unfortunate Lettice; but she takes care to hold her tongue."

"Do you think it will ever be found out, Miss Deveen?"

"I hope it will."

"But who—could have taken them?" And the thought of what I had said to Anna Whitney, that it might be Miss Cattledon herself, flashed over me as I put the question.

"I think"—Miss Deveen glanced round as if to make sure we were alone, and dropped her voice a little—"that it must have been one of the guests who came to Whitney Hall that night. Cattledon let out one thing, but not until after we were at home, for the fact seemed not to have made the least impression on her memory at the time; but it came back afterwards. When she was quitting her room after dressing that evening—I being already out of mine and gone down—she saw the shawl she had worn in the afternoon lying across a chair just as she had thrown it off. She is very careful of her clothes; and hesitated, she said, whether to go back then and fold it; but, knowing she was late, did not do so. She had been down-stairs about ten minutes, when I asked her to fetch my fan, which I had forgotten. Upon going through her room to mine, she saw the shawl lying on the floor, and picked it up, wondering how it could have come there. At that time the maids had not been in to put either her room or mine to rights. Now what I infer, Johnny, is that my jewel-case was visited and the studs were stolen *before* Lettice Lane and Mrs. Lease went near the rooms, and that the thief, in her hurry to escape, brushed against the shawl and threw it down."

" And cannot Miss Cattledon see the probability of that?"

" She will not see it.   Lettice Lane is guilty with her, and nobody else.   Prejudice goes a long way in this world, Johnny. The people who came to the dance that night were taking off their things in the next room to Miss Cattledon's, and I think it likely that some one of them may have found a way into my chamber, perhaps even by accident, and the sight of the brilliant emerald studs—they were more beautiful than any they were lying with—was too much for human equanimity. It was my fault for leaving the dressing-case open—and do you know, Johnny, I believe I left it literally *open*—I can never forget that."

" But Lettice Lane said it was shut: shut but not locked."

" Well, it is upon my conscience that I left it open.   Whoever took the studs may have shut down the lid, in precaution or forgetfulness.   Meanwhile, Johnny, don't you say anything of what I have told you; at the Whitney's or elsewhere.   They do not know that Lettice Lane is with me; they are prejudiced against her, especially Sir John; and Lettice has orders to keep out of the way of visitors.   Should they by chance see her, why, I shall say that as the case was at best doubtful, I am giving the girl a chance to redeem her good name.   We are going there after dinner.   So mind you keep counsel."

" To the Whitneys?"

" It is only next door, as you may say.   I did not mention that you were coming up," she added, " so there will be a surprise for them.   And now we will go down.   Here, carry my book for me, Johnny."

In the drawing-room we found a grey-haired curate, with a mild voice; Miss Cattledon was simpering and smiling upon him.   I gathered that he did duty in the church hard by, and had come to dinner by invitation.   He took in Miss Deveen, and that other blessed lady fell to me.   It was a good dinner,— Miss Deveen carving: uncommonly good to me after my journey.   Didn't Miss Deveen make me eat!   She said she knew what boys' appetites were.   After the salmon, before I had finished one joint she put on my plate another; first a leg and a merry-thought, then a wing and some bones, besides the stuffing and tongue. The curate took his leave, but Miss Deveen sat on; she fancied to have heard that the Whitneys were to have friends to dinner that night, and would not go in too early.

About half a dozen houses lay between, and Miss Deveen put a shawl over her head and ran the distance. "Such a mistake, to have taken a place for them so near Hyde Park!" whispered Cattledon as we were following—and I'm sure she must have been in a gracious mood to give me the confidence. "Neither Sir John nor Miss Deveen has much notion of the requirements of fashionable society, Mr. Ludlow: as to poor Lady Whitney, she is a very owl in all that relates to it."

Poor Lady Whitney—not looking like an owl, but a plain, good-hearted English mother—was the first to see us. There was no dinner party after all. She sat on a chair just inside the drawing-room, which was precisely the same in build and size as Miss Deveen's, but had not her handsome furniture. She said she was glad to see me, and would have invited me with Joe, but for want of beds.

They were all grouped at the other end of the room, playing at forfeits, and a vast deal too busy to notice me. I had leisure to look at them. Helen was talking very fast: Harry shouting; Anna sat leaning her cheek on her hand; Tod stood frowning and angry against the wall; the young ones were jumping about like savages; and Bill Whitney was stuck on a stool, his eyes bandaged, and the tips of a girl's white fingers touching his hands. A fairy, rather than a girl, for that's what she looked like, with her small, light figure and her gauze skirts floating: Miss Sophie Chalk.

But what on earth had come to her hair? It used to be brown; it was now light, and gleaming with golden spangles. Perhaps it belonged to her fairy nature.

Suddenly Bill shouted out "Miss Chalk," threw off the bandage, and caught her hands to kiss her! It was all in the forfeits: he had a right to do it, because he guessed her name. She laughed and struggled, the children and Helen were as wild Indians with glee, and Tod looked fit to bring the roof down. Just as Bill gave the kiss, Anna saw me.

Of course it created an interlude, and the forfeits were thrown up. Tod came out of his passion, feeling a little frightened.

"Johnny! Why, what in the world brings you here? Anything amiss with my father?"

"I am only come up on a visit, Tod, to Miss Deveen."

"Well, I'm sure!" cried Tod; as if he thought he ought to have all the visiting, and I none.

Sophie put her hand into mine. "I am so glad to see you, again," she said in her softest tone. "And dear Mrs. Todhetley, how is she? and the sweet children?"

But she never waited to hear how; for she turned away at some question put by Bill Whitney.

Sir John came in, and the four old ones sat down to their whist in the small drawing-room opening from this. The children were sent to bed. Sophie Chalk went to the piano to sing a song under her breath, Tod putting himself on one side, Bill on the other.

"Are *both* of them going in for the 'lady's favour?'" I asked of Anna, pointing to the piano, as she made room for me on the sofa.

"I think Miss Chalk would like it, Johnny."

"How well Bill is looking!"

"Oh, he has quite recovered; he seems all the stronger for his hurt. I suppose the rest and the nursing set him up."

"Is Sophie Chalk staying here?"

"No; there's hardly room for her. But she has been here every day and all day since we came up. They send her home in a cab at night, and one of the maids has to go with her. It is Helen's arrangement."

"Do you like London, Anna?"

"No. I wish I had stayed at home."

" But why ? "

" Well—but I can't tell you every reason."

" Tell me one ? "

Anna did not answer. She sat looking out straight before her, her eyes full of trouble.

" Perhaps it is all nothing, Johnny. I may be fanciful and foolish, and so take up mistaken notions. Wrong ones, or more points than one."

" Do you mean anything—*there ?* "

" Yes. It would be—*I* think—a terrible misfortune for us if William were to engage himself to Sophie Chalk."

" You mean Tod, Anna ? " I said, impulsively.

She blushed like a rose. " Down at Whitney I did think it was he ; but since we came here she seems to have changed ; to be—to be——"

" Going in for Bill. I put it plainly you see, Anna."

" I cannot help fearing that it would be a very sad mistake for either of them. Oh, Johnny, I am just tormented out of my peace, doubting whether or not I ought to speak. Sometimes I say to myself, yes it would be right, it is my duty. And then again I fancy that I am altogether mistaken, and that there's nothing for me to say."

" But what could you say, Anna ? "

Anna had been nervously winding her thin gold chain round her finger. She unwound it again before answering.

" Of course—what could I ? And if I were to speak, and —and—find there was no cause," she dreamily added, " I should never forgive myself. The shame of it would rest with me throughout life."

" Well, I don't see that, Anna. Just because you fancied things were serious when they were not so ! Where would be the shame ? "

" You don't understand, Johnny. *I* should feel it. And so I wish I had stayed down at Whitney, out of the reach of torment. I wish another thing with all my heart—that Helen would not have Sophie Chalk here."

"I think you may take one consolation to yourself, Anna—that whatever you might urge against her, it would most likely make not the smallest difference one way or the other. With Tod I am sure it would not. If he set his mind on marrying Sophie Chalk, other people's grumbling would not turn him from it."

"It might depend a little on what the grumblings were," returned Anna, as if fighting for the last word. "But there; let it drop. I'd rather say no more."

She got up to reach a photograph book, and we began looking over it together.

"Good gracious! Here's Miss Cattledon? Small waist and all!"

Anna laughed. "She had it taken in Bath, and sent it to William. He had only asked her for it in joke."

"So those studs have never turned up, Anna?"

"No. I wish they would. I should pray night and morning for it, if I thought it would do nobody an injury."

"Johnny!" called out Sir John.

"Yes, sir."

"Come you, and take my hand for five minutes. I have just remembered a note I ought to have written this afternoon."

"I shall be sure to play badly," I said to Lady Whitney, who had fallen to Sir John in cutting for partners.

"Oh, my dear, what does it matter?" she kindly answered. "I don't mind if you do. I do not play well myself."

The next morning Miss Cattledon went out to ten o'clock daily service. Miss Deveen said she had taken to the habit of doing so. I wondered whether it was for the sake of religion, or for that grey-haired curate who did the prayers. Sitting by ourselves, I told Miss Deveen of the commission I had from Mrs. Todhetley; and somehow, without my intending it, she gathered a little more.

"Go by all means, and learn what you can, Johnny. Go at once. I don't think you need, any of you, be afraid, though," she added, laughing. "I have seen very much of boy and girl love; seen that it rarely comes to anything. Young men mostly go through one or two such episodes before settling seriously to the business of life."

The omnibus took me to Oxford Street, and I found my way from thence to Torriana Square. It proved to be a corner house, its front entrance being in the square. But there was a smaller entrance on the side (which was rather a bustling street), and a kind of office window, on the wire blind of which was written, in white letters, "Mr. Smith, wine-merchant."

A wine-merchant! Well, I was surprised. Could there be any mistake? No, it was the right number. But I thought there must be, and stood staring at the place with both eyes. That *was* a come-down. Not but what wine-merchants are as good as other people; only Sophie Chalk had somehow imparted the notion of their living up to lords and ladies."

I asked at the front door for Mrs. Smith, and was shown upstairs to a handsome drawing-room. A little girl, with a sallow face, thin and sickly, was seated there. She did not get up, only stared at me with her dark, keen, deep-set eyes.

"Do you know where your mamma is, Miss Trot?" asked the servant, putting a chair.

"You can go and search for her."

She looked at me so intently as the maid left the room, that I told her who I was, and what I had come for. The child's tongue—it seemed as sharp a one as Miss Cattledon's —was let loose.

"I have heard of you, Johnny Ludlow. Mrs. Smith would be glad to see you. You had better wait."

I don't know how it is that I make myself at home with people; or, rather, that people seem so soon to be at home with me. I don't *try* for it, but it is always so. In two or three minutes, when the girl was talking to me as freely as though I were her brother, the maid came back again.

"Miss Trot, I cannot find your mamma."

"Mrs. Smith's out. But I was not obliged to tell you so. I'll not spare you any work when you call me Miss Trot."

The maid's only answer was to leave the room: and the little girl—who spoke like a woman—shook her dark hair from her face in temper.

"I've told them over and over again I will not be called Miss Trot. How would you like it? Because my mamma took to say it when I was a baby, it is no reason why other people should."

"Perhaps your mamma says it still, and so they fall into it also."

"My mamma is dead."

Just at the moment I did not take the meaning of the words. "Mrs. Smith dead!"

"Mrs. Smith is not my mother. Don't you insult me, please. She came here as my governess. If papa chose to make a fool of himself by marrying her afterwards, it was not my fault. What are you looking at?"

I was looking at her: she seemed so strange a child; and feeling slightly puzzled between the other Mrs. Smith and this one. They say I am a muff at many things. I'm sure I am at understanding complicated relationships.

"Then—Miss Chalk is—*this* Mrs. Smith's sister?"

"Well, you might know that. They are a pair, and I don't like either of them. There are two crying babies upstairs now."

"Mrs. Smith's?"

"Yes, Mrs. Smith's"—with intense aggravation. "Papa had quite enough with me, and I could have managed the house and servants as well as *she* does. And because Nancy Chalk was not enough, in addition we must be never safe from Sophonisba! Oh, there are crosses in life!"

"Who is Sophonisba?"

“She is Sophonisba.”

“Perhaps you mean Sophie Chalk?”

“Her name’s not Sophie, or Sophia either. She was christened Sophonisba, but she hates the name, and takes care to drop it always. She is a deep one, is Sophonisba Chalk!”

“Is this her home?”

“She makes it her home, when she’s not out teaching And papa never seems to see it as an encroachment. Sophonisba Chalk does not keep her places, you know. She thought she had got into something fine last autumn at Lord Augustus Difford’s, but Lady Augustus gave her warning at the first month’s end.”

“Then Miss Chalk is a governess?”

“What else do you suppose she is? She comes over people, and gets a stock of invitations on hand, and goes to them between times. You should hear the trouble there is about her dresses, that she may make a good appearance. And how she does it I can’t think; they don’t tell me their contrivances. Mrs. Smith must give her some—I am sure of it—which papa has to pay for; and Sophonisba goes in trust for others.”

“She was always dressed well down with us.”

“Of course she was. Whitney Hall was her great card place; but the time for the visit was so long before it was fixed, she thought it had all dropped through. It came just right: just when she was turned out of Lady Augustus Difford’s. Helen Whitney had promised it a long while before.”

“I know; when they were schoolfellows at Miss Lakon’s.”

“They were not schoolfellows. Sophonisba was treated as the rest, but she was only improving pupil. She gave her services, learnt of some of the masters, and paid nothing How old do you think she is?” broke off Miss Trot.

“About twenty.”

“She was six-and-twenty last birthday; and they say she will look like a child till she’s six-and-thirty. I call it a shame for a young woman of that age to be doing nothing for herself, but to be living on strangers; and papa and I are nothing else to her."

"How old are you?" I could not help asking.

"Fifteen: nearly sixteen. People take me to be younger, because I am short, and it vexes me. They'd not think me young if they knew how I feel. Oh, I can tell you it is a sharpening thing for your papa to marry again, and to find yourself put down in your own home."

"Has Miss Chalk any engagement now?"

"She has not had an engagement all this year, and now it's April! I don't believe she looks after one. She pretends to teach me—while she's waiting, she says; but it's all a farce, I won't learn of her. I heard her tell Mr. Everty I was a horrid child. Fancy that!"

"Who is Mr. Everty?"

"Papa's head-clerk. He is a gentleman, you know, and Sophonisba thinks great things of him. Ah, I could tell something, if I liked! but she put me on my honour. Oh, she's a sly one! Just now, she is all her time at the Whitneys, fire-hot for it. You are not going? Stay to luncheon."

"I must go; Miss Deveen will be waiting for me. You can deliver the parcel, please, with Mrs. Todhetley's message. I will call in to see Mrs. Smith another day."

"And to see me too?" came the quick retort.

"Yes, of course."

"Now, mind you don't break your word. I shall say it is me you are coming to call upon; they think I am nobody in this house. Ask for *Miss* Smith when you come. Good-bye, Johnny Ludlow!"

She never stirred as I shook hands; she seemed never to have stirred hand or foot throughout the interview. But, as I opened the door, there came an odd sort of noise, and I turned to look what it was.

She. Hastening to cross the room, with a crutch, to ring the bell! And I saw that she was both lame and deformed

In passing down the side street by the office, some one

rushed by, with the quick step of a London business man.
Where had I seen the face before? Whose did it put me in
mind of? Why—it came to me all in a minute—Roger
Monk's! He who had lived at Dyke Manor for a short while as
head gardener under false auspices. But, as I have not said
anything about him before, I will not enter into the history
now. Before I could turn to look, Monk had disappeared; no
doubt round the corner of the square.

"Tod," I said, as soon as I came across him, "Sophie Chalk's
a governess."

"Well, what of that?" asked Tod.

"Not much; but she might as well have been candid with
us at Dyke Manor."

"A governess is a lady."

"Ought to be. But why did she make out to us that she
had been a visitor at the Diffords', when she was only the
teacher? We should have respected her just as much; perhaps, made more of her."

"What are you cavilling at? As if a lady were never a
teacher before!"

"Oh, Tod! it is not that. Don't you see?—if she had kept
a chandler's shop, and been open about it, what should we
have cared? It was the sailing under false colours; the trying to pass herself off for what she is not."

He gave no answer to this, except a whistle.

"She is turned six-and-twenty, Tod. And she was not a
school-girl at Miss Lakon's but governess-pupil."

"I suppose she was a school-girl once?"

"I suppose she was."

"Good. What else have you to say, wise Johnny?"

"Nothing."

Nothing; for where was the use? Sophie Chalk would
have been only an angel in his eyes, though he heard that
she had sold apples at a street-corner. Sophie, that very
morning, had begged Lady Whitney to let her instruct the
younger children, "as a friend," so long as they were in town;

14

for the governess at Whitney was a daily one, and they had not
brought her. Lady Whitney at first demurred, and then
kissed Sophie for her goodness. The result was, that a bed
was found for Miss Chalk, and she stayed with them altogether.

But I can't say much for the teaching. It was not Sophie
Chalk's fault, perhaps. Helen would be in the school-room,
and Harry would be there; and I and Anna sometimes: and
Tod and Bill always. Lady Whitney looked upon this London sojourn as a holiday, and did not mind whether the children learnt or played, provided they were kept passably quiet.
I told Sophie of my visit to take the fichu, and she made a
wry face over the lame girl.

"That Mabel Smith! Poor morbid little object! What
she would have grown into but for the fortunate chance of my
sister's marrying into the house, I can't imagine, Johnny. I'll
draw you her portrait in her night-cap, by and by."

The days went on. We did have fun: but war was growing up between William Whitney and Tod. There could no
longer be a mistake (to those who understood things and kept
their eyes open) of the part Sophie Chalk was playing; and
that was the trying to throw Tod over for William Whitney
and to make no fuss about it. I don't believe she cared a
brass button for either: but Bill's future position in life
would be better than Tod's, seeing that his father was a baronet. Bill was going in for her favour; perhaps not seriously: it might have been for the fun of the moment, or to
amuse himself by spiting Tod. Sir John and my lady never
so much as dreamt of the by-play running on before their
face, and I don't think Helen did.

"I told you she'd fascinate the hair off your head, Bill, if
you give her the chance," said I to him one day in the school-
room, when Miss Chalk was teaching her pupils to dance.

"You shut up, Johnny," he said, laughing, and shied the
atlas at me.

Before the day was out, there was a sharp, short quarrel.

They were all coming for the evening to Miss Deveen's. I went in at dusk to tell them not to make it nine at night. Turning into the drawing-room, I interrupted a scene—Bill Whitney and Tod railing at one another. What the bone of dispute was I never knew, for they seemed to have got to the tail of it.

"You did," said Tod.

"I did not," said Bill.

"I tell you, you *did*, William Whitney."

"Let it go; it's word against word, and we shall never decide it. You are mistaken, Todhetley: but I am not going to ask your leave what I shall do, or what I sha'n't."

"You have no right to say to Miss Chalk what I heard you saying to-day."

"I tell you, you did not hear me say anything of the sort But if that you did—what business is it of yours? If I choose to go in for her, to ask her to be the future Lady Whitney—many a year may it be, though, I hope, before I step into my father's place, good old man!—who has the right to say me nay?"

Tod was foaming. Dusk though it was, I could see that. They took no more account of my being present than of Harry's little barking dog.

"Look here, Bill Whitney. If——"

"Are you boys quarrelling?"

The interruption was Anna's. Passing across the hall, she had heard the voices and looked in. As if glad of the excuse to get away, Bill Whitney followed her from the room. Tod went out and banged the hall-door after him.

I waited, thinking Anna might come in, and strolled into the little drawing-room. There, quiet as a mouse, stood Sophie Chalk. She had been listening, for certain; and I hope it gratified her: her eyes sparkled a little.

"Why, Johnny! was it *you* making all that noise? What was the matter? Anything gone wrong?"

It was all very fine to try it on with me. I just looked

straight at her, and I think she saw as much. Saying something about going to search for Helen, she left the room.

"What was the trouble, Johnny?" whispered Anna, stealing up to me.

"Only those two having a jar."

"I heard that. But what was it about? Sophie Chalk?"

"Well, yes; that was it, Anna."

We were at the front window then. A man was lighting the lamps in the road, and Anna seemed to be occupied in watching him. There was enough care on her face to set one up in the dismals for life.

"No harm may come of it, Anna. Any way, you can do nothing."

"Oh, Johnny, I wish she knew!" she said, clasping her hands. "I wish I could satisfy myself which way the *right* lies. If I were to speak, it might be put down to the wrong motive. I try to see whether that thought is not a selfish one, whether I ought to let it deter me. But then—but then—that's not the worst."

"That sounds like a riddle, Anna."

"I wish I had some good, judicious person who would hear all and judge for me," she said, rather dreamily. "If you were older, Johnny, I think I would tell you."

"I am as old as you, at any rate."

"That's just it. We are neither of us old enough nor experienced enough to trust to our own judgment."

"There's your mother, Anna."

"I know."

"What you mean is, that Sir John and Lady Whitney ought to have their eyes opened to what's going on, that they may put an end to Miss Chalk's intimacy here, if they deem the danger warrants it?"

"That's near enough, Johnny. And I don't see my way sufficiently clear to do it."

"Put the case to Helen."

"She would only laugh in my face. Hush! here comes some one."

It was Sophie Chalk. She looked rather sharply at us both, and said she could not find Helen anywhere.

And the days were to go on in public smoothness and private discomfort, Miss Sophie exercising her fascinations on the whole of us.

But for having promised that lame child to call again in Torriana Square, I should not have cared to go. It was afternoon this time. The servant showed me upstairs, and said her mistress was for the moment engaged. Mabel Smith sat in the same seat in her black frock; some books lay on a small table drawn before her.

" I thought you had forgotten to come."

" Did you? I should be sure not to forget it."

" I am so tired with my lessons," she said irritably, sweeping the books away with her long thin fingers. " I always am when *they* teach me. Mrs. Smith has kept me at them for two hours; she is gone down now to engage a new servant."

" I get frightfully tired of my lessons sometimes."

" Ah, but not as I do; you can run about: and learning, you know, will never be of use to me. I want you to tell me something. Is Sophonisba Chalk going to stay at Lady Whitney's?"

" I don't know. They will not be so very long in town."

" But I mean is she to be governess there, and go into the country with them?"

" No, I think not?"

" She wants to. If she does. papa says he shall have some nice young lady to sit with me and teach me. Oh, I do hope she will go with them, and then the house would be rid of her. I say she will: it is too good a chance for her to let slip. Mrs. Smith says she won't: she told Mr. Everty so last night. He wouldn't believe her, and was very cross over it."

" Cross over it?"

"He said Sophonisba ought not to have gone there at all without consulting him, and that she had not been home once since, and only written him one rubbishing note that had nothing in it; and he asked Mrs. Smith whether she thought that was right."

A light flashed over me. "Is Miss Chalk to marry Mr. Everty?"

"I suppose that's what it will come to," answered the curious child. "She has promised to; but promises with her don't go for much when it suits her to break them. Sophonisba put me on my honour not to tell; but now that Mr. Everty has spoken to Mrs. Smith and papa, it is different. I saw it a long while ago; before she went to the Diffords'. I have nothing to do but to sit and watch and think, you see, Johnny Ludlow; and I perceive things quicker than other people."

"But—why do you fancy Miss Chalk may break her promise to Mr. Everty?"

"If she meant to keep it, why should she be scheming to go away as the Whitney's governess? I know what it is: Sophonisba does not think Mr. Everty good enough for her, but she'd like to keep him waiting on, for fear of not getting anybody better."

Anything so shrewd as Mabel Smith's manner of saying this, was never seen. I don't think she was naturally ill-natured, poor thing; but she evidently thought she was being wronged amidst them, and it made her spitefully resentful.

"Mr. Everty had better let her go. It is not I that would marry a wife who dyed her hair."

"Is Miss Chalk's dyed? I thought it might be the gold dust."

"Have you any eyes?" retorted Mabel. "When she was down in the country with you her hair was brown; it's a kind of yellow now. Oh, she knows how to set herself off, I can tell you. Do you happen to remember who was reigning in England when the massacre of St. Bartholomew took place in France?"

The change of subject was sudden. I told her it was Queen Elizabeth.

"Queen Elizabeth, was it? I'll write it down. Mrs. Smith says I shall have no dessert to-day, if I don't tell her. She puts those questions only to vex me. As if it mattered to anybody. Oh, here's papa!"

A little man came in with a bald head and pleasant face. He said he was glad to see me and shook hands. She put out her arms, and he came and kissed her: her eyes followed him everywhere; her cheeks had a sudden colour: it was easy to see that he was her one great joy in life. And the bright colour made her poor thin face look almost charming.

"I can't stay a minute, Trottie; going out in a hurry. I think I left my gloves up here."

"So you did, papa. There was a tiny hole in the thumb and I mended it for you."

"That's my little attentive daughter! Good-bye. Mr. Ludlow, if you will stay to dinner we shall be happy."

Mrs. Smith came in as he left the room. She was rather a plain likeness of Miss Chalk, not much older. But her face had a straightforward open look, and I liked her. She made much of me, and said how kind she had thought it of Mrs. Todhetley to be at the trouble of making a fichu for her, a stranger. She hoped—she did hope, she added rather anxiously, that Sophie had not asked her to do it. And it struck me that Mrs. Smith had not quite the implicit confidence in Miss Sophie's sayings and doings that she might have had.

It was five o'clock when I got away. At the door of the office in the side street stood a gentleman—the same I had seen pass me the other day. I looked at him, and he at me.

"Is it Roger Monk?"

A kind of startled look came over his face. He evidently did not remember me. I said who I was.

"Dear me! How you have grown! Do walk in." And he spoke to me in the tone an equal would speak, not as a servant.

As he was leading the way into a kind of parlour, we passed a clerk at a desk, and a man talking to him.

"Here's Mr. Everty; he will tell you," said the clerk, indicating Monk. "He is asking about those samples of pale brandy, sir: whether they are to go."

"Yes, of course; you ought to have taken them before this, Wilson," was Roger Monk's answer. And so I saw that *he* was Mr. Everty.

"I have resumed my true name, Everty," he said to me in a low tone. "The former trouble, that sent me away a wanderer, is over. Many men, I believe, are forced into such episodes in life."

"You are with Mr. Smith?"

"These two years past. I came to him as head clerk; I now have a commission on sales, and make a most excellent thing of it. I don't think the business could get on without me now."

"Is it true that you are to marry Miss Chalk?" I asked, speaking on a sudden impulse.

"Quite true; if she does not throw me over," he answered, and I wondered at his candour. "I suppose you have heard of it indoors?"

"Yes. I wish you all success."—And didn't I wish it in my inmost heart!

"Thank you. I can give her a good home now. Perhaps you will not talk about that old time if you can help it, Mr. Ludlow. You used to be good-natured, I remember. It was a dark page in my then reckless life; I am doing what I can to redeem it."

I daresay he was; and I told him he need not fear. But I did not like his eyes yet, for they had the same kind of shifty look that Roger Monk's used to have. He might get on none the worse in business; for, as the Squire says, it is shifty world.

Sophie Chalk engaged to Mr. Everty, and he Roger Monk! Well, it was a complication. I went back to Miss Deveen's without, so to say, seeing daylight.

XV

THE GAME FINISHED.

THE ting-tang of the distant church was ringing out fiercely for the daily morning service, and Miss Cattledon was picking her way across the road to attend to it, with her thin white legs displayed, and a water-proof cloak on. It had rained in the night, but the clouds were breaking, promising a fine day. I stood at the window, watching the legs and the pools of water; Miss Deveen sat at the table behind, answering a letter that had come to her by the morning's post.

"Have you ever thought mine a peculiar name, Johnny?" she suddenly asked.

"No," I said, turning round to answer her. "I think it a pretty one."

"It was originally French: De Vigne: but like many other things has been corrupted with time, and made into what it is. Is that ten o'clock striking?"

Yes: and the bell was ceasing. Miss Cattledon would be late. It was a regular penalty to her, I knew, to go out so early, and quite a new whim, begun in the middle of Lent. She talked a little in her vinegar way at the world's wickedness in not spending some of its working hours inside a church, listening to that delightful curate with the mild voice, whose hair had turned grey prematurely. Miss Deveen, knowing it was meant for her, laughed pleasantly, and said if the many years' prayers from her chamber had not been heard as well as though she had gone into a church to

offer them up, she should be in a poor condition now. I
went with Miss Cattledon one Monday morning out of politeness. There were nine-and-twenty in the pews, for I counted
them; eight-and-twenty being single ladies (to go by the
look), some young, some as old as Cattledon. The grey-
haired curate was assisted by a young deacon, who had a
black beard and a lisp and his hair parted down the middle.
It was very edifying, especially the ten minutes' gossip with
the two clergymen coming out, when we all congregated in
the aisle by the door.

"My great-grandfather was a grand old proprietor in
France, Johnny; a baron," continued Miss Deveen. "I
don't think I have much of the French nature left in me."

"I suppose you speak French well, Miss Deveen?"

"Not a word of it, Johnny. They pretended to teach it
me when I was a child, but I'm afraid I was unusually stupid.
Why, who can this be?"

She alluded to a ring at the visitors' bell. One of the servants came in and said that the gentleman who had called
once or twice before had come again.

Miss Deveen looked up, first at the servant, then at me.
She seemed to be considering.

"I will see him in two or three minutes, George"—and the
man shut the door.

"Johnny," she said, "I have taken you partly into my confidence in this affair of the lost studs; I think I will tell you
a little more. After I sent for Lettice Lane here—and my
impression, as I told you, was very strong in favor of her
innocence—it occurred to me that I ought to see if anything
could be done to prove it; or at least set the matter at rest,
one way or the other, instead of leaving it to time and chance.
The question was, how could I do it? I did not like to apply to the police, lest more might have been made of it than
I wished. One day a friend of mine, to whom I was relating
the circumstances, solved the difficulty. He said he would
send to me some one with whom he was well acquainted, a

Mr. Bond, who had once been connected with the detective police, and who had got his dismissal through an affair he was thought to have mismanaged. It sounded rather formidable to my ears, 'once connected with the detective police;' but I consented, and Mr. Bond came. He has had the thing in hand since last February."

"And what has he found out?"

"Nothing, Johnny. Unless he has come to tell me now that he has—for it is he who is waiting. I think it may be so, as he has called so early. First of all, he was following up the matter down in Worcestershire, because the notion he entertained was, that the studs must have been taken by some one of the Whitneys' servants. He stayed in the neighborhood, pursuing his inquiries as to their characters and habits, and visiting all the pawnbrokers' shops that he thought were at available distances from the Hall."

"Did he think it was Lettice Lane?"

"He *said* he did not; but he took care (as I happen to know) to worm out all he could of Lettice's antecedents while he was inquiring about the rest. I had the girl into this room at his first visit, not alarming her, simply saying that I was relating the history of the studs' disappearance to this friend who had called, and desired her to describe her share in it to make the story complete. Lettice suspected nothing; she told the tale simply and naturally, devoid of fear; and from that very moment, Johnny, I have felt certain in my own mind the girl is as innocent as I am. Mr. Bond '*thought* she might be,' but he would not go beyond that; for women, he said, were crafty, and knew how to make one think black was white."

"Miss Deveen, suppose, after all, it should turn out to have been Lettice?" I asked. "Should you proceed against her?"

"I shall not proceed against any one, Johnny; and I shall hush the matter up if I can," she answered, ringing for Mr. Bond to be shown in.

I was curious to see him also; ideas floating through my brain of cocked hats and blue uniform and Richard Mayne. Mr. Bond turned out to be a very inoffensive-looking individual indeed; a little man, wearing steel spectacles, in a black frock-coat and grey trousers.

"When I last saw you, madam," he began, after he was seated, and Miss Deveen had told him he might speak before me, "I mentioned that I had abandoned my search in the country, and intended to prosecute my inquiries in London."

"You did, Mr. Bond."

"That the theft lay amid Sir John Whitney's female servants, I have thought likely all along," continued Mr. Bond. "If the purloiner felt afraid to dispose of the emeralds after taking them—and I could find no trace of them in the country—the probability was that she would keep them secreted about her, and get rid of them as soon as she came to London, if she were one of the maids brought up by Lady Whitney. There were two I thought in particular might have done it; one was the lady's maid; the other, the upper-housemaid, who had been ill the night of their disappearance. All kinds of ruses are played off in the pursuit of plunder, as we have cause to learn every day; and it struck me the housemaid might have feigned illness, the better to cover her actions and throw suspicion off herself. I am bound to say I could not learn anything against either of these two young women; but their business took them about the rooms at Whitney Hall; and an open jewel-case is a great temptation."

"It is," assented Miss Deveen. "That carelessness lay at my door, and therefore I determined never to prosecute in this case; never, in fact, to bring the offender to open shame of any sort in regard to it."

"And that has served to increase the difficulty," remarked Mr. Bond. "Could the women have been searched and their private places at Whitney Hall turned out, we might or might not have found the emeralds; but——"

"I'd not have had it done for the Lord Chancellor, sir,"

hotly interrupted Miss Deveen. "*One* was searched, and that was quite enough for me, for I believe her to be innocent. If you can get at the right person for me quietly, for my own satisfaction, well and good. My instructions went so far but no farther."

Mr. Bond took off his spectacles to ease his face for a minute, and put them on again. "I understood this perfectly when I took the business in hand," he quietly said. "Well, madam, to go on. Lady Whitney brought her servants to London, and I came up also. Last night I gleaned a little light."

He paused, and put his hand into his pocket. I looked, and Miss Deveen looked.

"Should you know the studs again?" he asked her.

"You may as well ask me if I should know my own face in the glass, Mr. Bond. Of course I should."

Mr. Bond opened a pill-box; three green studs lay in it on white cotton. He held it out to Miss Deveen.

"Are these they?"

"No, certainly not," replied Miss Deveen, speaking like one in frightful disappointment. "*Those* are not to be compared to mine, sir."

Mr. Bond put the bit of top cotton on, and the lid on that, and returned them to his pocket. Out came another box, long and thin.

"These are my studs," quickly exclaimed Miss Deveen, before she had given more than a glance. "You can look for yourself to the private marks I told you of, Mr. Bond."

Three brilliant emeralds, that seemed to light up the room, connected together on the inner side by a fine chain of gold. At either end, the chain was finished off by a small thin square plate of gold, on one of which was an engraved crest, on the other Miss Deveen's initials. In form the emeralds looked like buttons more than studs.

"I never knew they were linked together, Miss Deveen," I exclaimed in surprise.

"Did you not, Johnny?"

Never. My mind had always pictured them as tl ree loose studs. Mr. Bond, who no doubt had the marks by heart before he brought them up, began shutting them into the box as he had the others.

"Anticipating from the first that the studs would most probably be found at a pawnbroker's, if found at all, I ventured to speak to you then of a difficulty that might attend the finding," said he to Miss Deveen. "Unless a thing can be proved by law to have been stolen, a pawnbroker cannot be forced to give it up. And I am under an engagement to return these studs to the pawnbroker, whence I have brought them, in the course of the morning."

"You may do so," said Miss Deveen. "I daresay he and I can come to an amicable arrangement in regard to giving them up later. My object has been to discover who stole them, not to bring trouble or loss upon pawnbrokers. How did you discover them, Mr. Bond?"

"In rather a singular manner. Last evening, in making my way to Regent Street to a place where I had to go on business, I saw a young woman turn out of a pawnbroker's shop, whose shutters were put up, but its doors open. Her face struck me as being familiar; and I remembered her as Lady Whitney's housemaid—the same who had been ill in bed, or pretended to be, the night the studs were lost. Ah, ha, I thought, some discovery may be looming. I have some acquaintance with the proprietor of the shop; a very respectable man indeed, who has got on to wealth by dint of hard, honest work, and is a jeweller now as well as a pawnbroker. My own business could wait, and I went in and found him busy with accounts in his private room. He thought at first I had but called in to see him in passing. I gave him no particulars; but said I fancied a person in whom I was interested professionally, had just been leaving some emerald studs in his shop."

"What is the pawnbroker's name!" interrupted Miss Daveen.

"James. He went to inquire, and came back, saying that his assistant denied it. There was only one assistant, in the shop: the other had left for the night He, this assistant, said that no person had been in during the last half-hour, except a young woman, a cousin of his wife's; who did not come to pledge anything, but simply to say how d'ye do, and to ask where they were living now, that she might call and see his wife. Mr. James added that the man said she occupied a good situation in the family of Sir John and Lady Whitney, and was not likely to require to pledge anything. Plausible enough, this, you see, Miss Deveen; but the coincidence was singular. I then told James that I had been in search for these two months of some emerald studs lost out of Sir John Whitney's house. He stared a little at this, and asked whether they were of unusual value and very beautiful. Just so, I said, and described them minutely. Mr. James, without another word, went away and brought the studs in. Your studs, Miss Deveen."

"And how did he come by them?"

"He won't tell me much about it—except that they took in the goods some weeks ago in the ordinary course of business. The fact is he is vexed: for he has really been careful and has managed to avoid these unpleasant episodes, to which all pawnbrokers are liable. It was with difficulty I could get him to let me bring them up here: and that only on condition that they should be in his hands again before the clock struck twelve."

"You shall keep faith with him. But now, Mr. Bond, what is your opinion of this?"

"My opinion is that that same young woman stole the studs: and that she contrived to get them conveyed to London to this assistant, her relative, who no doubt advanced money upon them. I cannot see my way to any other conclusion under the circumstances," continued Mr. Bond, firmly.

"But for James's turning crusty, I might have learned more."

"I will go to him myself," said Miss Deveen, with sudden resolution. "When he finds that my intention is to hold his pocket harmless and make no disturbance in any way, he will not be crusty with me. But this matter must be cleared up if it be possible to clear it."

Miss Deveen was not one to be slow of action, once any resolve was taken. Mr. Bond made no attempt to oppose her: on the contrary, he seemed to think it might be well that she did go. She sent George out for a street cab, in preference to taking her carriage, and said I might accompany her. We were off long before Miss Cattledon's conference with the curates inside the church was over.

The shop was in a rather obscure street, not far from Regent Street. I inquired for Mr. James at the private door, and he came out to the cab. Miss Deveen said she had called to speak to him on particular business, and he took us upstairs to a handsomely-furnished room. He was a well-dressed, portly, good-looking man, with a pleasant face and quietly easy manners. Miss Deveen, bidding him sit down near her, explained the affair in a few words, and asked him to *help* her elucidate it. He responded to her frankness at once, and said he would willingly give all the aid in his power.

"Singular to say, I took these studs in myself," he observed. "I never do these things now, but my foreman had a holiday that day to attend a funeral, and I was in the shop. They were pledged on the 27th of January: since Mr. Bond left this morning I have been referring to my books."

The 27th of January. It was on the night of the 23d that the studs disappeared. Then the thief had not lost much time! I said so.

"Stay a minute, Johnny," cried Miss Deveen: "you young ones sum up things too quickly for me. Let me trace events back. The studs, as you say, were lost on the 23d; the loss was discovered on the 24th, and Lettice Lane discharged; on the 25th those of us staying at Whitney Hall began to talk of leaving; and on the 26th you two went home after seeing Miss Chalk off by rail to London."

"And Mrs. Hughes too. They went up together."

"Who is Mrs. Hughes?" asked Miss Deveen.

"Don't you remember?—that young married lady who came to the dance with the Featherstons. She lives somewhere in London."

Miss Deveen stared a little. "I don't remember any Mrs. Hughes, Johnny."

"But, dear Miss Deveen, you must remember her," I persisted. "She was very young-looking, as little as Sophie Chalk; Harry Whitney, dancing with her, trod off the tail of her thin pink dress. I heard old Featherston telling you about Mrs. Hughes, saying it was a sad history. Her husband lost his money after they were married, and had been obliged to take a small situation."

Recollection flashed over Miss Deveen. "Yes, I remember now. A pale, lady-like little woman with a sad face. But let us go back to business. You all left on the 26th; I and Miss Cattledon on the 27th. Now, while the visitors were at the Hall, I don't think the upper-housemaid could have had time to go out and send off the studs by rail. Still less could she have come up herself to pledge them."

Miss Deveen's head was running on Mr. Bond's theory.

"It was no housemaid that pledged the studs," spoke Mr. James.

"I was about to say, Mr. James, that if you took them in yourself over the counter, they could not have been sent up to your assistant."

"All the people about me are trustworthy, I can assure you, ma'am," he interrupted. "They would not lend themselves to such a thing. It was a lady who pledged those studs."

"A lady?"

"Yes, ma'am, a lady. And to tell the truth, if I may venture to say it, the description you have now given of a lady just tallies with her."

"Mrs. Hughes?"

"It seems so to me," continued Mr. James. "Little, pale, and lady-like : that is just what she was."

"Dear me !" cried Miss Deveen, letting her hands drop on her lap as if they were lead. "You had better tell me as much as you can recollect, please."

"It was at dusk," said Mr. James. "Not quite dark, but the lamps were lighted in the streets and the gas indoors; just the hour, ma'am, that gentlefolks choose for bringing their things. I happened to be standing near the door, when a lady came into the shop and asked to see the principal. I said I was he, and retired behind the counter. She brought out these emerald studs"—touching the box—"and said she wanted to sell them, or pledge them for their utmost value. She told me a tale, in apparent confidence, of a brother who had fallen into debt at college, and she was trying to get together some money to help him, or frightful trouble might come of it. If it was not genuine," broke off Mr. James, "she was the best actor I ever saw in all my life."

"Please go on."

"I saw the emeralds were very rare and beautiful. She said they were an heirloom from her mother, who had brought the stones from India and had them linked together in England. I told her I could not buy; she rejoined that it might be better only to pledge, for they would not be entirely lost to her and she might redeem them ere twelve months were past if I would keep them as long as that. I explained that the law exacted it. The name she gave was Mary Drake, asking if I had ever heard of the famous old forefather of theirs, Admiral Drake. The name answers to the initials on the gold."

"'M. D.' They were engraved for Margaret Deveen. Perhaps she claimed the crest, also, Mr. James," added that lady sarcastically.

"She did, ma am ; in so far as that she said it was the crest of the Drake family."

"And you call her a lady!"

"She had every appearance of one, in tone and language too. Her hand—she took one of her gloves off when showing the studs—was a lady's hand; small, delicate, and white as alabaster. Ma'am, rely upon it, though she may not be a lady in deeds, she must be living the life of one."

"But now, who was it?"

Yes, who was it? Miss Deveen, looking at us, seemed to wait for an answer, but she did not get one.

"How much did you lend upon the studs?"

"Ten pounds. Of course that is nothing like their value."

"Should you know her again? How was she dressed?"

"She wore an ordinary Paisley shawl; it was cold weather; and had a thick veil over her face, which she never lifted."

"Should not that have excited your suspicion?" interrupted Miss Deveen. "I don't like people who keep their veils down while they talk to you."

The pawnbroker smiled. "Most ladies keep them down when they come here. As to knowing her again, I am quite certain that I should; and her voice too. Whoever she was, she went about it very systematically, and took me in completely. Her asking for the principal may have thrown me somewhat off my guard."

We came away, leaving the studs with Mr. James; the time had not arrived for Miss Deveen to redeem them. She seemed very thoughtful as we went along in the cab.

"Johnny," she said, breaking the silence, "we talk lightly enough about the Finger of Providence; but I don't know what else it can be that has led to this discovery so far. Out of the hundreds of pawnbroking establishments scattered about the metropolis, it is wonderfully strange that this should have been the one the studs were taken to; and furthermore, that Bond should have been passing it last night at the moment Lady Whitney's housemaid came forth. Had the studs been pledged elsewhere, we might never have heard of them; neither, as it is, but for the housemaid's being connected with Mr. James's assistant."

Of course it was strange.

"You were surprised to see the studs connected together, Johnny. That was the point I mentioned in reference to Lettice Lane. '*One* might have fallen down,' she sobbed out to me, in leaving Whitney Hall; 'even two; but it's beyond the bounds of probability that three should, ma'am.' She was thinking of the studs as separate studs; and it convinced me that she had never seen them. True, an artful woman might say so purposely to deceive me, but I am sure that Lettice has not the art for it. But now, Johnny, we must consider what steps to take next. I shall not rest until the matter is cleared."

"Suppose it should never get on any further!"

"Suppose you are like a young bear, all your experience to come?" retorted Miss Deveen. "Why, Johnny Ludlow, do you think that when that Finger I ventured to speak of is directing a course onwards, that it halts midway? There cannot, I fear, be much doubt as to the thief; but we must get proof."

"You think it was——"

"Mrs. Hughes. How can I think else? She is very nice, and I could not have believed it of her. I suppose the sight of the jewels, combined with her state of poverty, must have proved the temptation. I shall get back the emeralds, but we must screen her."

"Miss Deveen, I don't believe it was Mrs. Hughes."

"Not believe it!"

"No. Her face is not that of one who would do such a thing. You might trust it anywhere."

"Oh, Johnny! there you are at your faces again!"

"Well, I never was deceived in any face yet. Not in one that I *thoroughly* trusted."

"If Mrs. Hughes did not take the studs, and bring them to London, and pledge them, who else could have brought them? They were taken to Mr. James's on the 27th, remember."

"That's the puzzle of it."

"We must find out Mrs. Hughes, and then contrive to bring her within sight of Mr. James."

"The Whitneys know where she lives. Anna and Helen have been to call upon her."

"Then our way is pretty plain. Mind you don't breathe a syllable of this to mortal ear, Johnny. It might defeat ends. Miss Cattledon, always inquisitive, will question where we have been this morning with her curious eyes; but for once she will not get satisfied."

"I should not keep her, Miss Deveen."

"Yes you would, Johnny. She is faithful; she suits m very well; and her mother and I were girls together."

It was a sight to be painted. Helen Whitney standing there in her presentation dress. Oh, she looked well. It was all white, with a train behind longer than three peacocks' tails, lace and feathers hanging from her hair. The whole lot of us were round her; the young ones had come from the nursery, the servants peeped in at the door ; Miss Cattledon had her eye-glass up ; Harry danced.

"Helen, my dear, I admire all very much except your necklace and bracelets," said Miss Deveen, critically. "They do not match : and do not accord with the dress."

The necklace was a row of turquoise beads, it did not look much : the bracelets were gold with blue stones in the clasps. The Whitney family did not shine in jewels, and the few diamonds they possessed were on Lady Whitney to-day.

"But I had nothing else, Miss Deveen," said Helen, simply. "Mamma said these must do."

Miss Deveen took off the string of blue beads as if to examine them, and left in its place the most beautiful pearl necklace ever seen.   There was a scream of surprise ; some of us had only met with such transformations in fairy tales.

"And these are the bracelets to match, my dear.   Anna, I shall give you the same when your turn for making your curtsey to your queen comes."

Anna smiled faintly as she looked her thanks.   She always seemed regularly down in spirits now, not to be raised by pearl necklaces.   For the first time her sad countenance seemed to strike Tod.   He crossed over.

"What is amiss, Anna ?" he whispered.   "Are you not well ?"

"Quite well, thank you," she answered, her cheeks flushing painfully.

At this moment Sophie Chalk created a diversion.   Unable to restrain her feelings longer, she burst into tears, knelt down outside Helen's dress, and began kissing her hand and its pearl bracelet in a transport of glad joy.

"Oh, Helen, my dear friend, how rejoiced I am ?   I said up-stairs that your ornaments were not worthy of you."

Tod's eyes were glued to her.   Bill Whitney called out Bravo.   Sophie, kneeling before Helen in her court furbelows, made a charming tableau.

"It is good acting, Tod," I said in his ear.

He turned sharply.   But instead of cuffing me into next week, he just sent his eyes straight out to mine.

"Do you call it acting ?"

"I am sure it is.   But not for you."

"You are bold, Mr. Johnny."

But I could tell by the subdued tone and the subdued manner, that his own doubts had been at last awakened whether or not it *was* acting.

Lady Whitney came sailing down-stairs, a blaze of yellow satin ; her face, with flurry, like a peony in full bloom.   She could hardly say a word of thanks for the pearls, for her wits were gone a woolgathering.   When she was last at Court herself, Bill was a baby in long-clothes.   We went out with them to the carriage, the lot of us; the lady's maid taking at least six minutes to settle the trains: and Bill said he hoped the eyes at the windows all round enjoyed the show. The postilion—an unusual sight in London—and the two men behind wore their state liveries of white and crimson; the bouquets in their breasts being bigger than full-blown cabbages.

"You will dance with me the first dance to-night?" Tod whispered to Sophie Chalk, as they were going in after watching the carriage away.

Sophie made a slight pause for consideration, before she answered; and I saw her eyes wander out in the distance towards Bill Whitney.

"Oh, thank you," she said, with a great display of gratitude. "But I think I am engaged."

"Engaged for the first dance?"

"Yes. I am so sorry."

"The second, then?"

"With the greatest pleasure."

Anna heard it all as well as I. Tod gave Sophie's hand a squeeze to close the bargain, and went away whistling.

Not being in the world of fashion, we did not know how other people finished up drawing-room days (and when Helen Whitney went to Court they *were* drawing-rooms), but the Whitney's programme was this: A cold collation in view of a dinner, when Fate should bring them home again, and a ball in the evening. The ball was our joint invention. Sitting round the school-room fire one night we settled it for ourselves: and after Sir John and my lady had stood out well, they gave in. Not that it would be much a ball, for they had but few acquaintances in London, and the house was small.

But now, had any aid been wanted by Miss Deveen to carry out her plans, she could not have devised better than this. For the Whitneys invited (all unconsciously) Mrs. Hughes to the ball. Anna came in to Miss Deveen's after they had been sending out the invitations (only three days before the evening), and began telling her the names as a slice of gossip. She came to Mrs. Hughes. "Mrs. Hughes," interrupted Miss Deveen, "I am glad of that, Anna, for I want to see her."

Miss Deveen's seeing her would not go for much in the matter of elucidation; it was Mr. James who must see her; and the plan by which he might do so was entirely Miss Deveen's own. She went down and arranged it with him, and before the night came, it was all cut and dried. He and she and I knew of it; not another soul in the world.

"You will have to help me in it a little, Johnny," she said. "Be at hand to look out for Mr. James's arrival, and bring him up to me."

We saw them come back from the drawing-room between five and six, Helen with a bright color in her cheeks; and at eight o'clock we went in. London parties, which begin when you ought to be in your first sleep, are not understood by us country people, and eight was the hour named in the Whitney's invitations. Cattledon was screwed into a rich sea-green satin (somebody else's once), with a water-lily in her thin hair; and Miss Deveen wore all her diamonds. Sir John, out of his element and frightfully disconsolate, stood against the wall, his spectacles lodged on his old red nose. The thing was not in his line. Miss Deveen went up to shake hands.

"Sir John, I am rather expecting a gentleman to call on me on business to-night," she said; "and have left word for him to step in and see me here. Will you pardon the liberty?"

"I'm sure it's no liberty; I shall be glad to welcome him," replied Sir John, dismally. "There'll be not much here but stupid boys and girls. We shall get no whist to-night. The plague only knows who invented balls."

It was a little odd that, next to us, Mrs. Hughes should be the first to arrive. She was very pale and pretty, and her husband was a slender, quiet, delicate man, looking like a finished gentleman. Miss Deveen followed them with her eyes as they went up to Lady Whitney.

"She does not look like it, does she, Johnny?" whispered Miss Deveen. No, I was quite sure she did not.

Sophie Chalk was in white, with ivy leaves in her spangled hair, the sweetest fairy (to look at) ever seen out of a moonlight ring. Helen, in her Court dress and pearls, look plain beside her. They stood talking together, not noticing that I and Tod were in the recess behind. The people had mostly come then, and the music was throwing out fits and starts. The rooms looked well; the flowers, scattered about them, had come up from Whitney Hall. Helen called to her brother.

"We may as well begin dancing, William."

"Of course we may," he answered. "I don't know what we have waited for. I must get a partner. Miss Chalk, may I have the honor of dancing the first dance with you?"

That Miss Chalk's eyes went up to his with a flash of gratitude, and then down in modesty to the chalked floor, I knew as well as though they had been behind her head instead of before.

"Oh, thank you," said she, "I shall be so happy." And I no more dared glance at Tod than if he had been a springing crocodile. She had told *him* she was engaged for it.

But just as William was about to give her his arm, and somebody came and took away Helen, Lady Whitney called him. He spoke with his mother for a minute or two and came back with a cloud on his face.

"I am awfully sorry, Sophie. The mother says I must take out Lady Esther Starr this first time, old Starr's wife, you know, as my father's dancing days are over. Lady Esther is seven-and-thirty if she's a day," growled Bill, "and as big as a light-house. I'll have the second with you, Sophie."

"I am *afraid* I am engaged for the second," hesitated Miss Sophie. "I think I have promised Joseph Todhetley."

"Never mind him," said Bill. "You'll dance it with me, mind."

"I can tell him I mistook the dance," she softly suggested.

"Tell him anything. All right."

He wheeled round, and went up to Lady Esther, putting on his glove. Sophie Chalk moved away, and I took the courage to glance sideways at Tod.

His face was as white as death: I think with passion. He stood with his arms folded, never moving throughout the whole of the quadrille, only looking out straight before him with a fixed stare. A waltz came next, for which they kept their partners. And Sophie Chalk had enjoyed the luck of sitting down all the time. When they were making ready for the second quadrille, Tod went up to her.

"This is our dance, Miss Chalk."

Well, she had her share of brass. She looked steadily in his face, assuring him that he was mistaken, and vowing through thick and thin that it was the *third* dance she had promised to him. While she was excusing herself, Bill came up to claim her. Tod put out his strong arm to ward him off.

"Stay a moment, Whitney," he said, with studied calmness, "let me have an understanding first with Miss Chalk. She can dance with you afterwards if she prefers to. Miss Chalk, *you know* that you promised yourself to me this morning for the second dance. I asked you for the first: you were engaged for that, you said, and would dance with me the second. There could be no mistake, on your side or on mine."

"Oh, but *indeed* I understood it to be the third, dear Mr. Todhetley," she said. "I am dreadfully sorry if it is my fault. I will dance the third with you."

"I have not asked you for the third. Do as you please. If you throw me over for this second dance, I will never ask you for another again as long as I live."

Bill Whitney stood by laughing; seeming to treat the whole as a good joke. Sophie Chalk looked at him appealingly.

"And you certainly promised *me*, Miss Chalk," he put in.

"Todhetley, it is a complication.   You and **I** had better **draw** friendly lots."

Tod bit his lip nearly to bleeding.   All the notice he took of Bill's speech was to turn his back upon him, and address Sophie.

"The decision lies with you alone, Miss Chalk.   You have engaged yourself to him and to me; choose between us."

She put her hand within Bill's arm, and went away with him, leaving a little honeyed flattery for Tod.   But Bill Whitney looked back curiously into Tod's white face, all his lightness gone; for the first time he seemed to realize that it was serious, nearly an affair of life or death.   His handkerchief up, wiping his damp brow, Tod did not notice which way he was going, and ran against Anna.   "I beg your pardon, child," he said, with a start, as if waking out of a dream.   "Will you go through this dance with me, Anna?"

Yes.   He led her up to it; and they took their places opposite to Bill and Miss Chalk.

Mr. James was to arrive at half-past nine.   I was waiting for him near the entrance door.   He was punctual to time; and looked very well in his evening dress.   I took him up to Miss Deveen; she made room for him on the sofa by her side, her diamonds glistening.   He must have seen their value.   Sir John had his rubber then in the little breakfast-parlor; Miss Cattledon, Old Starr, and another making it up for him.   Wanting to see the play played out, I kept by the sofa.

This was not the dancing-room: but they came into it between the dances in couples, to march around in the cooler air.   Mr. James looked and Miss Deveen looked; and I confess that whenever Mrs. Hughes passed us, I felt queer. Miss Deveen suddenly arrested her, and kept her talking for a minute or two.   Not a word bearing upon the secret subject said Mr. James.   Once when the room was clear and the measured tread could be heard to the tune of one of the best waltzes ever imagined by Strauss, Lady Whitney approached..

Catching sight of the strange gentleman by Miss Deveen, she supposed he had been brought by some of the guests, and came up to make his acquaintance.

"A friend of mine, dear Lady Whitney," said Miss Deveen.

Lady Whitney, never observing that no name was mentioned, shook hands at once with Mr. James in her homely country fashion. He stood up until she had moved away.

"Well?" said Miss Deveen to him, when the dancers were coming in again. "Is the lady here?"

"Yes."

I had expected him to say no, and could have struck him for destroying my faith in Mrs. Hughes. She was passing at the same moment.

"Do you see her now?" whispered Miss Deveen.

"Not now. She was at the door a moment ago."

"Not now!" exclaimed Miss Deveen, staring at Mrs. Hughes. "Is it not *that* lady?"

Mr. James sent his eyes in half a dozen directions at once.

"Which lady, ma'am?"

"The one who has just passed in black silk, with the simple white net quilling round the neck."

"Oh, dear no!" said Mr. James. "I never saw that lady in my life before. The lady, *the* lady, is dressed in white."

Miss Deveen looked at him, and I looked. *Here*, in the rooms, and yet not Mrs. Hughes!

"This is the one," he whispered, "coming in now."

The one turning in at that particular instant, was Sophie Chalk. But others were before her and behind her. She was on Harry Whitney's arm.

"Why don't you dance, Miss Deveen?" asked bold Harry, halting before the sofa.

"Will you dance with me, Master Harry?"

"Of course I will. Glad to get you."

"Don't you tell fibs, young man. I might take you at your word, if I had my dancing shoes on."

Harry laughed. Sophie Chalk's blue eyes happened to rest on Mr. James's face; they took a puzzled expression, as if wondering where she had seen it. Mr. James rose and bowed to her. She must have recognized him then, for her features turned a livid white, in spite of the powder that covered them.

"Who is it, Johnny?" she whispered, in her confusion, loosing Harry's arm and coming behind.

"Well, you must ask that of Miss Deveen. He has come here to see her: something's up, I fancy, about those emerald studs."

Had it been to save my fortune, I could not have helped saying it. I saw it all as in a mirror. *She* it was who had taken them, and pledged them afterwards. The same light flashed on Miss Deveen. She followed her with her severe face, her condemning eyes.

"Take care, Johnny!" cried Miss Deveen.

I was just in time to catch Sophie Chalk. She would have fallen on my shoulder. The room was in a commotion at once: a young lady had fainted. Fainted! What from? asked everybody. Oh, from the heat, of course. And no other clue was breathed.

Mr. James's mission was over. It had been successful. He made a bow to Lady Whitney, and withdrew.

Miss Deveen sent in for Sophie Chalk the next day, and they had it out together, shut up alone. Sophie's coolness was good for any amount of denial, but it failed here. And then she took the other course, and fell on her knees at Miss Deveen's feet, and told a pitiable story of being alone in the world, without money to dress herself, and the open jewel-casket in Miss Deveen's chamber (into which accident, not design, had really taken her) proving too much in the moment's temptation. Miss Deveen believed it; she told her the affair should never transpire beyond the two or three who already know it; that she would redeem the emeralds herself, and say nothing even to Lady Whitney; but, as a matter of course, Miss Chalk must close her acquaintance with Sir John's family.

And, singular to say, Sophie received a letter from somebody that same evening, inviting her to go out of town. At least, she said she did.

So, the quitting the Whitneys suddenly was smoothly accounted for; and Helen Whitney did not know the truth for many a day.

What did Tod think? For that, I expect, is what you are all wanting to ask. That was another curious thing—that he and Bill Whitney should have come to an explanation before the ball was over. Bill went up to him, saying that had he supposed Tod could mean anything serious in his admiration of Sophie Chalk, he should never have gone in for admiration of her himself, even in idleness; and certainly would not continue to do so or spoil sport again.

"Thank you for telling me," answered Tod, with indifference. "You are quite welcome to go in for Sophie Chalk in any way you please. *I* have done with her."

"No," said Bill, "good girls must get scarcer than they are before I should go in seriously for Sophie Chalk. She's all very well to talk and laugh with, and she is uncommonly fascinating."

It was my turn to put in a word then. "As I told you, Bill, months ago, Sophie Chalk would fascinate the hair off your head, give her the chance."

Bill laughed. "Well, she has had the chance, Johnny: but she has not done it."

Altogether, Sophie, thanks to her own bad play, had fallen to a discount.

When Miss Deveen announced to the world that she had found her emerald studs (lost through an accident, she discovered, and recovered in the same way) people were full of wonder at the chances and mistakes of life Lettice Lane was cleared triumphantly. Miss Deveen sent her home for a week to shake hands with her friends and enemies, and then took her back as her own maid.

And the only person I said a syllable to was Anna. I knew it would be safe; and I dare say you would have done the same in my place. But she stopped me at the middle of the first sentence.

"I have known it from the first, Johnny; I was nearly as sure of it as sure could be; and it is that that has made me so miserable."

"Known it was Sophie Chalk?"

"As good as known it. There was no proof, only suspicion. And I could not see whether I ought to speak of the suspicion even to mamma, or to keep it to myself. As things have turned out, I am very thankful to have been silent."

"How was it, then?"

"That night at Whitney Hall, after they had all come down from dressing, mamma sent me up to William's room with a message. As I was leaving it—it is at the end of the long corridor, you know—I saw some one peep cautiously out of Miss Cattledon's chamber, and then steal up the back stairs. It was Sophie Chalk. Later, when we were going to bed, and I was quite undressed, Helen, who was in bed, espied Sophie's comb and brush on the table,—for she had dressed in our room because of the large glass,—and told me to run in with them: she only slept in the next room. It was very cold. I knocked and entered so sharply that the door-bolt, a thin, creaky old thing, gave way. Of course I begged her pardon; but she seemed to start up in a terrible fear as if I had been a ghost. She had not touched her hair, but sat in her shawl, sewing at her stays; and she let them drop on the carpet and threw a petticoat upon them. I thought nothing, Johnny; nothing at all. But the next morning when the commotion arose that the studs were missing, I could not help recalling all this; and I quite hated myself for thinking Sophie Chalk might have been taking them when she stole out of Miss Cattledon's room, and was sewing them later into her stays."

"You thought right, you see."

"Johnny, I am very sorry for her. I wish we could help her to some good situation. Depend upon it, this will be a lesson: she will never so far forget herself again."

"She is quite able to take care of herself, Anna. Don't let it trouble you. I dare say she will marry Mr. Everty."

"Who is Mr. Everty?"

"Some one who is engaged in the wine business with Sophie Chalk's brother-in-law, Mr. Smith."

16*

XVI.

GOING TO THE MOP.

NEVER went to St. John's mop in my life," said Mrs. Todhetley.

"That's no reason why you never should go," returned the Squire.

"And never thought of engaging a servant at one."

"There are as good servants to be picked up in a mop as out of it; and you get a great deal better choice," said he. "My mother has hired many a man and maid at the mop: first-rate servants too."

"Well, then, perhaps we had better go into Worcester to-morrow, and see," concluded she, rather dubiously.

"And start early," said the Squire. "What is it you are afraid of?" he added, catching at her doubtful tone. "That good servants don't put themselves into the mop to be hired?"

"Not of that," she answered. "I know it is the only chance farm-house servants have of getting hired when they want to change their places. It was the noise and crowd I was thinking of."

"Oh, that's nothing," returned the Pater. "It is not half as bad as the fair."

Mrs. Todhetley stood at the parlow window of Dyke Manor, the autumn sun, setting in a glow, tinging her face and showing its thoughtful expression. The Squire was in his easy-chair, looking at one of the Worcester newspapers.

There had been a bother lately about the dairy-work. The

old dairy-maid, four years in the service, had left to be married; two others had been tried since, and neither suited. The last of them had marched herself off that day, after a desperate quarrel with Molly; the house was pretty nearly at its wits end in consequence, and perhaps the two cows were. Mrs. Todhetley, really not knowing what in the world to do, and fretting herself into the face-ache over it, was broken in upon by the Pater and his newspaper. He had just read in it the reminder that St. John's annual Michaelmas Mop would take place on the morrow: and he told Mrs. Todhetley that she could go there and hire a dairy-maid at will. Fifty if she wanted them. At that time the mop was as much of an institution as the fair or the wake. Some people called it the Statute Fair.

Molly, whose sweet temper you have had a glimpse or two of before, banged about among her spoons and saucepans when she heard what was in the wind. "Fine muck it 'ud be," she said, "coming out o' that there Worcester mop." Having the dairy-work to do as well as her own just now, the house hardly held her.

We breakfasted early the next morning and started betimes in the large open carriage, the Squire driving his pair of fine horses, Bob and Blister. Mrs. Todhetley sat with him, and I behind. Tod might have gone if he would: but the long drive out and home had no charms for him, and he said ironically he should like to see himself attending the mop. It was a lovely morning, bright and sunny, with a suspicion of crispness in the air: the trees were putting on their autumn colors, and shoals of blackberries shone in the hedges.

Getting some refreshment again at Worcester, and leaving the Squire at the hotel, I and Mrs. Todhetley walked to the mop. It was held in the parish of St. John's—which, as all the country knows, is a suburb of Worcester on the other side of the Severn. Crossing the bridge and getting well up the New Road, we plunged into the thick of the fun.

The men were first, standing back in a line on the footpath, fronting the passers-by. Young rustics mostly, in clean smock-frocks, waiting to be looked at and questioned and hired, a broad grin on their faces with the novelty of the situation. We passed them; and came to the girls and women. You could tell they were nearly all rustic servants too, by their high colors and awkward looks and manners. As a rule, each held a thick cotton umbrella, tied round the middle after the fashion of Mrs. Gamp's, and a pair of pattens whose bright rings showed they had not been in use that day. To judge by the look of the present weather, we were not likely to have rain for a month: but these simple people liked to guard against contingencies. Crowds of folks were passing along like ourselves, some come to hire, some only to take up the road and stare.

Mrs. Todhetley elbowed her way amidst them. So did I. She spoke to one or two, but nothing came of it. Whom should we come upon, to my intense surprise, but our dairy-maid—the one who had betaken herself off the previous day!

"I hope you will get a better place than you had with me, Susan," said the Mater, rather sarcastically.

"I hopes as how I shall, missis," was the insolent retort. "'Twon't be hard to do, any way, that won't, with that there overbearing Molly in your'n."

We went on. A great hulking farmer, as big a giant, and looking as though he had taken more than was good for him in the morning, came lumbering along, pushing everybody right and left. He threw his bold eyes on one of the girls.

"What place be for you, my lass?"

"None of yours, master," was the prompt reply.

The voice was good-natured and pleasant, and I looked at the girl as the man went shouldering on. She wore a clean light cotton gown, a smart shawl all the colors of the rainbow, and a straw bonnet that could not be seen for sky-blue bows. Her face was fairer than most of the faces around; her eyes were of the color of her ribbons; and her mouth, rather wide and always smiling, had about the nicest set of teeth I ever saw. To take likes and dislikes at first sight without rhyme or reason, is what I am hopelessly given to, and there's no help for it. People laugh mockingly: as you have heard me say. "There goes Johnny with his fancies again!" they cry: but I know that it has served me well through life. I took a liking to the girl's face: it was an honest face, as full of smiles as the bonnet was of bows. Mrs. Todhetley noticed her too, and halted. The girl dropped a curtsey.

"What place are you seeking?" she asked.

"Dairy-maid's, please, ma'am."

The good Mater stood, dubious whether to pursue inquiries or to pass onwards. She liked the face of the girl, but did not like the profusion of blue ribbons.

"I understand my work well, ma'am, please; and I'm not afraid of any much of it, in reason."

This turned the scale. Mrs. Todhetley stood her ground and plunged into the proper questioning.

"Where have you been living?"

"At Mr. Thorpe's farm, please, near Severn Stoke."

"For how long?"

"Twelve months, please. I went there Old Michaelmas Day, last year."

"Why are you leaving?"

"Please, ma'am"——a pause here——"please, I wanted a change, and the work was a great sight of it; frightful heavy; and missis often cross. Quite a herd o' milkers, there was, there."

"What is your name?"

"Grizzel Clay. I be healthy and strong, please, ma'am; and I was twenty-two in the summer."

"Can you have a character from Mrs. Thorpe?"

"Yes, please, ma'am, and a good one. She can't say nothing against me."

And so the queries went on; one would have thought the Mater was hiring a whole regiment of soldiers. Grizzel was ready and willing to enter on her place at once, if hired

Mrs. Thorpe was in Worcester that day, and might be seen at the Hare and Hounds inn.

"What do you think, Johnny?" whispered the Mater.

"I should hire her. She's just the girl I'd not mind taking without any character."

"With those blue bows! Don't be simple, Johnny. Still I like the girl, and may as well see Mrs. Thorpe."

"By the way, though," she added, turning to Grizzel, "what wages do you ask?"

"Eight pounds, please, ma'am," replied Grizzel, after some hesitation, and with reddening cheeks.

"Eight pounds!" exclaimed Mrs. Todhetley. "That's very high."

"But you'll find me a good servant, ma'am."

We went back through the town to the Hare and Hounds, an inn near the cathedral. Mrs. Thorpe, a substantial dame in a long cloth skirt and black hat, by which we saw she had come in on horse-back, was at dinner.

She gave Grizzel Clay a good character. Saying the girl was honest, clean, hardworking, and very sweet-tempered; and, in truth, she was rather sorry to part with her. Mrs. Todhetley asked about the blue bows. Ay, Mrs. Thorpe said, that was Grizzel Clay's great fault—a love of finery: and she recommended Mrs. Todhetley to "keep her under" in that respect. In going out we found Grizzel waiting under the archway, having come down to learn her fate. Mrs. Todhetley said she should engage her, and bade her follow us to the hotel.

"It's an excellent character, Johnny," she said, as we went along the street. "I like everything about the girl, except the blue ribbons."

"I don't see any harm in blue ribbons. A girl looks nicer in ribbons than without."

"That's just it," said the Mater. "And this girl is good-looking enough to do without them. Johnny, if Mr. Todhetley has no objection, I think we had better take her back in the carriage. You won't mind her sitting with you?"

"Not I. And I'm sure I shall not mind the ribbons."

So it was arranged. The girl was engaged, to go back with us in the afternoon. Her box would be sent by the carrier. She presented herself at the Star at the time of starting with a small bundle: and a little birdcage, something like a mouse-trap, that had a bird in it.

"Could I be let take it, ma'am?" she asked of Mrs. Todhetley. "It's only a poor linnet that I found hurt on the ground the last morning I went out to help milk Thorpe's cows. I'm a-trying, please, to nurse it back to health."

"Take it, and welcome," cried the Squire. "The bird had better die, though, than be kept to live in that cage."

"I was thinking to let it fly, please, sir, when it's strong again."

Grizzel had proper notions. She screwed herself into the corner of the seat, so as not to touch me. I heard all about her as we went along.

She had gone to live at her Uncle Clay's in Gloucestershire when her mother died, working for them as a servant. The uncle was "well-to-do," rented twenty acres of land, and had two cows and some sheep and pigs of his own. The aunt had a nephew, and this young man wanted to court her, Grizzel; but she'd have nothing to say to him. It made matters uncomfortable, and last year they turned her out: so she went and hired herself at Mrs. Thorpe's.

"Well, I should have thought you had better be married and have a home of your own than go out as dairy-maid, Grizzel."

"That depends upon who the husband is, sir," she said, laughing slightly. "I'd rather be a dairy-maid to the end o' my days—I'd rather be a prisoner in a cage like this poor bird—than have anything to say to that there nephew of aunt's. He had red hair, and I can't abide it."

Grizzel proved to be a good servant, and became a great

favorite in the house, except with Molly. Molly, never taking to her kindly, was for quarreling ten times a day, but the girl only laughed back again. She was superior to the general run of dairy-maids, both in looks and manners: and her good-humored face brought sweethearts up in plenty.

Two of them were serious. The one was George Roper, bailiff's man on a neighboring farm; the other was Sandy Lett, a wheelwright in business for himself at Church Dykely. Of course matters ran in this case, as they generally do run in such cases, all cross and contrary: or, as the French say, *à tort et à travers*. George Roper, a good-looking young fellow with curly hair and a handsome pair of black whiskers, had not a coin beyond the weekly stipend he worked for: he had not so much as a chair to sit in, or a turn-up bedstead to lie on; yet Grizzel loved him with her whole heart. Sandy Lett, who was not bad-looking either, and had a good home and a good business, she did not care for. Of course the difficulty lay in deciding which of the two to choose: ambition and her friends recommended Sandy Lett; imprudence and her own heart, George Roper. Like the donkey between the two bundles of hay, Grizzel was totally unable to decide on either, and kept both the swains on the tenter-hooks of suspense.

Sunday afternoons were the great trouble of Grizzel's life. Roper had holiday then, and came; and Lett, whose time was his own, though of course he could not afford to waste it on a week-day, also came. One would stand at the style in one field, the other at a style in another field: and Grizzel, arrayed in one of the light print gowns she favored, the many-colored shawl, and the dangerous blue-ribbon bonnet, did not dare to go out to either, lest the other should pounce upon his rival, and a fight ensue. It was getting quite exciting in the household to watch the progress of events. The spring passed, the summer came round; and between the two,

Grizzel had her hands full. The other servants could not imagine what the men saw in her.

"It is those blue ribbons she's so fond of!" said Mrs. Todhetley to us two, with a sigh. "I doubted them from the first."

"I should say it is the blue eyes," dissented Tod.

"And I the white teeth and laughing face. *Nobody* can help liking her."

"You shut up, Johnny. If I were Roper——"

"Shut up yourself, Joseph: both of you shut up: you know nothing about it," interrupted the Squire, who had seemed to be asleep in his chair. "It comes of woman's coquetry and man's folly. As to these two fellows, if Grizzel can't make up her mind, I'll warn them both to keep off my grounds at their peril."

One evening during the midsummer holidays, in bounding out of the oak-walk to cross the fold-yard, I came upon Grizzel leaning on the gate. She had a bunch of sweet peas in her hand, and tears in her eyes. George Roper, who must have been talking to her, passed me quickly, touching his hat.

"Good evening, sir."

"Good evening, Roper."

He walked away with his firm, quick stride; a well-made, handsome, and trustworthy fellow. His brown velveteen coat (an old one of his master's) was shabby, but he looked well in it; and his gaitered legs were straight and strong. That he had been the donor of the sweet peas, a rustic lover's favorite offering, was evident. Grizzel attempted to hide them inside her gown when she saw me, but was not quick enough, so she was fain to hold them in her hand openly, and make believe to be busy with her tin milk-pail.

"It's a drop of skim milk I've got over; I was going to take it to the pigs," said she.

"What are you crying about?"

"Me crying!" returned Grizzel. "It's the red sun a shinin' in my eyes, sir."

Was it! "Look here, Grizzel, why don't you put an end to this state of bother? You won't be able to milk the cows next."

"'Taint any in'ard bother o' that sort as 'll keep me from doing my proper work," returned she, with a flick to the handle of the can.

"At any rate, you can't marry two men: you would be taken up by old Jones the constable, you know, and tried for bigamy. And I'm sure you must keep *them* on the ferment. George Roper's gone off with a queer look on his face. Take him, or dismiss him."

"I'd take him to-morrow, but for one thing," avowed the girl in a half whisper.

"His short wages, I suppose,—sixteen shillings a week."

"Sixteen shillings a week short wages!" echoed Grizzel. "I call 'em good wages, sir. I'd never be afraid of getting along on them with a steady man,—and Roper's that. It ain't the wages, Master Johnny. It is that I promised mother never to begin life upon less than a cottage and some things in it."

"How do you mean?"

"Poor mother was a-dying, sir. Her illness lasted her many a week, and she might be said to be a-dying all the time. I was eighteen then. 'Grizzy,' says she to me one night, 'you be a likely girl and 'll get chose afore you be many summers older. But you must promise me that you'll not, on no temptation whatsoever, say yes to a man till he has got a home of his own to take you to, and beds and tables and things comfortable about him. Once begin without 'em, and you and him 'll spend all your after-life looking out for 'em; but they'll not come any the more for that. And you'll be at sixes and sevens always: and him, why perhaps he'll take to the beer-shop,—for many a man does, through having, so to say, no home. I've seen the ill of it in my days,' she says, 'and if I thought you'd tumble into it I'd hardly rest quiet in the grave where you be so soon a-going to place me.' 'Be at ease, mother,' says I to her in answer, 'and take my promise, which I'll never break, not to set-up for marriage without a home o' my own and proper things in it.' That promise I can't break, Master Johnny; and there has laid the root of the trouble all along."

I saw then. Roper had nothing but a lodging, not a stick or stone that he could call his. And the foolish man, instead of saving up out of his wages, spent the remnant in buying pretty things for Grizzel. It was a hopeless case.

"You should never have had anything to say to Roper, knowing this, Grizzel."

Grizzel twirled the sweet peas round and round in her fingers, and looked foolish, answering nothing.

"Lett has a good home to give you and means to keep it going. He must make a couple of pounds a week. Perhaps more."

"But then I don't care for him, Master Johnny."

"Give him up then. Send him about his business."

One would have thought she was counting the blossoms on the sweet-pea stalks. Presently she spoke, without looking up.

"You see, Master Johnny, one does not like to—to lose all one's chances, and grow into an old maid. And, if I *can't* have Roper, perhaps,—in time—I might bring myself to take Lett. It's a better opportunity than a poor dairy-maid like me could ever ha' looked for."

The cat was out of the bag. Grizzel was keeping Lett on for a remote contingency. When she could make up her mind to say No to Roper, she meant to say Yes to him.

"It is awful treachery to Roper; keeping him on only to drop him at last," ran my thoughts. "Were I he, I should give her a good shaking, and leave——"

A sudden movement on Grizzel's part nearly startled me. Catching up her can, she darted across the yard by the pond as fast as her pattens would go, poured the milk into the pig's trough with a dash, and disappeared in-doors. Looking round for any possible cause for this, I caught sight of a man in ligh' fustian clothes hovering about in the near field by the hay-ricks. It was Sandy Lett; he had walked over on the chance of getting to see her. But she did not come out again.

The next move in the drama was made by Lett. The following Monday he presented himself before the Squire,—dressed in his Sunday-going things, and a new hat on,—to ask him to be so good as to settle the matter, for it was " getting a'most beyond him."

"Why, how can I settle it?" demanded the Squire. "What have I to do with it?"

"It's a tormenting of me pretty nigh into fiddle-strings," pleaded Lett. "What with her caprices—for sometimes her speaks to me as pleasant as a angel, while at others her won't speak nohow; and what with dratted folk over yonder a-teasing of me"—jerking his head in the direction of Church Dykely—"I don't get no peace of my life. It is a shame, Squire, for any woman to treat a man as she's a-treating me."

"I can't make her have you if she won't have you" exploded the Squire, not liking the appeal. "It is said, you know, that she would rather have Roper."

Sandy Lett, who had a great idea of his own merits, turned his nose into the air. "Beg pardon, Squire," he said, "but that won't wash, that won't. Grizzel couldn't have nothing serious to say to that there Roper; nought but a day-laborer on a farm; *she couldn't:* and if he don't keep his distance from her, I'll wring his ugly head round for him. Look at me beside him!—at my good home wi' its m'hogany furniture in't. I can keep her a'most like a lady. She may have in a wench once a week for the washing and scrubbing, if she likes; I'd not deny her nothing in reason. And for that there Roper to think to put hisself in atween us! No; 'twon't do; the moon's not made o' green cheese. Grizzel's a bit light-hearted, sir; fond o' chatter; and Roper he've played upon that. But if you'd speak a word for me, Squire, so as I may have the banns put up——"

"What the deuce, Lett, do you suppose I have to do with my women servants and their banns?" testily interrupted the Squire. "I can't interfere to make her marry you. But I'll tell you thus much, and her too; if there is to be this perpetual uproar about Grizzel, she shall quit my house before the twelvemonth she engaged herself for is up. And that's a disgrace for any young woman."

So Sandy Lett got nothing by coming, poor unfortunate man. And yet—in a sense he did. The Squire ordered the girl before him, and told her in a sharp, decisive tone that she must either put an end to the state of things—or leave his service. And Grizzel, finding that the limit of toleration had come, but unable in her conflicting difficulties of mind to decide which of the swains to retain and which discard, dismissed the two. After that she was plunged over head and ears in distress, and for a week could not see to skim off the cream for her tears.

"This comes of hiring dairy wenches at a statty fair!" cried wrathful Molly.

The summer went on. August was waning. One morning that Mr. Duffham had called in and was helping Mrs. Todhetley to give Lena a spoonful of jam (with a powder in it), at which Lena kicked and screamed, Grizzel ran into the room in excitement so great, that they thought she was going into a fit.

"Why, what is it?" questioned Mrs. Todhetley, putting a temporary truce to the jam hositilities. "Has either of the cows kicked you down, Grizzel?"

"I'm—I'm come into a fortin!" shrieked Grizzel hysterically, laughing and crying in the same breath.

Mr. Duffham put her into a chair, angrily ordering her to be calm,—for anger is the best remedy in the world to apply to hysterics—and took a letter from her that she held out. It told her that her uncle Clay was dead, and had left her a bequest of forty pounds. The forty pounds to be paid to her in gold whenever she should go and apply for it. This letter had come by the morning's post: but Grizzel, busy in her dairy, had only just now opened it.

"For the poor old uncle to have died in June, and them never to ha' let me hear on't!" she said sobbing. "Just like 'em! And me never to have put on a bit o' mourning for him!"

She rose from the chair, drying her eyes with her apron, and held out her hand for the letter. As Mrs. Todhetley began to say she was very glad to hear of her good luck, a shy look and a half-smile came into the girl's face.

"I can get the home now, ma'am, with all this fortin," she softly whispered.

Molly banged her pans about worse than ever, partly in envy at the good luck of the girl, partly because she had to do the dairy work during Grizzel's absence in Gloucestershire: a day and a half, which was given her by Mrs. Todhetley.

"There won't be no standing a nigh her and her finery now," cried rampant Molly to the servants. "She'll tack her blue ribbons on to her tail as well as her head. Lucky if the dairy some fine day ain't found turned all sour!"

Grizzel came back in time; bringing her forty pounds in gold wrapped-up at the foot of a folded stocking. The girl had as much sense as here and there one, and a day or two after her arrival she asked leave to speak to her mistress. It was to say that she should like to leave at the end of her year, Michaelmas, if her mistress would please look out for some one to replace her.

"And what are you going to do, Grizzel, when you do leave? What are your plans?"

Grizzel turned the co'or of a whole cornfield of poppies, and confessed that she was going to be married to George Roper.

"Oh," said Mrs. Todhetley. But she had nothing to urge against it.

" And please, ma'am," cried Grizzel, the poppies deepening and glowing, " we'd like to make bold to ask if the master would let to us that bit of a cottage that the Claytons have went out of."

The Mater was quite taken aback. It seemed indeed that Grizzel had been laying her plans to some purpose.

" It have got a nice piece o' ground to grow pertaters and garden stuff, and it have got a pigsty," said Grizzel. " Please ma'am, we shall get along famous, if we can have that."

" Do you mean to set up a pig, Grizzel ?"

Grizzel's face was all one smile Of course they did. With such a fortune as she had come into, she intended herself and her husband to have everything good about them, including a pig.

" I'll give Grizzel away," wrote Tod when he heard the news of the legacy and the projected marriage. " It will be fun ! And if you people at home don't present her with her wedding gown it will be a stingy shame. Let it have a good share of blue bows."

" No, though, will he !" exclaimed Grizzel with sparkling eyes, when told of the honor designed her by Tod. " Give me away ! Him ! I've always said there's not such another gentleman in these parts as Mr. Joseph."

The banns were put up, and matters progressed smoothly, with one solitary exception. When Sandy Lett heard of the treason going on behind his back, he was ready to drop with blighted love and mortification. A three-days' weather blight was nothing to his. Quite forgetting modesty, he made his fierce way into the house, without saying with your leave or by your leave, and thence to the dairy where Grizzel stood making up butter, startling the girl so much with his white face and wild eyes that she stepped back into a pan of cream. Then he enlarged upon her iniquity, and wound up by assuring her that neither she nor her "coward of a Roper" could ever come to good. After that, he let her alone, making no further stir.

Grizzel quitted the Manor and went into the cottage, which the Squire had agreed to let to them; Roper was to come to it on the wedding-day. A daughter of Goody Picker's, one Mary Standish (whose husband had a habit of going off on roving trips and staying in them until found and brought back by the parish), stayed with Grizzel, helping her to get the cottage in habitable order, and arrange in it the articles she bought. That sum of forty pounds seemed to be doing wonders; I told Grizzel I could not have made a thousand go as far.

"Any left, Master Johnny, why of course I shall have plenty left," she said. "After buying the bed and the set o' drawers and the chairs and tables; and the pots and pans and crockeryware for the kitchen; and the pig and a cock and hen or two; and providing a joint of roast pork and some best tea and white sugar for the wedding day, we shall still have pounds and pounds on't left. 'Tisn't me, sir, nor George neither, that 'ud like to lavish away all we've got and put none by for a rainy day."

"All right, Grizzel. I am going to give you a tea-caddy."

"Well now, to think of that, Master Johnny!" she said, lifting her hands. "And after the mistress giving me such a handsome gownd!—and the servants clubbing together, and bringing a roasting oven and beautiful set o' flat irons. Roper and me 'll be set up like a king and queen."

On Saturday, the day before that fixed for the wedding, I and Tod were passing the cottage—a kind of miniature barn, to look at, with a thatched roof, and a broken grindstone at the door—and went in; rather to the discomfiture of Grizzel and Mrs. Standish, who had their petticoats short and their arms bare, scouring and scrubbing and making ready for the morrow. Returning across the fields later, we saw Grizzel at the door, gazing out all ways at once.

"Consulting the stars as to whether it will be fine to-mor-.

row, Grizzel?" cried Tod, who was never at a loss for a ready word.

"I was a-looking out for Mary Standish, sir," she said. "George Roper haven't been here to-night, and we be all at doubtings about several matters he was to have come in to settle. First he said he'd go on betimes to the church o' Sunday morning; then he said he'd come here and we'd all walk together: and it was left at a uncertainty. There's the blackberry pie, too, that he've not brought."

"The blackberry pie!" said I.

"One that Mrs. Dodd, where he lodges, have made a present of to us for dinner, Master Johnny. Roper was to ha' brought it in to-night ready. It won't look well to see him carrying of a baked-pie on a Sunday morning, when he've got on his wedding coat. I can't think where he have got to!"

At this moment, some one was seen moving towards us across the field path. It proved to be Mary Standish; her gown turned up over her head, and a pie in her hands the size of a pulpit canopy. Red syrup was running down the outside of the dish, and the crust looked a little black at the edges.

"My, what a big beauty!" exclaimed Grizzel.

"Do take it, Grizzel, for my hands be all a cramped with its weight," said Mrs. Standish: who, as it turned out, had been over to Roper's lodgings, a mile and a half away, with a view of seeing what had become of the bridegroom elect. And she nearly threw the pie into Grizzel's arms, and took down her gown.

"And what do Roper say?" asked Grizzel. "And why have he not been here?"

"Roper's not at home," said Mary Standish. "He come in from work about six; washed and put hisself to rights a bit, and then went out with a big bundle. Mrs. Dodd called after him to bring the pie, but he called back again that the pie might wait."

"What was in the bundle?" questioned Grizzel, resenting the slight shown to the pie.

"Well, by the looks on't, Mother Dodd thought 'twas his working clothes packed up," replied Mary Standish.

"His working clothes!" cried Grizzel.

"A going to take 'em to the tailor's, maybe, to get 'em done up. And not afore they wanted it."

"Why, it's spending money for nothing," was Grizzel's comment. "I could ha' done up them clothes."

"Well, it's what Mother Dodd thought," concluded Mary Standish.

We said good-night, and went racing home, leaving the two women at the door, Grizzel lodging the heavy blackberry pie on the old grindstone.

It was a glorious day for Grizzel's wedding. The hour fixed by the clerk (old Bumford) was ten o'clock, so that it might be got well over before the bell rang out for service. We reached the church early. Amidst the few spectators already there was cross-grained Molly, pocketing her ill-temper and for once meaning to be gracious to Grizzel.

Ten o'clock struck, and the big old clock went ticking on. Clerk Bumford (a pompous man when free from gout) began abusing the wedding party for not keeping its time. The quarter past was striking when Grizzel came up, with Mary Standish and a young girl. She looked white and nervous, and not at all at ease in her bridal attire,—a green gown of some kind of stuff, and no end of pink ribbons: the choice of colors being Grizzel's own.

"Is Roper here yet?" whispered Mary Standish.

"Not yet."

"It's too bad of him!" she continued. "Never to send a body word whether he meant to call for us, or not: and us a-waiting there till now, expecting of him."

But where was George Roper? And (as old Bumford

asked) what did he mean by it? The clergyman in his surplice and hood looked out at the vestry twice, as if questioning what the delay meant. We stood just inside the porch, and Grizzel grew whiter and whiter.

"Just a few minutes more o' this delay, and there won't be no wedding at all this blessed morning," announced Clerk Bumford aloud for the public benefit. "George Roper wants a good blowing up, he do."

Ere the words were well spoken, a young man named Dicker, who was a fellow lodger of Roper's and was to have accompanied him to church, made his appearance alone. That something had gone wrong was plain to be seen: but, what with the publicity of his present position, and what with the stern clerk pouncing down upon him in wrath, the young man could hardly get his news out.

In the first place, Roper had never been at home all night; never been seen, in short, since he had left Mrs. Dodd's with the bundle, as related by Mary Standish. That morning, while Dicker in his consternation knew not what to be at—whether to be off to church alone, or to wait still, in the hope that Roper would come,—two notes were delivered at Mrs. Dodd's by a strange boy : the one addressed to himself, John Dicker, the other to "Miss Clay," meaning Grizzel. They bore ill news; George Roper had given up his marriage, and gone away for good.

At this extraordinary crisis, pompous Clerk Bumford was so taken aback, that he could only open his mouth and stare. It gave Dicker the opportunity to put a few words in.

"What we thought at Mother Dodd's was, that Roper had took a drop too much somewhere last evening, and couldn't get home. He's as sober a man as can be—but whatever else was we to think? And when this writed note come this morning, and we found he had gone off to Ameriky o' purpose to avoid being married, we was downright floundered. This is yours, Grizzel," added the young man in as gently considerate a tone as any gentleman could have used.

Grizzel's hand shook as she took the letter he held out. She was biting her pale lips hard to keep down emotion. "Take it and read it," she whispered to Mary Standish,—for in truth she herself could not, with all that sea of curious eyes upon her.

But Mary Standish labored under the slight disadvantage of not being able to read writing : conscious of this difficulty, she would not touch the letter. Mr. Bumford, his senses and his tongue returned together, snatched it without ceremony out of Grizzel's hand.

"I'll read it," said he. And he did so. And I, Johnny Ludlow, give you the copy verbatim.

"Der Grisl, saterdy evenin, this comes hoppin you be wel as it leves me at presint, Which this is to declar to you der grisl that our marage is at an end, it hav ben to much for me and praid on my sperits, I cant stand it no longer nohow and hav took my leve of you for ivir, Der Grisl I maks my best way this night to Livirpol to tak ship for Ameriky, and my last hops for you hearby xprest is as you may be hapy with an-nother, I were nivir worthey of you der grisl and thats a fac, but I kep it from you til now when I cant kep it no longer cause of my conshunse, once youv red this hear letter dont you nivir think no mor on me agen, which I shant on you, Adew for ivir.

"your unfortnit friend George Roper.
"Ide av carred acros that ther blakbured pi but should have ben to late, my good hops is youl injoy the pi with another better nor you ivir could along with me, best furwel wishes to Mary Standish, G. R."

What with the penmanship and what with the spelling, it took old Bumford's spectacles some time to get through. A thunderbolt could hardly have made more stir than this news. Nobody spoke, however; and Mr. Bumford folded the letter in silence.

"I always knowed what that there Roper was worth," broke forth Molly. "He pipe-clayed my best black cloak on the sly one day when I ordered him off the premises. You be better without him, Grizzel, girl—and here's my hand and wishing you better luck in token of it."

" Mrs. Dodd was right—them was a change o' clothes he was a-taking with him to Ameriky," added Mary Standish.

"Roper's a jail-bird, I should say," put in old Bumford. " A nice un too."

"But what can it be that's went wrong—what is it that have took him off?" wondered the young man, Dicker.

The parson in his surplice had come along the aisle and was standing to listen. Grizzel, in the very extremity of mental bitterness and confusion, but striving to put a good face of indifference on the matter before the public, gazed around helplessly.

"I'm better without him, as Molly says—and what do I care?" she cried, recklessly, her lips and face quivering. The parson put his hand gravely on her arm.

"My good young woman, I think you are in truth better without him. Such a man as that is not worthy of a regret."

"No, sir, and I don't and won't regret him," was her rapid answer, the voice rising hysterically.

As she turned, intending to leave the church, she came face to face with Sandy Lett. I had seen him standing there, drinking in the words of the note with all his ears and taking covert looks at Grizzel.

"Don't pass me by, Grizzel," said he. "I feel hearty sorry for all this, and I hope that villain'll come to be drowned on his way to Ameriky. Let me be your friend. I'll make you a good one."

"Thank you," she answered. "Please let me go by."

"Look here, Grizzel," he rejoined, with a start, as if some thought had at that moment occurred to him. "Why shouldn't you and me make it up together? Now. If the one bridegroom's been a wicked runagate, and left you all forsaken, you see another here ready to put on his shoes. Do, Grizzel, do!"

"Do what?" she asked, not catching his meaning.

"Let's be married, Grizzel. You and me. There's the parson and Mr. Bumford all ready, and we can get it over afore church begins. It's a good home I've got to take you to. Don't say nay, my girl."

Now what should Grizzel do? Like the lone lorn widow in "David Copperfield," who, when a ship's carpenter offered her marriage, "instead of saying 'Thank you, sir, I'd rather not,' up with a bucket of water and dashed it over him," Grizzel "up" with her hand and dealt Mr. Sandy a sounding smack on the side of his left cheek. Smarting under the infliction, Sandy Lett gave vent to a word or two of passion, out of place in a church, and the parson administered a reprimand.

Grizzel had not waited. Before the sound of her hand had died away, she was outside the door, quickly traversing the lonely church-yard. A fine end to poor Grizzel's wedding!

The following day, Monday, Mrs. Todhetley went over to the cottage. Grizzel, sitting with her hands before her, started up, and made believe to be desperately busy with some tea-cups. We were all sorry for her.

"Mr. Todhetley had been making inquiry into this business, Grizzel," said the Mater, "and it certainly seems more mysterious than ever, for he cannot hear a word against Roper. His late master says Roper was the best servant he ever had; he is as sorry to lose him as can be."

"Oh, ma'am, but he's not worth troubling about—my thanks and duty to the master all the same."

"Would you mind letting me see Roper's note?"

Grizzel took it out of the tea-caddy I had given her—which caddy was to have been kept for show. Mrs. Todhetley, mastering the contents, and biting her lips to suppress an occasional smile, sat in thought.

"I suppose this is Roper's own handwriting, Grizzel?"

"Oh ma'am, it's his, safe enough. Not that I ever saw him write. He talks about the blackberry pie, you see; one might know it is his by that."

"Then, judging by what he says here, he must have got into some bad conduct or trouble, I think, which he has been clever enough to keep from you and the world."

"Oh yes, that's it," said Grizzel. "Poor mother used to say one might be deceived in a saint."

"Well, it's a pity but he had given some clue to its nature: it would have been a sort of satisfaction. But now—I chiefly came over to ask you, Grizzel, what you purpose to do?"

"There's only one thing for me now, ma'am," returned poor crest-fallen Grizzel, after a pause: "I must get another place."

"Will you come back to the Manor?"

A hesitation—a struggle—and then she flung her apron up to her face and burst into tears. Dairy-maids have their feelings as well as their betters, and Grizzel's "lines" were very bitter just then. She had been so proud of this poor cottage home; she had grown to love it so only in those few days of occupancy, and to look forward to years of happiness within it in their humble way: and now to find that she must give it up and go to service again!

"The Squire says he will consider it as though you and Roper had not taken the cottage; and he thinks he can find somebody to rent it who will buy the furniture of you—that is, if you prefer to sell it," she resumed very kindly. "And I think you had better come back to us, Grizzel. The new maid in your place does not suit at all."

Grizzel took down her apron and rubbed her eyes. "It's very good of you, ma'am—and of the master—and I'd like to come back but for one thing. I'm afraid Molly would let me have no peace in my life: she'd get tanking at me about Roper before the others. Perhaps I'd hardly be able to stand it."

"I will talk to her," said Mrs. Todhetley, rising to go. "Where is Mary Standish to-day?"

"Gone over to Alcester, ma'am. She had a errant there, she said. But I think it was only to tell her folks the tale of my trouble."

Molly had her "talking to" at once. It put her out a little; for she was really feeling some pity for Grizzel, and did not at all intend to "get tanking" at her. Molly had once experienced a similar disappointment herself; and her heart was opening to Grizzel. After her dinner was served that evening, she ran over to the cottage, in her coarse cooking apron and without a bonnet.

"Look here," she said, bursting in upon Grizzel, sitting alone in the dusk. "You come back to your place if you like —the missis says she has given you the option—and don't you be afeard of me. 'Tisn't me as'll ever give back to you a word about Roper; and, mind, when I says a thing I mean it."

"Thank you, Molly," humbly replied poor Grizzel, catching up her breath.

"The sooner you come back the better," continued Molly, fiercely. "For it's not me and that wench we've got now as is going to stop together. I had to call the missis into the dairy this blessed morning, and show her the state it was in. So you'll come back, Grizzel—and we'll be glad to see you."

Grizzel nodded her head: her heart was too full to speak.

"And as to that false villain of a Roper, as could serve a woman such a pitiful trick, I only wish I had the doctoring of him! He should get a—a—a——" Molly's voice, pitched in a high tone, died gradually away. What on earth was it, stepping in upon them? Some most extraordinary object, who opened the door softly, and came in with a pitch. Molly peered at it in the darkness with open mouth.

A cry from Grizzel. A cry, half of terror, half of pain. For she had recognized the object to be a man, and George Roper. George Roper with his hair and handsome whiskers cut off, and white sleeves in his brown coat—so that he looked like a merry Andrew.

He seemed three parts stupefied: not at all like a traveller in condition to set off to America. Sinking down in the nearest wooden chair, he stared at Grizzel in a dazed way, and spoke in a slow, questioning, wondering voice.

" I can't think what it is that's the matter with me."

" Where be your black whiskers—and your hair?" burst forth Molly.

The man gazed at her for a minute or two, taking in the question; he then raised his trembling hand to either side his face—feeling for the whiskers that were no longer there.

" A nice pot o' mischief *you*'ve been a-getting into ! " cried sharp Molly. " Is that your own coat ? What's gone of the sleeves ?"

For, now that the coat could be seen closely, it turned out that its sleeves had been cut out, leaving the bare white sleeves of the shirt underneath. Roper looked first at one arm, then at the other.

" What part of Ameriky be ye bound for, and when do the ship sail ?" pursued sarcastic Molly.

The man opened his mouth and closed it again ; like, as Molly put it, a born natural. Grizzel suddenly clung to him with a sobbing cry.

" He is ill, Molly ; he's ill. He has had some trick played on him. George, what be it ?" But still George Roper only gazed about him as if too stupid to understand.

In short, the man *was* stupid. That is, he had been stupe· fied, and as yet was only partially recovering the effects. He remembered going into the barber's shop on Saturday night to have his hair cut, after leaving his bundle of clothes at the tailor's. Some ale was served round at the barber's, and he, Roper, took a glass. After that he remembered nothing : all was blank, until he woke up an hour ago in the unused shed at the back of the blacksmith's shop.

That the ale had been badly drugged, was evident. The

question arose—who had played the trick ? In a day or two, when Roper had recovered, an inquiry was set on foot : but nothing came of it. The barber testified that Roper seemed sleepy after the ale, and a joke went round that he must have been drinking some previously. He went out of the shop without having his hair cut, with several more men—and that was all the barber knew. Of course Sandy Lett was sus-pected. People said he had done it in hopes to get himself substituted for the bridegroom. Lett, however, vowed through thick and thin that he was innocent; and nothing was traced home to him. Neither was the handwriting of the note.

They were married on the Thursday. Grizzel was too glad to get him back unharmed to make bones over the cut whiskers. No difficulty was made about opening the church on a week-day. Clerk Bumford grumbled at it, but the par-son put him down. And the blackberry pie served still for the wedding dinner.

XVII.

BREAKING DOWN.

AVE him here a bit."

"Oh! But would you like it?"

"Like it?" retorted the Squire. "I know this; if I were a hard-worked London clerk, ill for want of change and rest, and I had friends living in a nice part of the country, I should feel it uncommonly hard if they did not invite me."

"I'm sure it is very kind of you to think of it," said Mrs. Todhetley.

"Write at once and ask him," said the Squire.

They were speaking of a Mr. Marks. He was a relation of Mrs. Todhetley's; a second or third cousin. She had not seen him since she was a girl, when he had used sometimes to come and stay at her father's. He seemed not to have got on very well in life: was only a clerk on a narrow salary, was married and had some children. A letter now and then passed between them and Mrs. Todhetley, but no other acquaintanceship had been kept up. About a month before this, Mrs. Todhetley had written to ask how they were going on; and the wife in answering—for it was she who wrote—said her husband was killing himself with work, and she quite believed he would break down for good unless he had a rest.

We heard more about it later. James Marks was clerk in a great financial house—Brown and Co. Not particularly great as to reputation, for they made no noise in the world, but great as to their transactions. They did a little banking in a small way, and had mysterious money dealings with no end of foreign places: but if you had gone into their counting-house in London you'd have seen nothing to show for it, save Mr. Brown seated at a table-desk in a small room, and half a dozen clerks, or so, writing hard, or bending over columns of figures, in a bigger one. Mr. Brown was an elderly little gentleman in a chestnut wig, and the "Co." existed only in name.

James Marks had been thrown on the world when he was seventeen, with a good education, good principles, and a great anxiety to get on in life. He had to do it; for he had only himself to look to—and, mind you, I have lived long enough to learn that that's not at all the worst thing a young man can have. When some friends of his late father's got him into Brown and Co.'s house, James Marks thought his fortune was made. That is, he thought he was placed in a position to work up to one. But no. Here he was, getting on for forty years of age, and with no more prospect of fortune, or competence either, than he had at the beginning.

How many clerks, and especially bankers' clerks, are there in that City of London now who could say the same! Who went into their house (whatsoever it may be) in the hey-day of their youth, exulting in their good luck in having obtained the admission for which so many others were striving. They saw not the long years of toil before them, the weary days of close work, with no rest or intermission, save Sunday; they saw not the struggle to live and pay; they saw not themselves middle-aged men, with a wife and family, hardly able to keep the wolf from the door. It was James Marks's case. He had married. And what with having to keep up the appearance of gentlepeople (at least to make a pretence at it) and to live in a decent-looking dwelling, and to buy clothes, and to pay doctor's bills and children's schooling, I'll leave you to guess how much he had left for luxuries out of his two hundred a year.

When expenses were coming upon him thick and fast,

Marks sought out some night employment. A tradesman in the neighborhood—which was Pimlico—a butter and cheese-man doing a flourishing businesss, advertised for a book-keeper to attend two or three hours in the evening. James Marks presented himself and was engaged. It had to be done in a kind of secrecy, lest offence should be taken at .ead-quarters. Had the little man in the chestnut wig heard of it, he might have objected to his clerk keeping any books but his own. Shut up in the cheesemonger's small back closet that he called his counting house, Mr. Marks could be as private as need be. So there he was! After coming home from his day's toil, instead of taking needful recreation, the home-sitting with his wife, or the stroll in the summer weather, in place of throwing work to the winds and giving his brain rest, James Marks, after snatching a meal, tea and supper combined, went forth to work again, to weary his eyes with more figures and his head with casting them up. He generally managed to get home by eleven except on Saturday; but the day's work was too much for any man. Better for him (could he have pocketed pride, and gained over Brown and Co.) that he had hired himself to stand behind the even-ing counter and serve out the butter and cheese to the cus-tomers. It would at least have been a relief from the ac-counts. And so the years had gone on.

A portion of the wife's letter to Mrs. Todhetley had run as follows: "Thank you very much for your kind inquiries after my husband, and for your hope that he is not overwork-ing himself. *He is.* But I suppose I must have said some-thing about it in my last letter (I am ashamed to remember that it was written two years ago!) that induced you to refer to it. That he is overworking himself I have known for a long while: and things that he has said lately have tended to alarm me. He speaks of sometimes getting confused in the head. In the midst of a close calculation he will suddenly seem to lose himself—lose memory and figures and all, and then he has to leave off for some minutes, hide his eyes, and keep perfectly still, or else leave his stool and take a few turns up and down the room. Another thing he mentions—that the figures dance before his eyes in bed at night, and he is adding them up in his brain as if it were daytime and reality. It is very evident to me that he wants change and rest."

"And what a foolish fellow he must have been not to take it before this!" cried the Squire, commenting on parts of the letter, while Mrs. Todhetley wrote.

" Perhaps that is what he has not been able to do so, sir," I said.

"Not able! Why, what d'ye mean, Johnny?"

"It is very difficult for a banker's clerk to get holiday. Their work has to go on all the same."

"Difficult! when a man's powers are breaking down! D'ye think bankers are made of flint and steel, not to give their clerks holiday when it is needed? Don't you talk nonsense, Johnny Ludlow."

But I was not so far wrong, after all. There came a letter of warm thanks from Mr. Marks himself in answer to Mrs. Todhetley's invitation. He said how much he should have liked to accept it and what great good it would certainly have done him; but that upon applying for leave he found he could not be spared. So there seemed to be an end of it; and we hoped he would get better without the rest, and rub on as other clerks have to rub on. But in less than a month he wrote again, saying he would come if the Squire and Mrs. Todhetley were still pleased to have him. He had been so much worse as to be obliged to tell Mr. Brown the truth— that he believed he *must* have rest ; and Mr. Brown granted it to him.

It was the Wednesday in Passion Week, and a fine spring day, when James Marks arrived at Dyke Manor. Easter was late that year. He was rather a tall man, with dark eyes and very thin hair; he wore spectacles, and at first was rather shy in manner.

You should have seen his delight in the change. The walks he took, the enjoyment of what he called the sweet country. "Oh," he said one day to us, "yours must be the happiest lot on earth! No forced work; your living assured; nothing to do but to revel in this health-giving air! Forgive my freedom, Mr. Todhetley," he added a moment after, "I was contrasting your lot with my own."

We were passing through the fields towards the Court: the Squire was taking him to see the Sterlings, and he had said he would rather walk than drive. The hedges were spreading into green: the grass on either side us was yellow with buttercups and cowslips. This was on the Monday. The sun shone and the breeze was soft. Mr. Marks sniffed the air as he went along.

"Six months of this would make a new man of me," we heard him say to himself in a low tone.

"Take it," cried the Squire.

Mr. Marks laughed, sadly enough. "You might as well tell me, sir, to—to take heaven," he said, impulsively. "The one is no more in my power than the other.—Oh, hark! I do believe that's the cuckoo!"

We stood still to listen. It was the cuckoo, sure enough, for the first time that spring. It only gave out two or three notes, though, and then was silent.

"How many years it is since I heard the cuckoo!" he exclaimed, brushing his hand across his eyes. "More than twenty, I suppose. It seems to bring back my youth to me. What a thing it would be for us, sir, if we could only go into the mill that grinds people young again!"

The Squire laughed. "It is good of *you* to talk of age, Marks; why, I must be nearly double yours," he added—which of course was but random speaking.

"I feel old, Mr. Todhetley; perhaps older than you do. Think of the difference in our mode of life. I, tied down to a desk for more hours of the twenty-four than I care to think of, my brain ever at work; you, revelling in this beautiful, healthy freedom!"

"Ay, well, it is a difference, when you come to think of it," said the Squire soberly.

"I must not repine," returned Marks. "There are more men in my case than in yours. No doubt it is well for me," he continued, dropping his voice, with a sigh. "Were your favored lot mine, sir, I might find so much good in it as to forget that this world is not our true home."

Perhaps it had never struck the Squire before how much he was to be envied; but Marks put it strongly. "You'd find crosses and cares enough in my place, I can tell you, Marks, of one sort or another. Johnny, here, knows how I am bothered sometimes."

"No doubt of it," replied Marks, with a smile. "No lot on earth can be free from its duties and responsibilities; and they must of necessity entail care. That is one thing, Mr. Todhetley; but to be working away your life at steam point —and to know that you are working it away—is another."

"You acknowledge, then, that you are working too hard, Marks," said the Squire.

"I know I am, sir. But there's no help for it."

"It is a pity."

"Why it should begin to tell upon me so early I don't know. There are other men, numbers of them, who work as long and hard as I do, and are seemingly none the worse for it."

"The time will come though when they will be, I presume."

"As surely as that sun is shining in the sky."

"Possibly you have been more anxious than they, Marks."

"It may be so. My conscience has always been in my work, to do it very efficiently. I fear, too, I am rather sensitively organised as to nerves and brain: upon those who are so, I fancy work tells faster than on others."

The Squire put his arm within Marks'. "You must have a bit of a struggle to get along, too, on your small salary."

"True: and it all helps. Work and struggle together are not the most desirable combination. But for being obliged to increase my means by some stratagem or other, I should not have taken on the additional evening's work."

"How long are you at it, now, of an evening?"

"Usually about two hours. On Saturdays and at Christmas-time longer."

"And I suppose you must continue this night-work?"

"Yes. I get fifty pounds a year for it. And I assure you I should not know how to spare one pound of the fifty. No one knows the expenses of children, save those who have to look at every shilling before it can be spent."

There was a pause. Mr. Marks stooped, plucked a cowslip and held it to his lips.

"Don't you think, Marks," resumed the Squire, in a confidential, friendly tone, "that you were just a little imprudent to marry?"

"No, I do not think I was," he replied slowly, as if considering the question. "I did not marry very early: I was eight-and-twenty; and I had got together the wherewithal to furnish a house, and something in hand besides. The question was mooted among us at Brown's the other day—whether it was wiser, or not, for young clerks to marry. There is a great deal to be urged both ways—against marrying and against remaining single."

"What can you urge against remaining single?"

"A very great deal, sir. I feel sure, Mr. Todhetley, that you can form no idea of the miserable temptations that beset a young fellow in London. Quite half the London clerks, perhaps more, have no home to go to when their day is over; I mean no parent's home. A solitary room and nobody to bear them company in it; that's all they have: perhaps, in addition, a crabbed landlady. Can you blame them very much if they go out and escape this solitude?—they are at the age, you know, when enjoyment is most keen; the thirst for it well-nigh irrepressible——"

"And then they go off to those disreputable singing places!" exploded the Squire, not allowing him to finish.

"Singing places, yes; and other places. Theatres, concerts, supper-rooms—oh, I cannot tell you a tithe of the temptation that meets them at every turn and corner. Many and many a poor young fellow, well-intentioned in the main, has been ruined both in pocket and in health by these snares; led into them at first by dangerous companions."

"Surely all do not get led away."

"Not all. Some strive on manfully, remembering early precepts and taking God for their guide, and so escape. But it is not the greater portion who do this. Some marry early, and secure themselves a home. Which is best?—I put the question only in a wordly point of view. To commit the imprudence of marrying, and so bring on themselves and wives intolerable perplexity and care: or to waste their substance in riotous living?"

"I'll be shot if I know!" cried the Squire, taking off his hat to rub his puzzled head. "It's a sad thing for poor little children to be pinched, and for men like you to be obliged to work yourselves to shatters to keep them. But as to those others, I'd give 'em all a night at the treadmill. Johnny! Johnny Ludlow!"

"Yes, sir."

"You may be thankful that *you* don't live in London."

I had been thinking to myself that I was thankful not to be one of those poor young clerks to have no home to go to when work was over. Some fellows would rather tramp up and down the muddy streets than sit alone in a solitary room; and the streets, according to Marks, teemed with temptations. He resumed.

"In my case I judged it the reverse of imprudence to marry, for my wife expected a fairly good fortune. She was an only child, and her father had realised enough to live quietly; say three or four hundred a year. Mr. Stockleigh had been a member of the Stock Exchange, but his health failed and he retired. Neither I nor his daughter ever doubted—no, nor did he himself—that this money must come to us in time "

"And won't it ?" cried the Squire.

Marks shook his head. "I fear not. A designing servant, that they had, got over him after his daughter left—he was weak in health and weak in mind—and he married her. Caroline—my wife—resented it naturally ; there was some bickering on either side, and since then they have closed the door against her and me. So you see, with no prospect before us, there's nothing for me but to work the harder," he concluded, with a kind of plucked-up cheerfulness.

"But, to do that, you should get up your health and strength, Marks. You must, you know. What would you do if you broke down ?"

"Hush !" came the involuntary and almost affrighted answer. "Don't remind me of it, sir : sometimes I dream of it, and cannot bear to awake."

We had got to like Marks very much only in those few days. He was a gentleman in mind and manners, and a pleasant one into the bargain, though he did pass his days adding up figures and was kept down by poverty. The Squire meant to keep him for a month : two months if he would stay.

On the following morning, Tuesday, during breakfast-time, a letter came for him by the post—the first he had had. He had told his wife she need not write to him, wanting to have all the time for idle enjoyment : not to spend it in answering letters.

"From home, James ?" asked Mrs. Todhetley.

"No," said he smiling. "It is only a reminder that I am due to-morrow at the house."

"What house ?" cried the Squire.

"Our house, sir. Brown and Co.'s."

The Squire put down his buttered roll—for Molly had graciously sent in hot rolls that morning—and stared at the speaker.

"What on earth are you talking of?" he cried. "You don't mean to say you are thinking of going back?"

"Indeed I am—unfortunately. I must get up to London to-night."

"Why, bless my heart and mind," cried the Squire, getting up and standing a bit, "you've not been here a week!"

"It is all the leave I could get, Mr. Todhetley: a week. I thought you understood that."

"You can't go away till you are cured," roared the Squire. "Why didn't you go back the day you came? Don't you talk nonsense, Marks."

"Indeed I should like to stay longer," he earnestly said. "I wish I could. Don't you see, Mr. Todhetley, that it does not lie with me?"

"Do you dare to look me in the face, Marks, and tell me this one week's rest has cured you? Come! What on earth! —are you turning silly?"

"It has done me a great, great deal of good——"

"It has not, Marks. It can't have done it; not real good," came the Squire's interruption. "One would think you were a child."

"It was with difficulty I obtained this one week's leave," he explained. "I am really required in the office; my absence from it I know causes trouble. This holiday has done so much for me that I shall go back with a good heart."

"Look here," said the Squire: "suppose you take French leave, and stay?"

"In that case my discharge would doubtless arrive by the first post."

"Look here again: suppose in a month or two you break down and have to leave? What then?"

"Brown and Co. would appoint a fresh clerk in my place."

"Why don't Brown and Co. keep another clerk or two, so as to work you all less?"

Marks smiled at the very idea. "That would increase their

expenses, Mr. Todhetley. They will never do that. It is a part of the business of Brown's life to keep expenses down."

Well, Marks had to go. The Squire was very serious in thinking more rest absolutely needful—of what service *could* a week be, he reiterated. Down he sat, wrote a letter to Brown and Co., telling them his opinion, and requesting the favor of their despatching James Marks back for a longer holiday. This he sent by post, and they would get it in the morning.

"No, I'll not trust it to you, Marks," he said : "you might never deliver it. Catch an old bird with chaff!"

To this letter there came no answer at all; and Mr. Marks did not come back. The Squire relieved his mind by calling Brown and Co. thieves and wretches—and so it passed. It must be remembered that I am writing of past years, when holidays were not so universal for any class, clerk or master, as they are at present. Not that I am aware whether financiers' clerks get them now.

The next scene in the drama I can only tell by hearsay. It took place in London, where I was not.

It was a dull, rainy day in February, and Mrs. Marks sat in her parlor in Pimlico. The house was one of a long row, and the parlor just about large enough to turn in. She sat by the fire, nursing a little two-year-old girl, and thinking ; and three other children, the eldest a boy of nine, were playing at the table—building houses on the red cloth with little wooden bricks. Mrs. Marks was a sensible woman, understanding proper management, and had taken care to bring up her children not to be troublesome. She looked about thirty, and must have been pretty once, but her face was faded now, her grey eyes had a sad look in them. The chatter at the table and the bricks fell alike unheeded on her ear.

"Mamma, will it soon be tea-time?"

There was no answer.

"Didn't you hear, mamma? Carry asked if it would soon be tea-time. What were you thinking about?"

She heard this time, and started out of her reverie. "Very soon now, Willy dear. Thinking? Oh, I was thinking about your papa."

Her thoughts were by no means bright ones. That her husband's health and powers were alike failing, she felt as sure of as though she could foresee the ending that was soon to come. How he went on and did his work was a marvel: but he could not give it up, or bread would fail.

The week's rest in the country had set Mr. Marks up for some months. Until the next autumn he worked on better than he had been able to do for some time past. And then he failed again. There was no particular failing outwardly, but he felt all too conscious that his over-taxed brain was getting worse than it had ever been. He struggled on; making no sign. That he should have to resign part of his work was a fact inevitable: he must give up the evening book-keeping to enable him to keep his more important place. "Once let me get the Christmas work over," thought he, "and as soon as may be in the New Year, I will resign."

He got the Christmas work over. Very heavy it was, at both places, and nearly did for him. It is the last feather, you know, that breaks the camel's back: and that work broke James Marks'. Towards the end of January he was laid up in bed with a violent cold that settled on his chest. Brown and Co. had to do without him for eleven days: a calamity that—so far as Marks was concerned—had never happened in Brown and Co.'s experience. Then he went back to the city again, feeling shaken and dazed; but the evening labor was perforce given up.

No one knew how ill he was: or, to speak more correctly, how unfit for his work. how more incapable of it he was growing day by day. His wife suspected a little. She knew of his sleepless nights, the result of over-taxed nerves and brain,

when he would toss and turn and get up and walk the room;
and dress himself in the morning without having slept.

"There are times," he said to her in a kind of horror, "when
I cannot at all collect my thoughts. I am as long again at
my work as I used to be, and have to go over it again and
again. There have been one or two mistakes, and old Brown
asks what is coming to me. I can't help it. The figures
whirl before me, and I lose my power of mind."

"If you could but sleep well!" said Mrs. Marks.

"Ay, if I could. The brain is as much at work at night as
day. There are the figures mentally before me, and there am
I, adding them up."

"You should see a clever physician, James. Spare the
guinea, and go. It may be more than the guinea saved."

Mr. Marks took the advice. He went to a clever doctor;
explained his position, the kind of work he had to do, and
described his symptoms. "Can I be cured?" he asked.

"Oh, yes, I think so," said the doctor, cheerfully, without
telling him that he had gone on so far as to make it rather a
doubt. "The necessary treatment is very simple. Take
change of scene and perfect rest."

"For how long?"

"Twelve months, at least."

"Twelve months!" repeated Marks, in a queer tone.

"At least. It is a case of absolute necessity. I will write
you a prescription for a tonic. You must live *well*. You
have not lived well enough for the work you have to do."

As James Marks went out into the street he could have
laughed a laugh of bitter mockery. Twelve months' rest for
him? The doctor had told him one thing—that had he
taken the rest in time, a very, very much shorter period
would have sufficed. "I wonder how many poor men there
are like myself in London at this moment," he thought, "who
want this rest and cannot take it, and who ought to live better and cannot afford to do it!"

It was altogether so very hopeless that he did nothing, except take the tonic, and he continued to go to the City as usual. Some two or three weeks had elapsed since then: he of course growing worse, though there was nothing to show it outwardly: and this was the end of February, and Mrs. Marks sat thinking of it all over the fire, what she knew, and guessing at what she did not know, and her children were building houses at the table.

The servant came in with the tea-things, and took the little girl. Only one servant could be kept—and hardly that. Mrs. Marks had made her own tea and was pouring out the children's milk-and-water, when they heard a cab drive up and stop at the door. A minute after, Mr. Marks entered, leaning on the arm of one of his fellow clerks.

"Here, Mrs. Marks, I have brought you an invalid," said the latter gaily, making light of it for her sake. "He seems better now. I don't think there's much the matter with him."

Had it come? Had what she been dreading come—that he was going to have an illness, she wondered. But she was a trump of a wife, and showed herself calm and comforting.

"You shall both of you have some tea at once," she said, cheerfully. "Willy, run and get more tea-cups."

It appeared that Mr. Marks had been, as the clerk expressed it, very queer that day; more so than usual. He could not do his work at all; had to get assistance continually from one or the other, and ended by falling off his stool on the floor, in what he called, afterwards, a "sensation of giddy bewilderment." He seemed fit for nothing, and Mr. Brown said he had better be taken home.

That day ended James Marks' work. He had broken down. At night he told his wife what the physician had said; which he had not done before. She could scarcely hide her dismay.

A twelvemonth's rest for him! What would become of them! Failing his salary, they would have no means whatever of living.

"Oh, if my father had but acted by us as he ought!" she mentally cried. "James could have taken rest in time then.

and all would have been well. Will he help us now it has come to this? Will *she* let him?—for it is she who holds him in subjection and steels his heart against us."

Mr. Stockleigh, the father, lived at Sydenham. She, the new wife, had taken him off there from his residence in Pimlico as soon as might be after the marriage; and the daughter had never been invited inside the house. But she resolved to go there now. Saying nothing to her husband, Mrs. Marks started for Sydenham the day after he was brought home ill, and found the place without trouble.

The wife, formerly the cook, was a big, brawny woman with a cheek and a tongue of her own. When Mrs. Marks was shown in, she forgot herself in the surprise; old habits prevailed, and she dropped a curtsey.

"I wish to see papa, Mrs. Stockleigh."

"Mr. Stockleigh's out, ma'am."

"Then I must wait until he returns."

Mrs. Stockleigh did not see her way clear to turn this lady from the house, though she would have liked to do it. She made a show of hospitality, and ordered wine and cake to be put on the table. Of which wine Mrs. Marks noticed with surprise, she drank *four* glasses. "Now and then we used to suspect her of drinking in the kitchen!" ran through Mrs. Marks' thoughts. "Has it grown upon her?"

The garden gate opened, and Mr. Stockleigh came through it. He was so bowed and broken that his daughter scarcely knew him. She hastened out and met him in the path.

"Caroline!" he exclaimed in amazement. "Is it really you? How much you have changed!"

"I came down to speak to you, papa. May we stay and talk here in the garden?"

He seemed glad to see her, rather than not, and sat down with her on the garden bench in the sun. In a quiet voice she told him all: and asked him to help her. Mrs. Stockleigh had come out and stood listening to the treason, somewhat unsteady in her walk.

"I—I would help you if I could, Caroline," he said, in hesitation, glancing at his wife.

"Yes, but you can't, Stockleigh," she put in. "Our own expenses is as much as iver we can manage, Mrs. Marks. It's a orful cost, living out here, and our two servants is the very deuce for extravigance. I've changed 'em both ten times for others, and the last lot is always worse nor the first."

"Papa, do you see our position?" resumed Mrs. Marks, after hearing the lady patiently. "It will be a long time before James is able to do anything again—if he ever is—and we have not been able to save money. What are we to do? Go to the workhouse? I have four little children."

"You know that you can't help, Stockleigh," insisted Mr. Stockleigh's lady, taking up the answer, her face growing more inflamed. "You've not got the means to do anything: and there's an end on't."

"It is true, Caroline; I'm afraid I have not," he said—and his daughter saw with pain how tremblingly subject he was to his wife. "I seem short of money always. How did you come down, my dear?"

"By the train, papa. Third class."

"Oh dear!" cried Mr. Stockleigh. "My health's broken, Caroline. It is, indeed, and my spirit too. I am sure I am very sorry for you. Will you come in and take some dinner?"

"We've not got nothing but a bit of 'ashed beef," cried Mrs. Stockleigh, as if to put a damper upon the invitation. "Him and me fails in our appetites dreadful: I can't think what's come to 'em."

Mrs. Marks declined the dinner: she had to get back to the children. That any kind of pleading would be useless while that woman held the sway, she saw well. "Good bye, papa," she said. "I suppose we must do the best we can alone. Good morning, Mrs. Stockleigh."

To her surprise her father kissed her; kissed her with quivering lips. "I will open the gate for you, my dear," he said, hastening on to it. As she was going through, he slipped a sovereign into her hand.

"It will pay for your journey, at least, my dear. I am sorry to hear of your travelling third class. Ah, times have changed. It is not that I won't help you, child, but that I can't. She goes up to receive the dividends, and keeps me short. I should not have had that sovereign now, but it is the change out of the spirit bill that she sent me to pay. Hush! the money goes in drink. She drinks like any fish. Ah, Caroline, I was a fool—a fool! Fare you well, my dear."

"Fare *you* well, dear papa, and thank you," she answered, turning away with brimming eyes and an aching heart.

After resting for some days and getting no better, James Marks had to give it up as a bad job. He went to the City house, saw Mr. Brown, and told him.

"Broken down!" cried old Brown, hitching back his wig, as he always did when put out. "I never heard of such nonsense. At your age! The thing's incomprehensible."

"The work has been very wearing to the brain, sir; and my application to it was close. During the three-and-twenty years I have been with you I never had but one week's holiday: the one last spring."

"You told me then you felt like a man breaking down, as if you were good for nothing," resentfully spoke old Brown.

"Yes, sir. I told you that I believed I was breaking down for want of a rest," replied Marks. "It has proved so."

"Why, you had your rest."

"One week, sir. I said I feared it would not be of much use. But—it was not convenient for you to allow me more."

"Of course it was not convenient; you know it could not be convenient," retorted old Brown. "D'ye think I keep my clerks for play, Marks? D'ye suppose my business will get done for itself?"

"I was aware myself, sir, how inconvenient my absence would be, and therefore I did not press the matter. That one week's rest did me a wonderful deal of service: it enabled me to go on until now."

Old Brown looked at him. "See here, Marks—we are sorry to lose you: suppose you take another week's change now, and try what it will do. A fortnight, say. Go to the sea-side, or somewhere."

Marks shook his head. "Too late, sir. The doctors tell me it will be twelve months before I am able to work again at calculations."

"Oh, my service to you," cried Mr. Brown. "Why, what are you going to do if you cannot work?"

"That is a great deal more than I can say, sir. The thought of it is troubling my brain quite as much as work ever did. It is never out of it, night or day."

For once in his screwy life, old Brown was generous. He told Mr. Marks to draw his salary up to the day he had left, and he added ten pounds to it over and above.

* * *

During that visit I paid to Miss Deveen's in London, when Tod was with the Whitneys, and Helen made her first curtsey to the Queen, and we discovered the mal-doings of that syren, Mademoiselle Sophie Chalk, I saw Marks. Mrs. Todhetley had given me two or three commissions, as may be remembered: one amidst them was to call in Pimlico, and see how Marks was getting on.

Accordingly I went. We had heard nothing, you must understand, of what I have told above, and did not know but he was still in his situation. It was a showery day in April: just a twelvemonth, by the way, since his visit to us at Dyke Manor. I found the house out readily; it was near to E'bury Street; and knocked. A young lad opened the door, and asked me to walk in the parlor.

"You are Mr. Marks' son," I said, rubbing my feet on the mat: "I can tell by the likeness. What's your name?"

"William. Papa's is James."

"Yes, I know."

"He is ill," whispered the lad, with his hand on the parlor-door handle. "Mamma's down stairs, making him some arrowroot."

Well, I think you might have knocked me down with a feather when I knew him—for at first I did not. He was sitting in an easy chair by the fire, dressed, but wrapped round with blankets: and instead of being the James Marks we had known, he was like a living skeleton, with cheek-bones and hollow eyes. But he was glad to see me, smiled, and held out his hand from the blanket.

It is uncommonly awkward for a young fellow to be taken unawares like this. You don't know what to say. I'm sure I as much thought he was dying as I ever thought anything in this world. At last I managed to stammer a word or two about being sorry to see him so ill.

"Ay," said he, in a weak, panting voice, "I am different from what I was when with your kind people, Johnny. The trouble I foresaw then has come."

"You used sometimes to feel then as though you would not long keep up," was my answer, for really I could find nothing else to say.

He nodded. "Yes, I felt that I was breaking down—that I should inevitably break down unless I could have rest. I went on until February, Johnny, and then it came. I had to give up my situation; and since then I have been dangerously ill from another source—the chest and lungs."

"I did not know your lungs were weak, Mr. Marks."

"I'm sure I did not," he said, after a bad fit of coughing. "I had one attack in January through catching a cold. Then I caught another cold, and you see the result: the doctor hardly saved me. I never was subject to take cold before. I suppose the fact is that when a man breaks down in one way he gets weak in all, and is more liable to other ailments."

"I hope you will get better as the warm weather comes on. We shall soon have it here."

"Better of this cough, perhaps: I don't know: but not better yet of my true illness that I think most of—the over-taxed nerves and brain. Oh, if I could but have taken a sufficient rest in time!"

"Mr. Todhetley said you ought to have stayed with us for three months. He says it often still."

"I believe," he said, solemnly lifting his hand, "that if I could have had entire rest then for two or three months, it would have set me up for life. Heaven hears me say it."

And what a dreadful thing it now seemed that he had not!

"I don't repine. My lot seems a hard one, and I sometimes feel sick and weary when I dwell upon it. I have tried to do my duty: I could but keep on and work, as God knows. There was no other course open to me."

I supposed there was not.

"I am no worse off than many others, Johnny. There are men breaking down every day through incessant application and lack of needful interludes of rest. Well for them if their hearts don't break with it!"

And, to judge by the tone he spoke in, it was as much as to say that his heart had broken.

"I am beginning to dwell less on it now," he went on. "Perhaps it is that I am too weak to feel so keenly. Or that Christ's words are being indeed realized to me: 'Come unto me, all ye that labor and are heavy laden, and I will give you rest.' God does not forsake us in our trouble, Johnny, once we have learnt to turn to Him."

Mrs. Marks came into the room with the cup of arrowroot. The boy had run down to tell her I was there. She was very pleasant and cheerful: you could be at home with her at once. While he was waiting for the arrowroot to cool, he leant back in his chair and dropped into a doze.

"It must have been a frightful cold that he caught," I whispered to her.

"It was caught the day he went into the City to tell Mr. Brown he must give up his situation," she answered. "There's an old saying, of being penny wise and pound foolish, and that's what poor James was that day. It was a fine morning when he started; but the rain set in, and when he left Mr Brown it was pouring, and the streets were wet. He ought to have taken a cab, but did not, and waited for a omnibus. The first that past was full; by the time another came he had got wet and his feet were soaking. That brought on a return of the illness he had had in January."

"I hope he will get well."

"It lies with God," she answered.

They made me promise to go again. "Soon Johnny, soon," said Mr. Marks in a kind of eagerness that was suggestive. "Come in the afternoon and have some tea with me."

I had meant to obey literally and go in a day or two; but one thing or other kept intervening, and a week or ten days passed. One Wednesday Miss Deveen was engaged to a dinner-party, and I took the opportunity of going to Pimlico. It was a stormy afternoon, blowing great guns one minute, pouring cats and dogs the next. Mrs. Marks was alone in the parlor, the tea-things on the table before her.

"We thought you had forgotten us," she said in a half whisper, shaking hands. "But this is the best time you could have come; for a kind neighbor has invited all the children in for the evening and we shall be quiet. James is worse."

"Worse!"

"At least, weaker. He cannot sit up long now without great fatigue. He lay down on the bed an hour ago and has dropped asleep," she added, indicating the next room. "I am waiting for him to awake before I make the tea."

He awoke then: the cough betrayed it. She went into the room, and presently he came back with her. No doubt he was worse! my heart sank at seeing him. If he had looked like a skeleton before, he was like a skeleton's ghost now.

"Ah, Johnny! I knew you would come."

I told him how it was I had not been able to come before, **going** into the details. It seemed to amuse him to hear of the engagements, and I described Helen Whitney's Court dress as well as I could—and Lady Whitney's—and the ser ants' great bouquets—and the ball at night. He ate one bit of thin toast and drank three cups of tea. Mrs. Marks said he was always thirsty.

After tea he had a most violent fit of coughing and thought he must lie down to rest for a bit. Mrs. Marks came back and sat with me.

"I hope he will get well," I could not help saying to her.

She shook her head. "I fear he has not much hope of it himself," she answered. "Only yesterday I heard him tell Willy—that—that God would take care of them when he was gone."

She could hardly speak the last words, and broke down with a sob. I wished I had not said anything.

"He has great trust, but things trouble him very much," she resumed. "Nothing else can be expected, for he knows that our means are nearly spent."

"It must trouble you also, Mrs. Marks."

"I seem to have so much to trouble me that I dare not dwell upon it. I pray not to, every hour in the day. If I gave way, what would become of them?"

At dark she lighted the candles and drew down the blinds. Just after that, there came a most tremendous knock at the front-door, loud and long. "Naughty children!" she exclaimed. "It must be they."

"I'll go; don't you stir, Mrs. Marks."

I opened the door, and a rush of wind and rain seemed to blow in an old gentleman. He never said a word to me, but went banging into the parlor and sank down on a chair out of breath.

"Papa!" exclaimed Mrs. Marks. "Papa!"

"Wait till I get up my speech, my dear," said the old gentleman. "She is gone."

"Who is gone?" cried Mrs. Marks.

"*She.* I don't want to say too much against her now she's

gone, Caroline; but she *is* gone. She had a bad fall down stairs in a tipsy fit some days ago, striking her head on the flags, and the doctors could do nothing for her. She died this morning, poor soul; and I am coming to live with you and James, if you will have me. We shall all be so comfortable together, my dear."

Perhaps Mr. Marks remembered at once what it implied—that the pressure of poverty was suddenly lifted and she and those dear ones would be at ease for the future. She bent her head in her hands for a minute or two, keeping silence.

"Your husband shall have rest now, my dear, and all that he needs. So will you, Caroline."

It had come too late. James Marks died in May.

It was about three or four years afterwards that we saw the death of Mr. Brown in the *Times*. The newspapers made a flourish of trumpets over him; saying he had died worth two hundred thousand pounds.

"There must be something wrong somewhere, Johnny," remarked the Squire, in a puzzle. "*I* should not like to die worth all that money, and know that I had worked my clerks to the bone to get it together. I wonder how he will like meeting poor Marks in the next world?"

THE END.